DEATH

— BY —

PROPHECY

DEATH

— BY —

PROPHECY

A CONNOR HAWTHORNE MYSTERY

LAUREN MADDISON

alyson books
los angeles | new york

MANUFACTURED IN THE UNITED STATES OF AMERICA.

THIS TRADE PAPERBACK ORIGINAL IS PUBLISHED BY ALYSON PUBLICATIONS,
P.O. BOX 4371, LOS ANGELES, CALIFORNIA 90078-4371.
DISTRIBUTION IN THE UNITED KINGDOM BY TURNAROUND PUBLISHER SERVICES LTD.,
UNIT 3, OLYMPIA TRADING ESTATE, COBURG ROAD, WOOD GREEN,
LONDON N22 6TZ ENGLAND.

FIRST EDITION: NOVEMBER 2002

02 03 04 05 06 a 10 9 8 7 6 5 4 3 2 1

ISBN 1-55583-764-6

LIBRARY OF CONGRESS CATALOGING-IN-PUBLICATION DATA
MADDISON, LAUREN.
    DEATH BY PROPHECY : A CONNOR HAWTHORNE MYSTERY / LAUREN MADDISON.—1ST ED.
    ISBN 1-55583-764-6
    1. HAWTHORNE, CONNOR (FICTITIOUS CHARACTER)—FICTION. 2. WOMEN NOVELISTS—
FICTION. 3. CALIFORNIA—FICTION. 4. LESBIANS—FICTION. 5. MISSIONS—FICTION. I. TITLE.
PS3563.A33942 D426 2002
813'.54—DC21   2002027706

CREDITS
COVER PHOTOGRAPHY BY SANDRA SATTERWHITE.
COVER DESIGN BY MATT SAMS.

FOR SANDRA

MY GREATEST GIFT
MY DEEPEST JOY

Author's Note

Dear Reader,

Yes, Laguna Beach, Santa Ana, Orange County, and Irvine, California, are all real places. But rest assured, the San Peligro Nuclear Generating Station is a product of my imagination, as is the Cueva Antigua fault. All of the characters in this book are fictional. Any resemblance to actual persons, whether living or dead, is purely coincidental.

There is no Congregation for the Defense of Doctrine within the hierarchy of the Roman Catholic Church, although there is certainly a wide range of philosophy and political involvement among the clergy and staff of the curia. I'm probably safe in assuming that some might be more conservative than others. The Malleus Society and its history are my creation, as is the Cult of Magdalene and its long-treasured secrets. Yet I find myself wondering if we might not be in need of a few "Magdalenes" in the world right about now.

—*Lauren Maddison*

Prologue

The old monk scrubbed at the days-old gray stubble on his sunken cheeks, and stared with rheumy eyes at the small, battered casket before him on the tiny deal writing table. For hours he'd done nothing but write, the quill scraping across the ragged pieces of paper he'd secretly gathered so the old abbot wouldn't suspect him of this serious breach of the rules. The brothers were a dutiful and subservient lot, as much under the iron hand of the abbot as they were the uncertain mercy of a vengeful God. No minute of a monk's day was to remain unaccounted for. No books were read without permission, and certainly no unsanctioned writing was produced. Only those brothers assigned the task of painstakingly copying church manuscripts had access to pen and ink. Abbot Bellini enforced the rules with a zeal worthy of the Inquisitors at the peak of their investigations into the activities of witches and heretics.

The aged priest, his hands cramped and trembling with the sustained effort to keep his writing legible, knew that the punishment for his actions would be death, and not a speedy or merciful one at that. Fifteen years before, he'd endured six months in the underground cells of the east wing of the abbey in what the abbot had referred to as a penitential retreat. Before Brother Gandolfo had reported to the abbot to begin his 'sentence,' he'd heard the whispers among the brothers—tales of screams and sobs, murmurs of a few monks who had not reappeared after their retreats.

Brother Gandolfo knew why those wretched few had died, though he could not have explained why he had survived the abbot's "tests of faith." The monk had not screamed aloud, a circumstance that had sent the abbot into fits of rage. But Gandolfo had prayed long and loud. He had withstood the torments. He had answered no questions, stating only his fervent and unyielding commitment to God. In his heart, he knew the abbot would not let him die, for that would put an end to it once and for all. Thus Brother Gandolfo survived, albeit in a body twisted and bent, and the abbot, in an abrupt alteration of strategy, released him to return to his own tiny cell in the west wing of the abbey and join the other monks in their daily work and devotion. Yet the monk knew that eyes were always upon him as he struggled through his assigned labors in the gardens and the animal pens. He had only a few hours of privacy in his cell, and many of them he spent using the pen and ink he'd smuggled beneath his robe.

I shall die soon, he wrote, *and no one has come showing the sign of recognition to relieve me of the burden. I fear that it will fall into the hands of men like the abbot, men who are sprung from the purest evil known to humanity, as if born from the mind of the horned one whose true name I dare not even write. I am shamed by my weakness and despair. But if I do not survive until my successor is known to me, what is to become of that which I have held so long in trust? In truth, it is only a part of the whole; there are others whose burden is as great as mine, but without each part, nothing at all stands between us and our Lord's vengeance, and the Light of the Divine Mother will be forever extinguished. Even now I quake to write her name, though I would not blaspheme to write Her true name.*

I cannot risk a letter to the cardinal, who is, God be praised, one of us, and as my very bones are brittle with age and malnutrition, I stand no chance of reaching Rome.

He stopped writing, certain he had heard the familiar susurration of clerical robes just outside the door. His heart thundered in his ears. There was nowhere to hide what he was doing. It would be too late, and all would be undone. Seconds passed, then minutes. No one entered. He crept to the door and swung back the small iron hatch over the tiny observation hole through which the activities of the brothers could be observed by their superiors. His narrow view of the corridor revealed nothing. Cautiously, he tugged at the heavy oak until it opened enough to allow his head to slip through. The last fingers of the setting sun from the tall arched windows at the end of the corridor shone directly into his eyes. Shielding them, he squinted into the shadows of the niches that lined the hall. Still he could detect no human presence. But he was filled with a dread, an atavistic horror that propelled him back to his little table in a rush, unmindful of the flaring pain in his joints.

Now I must finish this quickly. I know it was forbidden to commit even this much to writing. The trust was to have been passed from my lips to the ears of my successor, along with the sacred object entrusted to me. But I am alone, and what I have held in my mind cannot be forever lost, or else the Truth is lost. He paused, listening again. *Something is here, something I cannot explain and do not have the strength to confront. Dear God, have mercy on my soul.*

Swiftly he rolled all the scraps of paper together, smearing the last one in his haste. He raised the lid of the casket only far enough to slip the papers inside, his eyes averted to avoid a careless glance. He would not violate the trust any more than he had already. Closing the hasp, the old monk slipped the box into the voluminous sleeve of his robes. With another cautious peek into the corridor, Brother Gandolfo slipped out, arms clasped tightly in front of him, the casket nestled against his chest.

He made his way as rapidly as he was able to the outbuildings on the eastern edge of the abbey grounds. There he had asked one of his few old friends to wait for him—Simon, the deaf-mute boy who'd grown up in the abbey and was now its blacksmith and ironmonger. Brother Gandolfo was counting on him to fasten shut the casket with bands of iron. Only then would he take it to the secret place he had chosen.

With another look behind him, the monk hobbled quietly into the blacksmith's shed. He did not see Simon. He'd expected the big, gentle man to be standing at his furnace, bellows pumping, with a strip of iron glowing red-hot in the tongs. It was too quiet and the forge was cool. He moved toward the back of the shed, to the stalls where Simon shod the abbey's few horses. His foot caught in the hay; he stumbled, looked down, and his heart constricted. Gandolfo backed away from the body. Simon lay there, the sharp ends of the big iron tongs buried deep in his chest. The man's eyes stared up at Brother Gandolfo in silent supplication. But the monk had no time to pray, no time to perform the prescribed offices for the dead. Even now his plan might be known to the abbot. The casket could not be properly sealed. Glancing about, he scooped up pieces of bridle and saddle straps. This was all he had.

With a fleetness of foot he had not believed he could still muster, he rushed out through the stable yard and along the path leading to the precipice. His breath came in rusty gasps, yet he pressed onward, ever listening for footsteps behind him. He reached the edge of the cliff and sought the narrow path leading downward. Awkwardly, with only one hand to steady him as he still clutched the casket, he crept down the path and forced his way into the narrow crevice he had discovered only a few months before. The opening would barely admit even his emaciated frame. Despite the attending pain, he knelt to use the hem of his robe to obliterate his footprints in the sandy soil, then pushed the scrubby bushes into the opening.

The sun had long since deserted the sky, and even the afterglow from the sea below the cliff no longer penetrated the fissures in the rocks. He felt his way along the tunnel, stooping as the height of the ceiling diminished. He had memorized this route, oh-so-carefully, and soon his searching hand felt the opening to the right. Into the little chamber he crawled on hands and knees, pushing the casket ahead of him until he reached the opposite wall. He stopped, took the bits of leather strapping from around his neck and tied them tightly around the box. Then he felt for the little recess and shoved the casket inside before piling up the stones in front of it, before collapsing against the wall, his chest heaving from the effort. This was all he could do, except for one last thing.

Brother Gandolfo was prepared to die in service to a cause he deemed more just than any other on earth, and he was even willing to lie there in the darkness until the Mother released him and the Father opened wide the gates to paradise. But if he simply disappeared, the abbot would be so enraged he would scour every inch of the abbey and its property for the monk's hiding place. That kind of intense search might well lead to the discovery of his little cave, his body, and necessarily, the precious casket.

Gathering the last of his physical resources, the old monk crept out to the entrance and listened carefully. He heard no sound, yet the boding presence of something he didn't care to think about still lurked near him. He murmured a prayer, then crawled out onto the ledge, once more obscuring the marks of his passage, and pulling the bushes into the opening.

Along the cliff face he went, balancing himself against the wind. Twenty yards, fifty, then a hundred, around a bend in the cliff, and another hundred yards until the ledge was petering out to nothing. Now he was much closer to the abbey walls and to the refectory. Here, too, was a well-worn path from the grounds to the cliff side. He began to shout, though his voice sounded weak in the swirling wind. Still, someone would hear, a monk hurrying to matins perhaps. Father Gandolfo removed the piece of rope and leather that served as a belt and tied it to a bit of branch. Next he pulled the wool cassock over his head, folded it lengthwise, and hung it over the branch, wrapping the sleeves around it. *They must be seen,* he said to himself. *They must be found.*

He shivered in the icy wind, his linen undergarments pitifully plastered to his gaunt frame. He waited, shouted again. Finally, an answering shout, "Where are you, brother? What is your distress?"

He delayed another moment until the voice was closer. He closed his eyes. "*In nomina matri et patri et filii et spiritu sanctu,*" he whispered. With arms outstretched, he waited for the strong embrace of the rising wind, waited for the Mother to release him and send him home with a swirl of the elemental forces of creation the church had long since forgotten. Brother Gandolfo smiled for the first time in thirty years as his body flew and his spirit soared.

Chapter One

My Lord, I am ready on the threshold of this new day
to go forth armed with thy power,
seeking adventure on the high road,
to right wrong, to overcome evil,
to suffer wounds, and endure pain if need be,
but in all things to serve thee bravely, faithfully, joyfully,
that at the end of the day's labor,
kneeling for thy blessing,
thou mayst find no blot upon my shield.
　—The Knight's Prayer
(Inscribed in Chester Cathedral)

Washington, D.C.

"This place is starting to give me the creeps," said Laura.

"The Bethlehem Chapel is giving you the creeps?" Connor raised one eyebrow. "You're kidding, right? You love art, and that reredos alone is one of the most beautiful carvings in the cathedral."

"I don't deny this place is magnificent on a grand scale. It's a marvel of craftsmanship and architecture and Gothic excess. We've seen the main altar, the rose windows, the gothic arches, the flying buttresses, the apse, the nave, the north and south transepts, five chapels, the view from the tower, the Bishop's Garden…"

Connor grinned. "Your point being that you've seen just about enough of the National Cathedral. I'm sorry. I get kind of carried away with places like this."

"Really big churches?"

"Yep."

"It's absolutely beautiful and all that, but it's almost on too overwhelming a scale. And it's so cold."

"We're in the crypt of an enormous stone cathedral, and it's still early spring. Actually, though, there is no temperature *except* cold down here, even in the middle of a D.C. summer."

"I wouldn't mind having my jacket on, but that isn't exactly the kind of cold I'm talking about. It feels sort of eerie in here." Laura shivered slightly.

Connor looked at her in mock alarm. "Please, I promise to sprint up the stairs and all the way to the car for your coat if you absolutely promise me you won't mention the word 'eerie' for this entire vacation."

Laura smiled. "I wasn't necessarily talking about the supernatural, but you've got to admit there's something about the silence, the heaviness of the tons of stone overhead, not to mention that everywhere you turn in here, there's a dead person in some niche."

"Okay, there are tombs. But you find those in just about every cathedral in the world. You've seen the crypts in Rome."

"*Very* briefly. And this is almost as creepy," answered Laura. "But you're right, it's their custom."

Connor nodded. "And the Navajo wouldn't dream of practicing their daily spirituality with dead bodies all around them." She looked closely at Laura. "I'm sorry. I guess I wasn't thinking when I suggested we come here. This must bother you more than you're letting on."

"Not because of my heritage, if that's what you mean. It took me a long time to reconcile some of my family's beliefs with the world outside the rez, but I did. I respect that some people do things I find odd, to say the least. But in this case, everything about this chapel feels oppressive."

"I'm sorry to hear that, my dear, but I understand what you mean."

They both turned, startled to see they were no longer alone in the chapel. An elderly priest clad in a simple black cassock stood beside the iron grille at the rear of the chapel. It was open now, though Connor was quite sure it had been locked when they first entered. A small sign on the iron door indicated that the crypt of Bishop Satterlee was not open to the public.

Laura was still staring at the priest, a slight blush creeping up her clear bronze skin. "I apologize, Father. I meant no disrespect."

The old man's deeply wrinkled face rearranged itself into a smile. "You need not apologize. There are very few of us left who feel at home in places like this." He waved his arm in a gesture that took in not only the Bethlehem Chapel but the entire cathedral towering more than 300 feet above their heads. "The dead will always have a home here, but one wonders if the living ever truly feel welcome."

Not entirely comfortable with the direction of the conversation, Connor asked, "Are you on the staff here, Father?"

"I am only a visiting priest," he said, "and far too old to be of much use. But this is not unlike churches in which I've served, much older churches." He paused for a moment, his eyes closed, then focused once again on the two women. "Forgive my manners," he said. "I am Father Angelico."

Laura held out her hand. "Laura Nez, Father, and this is Connor Hawthorne." The old priest held Laura's strong, slender hand in a grip that was surprisingly firm for an old man. For several seconds she met his steady gaze without blinking. "It is a pleasure to meet someone like you at last," he murmured.

Connor frowned slightly, and was about to ask what he'd meant by "at last," but before she could frame the question politely, he turned to her. "And you, my child." He left the sentence unfinished, or perhaps that was all he'd intended to say. But Connor was left with the sensation that many thoughts he might have shared were left unsaid as he locked eyes with her. She swallowed hard and waited for him to release her hand. She felt physically unable to break the contact, a sensation she didn't care for at all.

Then the moment had passed, and the priest was standing several feet away, his hand on the iron grille.

"I thought the Bishop's burial crypt was usually closed," she said, trying to cover her confusion.

"I suppose it is," he replied. "But I had work to do here." He paused, searching Connor's eyes. "I believe you would agree that there are times when even the darkest places must be opened and the doors of mysteries unlocked."

Connor shook her head. "I hate cryptic," she muttered under her breath, though loudly enough for Laura to shoot her a cautionary glance.

The priest seemed not to have noticed the exchange. "Before you continue your journey, might I say a brief prayer for you?"

Laura smiled at him. "We'd be grateful, Father."

He clasped his hands in front of his chest and closed his eyes. "Mother-Father God, may your wisdom continue to guide these young women, may your love embrace them, and may your light lead them in the ways of Spirit. As it is foretold, so it is. Amen."

He backed away from them and slid into the recess, pulling the iron gate toward him. He smiled at Laura. "Don't spend too much time worrying about the dead," he assured her. "The living are the ones who need our help." He melted soundlessly into the shadows of the crypt.

"What the hell was that all about?" Connor scowled, peering into the darkness behind the grillwork.

"Just a prayer. I know you're not much for organized religion, but I thought it was kind of nice of him to offer."

"That's not what I mean. I spent four years of my life at the Cathedral prep school and every Friday morning of the school year sitting in the choir upstairs for services. I never once heard an Episcopal priest say the phrase 'Mother-Father God.' That's almost heresy for traditionalists."

"So he's a heretic priest. Maybe he got tired of the party line of God being a 'he.'"

"Not likely," Connor frowned. "At his age, he's got to be an old-school priest. Maybe he's just a few fries short of a happy meal."

4

"Sh-h-h. He might be able to hear us." Laura put her fingers to her lips. "He seemed pretty lucid to me. Just an elderly priest with time on his hands." Laura shrugged. "But he was kind of spooky, wasn't he—especially that part about darkest places being opened?"

"All right, we're out of here. So far I've heard the words 'eerie,' 'spooky,' and 'creepy,' and I'm absolutely committed to one real vacation with you that does not include mysterious messages, psychic phenomena, bodies, ghosts, or criminals."

Laura's generous lips turned up slightly at the corners. "Given our history, don't you think that's asking a lot?"

"No, I don't," said Connor firmly, then sighed. "All right, your grandmother was," she hesitated, "or *is* a major-league medicine woman, whenever you can find her, and—"

Laura interrupted her. "And your grandmother, Gwendolyn…"

"I know, Celtic priestess, light-wielder, generally all-powerful woman of the outer dimensions, etcetera etcetera, but could we please not dwell on all that right now?"

Laura sighed. "You're impossible, you know that. Good thing I adore you." She laid her hand on Connor's cheek for a moment. "Sweetheart, you can't walk away from your birthright."

Connor's shoulders sagged. "I know that, but sometimes it would be nice to act like a normal person, live a normal life, and not wonder what evil weirdness might be lurking around every corner. Ever since Gwendolyn left and dumped all this stuff in my lap…"

"I don't think your grandmother's bequest to you is what made you cynical. I tend to think all those years prosecuting people you lovingly refer to as 'scumbags' and then more years writing about them is what got you started down that path. Besides, who says that your heritage is simply about hunting for evil?"

Connor sat in one of the pews and stared at the altar screen. "It certainly has seemed like that so far."

Taking a seat next to her, Laura placed a hand over one of Connor's. "Look, I know you're still processing what happened in England."

"Processing? Now don't go all psychobabble on me. I don't think I could stand it."

"Okay, wrong word maybe. But you know what I'm talking about. A lot of what we dealt with there *was* evil. I can't think of any other way to characterize it. Those people weren't your run-of-the-mill garden-variety scumbags. And you defeated that insane woman on Glastonbury Tor not just because you're Connor Hawthorne," she paused, "who is, I might add, a wonderful person in her own right, but because you're Gwendolyn's granddaughter and you can do some spectacular things."

"It's a lot easier to think of what happened in terms of collaring some greedy, crazy people who'd committed theft and murder and blackmail."

"Easier, but not true," said Laura gently. "You fulfilled a prophecy and you averted some pretty serious consequences."

"Not just me. You were there, and Dad, and Malcolm, and the Carlisles."

"Okay, I'll drop the subject. But I promise it's going to come up in the future. For now, we'll just be plain old sight-seeing civilians. But this cathedral is one sight I think I can honestly say I've thoroughly experienced, and my goose bumps have goose bumps."

Connor smiled as Laura held up her arm. "You know, my grandmother always called those God chills."

"And you wonder why Gwendolyn was who she was," said Laura. "I'm just about ready to race you back to the car. And Benjamin is expecting us for dinner."

At the top of stairs, Connor rounded the corner and almost collided with a tall man clad in a purple cassock and white surplice. She looked at him to excuse herself for her inattention and was greeted with a huge smile.

"Lydia—I mean, Connor Hawthorne!"

"Canon Edwards!" Connor stepped back a pace. "I didn't know you were still here at the cathedral."

"Thought I must certainly be past it," he chuckled, a faint trace of England in his accent.

"No, of course not," Connor answered politely.

"Oh, that's quite all right. It does seem as if I've been here a century or so. And you've been gone for—let's see, what must it be? Over twenty years?"

"At least." Connor's smile was rueful. "Seems much longer. I'm surprised you'd remember me."

"You're not a person one would be likely to forget. Nor those theological debates we sometimes enjoyed."

Connor reddened slightly. "I was pretty full of myself as a teenager. I can only imagine how rude I must have been at times."

"Never rude but always passionate. We didn't see eye to eye on a number of topics as I recall."

"I've mellowed over the years," she smiled. Then, remembering her manners, she gestured to Laura. "Canon Edwards, this is my friend, Laura Nez. Laura, Canon Edwards. He was on the cathedral staff when I went to school here."

The gentleman extended his hand. "A pleasure to make your acquaintance, Ms. Nez." He cocked his head to one side. "Nez is a Navajo surname, is it not?"

Laura nodded. "Yes, sir, it is."

"An intriguing people, the Navajo. Would that we had time to sit and chat about your religious traditions. I've made a study of comparative religion over the years. But I see you are on your way out. Did you enjoy our cathedral?"

"It was very…interesting," said Laura with her characteristic honesty.

The canon chuckled again. "Some find the grandeur overwhelming and the presence of the dead a little forbidding. Still others find it inspiring, and most don't know quite what they feel. But I like it because it still symbolizes man's yearning to reach the heavens."

"We met one of your priests downstairs in the Bethlehem Chapel," said Connor. "He must be comfortable with the idea of dead people, keeping company with the Bishop and all."

The canon looked at her quizzically. "Keeping company with the Bishop. You mean Bishop Satterlee?"

"He came out of the crypt while we were visiting the chapel."

"How odd. Few of our people have any reason to be in there. Which priest was it?"

"Father Angelico," offered Laura. "He's quite elderly."

7

The canon's frown deepened. "That name doesn't sound at all familiar. You say he's an older gentleman?"

"Could be in his eighties or more," Connor said. "And his cassock was rather frayed."

"He was wearing a cassock as well?" The canon shook his head. "That makes even less sense. Visiting priests often wear clerical garb—the collar I mean—but only our staff would be dressed..." His voice trailed off.

"Perhaps he's only a visitor," Connor assured him. "He was extremely old. Perhaps a little confused."

"You have grown kinder in your maturity, Connor—though I still must insist that your given name, Lydia, is much more to my old-fashioned tastes."

"My mother would agree with you, Canon." She looked at her watch. "I'm afraid we're late meeting my father, or we could chat more."

"And how is the senator these days?"

"He still manages to stay pretty busy, though it's been a few years since he gave up his senate seat."

"I imagine only in order to provide other services to his country," smiled the canon. "But I won't pry. A life spent in Washington has taught me a few things. I am often glad we don't follow the Catholic practice of hearing confessions. I'm not sure it wouldn't turn what's left of my hair completely white."

Connor smiled. "I think that's a reasonable possibility. Well, it's been a pleasure to see you again."

The canon extended his hand to her. "There's really no mystery to why I recognized you so quickly," he smiled, "since I've read all of your books and your picture appears on the dust jackets."

"You read *my* books?" Connor asked.

"Surely you don't think we of the religious life are only permitted to study Scripture," he teased. "And besides, your books are incisive, well-crafted, and highly literate. They afford a penetrating glimpse into the world of criminal law that I find fascinating."

"I'll be happy to send you a signed copy of the next one, Canon."

"I will look forward to it with anticipation." He turned to Laura. "Perhaps we shall meet again, Ms. Nez. I sense that you and Connor are quite close. My prayers are with you." He regarded them both for a moment, an unmistakable twinkle in his eye, then turned on his heel in the direction of the vestry.

Connor stared after him. "What do you suppose he meant by that?"

Laura smiled. "I think he's a lot smarter than you probably ever gave him credit for. Now, we really do have to hit the road. The traffic's going to be a mess."

"Are you worried we'll keep my dad waiting?" replied Connor, following Laura out through the south transept. "After all these years working for him, you should know his bark's a lot worse than his bite."

"He doesn't bark," said Laura, taking the shallow steps two at a time. "He mostly smiles, sometimes snarls, and occasionally roars. But he never barks."

»——«

Benjamin Hawthorne was neither smiling nor snarling, nor even roaring. He was, however, puzzled. The message he had received early that morning was rather out of character for his friend, Malcolm Jefferson, a D.C. captain of police. Jefferson was a man who, while imaginative and often innovative, generally took a very grounded approach to crime solving. Somewhat to his chagrin, his friendship with Benjamin's daughter, Connor, and involvement with her somewhat odd adventures of the last few years, had challenged Malcolm to explore ways of thinking that were neither ordered nor logical. Still, he didn't make a habit of looking for unreasonable explanations when rational ones would suffice. Thus, after reviewing the file Malcolm had sent with the message, Benjamin was frankly surprised at the conclusions his friend had drawn. But he'd never known Malcolm to go off half-cocked. *Well, on second thought,* he said to himself, *maybe I have, but that's why my daughter's alive today.*

The scraping of a chair interrupted his reverie. "Speak of the devil," he said, as Malcolm Jefferson's six-foot-six frame loomed over him.

"I think that qualifies as slander," Malcolm smiled, shaking Benjamin's hand. "I'll have to ask Connor."

"She doesn't practice law anymore, thank God. We have enough lawyers in this town as it is, including ones who would cheerfully sue their own fathers for a percentage."

"True enough. I seem to arrest more of them lately." He signaled to the waiter and ordered a bourbon and water. "How long before Connor and Laura show up?"

"They said they'd be here around seven. It's almost that now. I'm glad you were able to get in without the usual runaround."

Malcolm shrugged. "Ever since you insisted they get rid of that cracker they had on the door for so long, I haven't had to flash my badge to explain why even us black folk can stroll into this chummy men's club of yours."

"Bit of an exaggeration, my friend. This club has been integrated for over forty years, and you know perfectly well that that crotchety old bigot was a pain in everyone's behind. But he kept playing the 'wounded veteran' card to keep from getting fired."

"We all play games sometimes," Malcolm sighed. "I notice women still aren't allowed to live here. It's almost easier for *me* to get in."

"True, but if you bring that up so my daughter can have another go at me…"

"Have no fear, Senator, I wouldn't dream of it. Besides, I think she's glad to see you out of that hell you called a marriage. There are times when the thought of a quiet place to come home to like this, with creaky old waiters and hidebound rules seems kind of inviting."

"Speaking of lack of quiet, how are the kids?"

"All fine, except for my oldest boy. Still showing major attitude. And Eve's got her hands full trying to deal with him."

"I can't imagine your sister taking any crap from any of the kids."

"She doesn't. But he's getting too big for her to just smack his behind and yank him along by the ear. I think he's still angry that his momma's not around. He knew her the longest, maybe he still misses her the most."

"She's been dead a long time, Malcolm. Surely the kids would have adjusted to that for the most part."

"Maybe it's just an excuse to sound off at me and his aunt, but I'm worried he's going to get into some real trouble. Shit, with all the drugs on the streets and in the schools—yes, even the good schools," he added in answer to Benjamin's inquiring glance. "I know Connor hoped my having the kids in the public schools in Georgetown would make a difference. And it does. But money doesn't solve the kinds of problems kids are having now."

"True. And I don't imagine Connor saw it as a cure-all, just a little better opportunity for the kids."

"And that's the only reason I let her get away with all that."

Benjamin sat back in his chair. "If you start on that again, she'll probably want to deck you."

"I know, but it still galls me."

"Okay, so she should have told you that you weren't just house-sitting, that she'd put the town house in your name, but the fact is she would *never* have lived there again, not after everything that happened. Too many reminders of Ariana. You know that as well as I do."

"I suppose. But she could have sold it."

"She didn't want to. She has plenty of money from her family trusts, from her books…she's had how many best-sellers? She gives it away. You know that."

"Still feels like charity to me."

"Oh for God's sake, you're pouting, which is kind of silly for a 250-pound policeman with attitude."

"But—"

"Enough already! You saved my daughter's life. You almost killed yourself running across the desert in the middle of the night and for no good reason except that you thought she was in danger. You also helped save Laura, another thing for which Connor will always be grateful. And," he continued before Malcolm could interrupt, "you're one of the best friends any of us will ever have. So let's move on."

Benjamin declined the waiter's offer to refresh his scotch. "Now, you want to tell me what this is all about?" He gestured to the thin file folder beside his drink. "Granted these threats are alarming, but you're taking them seriously when very few others are."

Malcolm was silent for a moment, started to speak, then hesitated as the waiter returned with his drink. When they were alone again, he continued, "There's something about this that—well, you know how I told you one time about that little voice I have sometimes, the one that never steers me wrong?"

"I know exactly what you mean. Even a good intellect's not worth a damn if you ignore your intuition."

"Well, call it a hunch, but I don't think the source of these threats is just some crackpot fringe group. I don't know if it's in the wording, which as you probably noticed is sort of archaic for this day and age, or in the biblical references, or what."

"Surely you've dealt with your share of letters from cranks who are madder than hatters?" Benjamin paused. "You know, I've always wondered why a hatter is supposed to be mad."

Malcolm shook his head. "Something to do with *Alice in Wonderland,* I guess."

"Now that one I know," said a familiar voice from behind them. "It's because hat makers in earlier centuries used mercury in the process of making felt for hats. Inhaling the fumes eventually made most hatters insane."

"Is there any trivia you don't know?" grinned Malcolm, rising from his chair to envelop first Connor and then Laura in bear-size hugs.

"Yes, I don't know why flammable and inflammable mean the same thing, or why people go fifty in the fast lane on the Beltway, but I can live with it." She circled the table to hug her father who had stood as soon as he saw them. "Dad, those courtly manners of yours will get you into trouble one of these days. There are women out there starved for old-fashioned courtesy."

"I'm always careful to be rude if there are any eligible females on the prowl," he chuckled. "The last thing I need in my life is complication."

"As if your life is simple," teased Laura.

Benjamin shrugged. "I'm retired. What's so complicated about that?"

They all laughed. Benjamin's retirement was equal to just about anyone else's full-time job. While he no longer held either his senate seat or his subsequent post as presidential adviser for national security affairs, his influence in government circles was still a force to be reckoned with. His uncanny ability to identify and analyze political trends and espionage activities kept him not only in the loop but in demand as a sort of independent consultant. He had the ear of everyone of importance in Washington and had earned the respect of everyone who had ever worked with him. Neither was he a desk-riding bureaucrat. Only a few powerful individuals were privy to the operations Benjamin Hawthorne had undertaken in his lifetime and to the fact that he had never shirked a job because it was dangerous. Unlike a number of his colleagues in the intelligence community, the senate, and later, in service of the president, Benjamin's personal principles remained intact. As a result, he'd made a great many enemies and, fortunately, a number of intensely loyal friends.

They all took their seats as Benjamin asked his daughter, "You talk to your mother since you got into town?"

Connor sighed. "I tried. We had a barely civil conversation. At least she was sober for a change."

"She just got back from another 'vacation' at Betty Ford."

"I think that makes about a dozen trips so far. Apparently the effects don't last."

"They only last if you want them to," said Benjamin. "I'm afraid Amanda doesn't really want to be sober on a long-term basis. She's too angry and bitter, mostly with me."

"Dad, don't go there. You had no choice but to leave. She was making your life a living hell, and there wasn't a moment's peace between you."

"True, but every now and then I wonder if there isn't something more I could have done to help her get straightened out."

"You did it all for the last twenty years of your marriage. You sent her to every clinic. You bought her everything she ever wanted. You have to know when to say when."

Malcolm spoke up. "I've dealt with a lot of alcoholics over the years, from every walk of life, rich and poor, and no one can save them if they don't want to be saved.

"Besides," said Connor with only a faint trace of humor, "if we want to draw up a list of people who have disappointed my mother, I'd have to be right at the top."

Benjamin shook his head. "That's the one thing I could never get past. She has the most incredible daughter anyone could hope for, and she chose to throw away every chance at a relationship."

"Thanks for the compliment, Senator," said Connor with a smile, "but how about we find a more cheerful subject than the wild woman of Potomac."

"Speaking of incredible daughters," said Malcolm, "how's yours?"

"Pretending she's not nervous about exams. Laura and I didn't stay long at Oxford. Katy kept saying she had plenty of time for us, but I could tell she was distracted."

"You think she'll stay in England?" asked Benjamin.

"I try not ask her too much about her plans. Somehow, coming from a mother, even simple questions sound like prying. But I know she's always felt more at home in England than anywhere else. And she hinted at a possible job offer in London."

"You wish she'd come back to the States, don't you?" asked Malcolm.

"I suppose, I do. But she's incredibly grown up now. She'll be where she wants to be."

"Like you," smiled Benjamin.

"Too much like me." Connor shook her head and glanced at the file folder on the table. "Were we interrupting anything?"

"Something Malcolm was asking about," he said, beckoning the waiter. "Your usual, sweetheart?"

"Chivas on the rocks. I'm predictable that way."

"And *only* that way," he smiled.

"So is this a secret?" Connor persisted. "One of those need-to-know things?"

Malcolm shrugged. "Hardly a secret. The file's been passed around to every security nerd's desk in Washington. I seem to be the only person taking it seriously. And I'm probably obsessing about it. But there is one aspect you might find interesting."

"How so?" asked Connor.

"Do you remember a perp named Ricky Bell? Guy you prosecuted, must be ten years ago."

Connor frowned, concentrating. Her memory was almost encyclopedic, especially when it came to old cases, but man's face didn't immediately come to mind. "What were the charges?"

"Breaking and entering, theft of government property, vandalism—"

"Sounds petty, to say the least," Connor interrupted him.

"And abduction." Malcolm finished. "Guy broke into an office at a satellite facility of the Pentagon down on 14th Street where a couple of NSA types on loan to the Army were temporarily headquartered with some kind of investigation. He took a bunch of files, burned some, and grabbed the civilian secretary when she showed up unexpectedly on a Sunday. He let her go as soon as they got out of the building, but his car wouldn't start and he ran right into a couple of cops running up the street."

"Now I remember him. Skinny guy with a seriously bad attitude. Kept snarling at everyone about government conspiracies and spies everywhere and the avenging hand of God. We sent him to St. Elizabeth's for a psych eval, but they said he was no crazier than most of the inmates at the D.C. jail. So we got him on all the counts of the indictment, and he got what, twelve years?"

"Very good, Ms. Hawthorne, except it was fourteen years and he still got out in under seven."

"Hardly surprising. From what I hear, some prisons are stacking the inmates like cordwood. With no actual violence on his record, he'd be a good candidate for early release. As I recall, he didn't even have a record."

"Only because we couldn't find one. And his fingerprints weren't on file anywhere.

"Except he slipped his leash. Didn't see his parole officer even once. The P.O. violated him right away, but we couldn't find old Ricky so we could throw him back in jail."

"Typical," said Connor. "So what's the big deal with a small-time hoodlum running around? He's got lots of company."

Laura smiled. "Can you tell she's mellowed? There was a time when she would probably have gone out looking for this Mr. Bell right after we finished dinner, maybe even before."

Connor poked Laura's arm. "Gee, thanks. I expect some credit for being less obsessive than I've ever been before. But yes, I was a little gung ho about keeping creeps in jail. Bell had a lot of pretty nasty things to say to me and the judge. She had him removed from the courtroom twice."

"The big deal," said Malcolm, "is how he may tie in with something I'm looking into. Do you remember when we went over all the stuff we bagged from Ricky's apartment?"

"Lots of political pamphlets, and tirades about Big Brother watching, oppressing the people, proclaiming that God was going to punish us for our sins and heresies, something like that. It was all pretty rabid as I recall, an odd mix of right wing politics and fire-and-brimstone religious rhetoric. It was directed at just about everyone on earth. What was the name of his little group or club or whatever?"

"The Malleus..." he paged through the file, "The Malleus Society, although in a couple of places he wrote 'Malleus ab Deum.'"

"Ah, yes. Latin for 'hammer of God' or some such thing," said Connor. "Though if Ricky was an example of their collective might, I wouldn't worry too much about it. For that matter, I'm not entirely sure there *were* any other members."

"True, we never found a list or anything, but I'm beginning to think there were others involved."

"You check with the staff at the prison?"

"Yep. Bell was whatever passes for a model prisoner these days. In other words, he didn't kill anyone or try to escape. By their standards, he was an angel. But the psychologist there said she was concerned that the other inmates called him Preacher and he seemed to have a lot of influence." Malcolm frowned at the file, as if it still might reveal more details he'd somehow overlooked.

"Appropriate name for a fanatic," said Laura. "Was he actually proselytizing up there?"

"Indeed, he was. Dr. Cohen said she suspects some of Bell's followers were behind a spate of hate mail she got...anti-Semitic hate mail."

Connor frowned. "Bell still sounds like half the white supremacists running around in the woods."

"In some ways he does. But aside from all his other pet peeves, he's obsessed with what he calls the nuclear power conspiracy. He's convinced that it poisons the atmosphere, and that nuclear power plants are really fronts for military installations that promote Godlessness. Some of his old materials directly advocated violence against government installations and turning their weapons of Satan against them to cleanse the world."

"I take it Mr. Bell has surfaced again."

"Not surfaced in plain sight, but let's just say I can smell him. And not because of personal hygiene. Funny things stick in your mind, and I remember he was the cleanest, neatest perp I'd ever collared. But there's something a little familiar in a series of threats that various government agencies have received. All of them in some way threaten to neutralize every nuclear power plant in the country and also strike at the American imperialist war machine."

Benjamin, who had already read the file, said, "That phrase alone makes me think whoever's behind this is a little off—or a lot. I don't think we've been called imperialists or capitalist dogs since before the cold war."

"That's just it," said Malcolm. "That was the same sort of diatribe we found in Ricky's files before. We assumed he'd written a lot of it, and I don't doubt that he did. This new stuff sounds just like him."

Laura took a sip of her wine. "What makes you think he's any more dangerous now than he was then? As threats go…"

"I know, my theory's a little weak," answered Malcolm. "I'd like your take on it, too. You've worked for Benjamin a long time. The thing is, there's more *to* this. It isn't just his style of writing that's part of this. One envelope received at the Shady Springs generating plant in Maryland included detailed sketches of the entire facility, including security systems."

Connor's brow furrowed. "And no one is taking *that* seriously?"

"A lot of people took it seriously. I got copied on it because I'm heading up the anti-terrorism detail now. We turned D.C. upside down. We put out bulletins to every other jurisdiction. Hell, we had the FBI boys breathing down our necks. But after that packet was received, no one's heard a word."

"Nothing."

"It's as if whoever sent this stuff has dropped off the face of the earth. No more threats, no more hints, no more clues. Silence."

"So everyone else let this drop?"

"Yeah, they pretty much decided there were other fish to fry, and I don't blame them. Since 9/11," he shrugged, "they have to set priorities."

"But you don't want to let it go?" Connor studied her old friend. "And it's because you have a funny feeling about it."

Malcolm shrugged, his tone diffident. "Something like that. I don't like loose ends, maybe these people are just playing with us, but I don't think they're done."

"People?"

"The threats always say 'we' instead of 'I,' so this Hammer of God Society may really be a group."

"Or just one person with multiple personalities," suggested Connor. "Sort of a Sybil, the Environmental Avenger." She saw Malcolm bristle. "Come on, I'm only joking. I've never failed to take one of your hunches seriously, and I never will. What do you think, Dad?"

Benjamin had listened to the exchange with half an ear as he paged once more through the file. "I don't know. I can't say that what I've seen is setting off huge alarm bells in my head, but I have as much faith in our friend here as you do. So I'm going to make some in-depth inquiries. Discreet ones," he added, noting the look of apprehension on Malcolm's face. "No sense in getting people pissed off at you for staying on this case. And I'll light a fire under someone over at NRC to circulate a moderate sort of warning memo. Now, how about some dinner? I know the girls leave early in the morning."

"At long last," said Connor. "A real vacation. But that doesn't mean we have to rush dinner."

"Good," replied her father, "I'm thinking thick steaks and large baked potatoes with all the trimmings." He motioned to the waiter hovering nearby.

"I like your thinking," Malcolm smiled, some of the tension draining out of his face. "Make mine rare," he said to the waiter. "Just read it the last rites and walk it by the stove slowly."

They all gave their orders, the others opting for slightly more cooking time on their prime Nebraska corn-fed beef, and Laura adding a Caesar salad. "Someone has to eat the green stuff," she protested. "Want to share some?" she asked Connor who rolled her eyes heavenward.

"You're determined to make me like vegetables, aren't you?"

18

"You don't have to like them, just develop an amicable relationship with a few varieties. So," she said, switching gears, "let's consider how easy or difficult it would be for Mr. Bell, or anyone else, to gain access to a nuclear plant and possibly destroy it. Surely the security is very tight."

Benjamin thought about that for a moment. "You know, it isn't something I've reviewed personally in several years. But locations like that are never as safe as we think. And any determined person with an ax to grind can accomplish things we only have nightmares about. I think it's time I talked to a few people."

»——«

The old priest knelt on the frigid stone. His arthritic knees protested, but pain was no longer of great concern to him. What mattered was what had always mattered—the journal and the holy of holies. At least that is what they had come to call it over the past several decades. No one outside the limited circle of guardians entirely understood the nature of the secret he and his predecessors had kept century upon century. But he fully grasped the significance of what lay hidden. Time and again he'd looked to the ancient holy texts for a different meaning, a different interpretation that would obviate the need for him to make the journey at all. But his faith would not let him rest. His vows would not release him, though his heart yearned for another destiny.

The sound of feet in the passageway entered his consciousness. Odd that anyone would pass this way so late in the evening. He'd chosen this spot because few guards liked coming down all those stairs into the echoing emptiness at night. Fortunately, though, his gifts were quite special. Hiding in plain sight took on quite a different meaning for the old cleric.

Moments later a guard paused in front of the iron grille that protected the crypt. He pulled at it, confirming that it was secure. The old priest knew instantly that the two young women had mentioned his presence to someone, perhaps a person of authority in the cathedral. The guard, more diligent than strictly required, stepped close to the opening and shone his flashlight around the interior. He could see every corner of the crypt without actually opening the gate. After a few moments of probing every corner, he was apparently satisfied with his search, though he lingered briefly.

He's puzzled, thought the old priest. *His eyes tell him there is no one here, yet his instincts tells him he's seen something…a difficult contradiction for the human mind.* In fact, the beam of the flashlight had passed directly over the priest, for he was standing only a few feet from the iron grille. Yet to the guard's human perception there was only empty space. With a last look around the chapel, the guard continued on his rounds. The priest waited until the man's footsteps had died away before reaching his hand out to the gate. It swung open.

His time of waiting in this place was done. His heart told him that the final part of his journey was about to begin. But still he quailed at the thought, even while castigating himself for such unforgivable weakness. Certainly the work he had been given was not easy. It required a hardened resolve, immense knowledge of the history and destiny of humanity, absolute dedication, familiarity with every word of the holy texts, these things and more. The world might come to its end, finally, but he would not shrink from the task that God had set before him and his predecessors, no matter how much his human mind might rebel at the consequences. For all he knew, he was the last.

He knelt before the altar for a last prayer in this holy place. Perhaps before long there would be no churches, no cathedrals, no houses of worship left on the planet. Thus it was foretold, but was that enough to make it so?

Chapter Two

Heresy is only another word for freedom of thought.
—Graham Greene

Orange County, California

"Archbishop Johnston?"

"What is it, Grolsch?"

The young Jesuit closed the office door behind him. "The emissary from the Vatican is waiting for you in the outer office."

"You announced his presence an hour ago, as I recall."

"Yes, your Eminence, but—"

"He grows impatient, yes, I know. But there are times when a little gamesmanship is in order, don't you think?"

It was clear from the priest's demeanor that he didn't think so at all, that the presence of the Vatican messenger had thoroughly unnerved him. But it was hardly his place to contradict the archbishop of the archdiocese of Orange County, one of the largest in California. He stood there awaiting an order.

The archbishop sighed. He wondered how Grolsch had managed to complete his training as a Jesuit and still be so completely lacking in judgment, initiative, or personality. "In ten minutes, bring him to my office."

"Yes, Your Eminence," the young man replied, turning the old-fashioned door handle the wrong way for the hundredth time.

Archbishop Johnston leaned back in his comfortably broken-in leather chair, a piece of furniture specifically designed to accommodate his large frame. He'd been a wrestler in college, and even a back-alley fighter when necessary, but those days were long past. The once-hard muscle had softened enough that his 250 pounds were no longer arranged as neatly as he'd like. Still, at well over six feet tall, his physical presence would have dominated even if his personality had been gentle and meek, which it certainly wasn't. When the archbishop was angry, few dared oppose him.

In precisely nine minutes, rather than ten, he heard a gentle knock, the oak paneled door swung open to admit Monsignor Johann Kursk, a representative of the Vatican's Congregation for the Defense of Doctrine, an organization Johnston considered the modern-day equivalent of the old Inquisition—the protectors of dogma and hunters of heresy in the church. Johnston didn't like them, and at first glance he didn't like Kursk.

The visiting monsignor circled the desk to brush his lips against the archbishop's ring of office and then sat down without being asked to do so, immediately clicking open the brass clasp on his slim briefcase. Johnston knew the breach of etiquette was no mistake. Kursk was determined to establish his authority here. But two could play that game.

The archbishop pressed the send switch on the intercom. "Father Grolsch, would you ask Cecilia to bring us tea?" Then, without a word to Kursk, he rose from his desk chair and walked deliberately to the windows overlooking the citrus groves. "This view inspires me every day—the work of God so visible to our mortal eyes." He seated himself at the mahogany table beneath the window, then turned back toward his guest. "You'll join me for tea?"

Monsignor Kursk frowned slightly. Coming from the archbishop, the simple phrase sounded rather more like a command than an invitation, precisely as Johnston had intended. And he had to get up again, thus nullifying any advantage he might have enjoyed by presuming to sit down without being asked. Johnston watched him with an impassive expression, yet inwardly enjoyed the man's annoyance. *Amateurs,* thought the archbishop, who prided himself on his status as a chess master. *They never think far enough ahead.*

Kursk fumbled with the briefcase, apparently trying to decide whether to bring it over to the table or leave it in the chair by the desk. He chose to leave it. The archbishop smiled inwardly. If he'd brought it to the table, Johnston would have directed their conversation to every topic under the sun other than what Kursk had come to discuss. As it was, the archbishop waited until the man was seated again, looked him over for several seconds, and said, "So, Monsignor, what brings you to my neck of the woods?"

Kursk looked startled, then cast a longing glance at this briefcase, now fifteen feet away. He pushed his chair back with a sigh, and started back toward the desk just as the door swung open and Cecilia, the middle-aged matron who supervised the archbishop's residence, entered pushing a tea cart complete with silver tea service. Kursk paused and before he realized it, she was between him and his briefcase. He stopped, then she stopped the cart as if on cue, waiting to see which way he was going. The archbishop decided he couldn't have planned it better himself. Kursk started to his right and Cecilia went left. The monsignor barely avoided running into the cart. He backed away, and the performance was repeated in the opposite direction. By now, Kursk was red-faced. He stood stock-still and motioned Cecilia to push the cart to the table. She smiled and dropped the faintest hint of an old-fashioned curtsy. Cecilia was a holy terror in her housekeeping domain, but the epitome of respect when dealing with the clergy.

"Thank you, Cecilia," beamed the archbishop. "If you'll lay the table, we'll pour for ourselves."

Kursk had retrieved his briefcase but was now forced to stand as Cecilia finished setting the table. Her cart blocked his chair. The archbishop continued to chat with her, as if the monsignor weren't in the room. By the time the silverware and plates and napkins were set, and the tea service placed within the monsignor's reach, Kursk looked ready to explode. His mood didn't improve when the archbishop eyed the case under Kursk's arm and said lightly, "Let us not spoil a civilized ritual such as tea with the discussion of business. I take it you can spare an extra hour or so."

Considering that Kursk had already spent at least that much time cooling his heels in the waiting room, the archbishop's question verged on fighting words, but the monsignor kept his temper. "Of course, Your Eminence, but I do have a plane to catch early this evening."

"Then by all means, let me pour the tea. I'd be glad to hear your appraisal of this blend. It was suggested to me by a very old Tibetan monk of my acquaintance."

The archbishop sipped, nibbled, poured again, and ran the conversation along mundane lines for more than an hour. He actually began to feel sorry for the man across the table from him, though he knew the monsignor to be about as sympathetic a character as Himmler. The man's reputation for double-dealing, character assassination, and almost sociopathic disregard for people's lives and careers reflected the worst excesses of the curia in Rome.

Abruptly, the archbishop shoved back his chair and strode to his desk. "As you have such a tight schedule, Monsignor Kursk, shall we get down to the reason for your visit?"

Kursk scrambled for his briefcase and resumed his chair opposite the archbishop. He quickly removed some documents bearing the seal of the Vatican. "We have been concerned for some time about the activities of a priest in your diocese, a Father Rosario."

"Enrique Rosario?" inquired the archbishop.

"Yes. He is pastor of St. Mary of the Groves in—"

"Santa Ana. Yes, I know him personally. A dedicated young man who works very hard in the community."

Kursk scowled. "Parish charity work is not our concern, Your Eminence."

"And yet it should be, I think. For what reason does our Mother Church exist except to serve the people?"

"To perpetuate the Catholic faith and protect it against the attacks of heretics and nonbelievers."

"Ah, well, there are many ways to look at the same picture, are there not? One person may look at a tableau of human suffering and experience despair; another pair of eyes may see the need for hope."

Kursk's expression indicated that he couldn't care less about the archbishop's philosophy of life. "To return to the subject at hand, this Father Rosario."

"Yes," said the archbishop pleasantly.

"It is about his research, and some of the articles he has published."

"He is a credit to his Jesuit training," replied Johnston. "A very intelligent man, a true academic according to his college records, and yet he works with his hands as well as his mind, and shows great love and compassion for his parishioners. I am impressed that he asked for a parish assignment rather than a teaching post. That is most unusual."

"As I said, his work in the parish is irrelevant to this issue. The topics of his research are unacceptable to the Congregation."

The archbishop leaned forward and rested his chin on his clasped hands. "Unacceptable? How can search for knowledge and truth be unacceptable?" Johnston, who knew all too well the tendency of some in the church to try and control people's very thoughts, was baiting the monsignor.

"There are areas of inquiry that are inappropriate."

"Such as?"

Here was the crux of the matter. The archbishop had read Rosario's articles, had been intrigued by his theories. He'd also heard the rumblings from the Vatican. While he didn't know precisely what long-guarded secret (of which there were many) lay at the heart of the objection to the priest's research, he knew it must be serious to prompt the curia to send Kursk, frequently dubbed "the Enforcer" behind his back. Kursk's dilemma lay in explaining why he wanted the priest muzzled without revealing any more of this deep, dark secret, whatever it was. If he didn't make a strong case, the archbishop would feel free to ignore the warning. If he told too much, he would be in violation of his own code of secrecy on sensitive areas of church lore.

"Father Rosario has gained access to historical documents unearthed at one of the old missions."

"I believe his specialty is history," said the archbishop blandly. "He would be interested in the memoirs of the church's pioneering clerics in this country."

"This has nothing to do with the proper study of church history," Kursk snapped. "It is pure nonsense, this...this..."

"This what?"

"This obsession with folklore and legend with no foundation in fact. It's nothing but heresy...I mean, hearsay."

But heresy *is exactly what you mean,* thought Johnston.

"If there is nothing to Father Rosario's research, then why is the Congregation so concerned with it?"

The monsignor reddened. "It is my—that is to say, our responsibility to put a stop to the spread of gossip and innuendo that could be harmful to the church."

"The church's image?"

"Well, yes, but the issue is doctrinal, not a question of poor public relations."

"How so?" asked Johnston. "How does the study of the personal journals and private documents of priests who lived centuries ago constitute an assault on church doctrine?" He sat back in his chair, hands folded in his lap, looking for all the world like a student in need of instruction.

Kursk took the bait. "Some of those priests were operating far outside the established authority of our Mother Church. The examples of their departures from doctrine were frequent and highly disturbing."

"Such as when Father Canara tried to integrate the teachings of Catholicism with the natives' own beliefs so that they would be more comfortable with his attempts to save them?"

"Exactly," said Kursk, slapping the papers down on the desk. "Completely unacceptable. Pure heresy. What sort of example is that for parish priests?"

"A pretty good one," said Johnston, sitting forward abruptly. "If anything, it demonstrates the sort of sensitivity sorely lacking in the work of many of our missionary orders. And before you try to give me a history lesson, let me give you one. The church's history is rife with corruption, political infighting, tyranny, and, most importantly, adjustments to its so-called divine doctrines. The fact that one man chooses to investigate the motivations and feelings of some of the first priests to work on this continent is hardly any threat to an institution that has stood for 2,000 years, despite its innumerable mistakes and unquestionable faults."

The archbishop glared at Kursk, who struggled to maintain eye contact but failed.

"Is there something else about these documents you aren't telling me?" asked Johnston. "Something besides a record of the poor job performance of priests in Spanish California?"

Kursk stared at him. "No, nothing specific."

Liar, the archbishop chided silently. *If you and your keepers weren't very afraid of something, you wouldn't be here.*

"Then what is it exactly that you came here to ask me?"

The monsignor straightened the papers in his hand. "These are letters from Bishop Rinaldi, Bishop Kreitner, and a note from Cardinal de Marcos, asking you to see to it that Father Rosario ceases this current project of his and immediately surrenders all historical documents and artifacts in his possession to the Vatican."

"Artifacts? I thought you were disturbed about his review of old papers."

"The request is simply framed so as to be thorough, in case there are any items he has found that are not necessarily considered documentary in nature."

Ah, now it starts to become clear. I wonder what the young man has found in his digging. Johnston regarded Kursk as he might examine a specimen under glass. "I am not aware of any such 'artifacts,' Monsignor, but I will consider the matter, and if it seems prudent, I will discuss it with Father Rosario."

"Your Eminence," Kursk sputtered. "This is not a…these letters are not intended to be taken so lightly."

"Are you accusing me of showing less than the appropriate respect for communications from the curia?" A dangerous light flickered in the archbishop's dark blue eyes.

"No, Your Eminence, it is simply that…"

"That what, Monsignor?"

Kursk's anger sparked between them. Johnston waited. He knew the monsignor was smarting from having lost every round of the bout. But then the Vatican emissary had come unprepared for his opponent. The archbishop imagined that Kursk could grind most clerics into dust, even those who greatly outranked him. He'd come halfway around the world to deliver a warning and expected that his reputation alone would guarantee him success in seeing the will of his masters done. He hadn't done his homework.

"I will leave these letters and messages for your review," said Kursk, rising to his feet, and placing the sheaf of papers on the desktop.

"If you will be so kind as to leave those with my assistant, Father Grolsch, I will get to them in due time." He smiled, having taken the final point of the match. Kursk did not dare ignore the request, or question the archbishop about his lack of interest in following the directives of his superiors in Rome. He scooped up the papers and started toward the door.

"Good day, Monsignor. I hope you've enjoyed your stay here, and that your flight home is pleasant."

Kursk reluctantly turned to face his tormentor. "Yes, Your Eminence. Thank you."

The door closed none too gently behind him. The archbishop waited for a while, pondering the events of the last two hours, then picked up his private line and dialed a number. When a voice answered, he said, "I'm trying to reach Father Rosario… Fine, then would you tell him that his friend, *Mister* Johnston will be by the rectory this evening to see him?"

For that young man's sake, thought Johnston, *I'd better get to the bottom of this. If he's doing what I think he's doing, though, God help us all.*

Chapter Three

A good parson once said,
that where mystery begins, religion ends.
—Edmund Burke, *A Vindication of Natural Society*

"Why does the departure board say 'Orange County,' while the itinerary says 'John Wayne Airport,' and the luggage tags say 'SNA'?"

Laura held her hands up in the universal "who knows" gesture. "I've never figured out why they don't just pick one, but I do know that the airport is in Orange County, lies partly in the city of Santa Ana—thus the SNA—and is named for the quintessential tough-guy actor of all time."

"Tougher than Steven Seagal?" Connor quipped, a smile playing across her face.

"Yep."

"Bruce Willis?"

"Yep."

"Surely you can't mean tougher than Arnold Schwarzenegger?"

"Yes, I do. The Duke managed to be tough without automatic weapons, grenades, kickboxing, Chinese throwing stars, top-secret military aircraft, and large-scale explosions. He was a 'good guy' when that actually meant something in Hollywood."

"How have we gotten this far in our relationship without me discovering you're a closet John Wayne fan?"

"No closet for me, kiddo," Laura said, grinning slightly at the all too obvious double entendre.

"Thank heavens for that," said Connor. "But John Wayne? All those corny old movies?"

"I'll have you know those old movies are classics. And I'd rather watch them any old day than most of the stuff they're putting out now."

"Agreed. But I would have thought those Westerns where Indians are perpetually defeated for being bloodthirsty savages would offend you."

"Stereotypes are always offensive, so I try to look past them. John Wayne was a product of his era. Those are the movies the studios were making, and he gave people something to admire. Besides, they weren't all westerns."

"Yes, that's true. There were all kinds of war movies, too, driving home the not-so-subtle message that war is glorious."

"All right, I'll give you that. We tend to romanticize just about everything, no matter how dark a situation. But I don't hold John Wayne responsible for the themes of those movies. From what I understand, he was a pretty good human being. And besides, I don't think he personally ever shot any Indians.

"So it doesn't at least annoy you when they portray Native Americans as murdering savages who are always defeated in the end?"

"Some Indians were savage in the sense that they warred with other tribes and killed with impunity. Some were much more peaceful. My people—like everyone else—have a history of both. And they were all defeated in the end," said Laura thoughtfully.

"Don't forget Little Big Horn."

"Ah, yes, the miscalculations of the macho male of the species."

"And John Wayne isn't macho?"

"Of course he is. But his fans like to think he'd never have been as stupid as Custer. I guess what I'm saying is that people need their icons.

John Wayne, with the exception of his more curmudgeonly roles, was everyone's grown-up Boy Scout."

"All right. I'll give you that one. But are there any more surprises lurking behind that enigmatic countenance?"

"Absolutely," said Laura.

"Excellent," replied Connor.

»——«

The flight was uneventful and long, the meal unmemorable, but the journey was well worth it. They'd left behind a cool, rainy day in Washington and here, a bright sun hung hot and brilliant in a deep azure sky as they stepped out of the terminal.

"That's the biggest statue of him ever created," said Laura, pointing back over her shoulder to the enormous bronze figure of the actor clad in his trademark leather vest, boots, jeans and cowboy hat.

"Well, Mr. Wayne was a big, big man."

"I think you're quoting the lyrics of 'Big Bad John.' "

"Possibly. But if the boot fits—"

"All right, enough. I give up. How about if you wait here with the luggage and I'll go get the rental car."

Connor looked at her for a moment. "Why is it that I still sometimes get the feeling you can't stop acting like a secret agent–slash–bodyguard?"

"It would be hard to stop acting like what I've been for years," Laura said, "but I'm not bodyguarding you anymore. That was a long time ago, and if your father hadn't wanted someone to look out for you when you took that little jaunt to New Mexico, we'd never had met."

"And I'd be dead, too, as a matter of fact."

"Possibly. But since you returned the favor, why don't we not worry about it anymore? I'm going to get the car because you often let people take advantage of you and I always insist on the best car at the best rate."

"Am I that bad?" asked Connor sheepishly.

"Yes, like with that kid at the airport rental agency in London. You were so busy playing the kind celebrity to his hysterical fan worship you didn't notice that he charged you full price."

"I could afford it."

"Yes, but having money doesn't mean you're not entitled to a fair shake. You're the best tipper I've ever known. You're thoughtful, sensitive, generous to a fault, and never rude to anyone who doesn't deserve it. You never deprive anyone except yourself."

Connor regarded Laura with evident amusement. "Are you all done?"

Laura blushed. "Oops, was I getting carried away?"

"Yes, but I love that about you. And I'm not always all those virtuous things you said, but thank you for saying it anyway. I will stand here and obediently await your return with the rental car. Just one thing, though."

"Yes."

"Please can we have a convertible?"

Connor watched Laura walk back into the terminal and realized with a shiver that she loved everything about her.

Though the sun was edging close to the horizon when they drove into town on the Pacific Coast Highway, Laguna Beach was still hopping. Traffic was sluggish and they had plenty of time to take in the sights—shops, art galleries, and restaurants on their left, the broad expanse of Pacific Ocean on their right. People crowded the beach and the boardwalk. Sun worshipers were finally gathering up their towels, blankets, and beach paraphernalia as the more athletic types, unwilling to give up on the day, hurled themselves around the volleyball courts. Connor leaned her head back on the seat and soaked in the rays. "This is perfect."

Laura, at the wheel of the Volvo convertible she'd finally chosen, was equally happy. "You're right. This is one of those 'all's right with the world' moments, isn't it?"

"Indubitably," said Connor with a grin.

"You writers can never resist the twenty-dollar words, can you?"

"Nope."

The light turned red, and Laura slowed to a stop, glancing over at Connor basking in the sun.

Her thick mane of hair was skillfully cut to frame her face in soft, natural waves falling just to her collar, though Laura knew she had chosen the style more for the sake of convenience than out of an attempt to conform to fashion trends. Her chin was firm, though not overly prominent, as were the finely sculptured cheekbones. Behind the sunglasses, crystal blue eyes were set beneath dark, expressive eyebrows that contrasted sharply with a pale, creamy complexion. Her nose was subtle, well-proportioned. The sum total of Connor's features was harmonious and compelling, bordering on the androgynous, but retaining an unmistakably feminine energy.

Laura occasionally felt a little plain in comparison to Connor's black Irish intensity, but that was hardly an opinion anyone else would have seconded. A not too distant ancestor had added a trace of the oriental to her Navajo blood, creating the slightly almond-shaped brown eyes beneath luxuriant lashes. She wore her dark glossy hair long and sometimes braided in the traditional fashion, but more often loose, fanning across her back, nearly to her waist. Today she'd tied it back with a scarf in deference to the open car.

"The light's green, sweetheart," said Connor, bringing Laura our of her reverie.

"I was holding out for a different shade," Laura retorted, easing the car forward. "How many blocks to the hotel?"

Connor consulted the tiny map printed in the brochure. "It says 'not to scale' which is the same thing as 'not very helpful,' but I'd guess less than a half mile."

Just past a string of art galleries and shops, they pulled into the half circle driveway at the Laguna Vista Inn and a porter stepped to the trunk of the car. Laura popped the trunk release.

"I'll go check in," said Connor. "And then we can decide what to do for dinner."

Laura showed the porter what bags should be unloaded, then waited for the parking attendant to return to his desk and give her a claim check for the car. In less than a minute, she saw him sprinting across the parking lot toward her.

"Sorry to keep you waiting. We usually have quite a crowd downtown on Saturday nights in the summer, and we have to squeeze as many cars in as possible." His voice was deep and musical.

"That's all right," Laura smiled. "We're checking in, and I don't think we'll need the car tonight. So bury it if you need to."

"Thanks," the young man said.

Laura noticed the pendant glittering against his dark skin, dangling just beneath the hollow of his throat. "That's a beautiful crucifix," she said. "I don't think I've ever seen one with facets like that."

He held it up proudly. "My sister is an artist, a maker of beautiful jewelry. She made this for me for my confirmation."

Laura was intrigued by the craftsmanship. "Is your sister's work in one of the galleries around here?"

His face fell slightly. "No, she cannot afford a space here, and it is very difficult to convince people to sell your work in these shops. They are very…" he hesitated.

"Snooty?" said Laura, tipping her chin in the air and tapping her nose.

The young man laughed. "Yes, ma'am. Just that. But she does have some pieces on display at a shop in Santa Ana. Not a fancy place, you understand, but if you would like to go there sometime."

"As a matter of fact I would. My friend has a birthday coming up pretty soon. Could you give me the address of your the shop?"

Looking around, apparently to see if the coast was clear, he reached under the check stand and drew out a business card. "It's on here, ma'am. And here is your claim check."

"You don't have to call me 'ma'am.' My name is Laura Nez."

"I am Luis." He took her outstretched hand.

"A pleasure to meet you, and I hope we'll meet your sister as well."

"Thank you, Ms. Nez." Another car pulled into the driveway, and he grinned at Laura before sprinting over to it. She wondered if he did anything at a walking pace.

Just as she turned to go into the hotel, she saw a flash of movement at the corner of her eye, as if someone were standing right beside her. But when she swiveled her head, there was no doubt she was entirely alone standing under the portico of the hotel. Odd, she thought as a shiver crawled up her spine. What was Connor's phrase? As if someone had just walked over your grave.

»—«

He supposed there were those among the hard-line religious who would brand this scene sinful, all these near-naked bodies displayed in public, people with seemingly nothing on their minds except a day's play or a night's entertainment. And he was intelligent enough to imagine the form that entertainment might take. True, he had never partaken of those carnal activities for fear they might prove a fatal distraction from his work. His life was necessarily one of chastity, and in some cases, severe deprivation, but not because human pleasures were forbidden—far from it. His faith allowed him to rejoice in the human capacity to experience joy and pleasure.

To his occasional regret, however, the weight of his responsibilities dictated a solitary existence. Mostly, though, he saw only blessing in this, a gift of the Creator. His work was all, and he had been provided the training he needed to carry it out. All over the world he had traveled, cared for by first one then another of his sworn allies. They partly understood his burden and sought to help him in whatever way possible. But they could not walk the path with him to its conclusion.

A Tibetan mystic had taught him more than most of the others combined, though he had received wisdom in the words of many wise women and men. But the mystic, a wizened old woman from an ancient tradition that predated the repressively patriarchal phases of most religions, had guided him on the most dangerous and the most glorious of paths. He had almost become lost, had nearly allowed himself to escape into the void. But the spark that burned within him, ignited by his long-ago predecessor, and passed from one to another for hundreds of years, would not let his mind or his ego or even his desires choose a destiny different than that which his soul had freely chosen.

No one here could quite see him. The astute, the spiritually aware, they might glimpse a shadow, a flash of light, but the ability to remain outside their conscious perception was one of the gifts the old woman had given him.

He contemplated the men, women, and children around him and smiled a rare smile. *They are not sinners,* he thought. *Such an archaic concept, that natural behavior could be sinful, that carnality was neces-*

sarily evil unless sanctified by ritual and ceremony. Only love sanctified, and only fire purified. Those were the tenets of his faith and the principles on which he'd built his existence, an existence that was finally reaching its natural conclusion…he hoped.

A child laughed and the sound caught his attention. The tiny girl, perhaps only two years old, stood a few feet away, looking straight at him. She could see him. He knew that. He smiled at her and she giggled with delight. The child's mother looked to see what had amused her daughter. She shrugged. There was nothing there. Another flight of fancy. "You big silly," she teased the little girl.

The children see me, he mused. *They are still unburdened with cynicism and fear. They see with the eyes of angels. As soon we all will, God be praised.*

He was still a little puzzled about the two women he'd felt compelled to talk with at the cathedral. As he shook each one's hand, he saw their pasts, separately and together. The images were in some instances quite strange, though perhaps no stranger than some of the things he had seen in his journey in the other places of consciousness. The one with the shorter hair and the intense eyes—he'd seen her in his mind dressed quite differently, wearing a silvery gray robe girdled by a belt that shone like the brightest stars he'd ever seen. And the Native American woman, she had been there, too, on a hilltop in a place of great power. But also he'd seen a vision of her without her friend, standing instead beside a very old Indian woman in a cave beneath a mountain standing near a portal to those other places he'd sometimes visited on his spirit journeys. He wasn't sure what it meant, but he was convinced that they were a part of the Creator's plan. He would wait and he would watch. He knew the end of his search for the sacred object was within reach. Time could not be held back.

Chapter Four

Conscience is a coward,
and those faults it has not strength enough to prevent
it seldom has justice enough to accuse.
—Oliver Goldsmith, *She Stoops to Conquer*

San Peligro Nuclear Generating Station

Archibald Sims was frightened, but as fear had been his constant companion throughout the better part of forty-five years, the sensation was familiar. His stomach churned, and he reached for one of the economy-size bottles of antacid tablets he always kept within reach near his desk, on his nightstand at home, and in his car. As backup, he had smaller bottles and paper tubes of tablets stashed in his briefcase, coat pockets, desk drawers, and every nook and cranny of his luggage...just in case. A girlfriend had told him not too long ago how bad it was for his digestion to take so many antacids, but she had no idea that he wouldn't survive the nausea and heartburn for even a few hours without his trusty magic bullets. During the past thirty-six hours, he'd probably munched a hundred of them.

His office, with clear glass walls from waist level to ceiling, overlooked the control room. Below him he could see technicians at the various monitoring stations, others moving purposefully from one task to another. *They looked calm,* he thought, *as if they didn't know they were sitting on top of a nuclear pile.* Perhaps their imaginations didn't run to thoughts of "what if."

Archibald's did—at least once or twice a day.

Time and again he'd wondered why he even worked here, why he had chosen to be an engineer in the first place and a nuclear power expert in the second. The place terrified him. But he kept coming back to work, day after day, week after week, partly because he had nowhere else to go, and mostly because he was afraid to even contemplate disobeying the Preacher. There had been a time when everything about the secret society thrilled him. He finally belonged. He had some friends who respected him. He'd felt important for the first time in his life. But the situation had soured, first when he'd learned that the man who'd recruited him was a convicted felon who'd served time in prison back East for forgery and embezzlement and then when his new friends had disappeared rather suddenly. He'd been left alone again until recently, until the messages started coming—cryptic notes pushed under his door, or E-mails that couldn't be traced back to the sender. His loyalty was being questioned. But why?

He'd been so sure the society was little more than a game of pretend, like those people who ran around in a field, shooting paint balls at each other. All the talk of punishing the perverts and blasphemers who'd betrayed the word of God, defeating the government's conspiracies, and reasserting male superiority—it was all just right-wing propaganda, wasn't it? He didn't really agree that all women clerics should be thrown out of the churches, or that all adult females should be either wives or nuns. He rather liked women, though his love life was relatively pathetic since they didn't appear to like him.

The main problem was that he didn't welcome change in his life; no, more than that, he feared it. This particular phobia—and he had enough of them to inspire an article in a psychiatric journal—explained his brief and sadly unsuccessful relationships with women. They were attracted to his decent looks (except perhaps that increasing bald spot), his single status, and his obvious intelligence. Unfortunately, they were repelled, sooner rather than later, by his paranoia, obsessive fastidiousness, and of course, the munching of little white tablets, usually in place of meals. So Archibald remained unattached. The only outlet for his libido consisted of sessions of "compu-sex" with anonymous women who frequented Internet chat rooms. At least he hoped they were women. That they might not be gave him yet one more thing to worry about. Still, he needed something, didn't he?

He glanced at the special bulletin on his desk, the document that had made him reach for a handful of his tablets. The bold black letters leaped off the page: SECURITY ADVISORY. The page had oozed out of his fax machine only thirty minutes earlier and he still hadn't read it through completely. Now, while mentally repeating the various reassuring phrases his last therapist had taught him, he tackled the memo:

> *Various law enforcement agencies around the United States, both local and federal, have received increasing numbers of threats against nuclear power generating facilities. The actions threatened are not entirely specific, nor has any one facility been mentioned by name. No law enforcement agency has been successful in tracing the origins of these threats, which are not necessarily considered to pose an immediate danger. However, as they cannot yet be ruled out as entirely unsubstantiated threats, all management and security personnel at the above-addressed facilities are encouraged to maintain a state of enhanced alertness to possible security breaches.*

That was it. Archibald rubbed his temples. It was typical bureaucratic doublespeak—someone trying to cover his ass. If something happened, the desk jockey at the NRC could say he'd sent out an alert. If nothing happened, no one could accuse him of overreacting and stirring up anxiety. In the meantime, the recipients were left wondering. Was there cause for concern or not? For Archibald Sims, the situation was far worse than a mere state of uncertainty. The messages he'd received from the

Preacher weren't all that subtle. He was expecting Brother Sims to live up to his "oath" as a member of the society, to help wield the divine hammer of God, and the Preacher also hinted that it was Sims's profession that had made him so valuable to the society. Archibald shuddered at the thought of the nuclear pile beneath his feet.

He picked up the receiver, put it back, then picked it up again and stared at the keypad on the phone. Archibald was at least nominally the manager of the facility. But since he was loath to confront anyone over anything, the place pretty much ran without his participation. He was particularly leery of the security chief, a loud, overbearing, and physically imposing bully. Archibald had never once questioned Peter Holcomb's policies or actions. Besides, he was fairly sure the man would have received the same security alert memo. Why bother bringing it up? Holcomb knew his job. Still, what if Archibald did nothing and it later came out that Holcomb had never gotten the alert or a heads-up from his "boss?" The blame would then fall directly on Archibald's shoulders.

He chewed another antacid and pressed a button for an internal line. He punched in the extension.

"Holcomb!" The deep baritone vibrated the earpiece in Archibald's phone.

"This is Sims," he said.

"Yes, *Mister* Sims."

Archibald swallowed, ignoring the obvious sarcasm. "I'm checking to see if you got the security alert memo this morning about the potential terrorist threats."

Holcomb laughed. "Yeah, I got it. And I already put it where it belongs…in the round file." He laughed again. "Jesus, one of those pointy-head bureaucrats gets his panties in a twist because some zoned-out schizoid decides to play poison pen." He paused. "But I could see where you might take it seriously, *Mister* Sims. You being the *manager* and all."

Archibald gritted his teeth for a moment. Secretly, he hoped Holcomb was absolutely right about the alert being bogus, though he doubted it. But he couldn't let the remark go unchallenged, at least not completely.

"I think we should at least keep the alert in mind. After all, the people in Washington—"

"Those morons couldn't find their asses with both hands."

"Still, for the sake of our security—"

"Nothing wrong with our security. Nothing at all. This place is as tight as a virgin's—"

Archibald slammed the phone down before Holcomb could finish his obscene little analogy. God, how he hated that man. Plus, the bastard was lying through his teeth. Their security wasn't up to par at all. The last two new hires he'd seen at the gate looked not the least bit professional. The most complimentary adjective he could think of was 'scruffy.' He wondered if either of them could even pass a cursory background check. But he suspected that it all boiled down to money. For the last eighteen months, he'd been told one thing over and over: "Cut the budget—we're bleeding red ink." Archibald sensed that the claim was absurd, just as he had come to realize that something was very wrong with the way the plant was being utilized. California was in a full-stage energy crisis. Tens of thousands of homes were going dark for hours in rolling blackouts, and state bureaucrats were wringing their hands and demanding explanations. Archibald, were he not terrified of confrontation and notoriety, could have provided one simple answer: The generating plants were not operating at capacity.

He opened his desk drawer and pulled out the red folder in which he had compiled memos, documents that were to have been shredded after first reading. Why he'd been courageous enough to keep them he didn't know. Or perhaps he was more afraid that if his actions were questioned, he wouldn't have the proof at hand that none of this had been his idea. Simply put, he'd been told to periodically reduce the output of his plant. He had to use various excuses such as maintenance and overhauling of equipment, but all of that was just smoke. Somewhere far above his paltry management position were those who had decided to create a power shortage and make a great deal of money by generously providing additional power from outside the state. Electricity was being purchased at outlandish prices because the politicos knew people would eventually throw them out of office if the blackouts persisted.

Sighing, he closed the file, wondering, not for the first time, if he should somehow leak this information to the press. But he wouldn't, any more than he would reveal his involvement with the society. Principle-driven heroics were for others, not Archibald Sims. The security alert caught his eye again, and he shook his head. His plant's so-called security team was running at half the manpower he reported to the Nuclear Regulatory Commission. And of those, most were either young or inexperienced or both. Then Holcomb had added that pair who looked as if they might have just been released from a drug rehab center. He crumpled up the memo and did just what Holcomb had done—filed it where he thought it would do the least damage to his career.

Chapter Five

Habere non potest Deum patrem qui ecclesiam non habet matrem.
(He cannot have God for his Father
who has not the church for his mother.)
—St. Cyprian, *De Cath. Eccl. Unitate, iv*

St. Mary of the Groves Church
Santa Ana, California

"You have a visitor, Father," said the little old woman in a soft, quavery voice. "He says he is Mr. Johnston, but you know these old eyes of mine must be playing tricks. He looks exactly like our archbishop."

Enrique Rosario laughed, looking past his elderly cook housekeeper at the tall figure clad in black slacks, white open-collared shirt, and gray windbreaker. "I think Lucinda has your number, Eminence."

"I didn't think this ugly face was that well-known," the archbishop smiled. In truth, he kept out of the limelight. He firmly believed publicity-seeking on the part of church leaders was an ego fault, if not a venial sin.

"Yours is not a face I would forget, Your Eminence," said the old woman, nodding in deference as she left the room.

"So much for a low profile," said the archbishop. "Lucinda doesn't miss a thing, does she?"

"No, sir, she doesn't. Please sit down. I was about to have some coffee. Would you like a cup?"

"Too late in the day for me," said Johnston with a tinge of regret as he pulled out a chair from the old oak table. "I'd be up half the night."

Father Rosario poured his coffee and sat down across from his superior. "To what do I owe the honor of your visit, Your Eminence?"

"Enough with the 'Eminence' crap, Enrique. That may fly with some of the muddleheaded Roman collars in this diocese, but I know you better than that. You're obedient and demure only when it suits you."

The priest grinned. "So I'm that transparent, am I? Lucinda says the same thing."

"Smart woman. Now what exactly are you up to that's got the Vatican in a minor uproar?"

Father Rosario's face grew still. "What do you mean?"

"You're stalling, Enrique. You know perfectly well what I'm talking about because I know for a fact you've received copies of these letters." Johnston withdrew some folded sheets from the inside pocket of his jacket. "Monsignor Johann Kursk paid me a visit today with every intention of pinning my ears back about you."

The priest's face suffused with blood—a sure sign, Johnston knew, of Rosario's temper. "Yes, I've gotten a letter or two. I tore them up. They don't know what they're talking about."

Johnston regarded the young priest thoughtfully. "In all fairness to Kursk, and I hate even saying his name and the word 'fairness' in the same sentence, I think they have a pretty good suspicion of what you're up to."

"Look, it's just research. I worked on this same topic when I was at seminary. It was the heart of my dissertation."

"Ah, but then it was purely academic and not for public consumption...and your dissertation treated the matter as if it were nothing more than a quaint legend. You may as well know that even at the time there was some concern about your choice of topic."

"So that explains why old Father Jensen kept trying to convince me to start over with something else. I never knew why he backed off suddenly." Johnston smiled and Rosario stared at him for a moment. "It was you, wasn't it? You pulled strings."

"Yes, frankly, I did. As a matter of fact, there was a time when you were almost expelled from seminary for your unorthodox ideas, your lack of proper obedience…Need I go on?"

"No. You're right. I was all that and more. But I think I sensed I was walking a fine line. I swallowed a lot of what I was thinking during those last couple of years. Otherwise I'd never have gotten to be what I've always wanted—a priest."

"That's why you're here, isn't it? Working this old, run-down parish instead of teaching somewhere."

"Yes. I was always torn between vocations. The past fascinates me, especially the parts of our history that the 'system' tries to bury. But I couldn't be a priest and not minister to the people. I guess it's in my blood."

"Your mother was a woman of science, and from what you've told me, your father was an honorable man in the best possible sense of the word. It's a tragedy that illness took him."

Enrique's expression softened. His father had died only six months earlier. "He was a man of God, though he never became a priest. I've never known anyone who gave of himself so tirelessly. There was never a good cause he didn't support, never a hard job that he shirked. He worked with his hands all his life, you know."

"He was a stonemason, wasn't he?"

"From the old country. The last of a long line of gifted Italian artisans. Generations of men, all of the same honored profession."

"The builders of the cathedrals and churches."

"He came here when my grandfather was brought over from Europe to work on the National Cathedral. My father was an apprentice. He spent almost his entire life carving the stones of that church before he settled here in California. When he was almost thirty-five, he met my mother. She was touring the building site, stumbled over some stone, and a hand reached out to steady her. According to them, that's all it took to fall in love, even though she was ten years younger and the daughter of a minor Spanish diplomat."

"They were certainly an odd couple for that day and age. What was it, the 1950s?"

"Her family was furious because my father was a stonemason. His family was outraged because she wasn't Italian."

"And still they persevered."

"They were in love for more than forty years. Mama finally was able to teach at the university, published four papers, and after years of waiting for God to smile on them, she produced three kids. Dad adored us and her."

Johnston smiled. "You admire that loyalty, don't you?"

"Yes, I do."

"Even though as a priest you will never know the love of a woman, the warmth of your child in your arms?"

Enrique closed his eyes for a moment, as if in prayer. "I suppose I've accepted that, though not happily. I see no rational or defensible reason priests cannot marry. Neither do I believe that God requires it or that our Lord Jesus taught it. But I will content myself, I hope, with being a good uncle when the time comes."

"It's a position rather difficult to justify to most intelligent people," agreed Johnston. "Our leaders choose not to talk much about Saint Peter."

Enrique smiled slightly. "You mean that he was married. Otherwise, how could Jesus have cured his mother-in-law?"

"Exactly. There is really no sound theological or philosophical foundation for lifelong celibacy. But our Mother Church will cling to the past until change is literally forced upon it. But," he paused, "to get back to the subject at hand, tell me what you are doing, or what it is you have, that is scaring our Roman masters? This particular document," he unfolded the papers, "specifically requires you to turn over materials of any kind, document or artifact, that are in your possession. Just what is it you've gotten hold of, Enrique?"

Silence lay heavy in the room as the two men regarded each other. Johnston waited patiently, secure in the belief that the young priest would tell him the truth if given the chance.

"I don't...that is, I can't explain it."

Johnston frowned. "That answer isn't acceptable, Father Rosario. If you expect me to stand up to the Congregation for the Defense of Doctrine, and take on Monsignor Kursk, you'd better be more forthcoming. I have an idea of what you're doing, if only because I read your dissertation four years ago. This is about the Cult of Magdalene, isn't it?"

"Yes, and no." He held up his hand when he saw the irritation on the archbishop's face. "I'm not trying to be evasive. I'm just telling you that there's much more to this than I thought. When I first stumbled across the references to another branch of the faith, dating from the time of Jesus, I thought it was no more than the usual speculations based on fragmentary documents and apocryphal stories. But when I was working on my dissertation, I made a trip to Rome—to the archives. And I found something no one is supposed to see."

The archbishop's eyebrows went up. "They would never allow a seminarian access to secret materials, not without the permission of someone very high up in the curia, a cardinal…and not just any cardinal."

"I can't tell you the name, but your guess is close. While I was there I seemed to encounter very little resistance to my requests for various materials. Then I received a written message slipped under my door at the North American College where I was staying. It instructed me to ask for a particular file by catalog number and review its contents very thoroughly. The next day, I did. The clerk brought me the file enclosed in one of those clothbound hard covers. Most of it consisted of routine historical accounts of life in an Italian abbey toward the end of the seventeenth century. By all accounts, it was a pretty bleak place on the island of Corsica. Anyway, I read all that and was about to give up, thinking I'd been played for a fool, when I saw the edge of a parchment sticking out from between the binding of the cover and its endpaper."

"And what was in it?" Johnston was sitting forward on the edge of his chair now. His rigid posture belied the calmness of his question.

"A partial journal written by a novice monk at the abbey. When the buildings were torn down in the late 1800s, the sheets must have been found and tossed in with all of the documents beings shipped to the Vatican archives. They were never catalogued, though, because I couldn't find a reference in any index."

Father Rosario took a long swallow of coffee. "I kept the papers."

"You what?!"

"I had a strong hunch that whoever pointed me toward the file wanted me to have the document. Since it wasn't in the index, there was no way the clerk would know I had taken it."

"But there are security cameras, guards, X-ray machines—they even search some people as they leave."

"I was very careful, and I tended to think that if my original assumption was correct, and someone was trying to reveal some long-concealed secret, they would smooth the way for me at least a little. The guard only glanced inside my briefcase as I left."

"And didn't see the pages of parchment?"

"They weren't in the briefcase. They were wrapped around my ankle, inside my sock."

Johnston took a deep breath. "But what a chance you were taking. Your career could have been finished. It might have all been a trap."

"True, but it wasn't."

They sat in the silence for several moments and then both spoke at once.

"So what did the—"

"The gist of the journal was—"

They stopped, smiled at each other, and Johnston sat back in his chair, trying to relax the tension in his shoulder. "Sorry. I'm being impatient. Take your time."

"I couldn't decipher much of it that day in the library. Chunks of it were barely legible, given the age of the paper and the materials of that time. The text itself was written in a maddening and almost incomprehensible mixture of Latin, Greek, and archaic Italian. And the writer had tried to use every single centimeter of blank space by writing the tiniest characters you can imagine. Presumably there was little paper to be had. But I finally pieced most of it together. The monk had hidden the pages of his journal because unauthorized writing of any kind was forbidden. The abbot apparently was quite the tyrant and known to punish and even torture the disobedient among his monks."

"Sounds like a cleric the warm and friendly Monsignor Kursk would appreciate," said Johnston.

Father Rosario nodded. "Exactly. So the monks pretty much lived in fear and were afraid to discuss anything because spies of the abbot were everywhere. Why this monk dared to write a journal I'll never know, because he indicates the penalty could easily be the amputation of a hand, if not death."

"Then he must have been a man of principle. He was more disturbed about something at the abbey than he was afraid of the abbot."

"True. Although the journal ends abruptly, so perhaps he should have feared more for his life."

"So what exactly did he write, other than that the abbot was a sociopath?"

"I know it just about by heart now. He wrote of a Brother Gandolfo, an old monk who had been the object of the abbot's enmity for a very long time. The other monks had whispered of the brother's 'penitential retreat' from which he'd emerged physically broken. I haven't quite figured out what he meant by the retreat, but I'm assuming it was something cooked up by the evil abbot."

"Reasonable theory."

"Anyway, the writer of the journal says that the abbot was obsessed with having Brother Gandolfo watched at all times."

"Why?"

"The author doesn't know. But he cautiously befriended Brother Gandolfo, being careful not to be too chummy and draw unwarranted suspicion on himself. Still, he refers to the older monk as a kind and gentle soul who was always in great physical pain from many injuries."

"Sounds as if the good brother got on the abbot's bad side and spent some time in prison or being tortured."

Father Rosario shuddered. "I know the history of the church, but it still shocks me from time to time."

"Within every human being lies the potential to do cruel and unconscionable harm to their fellow humans, especially in the name of God. Why should Catholics be immune to that potential? But at least there is always room for improvement. Please go on."

"On the last few pages, the writing grew more emphatic and hurried. Brother Gandolfo was dead. He'd fallen into the sea from the edge of a precipice on which the abbey stood. His robe was found folded over a tree branch."

"So there was little doubt that the man had committed suicide."

"Exactly. Another monk had actually seen him dive out over the edge, and the abbot was furious."

"The worst of sins," Johnston acknowledged, "especially during that time. They had yet to develop a way around that, the 'mental disturbance, not of sound mind' theory."

"As I understood it, mortal sin was the least of the abbot's concerns. He immediately had the abbey turned inside out, searched by his close circle of—I don't know what you'd call them. Aides?"

"Henchmen?" the archbishop supplied.

"I suppose, but putting the term 'henchmen' in a story about an old abbey makes the story sound like an Ellis Peters novel."

"True but perhaps accurate. So the abbot was looking for something."

"Something he wanted very badly. I've theorized that Brother Gandolfo was only allowed to live because he had never revealed whatever the abbot wanted."

"Reasonable, but what could the secret possibly have been? And how does it relate to your dissertation topic?"

"When I first began to smooth out the translation, I couldn't imagine. The Cult of Magdalene, as it came to be called over the centuries, was only linked to this particular abbey in pure speculation. But I knew that whoever gave me access to this already was aware of my research topic. Otherwise, why bother?"

"True enough. But where does all this get you, except in serious hot water with Kursk and his people? They must have figured out that you have those pages of parchment. That's what they're trying to get back without mentioning them specifically."

"Which means something nasty may have happened to the person who sent me that note, I'm afraid."

"Possibly. But perhaps that person died and information was found in their files. It's taken them a very long time to figure this out, so they weren't aware of what you found until now."

"And now they're afraid."

"Yes, but of what? This still sounds like nothing more than a few more unsavory skeletons in the church's closet—a mad tyrannical abbot, a suicidal monk, a confused young novice."

"I haven't quite told you everything."

"Ah, then perhaps you should."

Father Rosario refilled his coffee cup. "There are two other important points. One is that the novice had occasionally glimpsed Brother Gandolfo slip away from his constant watchers. The young man was quick and apparently intelligent as well as curious. He followed Gandolfo to the same spot on three occasions and made note of a well-hidden path leading down to a shallow ledge. Gandolfo would apparently reappear within a short time and hurry back to the abbey."

"Sounds as if he were concealing something, but what on earth would a monk have to conceal?"

"I'm beginning to form an idea, a theory really, but the novice never figured out why the brother was going there."

"Planning his suicide, maybe?"

"No, the novice specifically says that the monk's robe and belt were found just below the garden's walls. The path he refers to earlier issues from the stable yard, which, according to the diagrams I've dug up, was more than 150 yards away."

The archbishop rubbed his chin. "Hmm, okay, so where does that leave us? You said there were two points."

"On the same day the monk leapt into the sea, the monastery's blacksmith, a deaf-mute giant of a man, was found murdered in the shed where he had his forge. According to the novice, who was ordered to help prepare the body for burial, he found what appeared to be an old marking that might have been burned onto the man's thigh, a symbol he reproduced in this journal. The older monk who was with him covered it immediately and threatened to have the young man whipped if he so much as mentioned it."

The archbishop took a deep breath and hesitated, almost as if reluctant to ask the obvious question. "The symbol?"

Rosario reached for a pen and pad on the table. "It looked like this."

He drew the simple shape quickly, and Johnston almost recoiled at the sight. He'd only seen that design once in his life and had been sure he would never see it again. His heart thrummed in his chest. "Sweet Mother of God," he whispered.

"Exactly," said Father Rosario.

A long silence enveloped the two men. The ticking of the old wall clock grew louder. Finally, Johnston raised his eyes to Father Rosario's. "But what has this to do with your research at the mission? The papers they say you took from the mission at Santa Maria."

Enrique shook his head. "I didn't steal anything from Santa Maria, or anywhere else. It's just an excuse they're using to find out what I do have."

"Then what is the connection to the missions? Is it Father Canara?"

Enrique's eyes widened. "How do you know that?"

The archbishop shrugged. "Kursk insisted that the work of heretical missionary priests like Canara was harmful to the image of the church. Don't tell me there is actually something to that absurd line of reasoning."

"Not the way they mean it, but I hope it's just a shot in the dark, another smoke screen." He lowered his voice and leaned across the table. "Canara was more than a disobedient, nondogmatic priest. He was a member of this." Enrique tapped his finger on the symbol that stared up at them from the scrap of paper.

"But why did you suspect?"

"I didn't! That's just it. I stumbled across something purely by accident. I was walking around Santa Maria, examining the ruins of some of the mission's outbuildings. Near the place where they boiled the soap, I was trying to take a photograph and stepped backward into a shallow vat. As I fell, a few of the stones from around the border came down on top of me."

"Lucky they didn't ban you from the place forever. It's part of the park system now, a historical landmark."

"No one saw me fall, thank heaven. I picked myself up and tried to put the stones back more or less where they'd been. Then I noticed something carved into one of them. I brushed off the dirt, and it was this symbol. Underneath the symbol was a stick figure and the initials A. C."

"Alejandro Canara?"

"His is the only name from that era that fits the initials. And if what I've learned of the history of the cult is true, his politics would make sense. Naturally I tried to get a look at all the documents I could locate from the mission's history. But there are very few on site, and the mission records, if they still exist, are in the Vatican Archives."

Johnston looked at Rosario closely, as if not entirely sure the young priest was telling the whole truth. But he let it drop. If Enrique had found something, he would tell Johnston sooner or later.

"So at least one of the Magdalenes was still around in the late-eighteenth century right here in California." The archbishop scowled. "You know you're playing with fire, Enrique. I can't fault you for seeking the truth, but surely you must realize that what this cult believed is as antithetical to the church's teachings as anything you could imagine."

"That doesn't mean they were entirely wrong, does it?"

"No, but don't think for a minute that Kursk and his cronies are going to let you get away with going public with any of this."

"The public isn't ready for it," said Enrique sadly. "And to be honest, I still don't know exactly what 'it' is. But I have a feeling the Magdalenes were a great deal more important than we've ever believed. They may still exist! I know I'm getting closer."

"No doubt someone or several someones at the Vatican have that same feeling. Please be careful, and for heaven's sake, pull together some useless but authentically historical material and send it to them. That, at least, will buy you a little time." He looked down at the paper again, then crumpled it in his large fist. "May the saints preserve us, my friend."

Chapter Six

It is the cause, and not the death, that makes the martyr.
—Napoleon Bonaparte

"I think this is the street," said Laura, consulting the Thomas Guide map book they'd purchased at a bookstore. "Yep, hang a right."

Connor spun the wheel of the convertible and slowed to a stop at the curb. "What's the name of the shop again?"

"*Fantasia de Oro,* according to this business card—'Fantasy of Gold' or maybe 'Golden Fantasy.' The number is 1325." She scanned the opposite side of the street. "There it is, that blue awning."

Spotting a parking place on the other side, Connor swung the car into a quick U-turn and backed smartly into the tight space.

"That's one of the things I love about you," said Laura. "You can parallel-park."

"Gee, and I've never even thought to put that on my résumé."

"Actually, you have many talents, some of which are probably not résumé material. But I still take note of them."

"And which talents would those be?" Connor smiled.

"Some we could discuss in public, some we could discuss with our

54

closest friends, and some we don't need to discuss at all because you demonstrate them regularly in a boudoir setting."

"Ah, let's hear it for multitasking capabilities." She leaned over and gave Laura a quick peck on the cheek. "Now, tell me again why we wandered around Santa Ana looking for a little jewelry shop. There were lots of places in Laguna Beach, and you know I love buying you things on those rare occasions when you let me."

"You didn't get a chance to see the crucifix that Luis was wearing, but you would have appreciated it."

"Luis? How is it that you manage to make friends and be on a first-name basis with people everywhere we go?"

"Because I'm an ardent egalitarian who likes people."

"And I'm not?"

"At heart, yes. You try, sweetheart, but I'm not sure you've entirely gotten over your reserved upbringing. You're unfailingly polite, and you treat everyone with equal respect, but you don't exactly come across as gregarious."

Connor thought about that for a moment. "I suppose you're right. I'm probably more like my grandmother than I admit."

"And I'm not knocking that. By all accounts, she was an elegant, charming, courteous, and typically British lady in the best sense of the word. From what I've felt of her spiritual presence, she's incredible. All I'm saying is that you're probably still a little young to take on the 'gruff but kindly matriarch of the village' role. There'll be plenty of time for that, maybe when we settle down some day in that very village."

"So I need to loosen up?"

"Just pretend you're an extrovert in training, and I'm your instructor. Now, let's go and meet this artist."

A bell over the door tinkled quietly as Laura and Connor entered. The place was small in square footage but bright and airy. There were pieces of sculpture, a few paintings hung on pale cream walls, and several glass cases displaying jewelry. A young man came through a curtained doorway.

"Good afternoon," he said pleasantly. "Is there something I can help you with, or did you just want to look around for a little while?"

Connor was on the verge of saying, "We'll look around," when Laura said, "We'd like to see the work of a particular artist. I understand her pieces are sold here."

"And who is that?"

Laura consulted the card once more. "Beatrice Rosario. I got her name from her brother."

"You've met Father Rosario?"

"Father?"

"He's the priest of our neighborhood church."

Laura was confused. "I don't think the young man I met could have a been a priest unless they're very young these days and have to moonlight. The person I'm talking about works at the hotel where we're staying in Laguna Beach."

The clerk smiled. "Oh, of course. I'm sorry for the confusion. That must have been Luis, her younger brother. We don't see as much of him since he's been working there."

"Do you have any of Ms. Rosario's pieces here? I saw the cross Luis was wearing. It was simply beautiful."

"No more so than your necklace," said the clerk, nodding toward Laura's squash blossom necklace. "It's on a smaller scale than others I've seen, and the detail in the craftsmanship is unusual. What sort of turquoise is that? It's quite different than the usual blue."

Laura smiled. "It's Manassa turquoise, mined in Colorado. The copper content and a few other minerals give it the dark striations and a more greenish cast to the stone."

"Very nice. I'm afraid we don't get much call for Indian jewelry here, or I'd love to carry some. But you were asking about Bea's work. Right over here are some excellent examples. Many are not for sale. She creates most pieces to order. They are never identical, though some are similar, based on her most popular designs."

Connor and Laura followed the clerk to the large display case occupying pride of place in the center of the back wall. The jewelry— bracelets, earrings, pendants, and rings—lay on black velvet, warm and luminous, the surfaces faceted to catch the light. Each item was indeed unique, though in several cases the symbology was clearly Christian. Laura saw a crucifix similar to the one Luis had worn, but not quite as detailed. Still, the figure of Christ was wrought with such care that it seemed almost alive.

"This piece," said Connor, pointing through the glass. "May I see that?" The clerk patted first one then another until he lit on the one she wanted and pulled it out, placing it on a black velvet display pad. It was a Celtic design cross with the circle passing through the shaft and enclosing both ends of the crossbar. The body of the cross was gold, but the raised carving of the delicate pattern was in sterling silver. The design, using a carefully executed contrast between the two precious metals was breathtaking.

Laura eyed Connor. "This is absolutely you, and I can tell you love it."

"It is unusual," she replied, picking it up. "I've seen a lot of Celtic crosses, but this one…I don't know. It's remarkable, the way it feels or something. And I like the way the circle encloses the top and sides of the cross itself. Do you have any idea what some of these symbols mean?"

"That's a one-of-a-kind design," said the clerk. "Bea only brought it in this week, and I haven't seen anything similar. I haven't really had a chance to get a full description from her about the meaning of the design.

"I'd like to buy it," Laura told the clerk.

"Now wait a minute," Connor protested. "Don't you think we ought to ask how much it is?"

"No. That cross was meant for you."

"Is this one of those 'psychic' things?" Connor laughed.

"Yes and no." She pulled out her wallet and handed the somewhat baffled clerk a credit card. "No need to wrap it. She'll want to wear it."

"Yes, ma'am," he said, still confused but clearly pleased with the effortless sale.

Connor was still shaking her head. "It isn't my birthday, and we don't actually have an anniversary that I know of, and it isn't a national holiday. This is too extravagant."

"Where is it written, my love, that only you can bestow gifts and spend money impulsively?"

"Well, I didn't mean that but…" She couldn't think of a reason, so she changed tactics. "You hardly ever let me buy you anything."

"I have just about everything I need."

"You think I need this cross?"

"Yes, I do."

The clerk returned with the credit card voucher. Laura looked at it, signed her name, took her receipt, and card and shoved them into her wallet. "That's much less than I would have expected," she said to the clerk. "Surely the price should be more."

The clerk shrugged. "I agree, especially considering the many hours of work that go into each piece. But Bea is determined to keep her art-work as affordable as possible. She also tithes to our church, St. Mary of the Groves."

"She tithes?" asked Connor. "That sounds so old-fashioned."

"Bea is the sister of a priest, ma'am, and a devout member of our church. She firmly believes her talent comes from God, and she never fails to give back to God a tenth of what she earns."

"That's very generous of her," said Laura.

"Not really," replied the clerk, his expression earnest. "Father Rosario teaches us that all bounty comes from God. The wonderful gift is that we get to keep ninety percent."

"I suppose if you look at it that way," Connor shrugged uncertainly. "But in that case she probably ought to charge more."

"She wouldn't let us. Besides, we can't ask Laguna Beach prices here in Santa Ana."

Laura picked up the cross on its fine gold and silver serpentine chain. "Turn around," she instructed. Connor obeyed with a rueful smile, stooping slightly since Laura was a couple of inches shorter and had to reach over Connor's head with the necklace. Laura fastened it in place and grinned when Connor turned around. "It looks fabulous, sweetheart."

The clerk quickly handed Connor a mirror. The cross lay against the lightly tanned skin just below the hollow of her throat. She smiled, almost in spite of herself. "All right, you win. I love it."

"I think it's something your grandmother would like, too," said Laura. "Right up her alley, so to speak."

"Yes, she definitely would like it."

The clerk was back with a paper bag, a jewelry box, and a small brochure. "Even though you're wearing it, Bea would want you to have a box, and here's some more information about her."

Laura was still examining the various pieces in the case. "She's a truly gifted artist. I'd love to meet her sometime."

"Then you're in luck. She isn't always in town since she travels to art and jewelry shows around the country. But tonight she's teaching a class in jewelry making, and all are welcome to attend."

"I don't know a thing about making jewelry," said Connor.

"You needn't make anything if you don't want to," responded the clerk. "And the first part of the class is a brief lecture and slide presentation. Here, let me write down the address for you." He returned in less than a minute with a slip of paper. "It starts in a couple of hours and it's only a few blocks from here."

Laura took the paper from him. "It's at your church," she said.

"Yes, ma'am. There are classrooms in the basement and in part of the rectory. Father Rosario lets people from the community used them free of charge to teach classes in job skills and English, things like that. You'll also like seeing the church itself," he added. "It has lovely frescoes and stained glass."

"Sounds perfect, almost preordained," she said, hoping to get a rise out of Connor, who still squirmed in the face of reminders that the universe was nowhere near as controllable as she'd like.

"You think that about almost everything that happens to us," said Connor.

"That, my love, is because there is no such thing as coincidence."

»——«

A short distance away, Father Enrique Rosario was also thinking about coincidence, about all the seemingly unrelated events that had conspired (though that was perhaps the wrong word) to bring him to the verge of committing the greatest heresy he could imagine.

He sat in his small office in the rectory, in an old wooden desk chair that would tip over if you tilted back too far. Everything about the office was used, old, shabby, and tired. It mattered little to him. He hadn't grown up in luxury and thus never missed it. His only vice was coffee— very good, very strong coffee—and his parishioners had banded together to buy him a first-class espresso machine and bean grinder. At least twice a day he silently thanked them (along with the good Lord) for the blessed aroma that permeated his office.

Today, however, he hadn't yet made himself a single cup. His stomach churned with the knowledge of what he had done—and what he might do. The archbishop had left him the night before with a stern warning to do nothing until they talked again. But Father Rosario had not promised, and for good reason. He could not involve his mentor in something so dangerous. The potential for the ruination of both their careers was all too real, but removal from office and excommunication could almost be the least of their worries if what Father Rosario suspected were true. His palms felt sweaty at the thought, and his mind strayed to what was buried beneath a slab of flat rock in the old mission church.

This was also why he hadn't told the archbishop everything. The only person who knew how far Enrique had gone to pursue this mystery was his father, and now his father was dead. That there might be a connection was something Enrique desperately avoided thinking about. But guilt lay heavy on his heart. What if he hadn't told Bruno about the notes, the hints about something hidden in the cliffs near the monastery? What if he hadn't half-convinced him to take a trip there? Enrique knew full well that with no associate priest on his staff, he couldn't easily leave for two or three weeks. He'd also been a little afraid to go to the old monastery, as if he might draw the suspicions of the curia in Rome just by visiting the location.

So Bruno had gone instead with the energy of an adventurer setting out to discover treasure. Enrique had given him every clue he could distill from the writings of the novice who'd illegally kept a journal, clues he still hadn't shared with Archbishop Johnston. Bruno had made cryptic notes in Italian, in his almost illegible hand. He assured his son he would be the soul of discretion. Apparently he had been. He played the part of tourist, an old man returning home for a glimpse of the old country. After checking out the monastery by day, and admiring some, though certainly not all, of the stonework, he'd returned surreptitiously just at sunset. A wiry little old man, he'd crept down the cliff path and explored every nook and cranny with a covered flashlight. He went back for three nights in a row, always careful to remain unseen.

It was on the third night that he'd discovered the crevice—completely by accident. He stumbled slightly and reached for a clump of brush to steady himself. It was not entirely anchored to the dirt in which it sat. Pushing the branches aside, he thought perhaps there was an opening beyond. He pulled harder and it loosened some more. After several minutes of hard effort, it came away in his hand. Yes, he could just detect variations in the darkness beyond. He shone his light into a narrow opening and his heart leaped at the thought that this might be the hiding place of whatever his son was seeking. Turning sideways, he took off his canvas knapsack and held it to one side, then slipped his small frame into the opening. Had he been much heavier or taller, the maneuver would have been impossible. Enrique could not have fit there. *The old monk must have been a pretty skinny fella,* thought Bruno as the crevice finally widened enough for him to turn sideways. Before him, in the beam of the flashlight was the opening of a tunnel that appeared to narrow quickly. Bruno, who'd worked in small spaces many times in his life, was not troubled by the close quarters. He stooped, then crawled into the tunnel, going very slowly and playing his flashlight across the floor and walls, dragging his knapsack along with him.

Just as he reached the point where he thought he could go no further, he detected a small chamber to his right. On the floor he could see odd markings in the dirt, as if something soft had passed over the surface, smoothing it down. If this had been a hiding place for one of the brothers, he reasoned, a monk's robes maybe might make that pattern. Perhaps he had crawled back out with the robe trailing behind him. Worth a look. Bruno squeezed into the opening and carefully examined the small cave. Empty. But he tried again, unwilling to disappoint his son, who seemed so sure there was something very important here. He went over the perimeter again, this time even more slowly. Then he saw it— scrape marks in the dirt, marks made by rough stones. He crawled over to the small pile of rocks and began moving them one by one. Behind the pile was a small opening. Hunkering down, Bruno shone the light into the hole. Yes, there was something there.

Laying the flashlight on the floor so that its beam illuminated the opening, he reached in and touched a rough surface that was not stone. Then, with both hands, he felt for the edges of the object and pulled it toward him. The space was very tight and he worked the thing gently back and forth before he finally freed it and dragged it out onto the floor of the little cavern. It was a very old and crudely fashioned box of darkened wood, bound around and around with rotting leather straps. Bruno touched them gently, afraid they might fall apart. From his knapsack he withdrew a folded sheet of heavy gauge plastic. He unfolded it and lay it flat on the floor, then carefully placed the box in the middle. Wrapping it like a Christmas package, he used a flattened roll of duct tape to secure the plastic. Finally, he put it in his knapsack.

By now it would be fully dark outside and he could exit undetected. The trip along the ledge would be a little hairy, but for a man who'd climbed rickety scaffolding and perched on the edges of platforms a hundred feet above the stone floors of cathedrals, it was almost child's play. When he reached the crevice, Bruno held the knapsack over his head so he could slide sideways through the opening. The box felt surprisingly heavy for such a small item and he couldn't help but wonder what it held that was apparently so important. Nonetheless, he'd promised his son he wouldn't open it. Bruno had recognized something almost akin to fear in Enrique's eyes, though he didn't know what could have caused it. His son was a brave man. Yet he had to admit, now that he'd touched the little box, something about it was disturbing. He couldn't quite put his finger on it. So, as with most puzzlements in his lifetime, Bruno chose not to waste any effort on figuring it out. He firmly believed that some of God's mysteries were simply too complex for human beings. He made the sign of the cross, slung the knapsack over his shoulder, and set off up the path. Just as he cleared the top of the precipice he heard something, a snap of a twig or the clatter of a small pebble somewhere below him. He stopped, barely breathing. Silence. Bruno's pulse was racing, and he felt a slight twinge in his chest.

It's nothing but the wind and your imagination, he said to himself. Still he hurried along faster. He suddenly wished very much for the sight of orange groves under the California sun, and the faces of his beloved children.

»——«

Beatrice Rosario had the face of an angel—at least that was Connor's first impression. Come to think of it, her name, "Beatrice" must come from the same Latin root as beatific, which, as she recalled, meant saintly or virtuous. So far, however, she had shown herself to be wonderfully human. Connor and Laura watched as she helped students with their work, laughed at their jokes, and hugged those who had managed to complete a piece. Once the class was over, she asked Laura and Connor to join her for a cup of coffee.

"So you like my work." She eyed the cross around Connor's neck. "That's a new design for me, something I could almost say I dreamed rather than thought up. I hadn't done much work with silver and gold combined, but that's the way I envisioned it. Frankly I was afraid it was too expensive for anyone to buy it."

"Too expensive? Hardly. You should see what original designs go for in Santa Fe shops and galleries," said Laura.

Bea's eyes twinkled. "I have seen them, but I don't know if what they charge is altogether honest."

"I've heard it said that tourists are fair game," Laura smiled.

"We don't get many tourists in Santa Ana, so I don't have to ponder any moral dilemmas," Bea replied. "I'm rather surprised you found that little shop. It's definitely off the beaten path for out-of-town visitors."

"We only found it because of your brother, Luis."

Bea grinned. "I should probably pay him a commission. That boy almost never ceases promoting my work. I keep telling him he's going to get fired if he goes too far."

"I'm the one who asked him, actually, about the crucifix he was wearing. It was so finely wrought I wanted to see more of the work," said Laura.

63

"And I imagine he was not the least bit reluctant to give you my card," Bea chuckled.

"Had to twist his arm a little," said Laura with a smile. "But seriously, there's nothing wrong with having a fan who spreads the word about what you do."

"Trouble is, I can't produce enough pieces to keep up with a great demand. Sometimes I have the designs in my mind and I have to wait for something to sell so I can buy more gold." She looked again at the cross. "Thanks to this sale, however, I will be able to start on something new tomorrow. What a blessing."

Connor spoke up. "We're the ones who feel blessed. Your talent is obvious."

This time Bea blushed but was saved from further compliments by a sound at the far end of the room. They turned to observe the tall, well-built man coming toward them. He was dressed in a black suit with a Roman collar. Clearly this was Father Rosario. He looked so much like his sister it was startling. The same thick black hair, hers long and loose, his trimmed short. The same brown eyes and classical nose. Bea's firm chin and sculpted cheekbones found male expression in the priest's strong jawline, and slightly broader face.

"Enrique! I didn't know you were still in the church. I thought you'd gone back to the rectory."

"A few things to do in the chapel, *mi hermanita*. I see you have visitors."

"And not only that, they're customers. Luis sent them over from the shop. They purchased the Celtic cross."

Connor, who was looking directly at the priest when Bea said this, could have sworn a frown of displeasure passed over the man's features, but it happened so quickly she couldn't be sure. And, besides, of what could he possibly disapprove? Still, his eyes were focused on the cross. "That's one of my sister's most unusual pieces."

"It's unlike others I've seen," said Connor. She looked at Bea. "Perhaps you'll tell me more about the symbols carved on the circular part."

"I'd be happy to, though my brother is really the expert."

Laura held out her hand. "A pleasure to meet you, Father. I'm Laura Nez and this is my friend, Connor Hawthorne."

"The author?" he asked.

Connor smiled. "Guilty as charged."

The priest's face lost its rigidity. "I really love your books. You were an attorney once, weren't you?"

"Another guilty plea is in order," said Connor.

"Not all lawyers are sinners," he said, "and not all priests are saints."

"Hard to overcome stereotypes, isn't it?" Connor said.

"Absolutely. But we sometimes have to live up to them anyway." He gave his sister a quick hug. "I'm glad you're back." He addressed himself to Laura and Connor. "Sorry to have interrupted your conversation, ladies. I haven't seen Bea in weeks, and I knew her class would be over by now."

Laura took the hint. "We had better be going anyway. It's after eight, and we haven't had dinner yet. Perhaps you could recommend someplace nearby."

"What sort of food did you have in mind?" asked Bea.

"We're always open to culinary experiments," replied Connor. "So long as it's good."

"We have a wonderful Spanish restaurant three blocks from here," Bea suggested. "I know the owners and they're both excellent cooks. The place isn't elegant, but…" She shrugged eloquently.

"Who needs elegant?" said Laura. "I'm in the mood for something very spicy."

"Ah, you're accustomed to green chile, aren't you?" said Father Rosario.

Laura smiled. "You've spent time in New Mexico, Father?"

"I was assigned briefly to a small church north of Santa Fe. I fell in love with the people, the land, and the green chile."

"In that order?"

He grinned. "Perhaps. Each has its merits. The land is eternally present in one's thoughts, the green chile is almost always fiery, and for the most part the people are entirely unpredictable, despite their long Catholic heritage. So you have the gamut of life experiences."

Connor looked at the priest curiously. He was more than a simple parish pastor, of that she was sure. "You sound as if you are a student of life," she said.

"A student always," he smiled. "Best never to stop learning."

Bea piped up. "My brother is a Jesuit. Many expected him to teach at a college, but he chose this work instead. Still, he keeps up his research."

Father Rosario's good humor vanished. "No," he said with a frown, "I don't spend time on that anymore. I have more important responsibilities than intellectual pursuits. What good does it do? The people of my parish need a priest, not an academic dilettante. Now, if you will excuse me, I must be going."

"But I thought…" Bea started to speak, then paused, her expression puzzled.

"I'll call you later, Beatrice" he said, then nodded in the direction of the two visitors. "It was a pleasure to have met both of you. Perhaps you will care to come to Mass on Sunday."

Without waiting for a reply, he strode hurriedly from the room. Beatrice stared after him. "I don't know what's going on with Enrique. These past few months he's been short-tempered, and he's not sleeping or eating properly. And he hardly speaks to us, even to Luis who idolizes him." As if remembering that Laura and Connor were standing beside her, she stopped abruptly. "You must excuse my rudeness. Here I am boring you with family dynamics. Now where were we? Oh, yes, I was going to give you the name of the restaurant." She paused. "I thought I had dinner plans," she said, her eyes straying to the door through which the priest had left. "I hope you don't think me presumptuous, but I would be happy to take you to the restaurant and give you a tour of some of the delicacies from my mother's country."

"We'd be delighted," said Laura.

Connor nodded her agreement. "I'm ready for an excellent food experience."

»——«

Father Rosario stood in the center aisle of the church, facing the altar. What had gotten into him? He'd been unreasonably curt with his sister and the two visitors. He'd skipped the planned dinner with Bea. And all he could think about was that damned box. He didn't dare open it—didn't dare because although he did not know precisely what was inside that he was afraid of it. That was why he'd hidden it far from the rectory, to keep temptation out of reach. None of this made sense for a logical, intelligent person, but he was torn. Enrique was a man both of faith and of intellect. His intellect prodded him to investigate and unveil a secret that might have been kept for almost 2,000 years. His faith nagged at him to stay true to his vows to the church and to God rather than indulge in purely academic curiosity. But was it only that? Surely his soul, too, yearned for truth, that part of him that had never been quite satisfied by the doctrines of the Catholic faith, that fought against the rigidity of the authoritarian control of the curia in Rome.

Did what lay inside that little wooden casket threaten him, his church, the world? Perhaps, if there was any substance to the centuries of rumors and whispers. Was there any secret so powerful that no human being had a right to reveal it?

A quiet shuffling noise caused him to swivel around and peer at the side aisle where the confessional boxes stood. The small lightbulb over the penitent's door came on. He sighed. The hour for confession was long past, but he would not turn away someone in need. He walked to the head of the aisle, genuflected at the altar, and circled the pews to reach the confessionals.

As he opened his door he considered that perhaps he would have to visit the archbishop soon. He needed advice and now wished he'd been more forthcoming. He knew in his heart that Johnston wouldn't betray him. Besides, the archbishop was his confessor and Father Rosario felt desperately in need of absolution.

》——《

Beatrice, Laura, and Connor were sipping strong coffee and nibbling at the last of a sugary confection. Three hours had passed almost unnoticed, a not unusual situation when three intelligent, accomplished women get together. They talked about Connor's career as a district attorney and later a novelist and Laura's work as a government investigator—though in little detail because Laura's actual work was classified. And the conversation turned once again to Beatrice's designs.

"You mentioned that you'd had a 'vision' or something like that of the design of this cross," said Connor. "You know, I may be wrong, but your brother didn't seem entirely pleased that we'd bought this piece."

Beatrice nodded. "I know. But please don't hold it against him. He gets funny ideas sometimes. And ever since I sketched out the patterns and symbols, he's been irritated with it somehow. He kept asking me where I'd seen the design before, and all I could tell him was that I'd seen it in a dream, and when I woke up it was still vivid. I couldn't understand why it bothered him. He actually tried to get me to tear up the sketches and not make that piece."

Laura peered at the necklace Connor wore. "But there's nothing wrong with it at all. I admit I don't entirely understand each element of those engravings, but I don't get a negative charge off it."

Beatrice smiled. "It's nice to talk to someone who isn't embarrassed to discuss the spiritual world around us." She looked across the table at Connor. "You, too, are a gifted individual, are you not?"

Connor hesitated for a moment. "I suppose. I guess you could say it runs in the family. Sort of an inheritance I got, whether I wanted it or not. My grandmother was the leader of a...circle...in England."

"A Celtic coven!" exclaimed Beatrice. "How wonderful!"

"Not a coven exactly, more of a council of—I guess you'd call them guardians."

"Ah, guardians of all that is good in this world and the other places."

"Like the Dreamtime," said Laura.

"Yes. There are many places I have traveled in my dreams, but I'm not able to do so at will, only by accident."

Connor started to squirm in her seat and Beatrice eyed her thoughtfully. "You don't like this power that flows through you, the connection with your beloved grandmother?"

"No, I'm not comfortable with the power part, partly because I don't know what it really means, but I have to say that I've gotten used to the idea that my grandmother and I share something special."

"Good, then perhaps you will also soon learn that all of these different pieces are one."

"I'm sorry, I don't know what you mean."

"I suspect, my friend, if I may presume to call you that, that you worry because you do not understand how all these puzzles and mysteries and religions and supernatural spookiness fit together. Am I right?"

Connor nodded and Laura smiled to herself. It was sometimes hard to keep Connor's attention when the "woo-woo" stuff came up in conversation, partly because it made her nervous. But Beatrice was hitting the nail on the head, and Connor was predictably intrigued when anyone pierced her veil of defensive cynicism.

"So what if I were to tell you that none of it is separate?"

"I'm sorry, I don't follow," said Connor.

"Think about it this way: For me, God is everywhere."

A twinge of skepticism crept into Connor's voice. "You'll forgive me if I tell you that I've heard that phrase since I was a child, and it doesn't make any more sense now than it did then. Everyone made it sound as if God were some sort of superhuman voyeur."

Beatrice chuckled. "That's why so many children grow up in fear of God. My father and mother, rest their souls, only taught us to respect the Creator and believe in miracles like angels and fairies and the presence of spirits. They also taught us that we lived many lifetimes, and there were many more to come."

"But weren't your parents Catholic?" asked Connor.

"Of course. But my mother was never one to ignore her traditions. Her great-grandmother was known as a *curandeira*—what some might call a witch or a natural healer—and my mother heard the stories of her ancestors all during her childhood." Beatrice shrugged in a gesture that conveyed more than words.

"These symbols on the cross you made," said Laura. "Are they part of your tradition?"

"Since I drew those, I did some research. Some bear a faint resemblance to carvings I found in my father's sketchbooks. He was a stonemason who worked on cathedrals his entire life."

"Did he happen to work on the National Cathedral?" asked Connor.

"Why, yes. He was there for much of his career. Why do you ask?"

"It's just that I went to the girl's prep school affiliated with the cathedral, and we were there only a couple of days ago."

"So perhaps you saw some of my father's work. He carved many of the smaller stones." Beatrice looked at her watch. "Oh, look at the time. And we're the only people left. I have a feeling the owners would like to close up." She started to pull out her wallet.

Connor laid a hand gently on Beatrice's arm. "Please, let this be my treat. The meal was outstanding, and the company couldn't have been better."

Laura smiled into her napkin. Connor was a charmer when she put her mind to it.

Beatrice looked a little reluctant. "But you've spent so much buying my jewelry."

"And I will enjoy owning this piece for many years. Let's call dinner a little advance on the enjoyment royalties."

The artist held up her hands in mock surrender. "So you think we jewelers should collect annual royalties?"

"Why not?" said Connor, signaling an obviously relieved waiter for the check. "Every time I see this in the mirror, I'll get a thrill out of it. That kind of feeling is almost priceless."

They left the restaurant and walked back toward the church where Connor and Laura had left their car. Just as they reached the foot of the stone stairs leading up to the entrance, one of the large central doors of the church crashed open and a figure hurtled down the steps. "*Madre de Dios!* Help! Someone, help!

Beatrice grabbed at the figure and swung her into the light of a streetlamp. Her eyes widened. "Lucinda, what is wrong? What is it?"

The old woman half collapsed into Beatrice's arms, sobbing hysterically. "Senorita Bea, Senorita Bea ...*il padre, il padre...*"

"What about the *padre*?" asked Bea, her voice sharp with anxiety. Connor and Laura moved closer to help keep the woman from collapsing completely.

"*Il padre...es muerto!*" she screamed, pointing back toward the church.

Sitting her down none too gently on the steps, Beatrice sprinted up the stairs with Connor and Laura close behind her. They ran into the silent church and stared around the sanctuary. Connor dashed up the aisle toward the altar. "Where is he?" Beatrice shouted. "Luis! Luis!"

Laura turned to the left and started up the far aisle. She saw the door of the confessional open and the dark stain spreading out along the pale marble floor. She swallowed hard and said, "Over here," instantly regretting she'd alerted the priest's sister. She wheeled around and sprinted to intercept Beatrice before she could see what must be inside the confessional booth. Connor, taking in the situation in a heartbeat, had the same idea. They corralled Beatrice thirty feet from the confessional. She fought them like a wildcat. It took their combined and not inconsiderable strength to restrain her.

"I have to go to him. I have to go to my brother."

"No!" said Connor sharply. "You're going to stay right here until I see what's happened. And if it's what I suspect, we're not going to touch anything, and we're not going to do anything except call the police."

Assured that Laura had a firm lock on Beatrice, Connor walked deliberately toward the confessional, neither delaying nor rushing. She took a few deep breaths and instantly the coppery tang of fresh blood filled her nose and mouth. Connor gritted her teeth. This wasn't the first crime scene she'd ever visited, nor even the one hundred and first. But experience didn't make this any easier. Her mind tried to invent all sorts of benign reasons why there was fresh blood pooling on the floor, but there were none. Just a little defense mechanism to ward off the fury she felt when confronted with the human capability for cruelty and violence.

Carefully avoiding the crimson puddle, she reached into her pocket, pulled out a tissue, and swung the door fully open. She swallowed hard, taking in the long wooden stake protruding from the chest, the handsome head thrown back against the wall, the face twisted in agony. On the floor of the confessional lay a wooden mallet, painted white with dark rings and markings on the handle. She couldn't decipher it all from this distance. But there was a phrase painted in black on the head of the mallet: "*Malleus Caelistis ab Deum,*" the Divine Hammer of God.

Then she saw the collar. One end of it had popped out of the black shirt. On it, written by a fingertip, in the priest's own blood, was the word TRAITER. She focused on the absurd irrelevancy that the murderer couldn't spell because she didn't want to think about the rest of what she was seeing. Father Enrique Rosario was most assuredly and most horribly dead.

Chapter Seven

Man prefers to believe what he prefers to be true.
—Francis Bacon

"Jefferson!" he barked into the phone.

"Malcolm, it's Connor. I didn't want to call you this early at home. I took a chance you might be in your office."

He looked at his watch, doing a quick mental calculation. "It's seven o'clock here. What are you doing up at four in the morning?"

There was no response, though he could still hear that the connection was open. His pulsed increased slightly. "Connor! What's wrong? Is Laura all right?"

"Yes, yes, Laura's fine and so am I. But some things have happened out here that I thought you should know about."

"What is it?" he asked, faintly puzzled.

"It's kind of a long story," she said.

"I've got all the time in the world. Hang on a minute. Let me shut my office door." In a couple of seconds he was back on the phone. "Okay, now what's going on?"

In concise sentences, typical of her days as a prosecutor, Connor recounted their first two days in California, including Laura's discovery of a gifted jewelry artist through the woman's brother, their meeting with Beatrice Rosario and her other brother, the priest of a Santa Ana church, and last, the discovery of the priest's body in the confessional.

"Geez, Connor. I'm sorry. How is it you get involved in this shit?"

"I don't know, but if I've learned anything this past year, it's that there's no such thing as coincidence."

He thought about that for a moment. "You're saying that somehow you're supposed to be involved in this?"

"I don't know if 'involved' is the right word, but there's one more little factor that's going to hit home for you, whether you want to call it a coincidence or not."

"And what's that?"

"Malleus Caelistis—it's part of a phrase I saw at the crime scene. Remember the Malleus Society? Sound familiar?"

"You're kidding. What does that lunatic group have to do with the murder of a priest in California?"

"I have no earthly idea, but that's part of the phrase that I think translates Divine Hammer of God, even if my Latin's a little rusty. I saw it carved or painted on the mallet used to hammer a stake through the chest of a parish priest whom everyone loved."

"Not everyone apparently. But for crying out loud—a stake? Please tell me this isn't some sort of weird vampire thing. I think I've gotten just about as far into the supernatural, metaphysical, stranger-than-fiction world of Connor Hawthorne as I ever want to."

"Gee, thanks," she said. "And no, I don't think the stake has anything to do with vampires. Believe me, I met the priest. Seemed nice but kind of tense. No, I think the message wasn't the stake; it was the hammer, as in Malleus."

"So some psycho is actually taking the hammer thing literally. Have you talked to the police out there about this?"

"They're still processing the crime scene and told us to come in tomorrow to give statements. That's why I wanted to talk to you first. Maybe it's better if you lay it out for them. I'm just a civilian as far as they're concerned."

"Not for long."

"What's that supposed to mean?"

"Once Benjamin gets wind of this, you know perfectly well that the word will filter down very quickly that talking to his daughter is virtually the same thing as talking to him. You'll get all kinds of courteous cooperation."

Connor sighed. "I know. Sometimes that's a good thing, sometimes not. Maybe we ought to hold off telling him for a day or two."

Malcolm snorted. "Yeah, and assuming he hears it from someone else, since all information generated on earth seems to find its way to Benjamin, then he'll just have my balls on a platter for not mentioning his daughter stumbled across a body."

"You're right. So how do we want to play this? Do I mention the Hammer of God people and Ricky Bell, or do you?"

"Go ahead. You had legitimate access to the files as the prosecutor on that case. They can call me for confirmation, and chances are, I'll have Benjamin pull a few strings and get me cleared for a fact-finding, helping-out-my-colleagues sort of trip to the coast."

"You can't clear *yourself* for that?" asked Connor.

"I didn't mention it to you when you were here, but I'm not all that popular with the powers that be in the District these days. A certain few seem to think I took my job with the anticorruption task force a little too seriously."

"Ah, I see. That explains the transfer to antiterrorism."

"Yes, it does. There's all kinds of ways to fuck up running this unit, mostly because our intelligence usually sucks, and we can't necessarily tell the real threats from the phony ones. One good-size bomb goes off, or someone takes a few hostages, and I get to be the sacrificial goat. Fortunately for me, your Dad has been supportive."

Connor knew better than to ask him to elaborate. She caught the hint, and he was, after all, talking on a department phone system. She knew her father's "support" meant that Malcolm was getting top-notch intelligence reports and was thus able to avert some potential disasters. If the so-called powers had expected him to fail, they were doubtless doomed to disappointment. Still, it wouldn't do for him to go running off without solid reasons and preferably the backing of federal rather than local authorities. Benjamin could certainly handle the federal part, and she'd just handed Malcolm the reasons: Ricky Bell, supposed wielder of the Divine Hammer of God, was in California. Someone had better find out why.

"Do me a favor, will you?" she asked.

"Anything for you, kiddo," he said, although at forty-six he wasn't that much older than Connor. Still, at heart, he would always be a big brother to her.

"Call my dad and tell him about this. Laura and I are both worn out, and we need to get a few hours sleep before we head over to the police station."

"Will do. Give me your number there."

Connor read off the hotel's phone number from the small plastic plate and added their room extension.

"I'll leave you a message about when I'll be arriving. And in the meantime, could you two try and stay out of trouble? Give your statements to the locals, then go to the beach, lie in the sun, and play tourist— please."

"Whatever you say, Captain Jefferson," Connor said, her voice tired but less strained than when she'd first called.

Malcolm didn't believe her one bit.

»——«

Beatrice Rosario was deeply in shock. She had not spoken a word to the police. Even though Connor Hawthorne and Laura Nez had hustled her out of the church before she could see the horror of the scene, she could still sense her brother's terror, his utter disbelief that someone had come to kill him. They had shared a deep connection, and while that connection still existed, it now vibrated painfully within her. Enrique's half of the soul they often seemed to share now projected sorrow, longing, anger, and fear. It was as if he were somewhere nearby, hovering anxiously, confused and outraged.

Now she sat, hours later, in the kitchen of the rectory, an old cotton blanket wrapped around her. Twice, Lucinda had placed hot mugs of tea on the table in front of her. Twice, they'd grown cold. Somewhere inside, Beatrice was trying to smother the same grief that had devastated the elderly Lucinda. She couldn't bear to let it out. And she had no strength with which to comfort Lucinda. Later perhaps.

She heard the doorbell, Lucinda's slow steps, the heavy front door opening then closing. More footsteps, these much heavier. *Please, not the police, not now,* she prayed to no one in particular. *Not now.*

But it was not a police officer who walked into the kitchen. She looked up into the red-rimmed eyes of Archbishop Johnston. She rose out of habit. "Your Eminence," she whispered, her voice almost failing her. "Enrique…he's…" Sobs erupted from deep within her chest. "He's…"

He stepped forward and drew her into his arms. "I know, Beatrice, I know."

»——«

At nine-thirty, Connor and Laura had finished their separate interviews with Detectives Jaramillo and Consadine, signed their statements, and been asked to leave their local contact information. Patiently and politely, Connor had explained her connection to the case, beginning with her prosecution of Ricky Bell some eight years earlier. The gray-haired Consadine hadn't seemed particularly impressed with her contribution. He wasn't interested in an old case far from his jurisdiction. He'd barely changed expression when Connor reminded him of the lettering etched and painted on the mallet, seeming more suspicious that she'd noticed it at all than interested in Ricky Bell's potential connection to the murder. She'd quickly recognized him for what he was and didn't bother arguing. He was a relic of the old school who operated under the assumption that women who found dead bodies should run screaming into the street for help, not stand there and mentally catalog the details of a grisly scene. Apparently he didn't know many women like Connor, or the only prosecutors he worked with were men.

When the two cops switched interviews, presumably to compare notes, Connor had found Detective Ray Jaramillo a ray of sunshine in comparison to his partner. He was probably fifteen years younger and about three centuries more enlightened. He'd made precise notes about Ricky Bell, asked Connor for a contact person in the district attorney's office in Washington, and thanked her for her careful observations. Connor had made a mental note to warn Malcolm about Consadine. She wondered if his various prejudices extended to African-Americans as well as women, especially gay women. She suspected Malcolm would get a lot more interdepartmental cooperation from Ray Jaramillo.

Standing in the sunshine outside the station, Laura slipped her arm through Connor's. "You okay?" she asked.

"Yeah, just a little down."

"Detective Consadine?."

Connor smiled. "I think I'm just tired of all this, and I hate looking at dead bodies. And as for Mr. Charming, I'm long past the point where jerks like that get under my skin. They're who they are."

"What a fatalist you're getting to be, my love."

"Sort of. There will always be things we can't fix or change, and we can't lose sleep over it."

"Oh, the old 'It is as it is' philosophy. When my grandmother tried to teach you that, you thought she was a little naïve."

"I was an idiot," smiled Connor. "But frankly, all this maturing is wearing me out."

"Do you think we ought to go and see Beatrice?"

"You're in my head again, aren't you? That's just what I was thinking."

"But you're not sure if it's appropriate, and we hardly know her, and what if we're intruding?"

"Exactly."

"I think we ought to go. If she doesn't want to see us, we'll go away quietly and send flowers when the time is right. But last night I felt a strong empathy for her, and maybe we share some sort of connection, a past-life connection."

Connor laughed. "Woo-woo stuff alert! Malcolm warned me about that early this morning."

"Sorry, darling. Like it or not, we're who we are."

"I know. And you're right—I don't have to like it. But for whatever reason, I think we ought to go and see Beatrice. I have a feeling she needs some help."

They found a place to park their rental car on a street behind the rectory next to the church and walked around the building. On the stoop sat a young man with his head in his hands. When they started up the short flight of steps, he raised his face to them. Laura felt a pang of sadness. It was Luis, the youngest brother. Clearly he had been crying, but he quickly wiped his face on the sleeves of his shirt. She noticed he was still wearing his parking attendant uniform.

"Luis, I'm so sorry about your brother," she said, sitting down beside him. She put her arm around his shoulders. "It's a terrible thing."

He looked at the cars passing by on the street, but she doubted he saw them, or saw anything. She was grateful he hadn't been the one to discover his brother's body. A scene such as that would have stayed with him for a lifetime. The young man finally seemed to take notice of Connor. "This is your friend?" he said. "The one from the hotel?"

Laura nodded. "This is Connor. We met Beatrice yesterday, and I know it may seem strange, but we feel we became friends in a very short time, and we thought we might be able to help in some way. But we don't want to intrude on the family."

At the mention of his sister, Luis sat up straighter and squared his shoulders. "Bea and I are the only family left. I will take care of her. But if you've come here to help, who am I to say 'no' to your kindness? We will go inside. She is with the archbishop."

»——«

Laura had never met an archbishop in the flesh, but she did harbor certain preconceived notions about what a ranking Catholic clergyman would look like. Archbishop Johnston dashed all of her expectations and then some. He looked like a gray-haired version of Robert Parker's "Spenser" character—well over six feet tall, a muscular, tough ex-boxer with a crooked nose and penetrating dark eyes. Whether he also had a soft spot for damsels in distress remained to be seen. But he looked as if wouldn't balk at a challenge. Nor was he dressed in religious garb.

Instead he wore a monochromatic ensemble of black slacks, white open-collared shirt, dark-gray loafers and a light-gray windbreaker. Laura wondered if the outfit constituted "civvies" for a priest.

He rose from the table where he'd been sitting with his arm around Bea's shoulders. Bea looked at the visitors in puzzlement but said nothing. Laura was immediately concerned they'd interrupted something private. "If this is a bad time, I'm sorry. We just wanted to see if there was anything we could do, and Luis thought it might be all right if we came in."

The woman nodded, then tilted her head back to look up at the archbishop. "These are my friends, from last night. They…they found Enrique…and they wouldn't let me see him."

Laura tensed and looked at Connor, not sure if Bea was angry at them for hustling her out of the church and physically restraining her. *Should we leave?*

Connor, reading the question in Laura's eyes, shrugged almost imperceptibly. They waited. After an awkward silence the young woman added, "They protected me from the worst. I would not have wanted to see him like that."

Laura relaxed a little and turned her attention to the archbishop who stepped around the table to offer his hand. "I'm Robert Johnston," he said.

"Laura Nez, and this is my friend, Connor Hawthorne."

He shook Connor's hand. "Under other circumstances I would say it's a pleasure to meet you both, but, as it is…" He stopped speaking somewhat abruptly, and Laura saw that he was gazing intently at Connor's chest. For a moment she was tempted to be both shocked and even a little amused. But he saved her from making an unfair judgment about his moral character when he said, "That necklace you wear—may I ask where you got it?"

Connor appeared startled by the non sequitur, but took it in stride. "I—that is, Laura bought it for me yesterday at a shop near here. It's one of Bea's pieces."

The archbishop's head snapped around and he stared searchingly at Bea. "Where did you get the idea for this design?" he asked. "The symbols carved on the circle of the cross?"

Laura was beginning to find the archbishop a bit odd. Here they were in the kitchen of a man, a priest, who'd been brutally murdered, and the head church guy in the area was asking about jewelry making. This just got stranger and stranger. Apparently Beatrice was just as bewildered by the question.

"I don't know exactly. It appeared in my dreams over and over. But now that I think about it, maybe I saw it somewhere, perhaps in all those odd drawings that Enrique used to make of his archaeology finds. I was there one day when he had several sketches on his desk when he was working. Maybe it sort of stuck in my mind, and later on I guess I reproduced the symbols without really being aware that I was doing it. Why? What does it matter?"

"It doesn't," said the archbishop, regaining his composure. "It reminded me of something, that's all. I'm sorry. I must sound like a complete idiot. Please, won't all of you sit down?"

Luis, who had hovered in the doorway during the conversation, looked on the verge of slipping out again, but the archbishop held out his hand. "Come and sit, Luis. You need to be with family, and Lucinda has made a fresh pot of tea for us."

Laura still felt a little out of place and sensed Connor did, too. "We don't mean to be a nuisance. But we both had the feeling we ought to be here. Still, perhaps another time would be better."

"No," said Beatrice. "Please stay. You proved yourselves as friends last night. Many strangers would have run away so as not to be involved."

Laura spoke up. "When you get to know us a little better, you'll discover that whatever our faults, we aren't the type to scare easily, or abandon people in need."

They sat in awkward silence for several moments.

"You've seen this before, Connor," said Bea suddenly, realization dawning on her face. "I remember last night you mentioned you were a district attorney. You prosecute criminals. You've seen murderers, like whoever…" Her voice broke and her shoulders sagged. The archbishop and Luis reached for her at the same time. The archbishop pulled back and watched the young man comfort his sister. He gestured slightly with his chin toward the door. Laura took the hint immediately.

"Bea, we're going to come back later and see what we can do to help."

She and Connor quickly stepped out of the kitchen, but the archbishop was right behind, shadowing their footsteps down the corridor and into the vestibule. They went through the inner door, and he closed it behind them. "I didn't really mean you had to leave," he said. "I simply wanted to speak to you about Enrique. Beatrice doesn't really know how it happened—a blessing for which I thank both God and you." Laura thought that under other circumstances he would have smiled, and there would have been a discernible twinkle in those dark eyes.

"Can you tell me more about how he died?"

Laura looked at Connor. Of the two of them, only she had seen the body.

"Is it important that you know?" asked Connor. Her tone was neutral, but Laura suspected Connor was reluctant to satisfy what seemed like ghoulish curiosity. Laura, on the other hand, didn't think the man's motivations had anything to do with simple inquisitiveness. He struck her as someone who always had a purpose.

"Yes, it is important, though I don't know that I'm at liberty to tell you why I think so."

Connor looked at him for few seconds, as if weighing her decision. "Not a very persuasive argument, considering that the police asked me to keep what I know in absolute confidence. But if you can't trust an archbishop…" She left the sentence unfinished, and the ghost of a smile played around his lips.

"Actually, that's probably the worst reason you could think of," he said. "I rarely trust archbishops and cardinals as far as I could throw them. But I would like you to trust *me* for the time being."

Connor described the murder scene in clinical detail, keeping her emotions well in check as far as Laura could tell. She knew the tableau of the priest had been deeply disturbing to her lover, but recognized that Connor had chosen to deal with the trauma by slipping into her prosecutor persona—the Connor Hawthorne who could view the goriest of crimes, read the most graphic details of the medical examiner's report, and never flinch. Laura knew Connor would have to actually let herself feel all this, but it would come later, when she felt safe enough to let go.

Laura watched the archbishop's reactions and saw his jaw tighten slightly when Connor described the epithet written on the dead priest's collar. He positively paled when Connor mentioned the mallet, and the Latin inscription that had appeared on it. Laura felt the tingle along her spine, the one that crawled upward until it raised the hair on the back of her neck. From past experience, it was a sure sign that there were spiritual forces at work and that the tragedy, albeit macabre, was much more complex than it appeared. She would not be surprised if her grandmother paid her a visit in the Dreamtime before too long. She refocused on the conversation.

"And you're quite sure that you've remembered the inscription precisely?" the archbishop was asking.

Connor frowned. "Yes...Your Eminence, if that's the proper title."

"Please, first and foremost, I'm a priest. 'Father' will do very nicely."

"Well, then, Father, although I can understand why you might think I'd get it wrong, I should tell you that my British grandmother insisted I learn Latin and classical Greek. So it isn't a question of having to remember something that didn't make sense to me in the first place."

The archbishop shook his head. "I'm sorry. I was being arrogant. We so often forget that there are some educated people in the world besides us Jesuit priests."

"Apology accepted. But I'd still like to know why you seem almost more concerned with the *manner* of Father Rosario's death than the fact that he's gone."

"Do I? Well, I don't want to seem callous, because I'm not a callous person. I loved that young man and had the greatest respect for him, both as a human being and as a fellow priest. You could almost say, if you wanted to get maudlin about it, that Enrique was like a son. But my grief is personal, and I'll mourn in my own way. In the meantime, the manner of death, as you say, is of gravest concern to me. Perhaps once I've considered the matter, I will be able to discuss it with you both further."

"Perhaps with the police as well," said Connor. "I imagine they can use all the help you could provide in figuring out who murdered Enrique."

"The aspects of this horrible crime that may be the most disturbing are far outside the purview of the police, Ms. Hawthorne. I'm sorry if you don't like that, but there it is. Frankly, I'm not a man who scares easily, and I'd have to tell you that the twisting in my gut feels an awful lot like fear." He reached into his wallet. "Here's my card. Please feel free to call me at any time. And if I may be in touch with you..."

Laura pulled one of her business cards from her wallet and wrote the name of their hotel on the back. She handed it to him and their hands brushed. She sent out her own energy, probing him ever so slightly in the way her own grandmother had taught her. To her surprise, she saw a flicker of understanding in his eyes. Had he actually felt her gentle and non-intrusive "scan" of his energy field? She found she rather liked his aura—gold in general with some warmish pink and a darker area around his heart chakra, a density that reflected his inner sadness. The archbishop smiled a tiny bit, and she had a strong feeling he knew a lot more than he let on.

"Ms. Nez, we'll see each other again. Ms. Hawthorne," he added, taking her hand. "Might I offer one rather presumptuous bit of advice?"

"Perhaps," she said, her eyes narrowing slightly. "What would that be?"

"Don't wear that cross for a while. Put it away."

Connor bristled visibly, and Laura could imagine how annoyed she was at being told not to wear a beautiful piece of jewelry she'd just been given as a gift. But she also suddenly remembered the expression on Father Rosario's face when he'd first seen Connor wearing the cross. He'd look angry, but she couldn't imagine why.

"Please," he continued. "I wish I could explain more, but I can't, at least not yet. Beatrice doesn't really know what she's done by creating it, or what those symbols mean. But I do. And there may be more consequences to all this than we can imagine. If I try to tell you, it's all going to sound too strange for words."

"You know what, Father?" said Connor. "You'd be amazed at how comfortable we can be with the strange—the really strange and the absolutely unbelievable." She opened the outer door and Laura followed her out. "I hope you'll be in touch soon, Archbishop. You may need our help more than you think."

They both got into the car, but Laura didn't start it right away. She turned in the seat to look at Connor and smiled. "Laying it on a little thick there at the end, weren't you? 'The strange—the really strange and the unbelievable.' I was beginning to think I was in an episode of *Tales from the Crypt.*"

Connor grinned sheepishly. "Okay, he sort of got to me, acting like we're too innocent to understand anything esoteric or, God forbid, spooky."

"So you decided to do your Rod Serling imitation?"

"Yeah."

"Good. I love that one. Now how about we imitate regular human beings and go have lunch by the ocean?"

Laura wiggled the car out of the tight space and headed back toward the beach. After a few minutes, Connor reached for the clasp of the necklace. "Will it hurt your feelings if I take this off?" she asked.

"Not in the least. I'd be more worried if you wouldn't listen to a well-meant warning. I care a lot more about you than one impulsive gift. Besides, I don't think he was trying to tell you never to wear it again, just that it might attract the wrong sort of attention for some reason."

Connor dropped the cross and chain into her blazer pocket. "Maybe it already has," she said.

Laura nodded and studied the rearview mirror a little more carefully. After all, her spine had tingled, and the hair on her neck had stood up. Some professional precaution might be in order.

Chapter Eight

No exorciser harm thee!
Nor no witchcraft charm thee!
Ghost unlaid forbear thee!
Nothing ill come near thee!
Quiet consummation have:
And renowned be thy grave!
—William Shakespeare
Cymbeline, Act IV, Scene 2

"Do you know how much I hate hearing this?"

"Do you know how much I hate *telling* you this?" replied Malcolm. "I'm surprised you haven't already heard the news, reviewed the police reports, and booked a flight to California."

Benjamin sighed. "I'm sorry. I don't mean to take it out on you. But why does she get herself into these things? They went out there for a vacation."

"Yes, they did. But there's something Connor said to me that kind of makes sense in a weird way."

"What's that?"

"She said 'there's no such thing as coincidence,' and I'm starting to wonder if maybe she isn't right about that."

"My daughter is sounding more and more like her Grandmother Broadhurst every day. That's just the sort of cryptic, open-ended commentary Gwendolyn employed most of the time."

"And that surprises you? After all the weird shit that went down in Glastonbury? Not to mention New Mexico. I'm not too crazy about it, but I'm starting to accept it."

"I, too, Malcolm, though reluctantly."

"Why reluctantly? You've done better with it than I have."

"Theoretically, all these paranormal phenomena are fascinating. I was always in awe of Gwendolyn, and I loved her. Besides, how often does a man get a powerful Celtic witch for a mother-in-law?"

"I still have trouble understanding why your wife hated her mother so much."

"The gift—or whatever you call it, the magic maybe—skipped Amanda either because that's what she chose, or because her character just wasn't up to the responsibility. Sometimes I wish it had skipped my daughter, but my reasons are absolutely selfish. I don't want her always at risk."

"I don't like it either. But you remember some of what the old lady wrote to Connor? That letter she found in the house in England."

"Yes, I can still hear every word echoing in Gwendolyn's crusty British accent. She explained to Connor what this responsibility was and gave her the choice of accepting it or not. I have to tell you I was secretly voting for 'not.'"

"Me, too, but what's done is done. And for all the complaining she does about this bizarro stuff, she's committed to it. I saw her face on that hill in Glastonbury—the way it was shining and that light coming from her. It was scary, but—"

"Kinda cool?" laughed Benjamin.

"For lack of a better word, yeah."

"I agree. Now let's see what we can do to get you on your way to California with the blessing of federal law enforcement."

"You're coming, too, aren't you?"

"Wild horses couldn't keep me away. But I need to do a little research that might prove helpful to us."

Malcolm smiled at the understatement. For most people, research meant a trip to the library, a few hours surfing the Net, or making some phone calls. The state-of-the-art computers and communications systems in Benjamin's home office rivaled the data-gathering capabilities of any intelligence agency in the world. And the ex-spymaster possessed an almost uncanny ability to distill enormous amounts of raw data into patterns that could be identified, analyzed, and acted on if necessary.

"You've been looking into the Divine Hammer of God people?"

"Yes, and while there isn't a lot of information on the group itself, I think I've turned up some interesting connections. But what you've told me about the priest being killed tends to point me toward one lead in particular."

"Which is?"

"Let me give you a little background on this. A few months ago one of the European agencies identified and eventually broke up a computer network run by some first-class hackers operating all over the continent. Predictably, most of their projects were designed to relieve their targets of various sums of money, but there was one guy working with them whose hobby was just plain snooping. He apparently got his kicks digging up dirt on people, which also might explain why not every victim of theft hurried to report it. But I'm digressing. The point is, this man's files were confiscated and not destroyed. Some bureaucrat or other in Italy must have seen a potential gold mine in the information and arranged to have the drives and disks stolen from the intelligence agency involved in the original sting operation."

"And there's something in those files related to these Hammer nut-jobs?"

"I think so. I was running a really broad search over several different networks to see what sorts of hits I'd get on both *'Malleus Caelistis ab Deum'* and its English translation, even though I thought the Latin probably wouldn't produce much. Funny thing is, the Latin phrase cropped up several times, mostly in historical text references. Apparently this society has its roots in a much older organization. But one hit traced back to the stolen data files from the hacker. At least that's what the site implies. He's mentioned by his hacker name, and apparently he'd posted a few juicy tidbits on the Net to get the attention of potential victims. He wrote barely veiled threats to expose a conspiracy that involved bigwigs in the Catholic Church, and he mentioned Malleus Caelistis by name."

"Anyone talk to this hacker?"

"He was interrogated thoroughly and refused to talk. The intelligence people were going to take another crack at him, but he died."

"How?"

"In his cell, of unknown causes."

Malcolm frowned. "The autopsy showed *nothing*?"

"There was no autopsy. Somebody paid somebody. And the sketchy information I got implies that some individual or maybe even a sub-rosa security group from the Vatican was somehow involved."

"Vatican? As in the Catholic Church, the pope, and the guys with pointy hats?"

"Yes, that one."

"Damn! And that puts a whole new spin on this dead priest and the way he was whacked."

"Whacked? You've been reading Dashiel Hammett again, haven't you?"

Malcolm chuckled. "I admit nothing."

"Who would? But you're right about taking a second look at this. This is starting to feel less like a fly-by-night fringe group and more like something that's...I don't know...organized."

"Please don't say that. Organized killers are a pain in the ass," said Malcolm. "The stupid ones we catch a lot quicker."

"I don't know about Bell. But someone in this group is. I've also analyzed all those pamphlets and flyers in the file, along with some correspondence that might be his. The letters aren't particularly intelligent. Some of the material in the pieces meant for publication is entirely different."

"Maybe he borrowed it," suggested Malcolm.

"Possibly, but if that's the case, I should be able to track down the source. I can't. So if the text was original, maybe Bell wasn't the author.

As to whether he could pound a stake into some man's chest, you'll have to figure that out."

"When he went into prison, I would have said he wasn't the right type for that kind of bloody killing."

"But somewhere along the line he appears to have taken on a different persona than the guy you thought was a raving lunatic. He turned into the Preacher. Who knows how much weirder he got?"

"We don't know. And we also don't know whether his threats against nuclear facilities are for real."

"True."

"And what does that have to do with the priest anyway?" asked Malcolm in frustration. "It's like we're talking about completely unrelated issues, and yet it's the same guy who's involved."

"*May* be involved. Remember, no one has seen Ricky Bell since he got out of prison. I haven't found a trace of him in any database. He doesn't have any credit cards in his name. His Maryland driver's license expired years ago. He hasn't held a regular job anywhere that taxes are withheld, and he hasn't tried to collect unemployment benefits. He has no cars or real property that I can find. There's no record of admission to a hospital—mental or otherwise—or arrest in any reporting jurisdiction."

"Meaning he could be dead."

"Yes, but anyone who's determined enough can drop out of sight completely if they already know all the ways we have of tracking them down. If he's alive, he knows exactly how to stay out of the system."

"And you think he could be connected with some Catholic secret society?"

"It's a stretch, given his background, but what the hell. I've got that itch, just like you have your little voice that tells you when something isn't quite right."

"Yeah, but let's just keep that between us."

"Little voices aren't sufficiently macho for the D.C. police, are they?" said Benjamin with a chuckle.

"Not hardly."

"All right. You go home and pack. Before you know it, your boss will be getting a call from one of my friends. He'll be asked to send you immediately to California to investigate a potential connection between a crime there and a recent spate of terrorist threats."

"Aw, you know how much he hates it when people from Capitol Hill call him."

Benjamin could hear Malcolm's grin. "Yes, but the poor man will just have to suck it up, won't he? In the meantime, all I have to do is find out what Signore Albertini, our venal Italian bureaucrat, has done with his little cache of blackmail material and see if there's anything in it that might indicate Ricky Bell is a twisted front man for something more dangerous than we thought."

"But we don't really want to mess with the Vatican, right? If you think I'm not popular in Washington right now, can you imagine the shit they'd give me if I even mentioned investigating Catholic clergy?"

"Don't worry about that right now. I'm not suggesting anything quite so provocative. You know me. I like to gather information and then see where it leads us."

Malcolm sighed. "Sometimes I hate where it leads us."

"Me, too."

»——«

The old priest sat quietly in the pew furthermost from the confessional. He'd slipped unnoticed past the police cordon outside the church. Inside it was deathly quiet. The body had been removed, then a dozen women and men had scurried about the place taking photographs, dusting powder onto a hundred different surfaces, and occasionally cracking jokes, or what he supposed passed for jokes in their profession. Finally they'd left, locking the door behind them. There would be no Mass said this Sunday at St. Mary of the Groves.

He waited. Just as he felt his energy begin to shift and prepared to let his consciousness transition from this reality to another, a noise distracted him. Pulling completely back into his body, the elderly priest made himself virtually invisible to any but a trained and powerful mystic. At the far end of the church, to the right of the main altar, a man emerged from the sacristy door. His energy was potent, and to the old priest's well-honed senses, it preceded him in the gloom. *One of ours perhaps?*

He reached out with his mind, but there was no response from the intruder. *Maybe not.* The old priest studied the man, who walked slowly through a pool of light from a wall sconce. He was quite tall, with thick silvery hair. He was dressed in black, gray, and white and might have been a cleric. But his face was not peaceful. Carefully the man drew open the confessional door and stood there for a long time staring at the place where the blasphemous killing of a priest had occurred. *Was the killing of any priest blasphemous,* the old priest wondered, *or just the good ones?* Perhaps what bothered the old wanderer even more was the place where the killing was done: a house of the Blessed Mother. She who had ordained that the world would be at peace, had commanded mankind to rejoin what had been put asunder—she has been dishonored. Someone, some devil, had desecrated her house. The old priest almost wished there were truth in the myth of hell, for it was a place he might gladly send whoever had done this. Then he gently chided himself for the vengeful thought. Now was not the time to abandon the path of Light.

The stranger was leaving now, walking down the aisle toward the front of the church. His wide shoulders sagged, his head was bowed. The man stopped, faced the altar. The old priest knew the man's lips were moving in prayer, making supplication for understanding, for strength. The litany was familiar, but its words were hollow.

He knew that She would not hear the man clearly, nor would he hear Her, not until he learned to speak the language of the Divine Mother: *"She Who Is"…a holy song forgotten…a prayer only whispered in the shadows…a sacred promise not yet fulfilled.*

The visitor was gone. The old priest prepared himself once more and quickly reached out through the layers of density of normal consciousness. The objects and walls became less substantial, shimmering slightly as a mirage in the desert. *Illusion,* he repeated to himself, *and beyond the Illusion is God.* He breathed deeply and allowed the shift to take place.

He was searching, and the object of his search was close. That much he knew. It emitted a sort of pulse that only a few people on earth could possibly detect—only those who were sworn to protect it, or students of the mysteries so advanced in their understanding there was very little they could not see. The old priest was both, but he nonetheless could not pinpoint the source of the pulsation that surged and fell in synchronicity with all of creation. His essence pursued the living heartbeat of it, the sensation of proximity growing stronger. Then, suddenly the connection was distant and fuzzy. The old man instantly sensed another presence. He tried to reestablish the focus, but couldn't. His thought projections were met with waves of sadness, anger, fear, and confusion.

Then he understood. At the foot of the altar a shape huddled, a gray, rather forlorn assemblage of spiritual energy. Its attention was turned inward so that it did not perceive the growing corona of light emanating from the side chapel where stood the statue of the Mother. But the old priest saw it and understood immediately that his purpose today had changed.

He sent forth his essence to embrace the gray being. *You are lost, my son. I will help you. Come with me.* Slowly, the mist coalesced into a more defined shape—the outlines of a man. The old priest felt a human consciousness answer his summons. It was weak and yet alive. *Look to the Mother: Her light will guide you.* He repeated the instruction again and again like a simple mantra, until the confused and frightened young soul drifted toward the side chapel. The corona of light expanded to fill the entire church for a brief second, and the brief glimpse of what lay beyond made the old priest's spirit ache. If only he might follow the soul…Yet he had no more completed the thought than the light was extinguished, the portal closed.

The old man sighed, finding an antidote to his disappointment in that he had again done his work—Enrique Rosario was home.

>—《

Monsignor Johann Kursk stood on the balcony of his hotel room at the Hilton. His hands gripped the metal railing until his knuckles were white. In his fury he would have liked to tear it from its fastenings and fling it out into the parking lot below. His superiors had sent him here, to this vile godless place, to muzzle Father Rosario, that damned heretic and traitor to the church, and get hold of the one thing that still seemed to hold together the heathen Cult of Magdalene. He was hampered by not knowing precisely what the thing was. But Cardinal de Marcos had been adamant that he would know it when he saw it. And his superiors always counted on Kursk to take care of difficulties. They didn't inquire into his methods, and he repaid the favor by not burdening them with distasteful details. He served without complaint. He used whatever tools presented themselves. His conscience ran in a very narrow channel bounded by the interests of Malleus Caelistis. Anything or anyone who did not share those interests was irrelevant; anyone who threatened them was expendable. Conveniently, even some of the rank and file of the society were expendable, too. There were lots of hangers-on who barely even understood the principles of the movement to which they nominally belonged. They were useful at times. When they were "expended," Kursk liked to think of them as acceptable casualties of war, the foot soldiers who died for the good of the many.

The more he thought about the events of the past two days, the more he shuddered with rage. First he'd been humiliated by that stupid old fool, Johnston, who'd refused to obey the extremely unambiguous orders from the Congregation and help him put a leash on the damned Jesuit priest. So Kursk had canceled his flight back to Rome and decided to deal with Rosario himself. But the bastard had refused to come to the phone, which led Kursk to suspect that Johnston had warned him. Now the son of a bitch was dead, which took care of one problem, but who knew what he'd left behind? Who knew what might be found in his papers, his notes? And where was this terrible "thing" Kursk was supposed to find and retrieve? He had worked for years to track down the mongrel heathens who dared to question the true nature of God, who dared to attack the very foundations of the church, who would defile the priesthood itself with scurrilous lies and rumors intended to deny their noble heritage. But he had still never even come close to discovering what lay at the heart of this cult that had lived on for century after century, that dated, it seemed, from the very founding of Malleus Caelistis. Some even believed that the histories and fates of the two groups were inextricably intertwined by divine intention. He disagreed, and now he would put an end to it.

The monsignor had intended to sneak into the rectory well before dawn, but hadn't counted on the presence of several dozen mourners who'd been holding an all-night vigil there in the large living room because the church itself was off-limits to the public. He'd been stunned to see all the windows of the rectory ablaze with light and people moving back and forth in most of the rooms, including the kitchen. He was also annoyed that good Catholics would be so easily duped into praying for a man who wasn't fit to wear the collar. They didn't deserve to belong to the church. He'd see that this particular parish was closed; indeed, he would. And something would have to be done about Archbishop Johnston as well. A well-crafted scandal, a few improprieties uncovered, and the stubborn bastard would be lucky not be excommunicated.

But that would have to wait until he returned triumphantly to Rome. Tonight he'd go back to the rectory. By God, he'd go back. No matter how much he hated this place with its plastic facades and shiny cars and trendy restaurants and sullen, rebellious, half-naked young people engaging in mortal sin, he'd stay here until his tasks were complete. He'd find every scrap of paper, every document, every file, no matter where it was hidden, and he would burn it all, just the way he knew Enrique Rosario was burning in hell.

Chapter Nine

*I do not feel obliged to believe
that that same God who has endowed us
with sense, reason, and intellect
has intended us to forego their use.*
—Galileo Galilei

Washington, D.C.

One sharp knock and his office door swung open before he had a chance to respond.

"Captain Jefferson?"

Malcolm looked up from the morning report on the previous night's crime statistics, prepared to bark at whoever had entered his private domain so abruptly. The reprimand died on his lips. This was not a woman he wished to chide. She was a stranger, and by any thinking person's definition, just this side of gorgeous.

"Yes," he said, standing up because it seemed polite under the circumstances.

"Ayalla Franklin." She flipped open a leader badge folder with her left hand, extending her right hand toward Malcolm. Reaching to shake hands, he glanced down at the I.D. and allowed himself a momentary sinking feeling. FBI: Just what he needed to complicate his life.

As if reading his mind, she smiled slightly. "The locals are hardly ever glad to see us, but I'm used to it. Cooperation is usually minimal since they're more interested in getting credit than solving a case."

"Pretty broad generalization," Malcolm replied, trying to keep the irritation out of this tone.

"Let's just say it describes my experiences to date."

"There's another way of looking at it," he said. "My impression has been the tendency of the Fee—that is, the FBI to come storming in on local cases when it suits them and treat the local authorities like a bunch of yahoos who wouldn't know where to point their guns unless someone told them."

"I believe you were about to say 'the Feebies,'" she replied.

"Sorry, that was uncalled for. Old habits die hard."

"That's hardly the worst thing we've been called. I know there's even more tension in Washington with agencies literally tripping over each other. But I'm not here to get into a pissing match with anyone. I'm here because our interests coincide. If you don't care to cooperate, let's get that out in the open right up front." Her tone was icy, but Malcolm couldn't help registering that she had a rather nice voice.

They stood there for a moment, facing off across his desk. He had time to notice that she was looking him almost in the eye, a rare occurrence for someone his height. She must have been very near six feet tall—in her low-heeled shoes. She wore the FBI "uniform"—dark suit, white shirt (in her case, a white silk blouse). The jacket bulged only slightly where her service weapon nestled at her waist. Her brown hair, flecked with blond highlights, was swept back from her face. Her skin was only a shade lighter than Malcolm's, but where his eyes were a soft brown, her eyes were a stunning crystal blue, and her high cheekbones subtly implied a more exotic heritage than his own.

"Please," he said. "Sit down." She stared suspiciously at the chair for a second or two, then sat, her spine rigid. Malcolm resumed his chair. "We're getting off on the wrong foot. I'm not one of the 'yahoos' you may be used to dealing with, and I don't like getting into 'pissing matches,' at least not with—"

"With a woman," she finished his sentence, her eyes sparking.

"No. If you'll let me do my own talking, you can jump all over me when I'm done. I was going to say…at least not with people whose goals are the same as mine—catching the bad guys—and who don't bring a lot of attitude to the table."

She glared at him for a moment, then her shoulders relaxed ever so slightly. "Okay. You're right. It's just that I try to be prepared for the worst right from the start."

"Because everyone loves to hate the FBI?"

"It's partly that. Every other agency competes with us. The public thinks we're either inept or trigger-happy."

"Ruby Ridge and Waco," said Malcolm quietly.

"Yep. And September 11."

"You know, Agent Franklin, the public doesn't really think much of any of us in law enforcement. About the only public servants left who command any respect at all are the firefighters and the paramedics. Maybe if we'd come up in a different time, when people felt differently."

"You mean as in the days of *Dragnet* and Jack Webb?" she looked at him incredulously.

"At least then cops were perceived as good guys."

"And you think you'd be a police captain?"

He hesitated. "No, probably not."

"And the closest I'd get to working for the FBI would be scrubbing J. Edgar's toilets. So much for the good old days."

Malcolm smiled. "Okay, you're right. There are no good old days, and the last FBI agent the public could warm up to was Efrem Zimbalist Jr. So let's take it from there."

She actually smiled. "Efrem Zimbalist Jr.? You know, Senator Hawthorne was right. You do have a sense of humor."

Malcolm's eyes widened. "Benjamin Hawthorne?"

"Yes."

"He sent you?"

"He spoke to me briefly. As he does not currently hold a position of executive authority in the federal government, Captain Jefferson, it would not be accurate to say he sent me. The special agent in charge of our Washington office sent me."

"Of course," said Malcolm slowly, wondering if he had once again stepped on her toes.

"However, it would be accurate to say that he discovered we are both working on what is basically the same case and gave my office a friendly heads-up."

His head cocked slightly to one side, a habit he had when pondering a question, Malcolm regarded her thoughtfully. "So instead of saying right off that Benjamin suggested this meeting, you decided to come in here and yank my chain just for the hell of it?"

Special Agent Franklin chuckled. "Not entirely for the hell of it. If I'm going to work a case with someone, I like to know what sort of person might end up watching my back."

"And if we work together, Agent Franklin, what sort of person will be watching *my* back?"

"Someone who keeps her eye on the target, Captain Jefferson, and holds records for marksmanship at Quantico."

"I'm duly impressed," he replied, "but how is it you're interested in the Ricky Bell investigation?"

Her brow furrowed slightly. "Bell? Oh, you mean the ex-con from the old NSA burglary. I'm not all that interested in him. What I am pursuing, though some of my superiors think it's a waste of time, is the Divine Hammer of God group."

"But that *is* Ricky's group."

"Not exactly. I'm afraid you've only got hold of one of the tiger's ears, Captain. Bell is small-fry. Little cells of this group have been cropping up all over the country for years."

"So you're taking the potential nuclear plant threats seriously?"

"Maybe. At least I'm a lot more willing to be convinced than some of the bureaucrats in this town. Most of them are like those three monkeys."

"See no evil, hear no evil…"

"Speak no evil," she finished the old axiom. "They don't like hearing that we're vulnerable."

"Do you have any idea what their real agenda might be?" asked Malcolm.

"You've read their manifestos and pamphlets, haven't you?"

"Yes, from the old files on Ricky Bell. I've looked at all of them at least a dozen times. But their—or at least *his*—anger isn't focused. It's too scattered. They hate the government, they're suspicious of the military, they're rabid about the United Nations, and sure that one world government is just around the corner. On the other hand, they espouse one religion—extreme fundamentalism—for the entire globe. They also appear to be white supremacists, misogynists, and separatists."

"That profile isn't exactly unusual, and it does sound unfocused. I think it's because there *was* no focus. It sounds like someone trying to be all things to all malcontents in the world."

"So why are they now targeting nuclear generating plants?" he asked. "Why have they gone from the very general to the extremely specific?"

"I can't answer the first question, though that's the one that concerns me the most. As for the second one, my theory is that something has happened, or someone new has taken a more active leadership role in the Hammer of God."

"Someone with brains as well as power."

"I'm afraid so. I've also looked at copies of the police file on Ricky Bell, and I've read some of his 'literature.'" She crooked her fingers into quotation marks around the last word. "But the person who drafted these current threats, especially the one that included the facilities plans, sounds like…" She paused, as if groping for the right way to explain her hunch.

It hit Malcolm in a flash of understanding. "Like someone repeating Bell's rhetoric but with a different agenda."

Her eyes widened in surprise. "Yes, but I thought I was the only one who saw that. For that matter, I was beginning to think I was manufacturing the whole idea."

"I don't think so at all. Though I'll have to admit that up until this moment, I hadn't really seen it myself. I just sensed something was off about it."

"I'm beginning to think this temporary partnership could work after all," she said.

"I take it you had your doubts?"

"Didn't you?"

"At first. But once you mentioned Benjamin—"

"What is it with that guy? He sounded perfectly nice on the phone. Everyone seems to have heard of him, which is hardly a surprise considering his career, but no one seems to know quite what it is he does now. And when he 'suggests' a course of action, people right up to the director go along with it. What *does* he do?"

Malcolm smiled. "I think he prefers a low profile. Whatever you want to know about his...uh...work, you'll have to ask him yourself. Personally, he's one of the best friends I've ever had, or ever will have. I'd trust him with my life."

Agent Franklin was quiet for a few moments. "Coming from a cop, that's high praise indeed."

"And not the least bit overstated. But you can decide for yourself when you meet him."

"*Meet* him?"

"Of course. I assume you're going to California."

"You mean he's planning on being actively involved in this investigation? I thought he was simply sharing some information."

"He could hardly avoid being involved, considering that his daughter was one of the people who discovered the priest's body at the church."

"Body?" she asked, baffled. "What the hell are you talking about?"

The tables were turned and Malcolm permitted himself a moment to savor the sensation of knowing more than Agent Franklin. "Night before last, the senator's daughter, Connor Hawthorne—"

"The author, right?"

"Also ex–assistant district attorney who used to practice right here in town."

"Wait a second. She's the one whose lover was murdered down by the C&O Canal. I remember the case. We worked on it, too. Not me personally, but—"

"Yeah, and we threw everything we had at it, too. But, believe it or not, it was Connor and her father and…a couple of other people who broke it."

"The murder vic, her lover, was a woman, right?"

Malcolm paused. "Yes."

"So the daughter, she's—"

"Gay. Is that what you're asking?"

"Well, not exactly asking. I mean it was in the papers where anyone could read it. I just wondered if she was still…you know."

"Yes, she is. Her lifestyle is part of who she is, not a temporary condition. Do you have a problem with that, Agent Franklin?" His tone was icy. There was no trace of friendliness in his expression. "Because if it is, you and I are going to have a problem."

She had the good grace to look embarrassed. "I really didn't mean it that way. It's just how I was raised. My brothers and sisters and I, we went to church every week and sabbath school. I mean, I don't buy into all that so much now but…" The special agent looked as if she knew she'd backed herself into a verbal corner.

"Your personal beliefs are your business," said Malcolm, with little sign of his former warmth. "But if those beliefs in any way impact on this investigation, or on my friends, then it becomes my business. Are we clear on that?"

"I don't need your blessing to pursue this investigation, Captain Jefferson, nor do I require your involvement. And, as a matter of fact, it seems pretty clear that *you* are the one with personal involvement."

Malcolm leaned forward. "Damn right I am. And I'm not going to waste my time explaining why. Far as I'm concerned, you can do whatever you want. But since you obviously came in here without a goddamn clue about what's been happening in California, and since I'm the one the local cops are expecting to liaise with, you might want to weigh your personal prejudices against your desire to solve this case. You need me, and you're going to need the Hawthornes. So make up your mind, Agent Franklin. I've got a plane to catch."

She was silent. Malcolm watched her inner struggle play out across her expressive features. They were very nice features, he thought, but if they were attached to a bigot, it was a waste of good genetics as far as he was concerned.

"I'm sorry." She shook her head. "God, I don't think I've done this much apologizing all year. Frankly, I hate it. But I do know what my priorities are. The personal stuff I'll deal with later. Now, would you please fill me in on the dead priest and explain what this has to do with the Divine Hammer of God."

Malcolm nodded, not quite willing to unbend, at least not yet. "Yes, but I suggest we discuss it on the way to the airport."

"What makes you think I'm on the same flight?"

"I know Benjamin," he said with a slight smile. "If you weren't on this flight, I'd be majorly surprised."

He picked up his briefcase and the two-suit carry-on his sister, Eve, had packed for him the night before because she was convinced he'd forget some critical item. Malcolm opened the door. "After you, Agent Franklin."

She stood up, turned toward the door. "Please. Call me Ayalla…and I'll hold the door for *you*. My carry-on's in the car."

"Then we'll take your car," he said. "I've heard the Feebs know how to drive *and* shoot their guns."

"I can also walk and chew bubble gum at the same time." She paused and met his eyes. "This is going to get easier, isn't it?" she asked, looking and sounding a little less certain than when she'd walked in.

"Up to you," he said. "Entirely up to you."

»—«

Unaware that she was a current subject of debate between two somewhat prickly law enforcement types back East, Connor Hawthorne rolled over in the king-size bed and stretched her arms luxuriantly.

"Ouch, that's my nose," a muffled voice said. Laura emerged from beneath the sheet.

"Sorry, sweetheart," Connor replied, seriously studying the facial feature in question. "Doesn't look broken."

"I'm not all that delicate," Laura smiled. "I was just giving you a hard time. And speaking of time," she added, peering around Connor at the digital clock. "Good Lord, it's past noon. How long have you been awake?"

"Not long. We were up talking to Beatrice and the archbishop until almost five o'clock this morning. I figured we could use the sleep."

Laura kicked back the covers and slipped a silk robe around her, before going to the window. "Looks like another beautiful day in the neighborhood," she said. "You gotta love the weather here."

"At least until you get completely bored with bright, sunny, and temperate."

"That could take years," Laura replied. "I've got a very high boredom threshold when it comes to perfect weather." She turned back to Connor. "Please don't tell me you are emotionally attached to the slush, snow, and misery of a winter in the Northeast."

Connor grinned and Laura held up her hand. "At least don't tell me yet. Give me a chance to delude myself into thinking we could hang out in paradise indefinitely."

Pulling on her own robe, Connor came to stand behind Laura and put both arms around her waist. Laura leaned back into her with a small sigh of contentment. "To be honest, it doesn't matter. Would it sound really corny if I told you I didn't care where we live as long as we're together?"

Connor gently moved Laura's hair to one side and kissed the back of her neck. "Yes, it does sound undeniably corny, but I love it anyway. I'm a secretly corny person myself. So as long as no one hears us…"

"And discovers that the queen of cynical legal dramas is a total marshmallow…"

"Then our secret is safe," finished Connor.

"So I have carte blanche to say whatever romantic thoughts come to mind?"

"Unless you get completely carried away and I end up in a diabetic coma."

"Not much risk in that," replied Laura. "I'm not all *that* sweet." She turned in her lover's arms and brushed the lock of hair off Connor's forehead. Her hair had always defied any restraints imposed by spray and mousse. "How about breakfast? I'm starving."

"Me, too" said Connor, tracing the outline of Laura's lips with her fingers. "But could we hold off on the food part for just a little while?"

»——«

Archbishop Johnston pushed his chair back in frustration and glared at the computer beside his desk. He rarely used it because technology annoyed him. When he wanted something done, he asked Grolsch, who had formed some sort of symbiotic relationship with the damned thing. The young man was a disaster in most other areas, but he was transformed into an expert when you put him in front of a computer. On this occasion, however, the archbishop wanted to do his own research—privately.

Hours later he was convinced that if there were a hell, the Internet was the way to get there. Every time he tried to search for something, he was given several million locations as possibilities, and he had to wade through thousands of words of worthless information. Yet there had been a few rewards along the way.

He'd learned slightly more about the Cult of Magdalene, though not historically speaking. He already knew every fragment of its history by heart. What he'd discovered was that there were others out there talking about it. The Cult wasn't quite as much of a deep, dark secret as he'd thought. But he hadn't gotten any closer to understanding why the esoteric theology of the cult could be of interest to anyone now. It had been little more than a splinter group of its time.

His search for "*Malleus Caelistis ab Deum*" as well as its English version, The Divine Hammer of God, had produced a number of "hits" as Grolsch informed him they were called. But he grew exhausted going back and forth from one page to another finding tangential references that had little to do with the true object of his search. Many of the pages he read spewed out a lot of prejudice, violence, and antigovernment rhetoric. But surely these were the product of sick minds who had somehow co-opted the name of the Malleus Society to lend legitimacy to their rantings. Their philosophy, it if could dignified with such a term, was alien to him.

From what he understood of the original Malleus organization, its purpose was purely religious in nature—religious discipline, that is. He sincerely hoped it no longer existed. In its most virulent seventeenth-century manifestation, it had played a significant role in the atrocities of the hated Inquisition. Over the centuries, the society was said to have withered and just about died out completely, retaining among its members perhaps few elderly clerics whose politics remained to the right of Mussolini. The archbishop had heard a few rumblings that younger priests at the curia might be trying to kick-start the old society, in reaction to what they perceived as a sinfully liberal trend in the church's leadership. By and large he'd discounted it as foolishness. But the death of his friend, Father Rosario, had changed his attitude. This was no longer a matter of idle curiosity.

The young woman, Connor Hawthorne, had pulled him aside at the rectory a few hours earlier and shared the details of the inscription and symbols painted on the white mallet that had been used to murder the young priest. While she hadn't been able to decipher or remember them all in her brief look at the scene, she was sure of the name and of a few other details.

He had noticed Connor was not wearing the cross Beatrice had made; she had apparently taken his advice. That was at least partly reassuring. The woman obviously had a brain in her head and was equally capable of figuring out that there was much more to this murder than what appeared on the surface. She also seemed the sort of person who might not let go of it once she started poking around in it. He shuddered to think that she and her friend, and possibly Beatrice as well, might be in some jeopardy from whoever had killed Enrique.

He flipped the switch on the computer to turn it off. The damn thing beeped loudly, and he remembered that he wasn't supposed to just turn the power off. There was some special procedure one needed to follow. He didn't care. There was a lot more to worry about right now than the bad attitude of a piece of silicon circuitry. He had a feeling the Society was alive and well—and doing something potentially nasty.

The archbishop was deeply angry, and somewhere inside (though he tried to deny it to himself) he was profoundly afraid.

Chapter Ten

Building one's life on a foundation of gold
is just like building a house on foundations of sand.
—Henrik Ibsen

Greed is a powerful motivator. Born of fear, it is a sadly common feature of the human condition, encompassing as it does the obsession to acquire and to defend at all costs what one has acquired. Sometimes the consequences of greed are restricted to a few individuals; in other instances, a host of innocents pay the price.

In the early 1980s, a federal panel approved the plans and specifications for the San Peligro Nuclear Generating Station. There should have been a thorough investigation of the proposed site. Yes, the fairly desolate location appeared, at least on the surface, to be ideal. The facility would be many miles from heavily populated areas and only thirty miles from an air force base should security become an issue. Groundwater was present in sufficient quantity, and the terrain was not so rough as to hinder the construction of the pylons and towers that would carry the generated power to urban areas. Even the environmental impact statements and reports had passed muster with all the watchdogs, both public and private.

The proposal reviewed by the panel and their staff comprised some 11,480 pages. Most of the people privy to the proposal had not been aware that fourteen pages were missing from the section devoted to geological reports compiled by a private surveying group. Dr. Calvin Finch, whose report was missing entirely from the files, was the only dissenting voice in a sea of support for the plant's location. Like the much-ridiculed Cassandra of ancient Troy, whose dire warnings regarding the large wooden horse outside the gates were patently ignored, Finch was absolutely convinced the choice of site was potentially dangerous, but no one cared to listen to him. This plant would sit squarely astride the Cueva Antigua fault, a fact that any college student with a GPS unit, a calculator, and a meticulously detailed survey map could have figured out.

Dr. Finch's opinions were not really that outlandish. A number of individuals might well have shared his concerns, particularly if they'd understood that he wasn't primarily worried about what a potential earthquake could do to the structural integrity of the plant, most of which would be sunk more than a hundred feet underground. A nuclear accident would be nasty, yes, but Dr. Finch recognized a more frightening risk. What would happen if a nuclear disaster far below ground set off a chain reaction along the fault itself? He believed the consequences would be disastrous beyond measure. He mentioned massive earthquakes, tidal waves, and volcanic eruptions as just a few of the possible scenarios.

For that very reason, those fourteen pages had been removed by persons unnamed. Their justification: Why muddy the waters with opposing views? Nonscientific government types were so easily confused.

Two of the panel members were acutely aware of the missing pages and did not object. Both individuals were key in guaranteeing approval without a great deal of oversight. One of them, a career bureaucrat, had recently "inherited" a substantial sum from a distant relative in Canada. The windfall had enabled him to pay off his mortgage and half a dozen credit cards. The other, a one-time real estate mogul, owned a partial interest in the proposed parcel of land. The ownership, naturally, was obscured by several layers of dummy corporations registered in Nevada, but in the end the profits would make their way into her pockets.

To ease her own conscience, she'd read the report herself and decided that Finch really was one of those namby-pamby Chicken Little types who always found a reason to hold up progress. Besides, her income from the land and from the rights to use adjoining land would keep her in extremely comfortable retirement in Florida, along with her husband, Leland. She also intended to set up a trust fund for her son, Lee Jr., whose long list of dubious achievements included a recently completed stretch in a prison back East. She doubted he'd ever find a decent job, so she was resigned to employing him herself, if only to keep him out of jail. He ran errands, transported boxes of files between her office and home, and at least pretended to be her conscientious personal aide while she served on the federal panel in question.

Thus the plant was constructed and brought on line. An electric fence was built around it, and pretty soon hardly anyone cared about its history. But that did not mean the facts of its birth could not be discovered by someone with a reason to look.

A few months later, the real estate mogul's son was arrested on drug charges and sent back to prison. She debated cutting him off without a dime, but finally relented and hired a lawyer to file an appeal. Her son was, after all, her son.

»—«

"Archie, old pal, you're lookin' kinda pale. What's up? Thought you'd be out cruisin' for beach babes all weekend? The weather was truly fine."

"The name is Mr. Sims," Archibald corrected the grinning guard, Leonard Zemecka, one of the new hires he particularly disliked.

The scruffiest of the two, with hair that fell past his uniform shirt collar, laughed. "Oh, sorry, *Mister* Sims." He glanced at the monitor where Archibald's briefcase was being X-rayed. In an exaggerated stage whisper, he said to his partner who manned the metal detector, "Maybe he don't do girls. Check out that *pink* shirt."

Archibald stepped through the detector and grabbed his briefcase off the conveyor belt. "I've had enough of you two. You're a disgrace to the security team. I'll see to it that as of the end of shift, you will no longer be employed here."

He stood there almost hyperventilating from the stress of being confrontational, and the two men pointedly ignored him.

"Did you hear what I said?" he shouted, his hysteria rising.

The metal detector guard, Garvey Hull, stepped right up to the trembling manager, his nose inches from Archibald's. His tone was insolent and derisive with a touch of threat. "Yeah, we heard you, little man. You think Holcomb's gonna listen to you, then you're stupider than he said. But me and Leonard, we don't appreciate being treated like dog turds you wanna step over. You get my drift?" He backed away slightly and just as Archibald was trying to find the courage for some sort of pithy comeback, Hull leaned in again, almost whispering. "And, oh, by the way, the Preacher sends his regards."

Archibald stared at him, trying to decide if he'd heard the man right. His chest was so tight he couldn't breathe. The plant manager wheeled around, almost tripped over his own feet, and fled up the corridor, arms flapping beside him. The sound of laughter accompanied his retreat. Small wonder—Archibald Sims looked for all the world like a drunken flamingo on the run.

Chapter Eleven

Beware of false prophets,
which come to you in sheep's clothing,
but inwardly they are ravening wolves.
—Matthew 7:15, The King James Bible

Orange County, California

Richard Timothy Renard La Cloche…Ricky…the Preacher: A man who looked absolutely nothing like his arrest mug shots and whose crimes to date merited far more incarceration than the relatively brief seven years he'd served. Still, those years had been surprisingly productive. He had not only established a network of loyal, if not terribly bright, followers, but he had also mapped out his destiny in painstaking detail. He personally thought that was a remarkable accomplishment for a prison inmate, even one of his intelligence and foresight. He was a different man now, outwardly and inwardly.

He sat at the kitchen table in his Newport Beach condominium, tracing his finger along the diagrams and illustrations neatly reproduced in the blueprints. He could read them clearly and accurately, including the engineering data and construction specifications. Ricky, who rarely used that name anymore, was thoroughly self-educated, primarily because his life had not lent itself well to formal study.

He'd been the child of a Creole woman with a café au lait complexion whose luck in the birth control department had run out just before an otherwise profitable encounter with a Baptist minister who'd occasionally strayed from his shepherd duties at the Holy Roller Traveling Revival Ministry. The reverend had shown no interest in providing ongoing financial support for the living proof of his human weakness, perhaps because the infant bore a startling resemblance to his father. Understandably, Emmiline's workplace in the Quarter did not provide child care. An erstwhile Catholic girl, she had the child baptized and then turned him over to the Sisters of Mercy who ran an orphanage in Baton Rouge. She didn't return to check on him in the twelve years he stayed with the sisters.

Ricky liked the nuns. He didn't mind the discipline. He soaked up the Bible verses they taught and scrupulously adhered to all the rules, no matter how strict. He even appointed himself an enforcer of those rules. Other children quickly learned to keep their transgressions a secret from Ricky. He not only beat the crap out of those who stole, smoked, cussed, or talked about "lewd" subjects, but he then told the nuns, who sent offenders to Father Crillon and his leather belt for attitude adjustment. Ricky was never punished, but he spent all the time he could with the gray-haired priest, asking question after question about being a soldier of God. If Crillon seemed occasionally taken aback by the child's interests, Ricky chose not to notice.

He gave up on Crillon, though, the day he saw the old man forgive a boy for stealing instead of whipping him so he couldn't sit down. Weakness. Ricky hated weakness, especially in a man of God.

He'd also pretty much hated the wimpy, soft-spoken psychologist who saw him on occasion. The nuns had become a little worried about Ricky's fierce temper and tendency to judge harshly everyone around him. He was, as Sister Mary Paul once put it, like a pint-size Hitler on a religious tirade. Ricky thought the psychologist was a pathetic excuse but humored the man anyway. He answered the stupid questions the way he knew they should be answered. The doctor was particularly fond of harping on the subject of Ricky's birth parents. Did he think about them? Resent them? Want to find them? In all honesty, he had no strong emotions one way or the other about Emmiline or the reverend. Later, when he was almost nineteen, he killed them both, but that had been purely a matter of meting out appropriate penalties for their sinful behavior. Emotion didn't enter into it. Emmiline had been dispatched quickly, a slender knife thrust into her heart. She'd never suspected that the client she'd taken to her room was her abandoned son, and he had no intention of enduring the sight of her sinful nakedness. Thus his haste in sending her to hell. There had been more time with the good reverend. Ricky attended a couple of revival meetings and familiarized himself with the routine. He especially paid attention to how the money was collected during the offering, and where it was stashed in the minister's big RV. One night, when everyone was asleep, Ricky let himself into the RV, tied the evangelist to a chair and had a chat with him—a one-sided chat since the man's mouth was sealed with duct tape. The next day, his wife alternated between hysteria over the frozen grimace on her deceased husband's face, and rage that more than $3,000 was missing from the safe.

Ricky stayed at the orphanage until he was jut shy of his thirteenth birthday. He was still inclined to obey the nuns in most things, and was strongly considering the priesthood as a vocation, at least until one of the sisters showed up in the newly approved modified habit of their order—no wimple, no long, heavy, and decidedly chaste robes. Instead, Sister Anicetus wore a calf-length black skirt, a white blouse, gray sweater, and a half scarf on her head. Ricky was outraged. He might have killed her, too, at some point, but he wasn't entirely clear on whether God's teachings allowed him to do that. After all, she was a bride of Christ, and perhaps it wasn't his place to mete out the punishment. He satisfied himself with the thought that she would burn in hell for having displayed her legs to adolescent boys. One night he packed his few belongings and left Baton Rouge. The authorities were notified, of course, but, if truth be told, some of the nuns slept much better after Ricky left, and not one of them nagged the police to search harder for him.

In his own estimation, Ricky led a charmed life. Where other boys his age were forced into crime or prostitution by adult criminals, Ricky ran his own affairs. He relieved every church in greater New Orleans of money at one time or another, firmly convinced that God was supporting him. Contribution boxes, offerings from those who lit candles, even the Sunday receipts locked in safes—all were available to him as if by divine edict. He slept in church basements, swept out sanctuaries in exchange for food, and impressed every clergyman who met him because of his knowledge of the Bible and the dictates of the Catholic faith. No one ever suspected the angelic boy of anything other than unusual piety, except of course for Father Brainard, a sharp-eyed Jesuit who found Ricky a little too good to be true. He had shared that conviction with his friend, a police sergeant on the New Orleans police force, but the priest's inquiries ceased when he fell victim to an unfortunate accident. It was so like Father Brainard to jump in and do repairs at the church to save money on the maintenance budget; no one thought to question how on earth he had managed to fall over the choir-stall railing he was in the process of repairing. He was neither inept nor awkward. But as the priest was completely alone in the church at the time, there was no suggestion of foul play.

That had been Ricky's first experience of exercising his substantial intellect in exacting the ultimate penalty, but hardly his last. Father Brainard, in grilling Ricky about his extracurricular activities, and questioning the source of his ample pocket money, had shown disrespect for one who was undeniably one of God's chosen. Others guilty of that offense would meet the same fate. He was so good at punishing people (Ricky didn't call it murder; murder was a mortal sin) that not only was he never caught, he was never even suspected…except perhaps by one person, the old friend of the deceased Father Brainard, a detective sergeant by the name of Henri Duchamps who made it clear that he had pegged Ricky as nothing more than a well-spoken con artist and hooligan. He'd nabbed the kid a week after Father Brainard's funeral Mass was said, but he had no evidence against him, and even after two hours of verbal battering, Ricky didn't so much as break a sweat. Duchamps had to let him go, but he didn't have to like it. He swore he'd keep tabs on the little brat, but Ricky disappeared.

When he was finally arrested in Washington, an event that still troubled him because he'd let his obsessions override his good sense, Ricky had no criminal record, other than failure to register for the draft. He wouldn't have minded serving if they'd been true Christian soldiers, but he discovered that they'd let almost anyone in.

The Washington debacle had been his only real mistake. Prior to that he'd continued his education, starting with a large cache of books stolen from church libraries and personal collections in rectories throughout New Orleans. He was most intrigued with a small, very old, leather-bound volume he'd discovered hidden behind several others in one priest's room. On the frontispiece was the phrase he later understood to be the name of a secret society: "*Malleus Caelistis ab Deum*," and underneath it what could almost be a coat of arms—the crucified Christ in the center, hands clenched around the hilts of swords at each corner of the design, and at the bottom a booted foot crushing a naked sinner under its heel. Ricky loved it, copied it, and eventually had it tattooed on his chest. He kept the book with him at all times.

He did not neglect his research into the darker side of human nature. Firmly believing that all occult practices were guided and infused with the power of Satan, he took to heart the ancient admonition, "Know thy enemy." He'd learned that his mother (before she died) and some of the other whores who plied their trade at La Maison de La Femme Jolie were in the habit of visiting an old harridan who lived in a crumbling building in the worst part of the Quarter. He soon discovered why. She was a witch, a voudun, or voodoo priestess. He spied on her for weeks before breaking into her apartment during one of her rare journeys to visit relatives who lived in the swamplands. He bagged up a few of the evil items for further study, then burned the building to the ground.

For years, Ricky's life proceeded precisely according to his wishes. His temporary downfall in the nation's capital had been the result of miscalculation, misinterpretation of the Scriptures, and the machinations of a woman. Frustrated that he would likely never be admitted to a real seminary, Ricky had enrolled in a correspondence course guaranteed to provide an ordination upon completion of the course. One night while at a library in the District to find a book he needed, Ricky met the woman. She looked at the subject matter of the books he was carrying and said that she'd always wanted to be a nun. Ricky, still naïve, thought this was a sign. He would teach her what she needed to know to be a truly obedient servant of God.

As it turned out, she also wanted to teach him a couple of things. Lillian was a card-carrying member of some fringe resistance group that didn't even have a formal name. Since Ricky knew the government was entirely corrupt and thoroughly godless, he humored her by helping her write pamphlets, adding numerous scriptural references to support their platform, some of which he privately thought was rather naïve. Upon further consideration, he concluded that this was his opportunity to create a new generation of adherents to Malleus Caelistis. He boldly put the name on the materials he prepared and began to wonder if perhaps the fire that would cleanse the earth would be born in a nuclear blast. Or was this particular type of fire the work of Satan? His indecision was reflected in his writing, which began to deteriorate along with Ricky's rigid self-control and sharp intellect, possibly because his new friend found it amusing to slip the occasional hallucinogenic substance into his iced tea.

Then the woman had tried to seduce him. He was infuriated. Her plan to join a religious order was an utter lie. Naturally, he punished her and buried her body in the forests of western Maryland. But something in his mind was no longer functioning properly. He couldn't plan, couldn't approach life with his usual efficiency. Why he'd thought he needed information from that office in Washington he still couldn't remember. But once they had him handcuffed, it didn't matter. He needed only to protect his true self from their probing. That was the day he became Ricky Bell. The little group had scattered; the woman was dead. There was no one in the city who could claim to know him by name. Thus, a little translation from the French and La Cloche became the mundane Bell. Since he had no criminal record of any kind, no fingerprints on file in any jurisdiction, and insisted he'd never had a social security number in his life (not true, since the Sisters of Mercy were very meticulous about such things), he was tried, convicted, and sentenced as Richard R. Bell. He told them the "R" stood for Renard, which was true. And he laughed that they didn't quite get the joke. Renard, a fox, and in this case, truly a fox in the henhouse. But they only cared that he go to jail and serve his time.

Once his mind felt more at ease, he immediately began his own ministry in the prison. He was choosy. For his inner circle, he only selected those whose attitudes and beliefs were already similar to his own. To them he preached about Malleus Caelistis and molded their minds accordingly. To them he promised ultimate salvation both in this world and in the next. Ricky needed expendable foot soldiers, and in prison he found plenty of what the infantry once called cannon fodder—the not too bright but nonetheless obedient arm-breakers who might come in handy further down the line.

Seven years of careful work in prison, then three more years of meticulous planning, including all kinds of misdirection like the nuclear plant threats phrased as antimilitary propaganda, the shift from incoherent whining to more intelligent-sounding rhetoric, the use of the society's name to instill the appropriate fear in their hearts. It all worked.

The ideas came to him in a steady flow. It was effortless. He hadn't had to punish anyone since he'd been released from prison, although he'd briefly considered intervening in the fate of the woman who'd prosecuted him. She was clearly a godless sinner. But she'd quit her job and gone somewhere else. Ricky knew that God would make time for him to punish her later if it became necessary. For now, his focus was perfectly clear.

He pushed aside the blueprints and reached first for the well-worn leather book that was second only to the Holy Bible in its importance to him, then changed his mind and picked up the Bible instead. He went to stand by the window and look at the vast Pacific stretched out before him. *What a wondrous creation,* he thought. *Will it survive the revelations?* He began to read the words aloud, though he hardly needed to refer to the tiny print. He knew it well.

> *Then the seventh angel poured out his bowl into the air, and a loud voice came out of the temple of heaven, from the throne, saying, "It is done!"*

And there were noises and thunderings and lightnings; and there was a great earthquake, such a mighty and great earthquake as had not occurred since men were on the earth. Now the great city was divided into three parts, and the cities of the nations fell. And great Babylon was remembered before God, to give her the cup of the wine of the fierceness of His wrath. Then every island fled away, and the mountains were not found. And great hail from heaven fell upon men, each hailstone about the weight of a talent. Men blasphemed God because of the plague of the hail, since that plague was exceedingly great. [Book of Revelation 16:17, The King James Bible]

Chapter Twelve

Say what you have to say,
not what you ought.
Any truth is better than make-believe.
—Henry David Thoreau

"We're going to be late," Connor grumbled from the other side of the bathroom door.

"Their flight doesn't get in until quarter of five."

"But the desk clerk told me that one-lane road can get backed up."

Laura sighed and gave her long hair one last stroke with the brush. "I always thought punctuality was a virtue, but I'm beginning to wonder about that." She opened the door and stepped out. "You hate to wait, don't you?"

Connor took one look at Laura and smiled her happy-to-be-alive smile. "You, however, are worth waiting for."

"Why, thank you, ma'am," said Laura in a startlingly authentic Texas drawl. "I'm mighty glad to hear you say that. So how about we mosey on over to John Wayne Airport and pick up the rest of the posse."

As they approached the parking lot attendant's stand, they saw that

Luis was there. "Please don't tell me they made you work today," said Laura. "You should have time to be with your sister."

He took a deep breath and his voice caught in his throat. He swallowed hard and tried again. "She is busy with Archbishop Johnston. The police were finally done, and they are going through my brother's things at the rectory. Bea already decided everything about the arrangements. She…she didn't need me. I didn't know what else to do, so I came to work." Tears glistened in the corners of his eyes.

Connor put a hand on his shoulder. "I'm so sorry, Luis. You know, if there's anything we can do, anything at all—"

"Bea tells me you have been very kind. You were at the prayer vigil all night." He paused and looked at them both intently. "You found my brother," he said, though it was difficult to tell if it was a question or a statement.

"Yes, we did," said Connor without elaborating.

"No one will tell me exactly what happened. Bea is always trying to protect me from everything. But she doesn't see that I'm a man. I'm not a little boy anymore. The police hardly talked to me except to ask where I was that night." He leaned close to Connor. "But you will tell me, please? What happened to Enrique?"

"He was murdered, Luis."

"I want to know how."

Connor frowned. She hated the thought of the young man carrying an image like that in his mind for the rest of his life. Besides, she was bound to confidentiality. The Santa Ana police had kept the details of the crime out of the public information trough, where there would have been, no doubt, a feeding frenzy over the gorier details. The detectives had specifically asked (Jaramillo politely, Consadine rudely) that she keep what she'd seen to herself.

She glanced at her partner for a second opinion. Laura shrugged slightly, and raised an eyebrow. The message was clear: *I don't know either.* Connor made up her mind to compromise.

"Luis, Father Ro—I mean, your brother—was stabbed. I found him in the confessional."

"But someone at the vigil was talking about evil spirits, the evil eye, or something like that. They said…well, they made it sound as if my brother might have been evil, that it might have been his fault. But that couldn't be. It just couldn't."

Connor shook her head. "No, that isn't true." Obviously someone had gotten wind of the wood stake part and jumped to an ignorant, superstitious conclusion. The jury might still be out on the existence of vampires, but Connor was quite sure Enrique Rosario was a flesh-and-blood human being and a good soul.

Laura put her arm around the young man's shoulders. "You know, Luis, some people are very foolish, and they have a lot of strange beliefs and superstitions. They tend to think of churches as sanctuaries, places where bad things don't happen. But when a tragedy like this occurs, they start looking for all kinds of wild reasons. Don't let them get to you, okay?"

He nodded slightly, his eyes squinched shut to hold back the tears. "It's hard."

"I know what it's like to lose someone you love," said Connor. "Believe me, I know."

Luis straightened his spine and took a gulp of air. "I'm sorry to bother you with this. I'll get your car."

He started to turn away, but Laura caught his hand in both of hers. "Luis, don't apologize. You haven't known us very long, but you can depend on us."

He stared hard at her, then at Connor. "If that's true, then I need you to help find out who did this to my brother."

"That's really a job for the police," said Connor reflexively.

"You think they care about a Latino priest in a church that poor people go to?"

Connor, who understood political realities from her years in Washington, didn't honestly know how much priority the crime would receive. The neighborhood in which the church stood hadn't looked particularly prosperous, and she wasn't naïve enough to think that poor people, no matter what color their skin, could expect quite the same amount of justice as rich folk living in expensive enclaves.

"I think the police want to solve this crime, Luis," she said. "They wouldn't be very pleased if we interfered." Connor knew full well that she and Laura, along with Malcolm and Benjamin, had every intention of investigating. But that had to be done fairly quietly to avoid territorial disputes.

"But my sister says you were a lawyer for the government."

"Yes, but I'm not anymore."

"Then perhaps you can't help," he said, his shoulders sagging. "I'll get your car."

He trotted off, and Connor looked at Laura. "I hate this. If I tell him we're going to dig up everything we can about this, he'll be all over us for an update every half hour. And if he tells anyone else and it gets back to that Neanderthal detective—"

"Consadine?"

"Yep. Then he'll be all over us for much less pleasant reasons. I just bet he knows how to recite whatever the California penal code has to say about obstructing justice and interfering with a police investigation."

"Luis needs hope, Connor."

She sighed. "Yes, he does. And Beatrice is wrong to leave him out of the loop. I imagine she's trying to protect him, but that just makes him feel worse."

Luis pulled the convertible up in the front of the hotel and hopped out. Connor walked around to the driver's side and extended the customary tip. Luis shook his head. "No, please. I couldn't take it from you, not from a friend of my family."

Connor slipped the money in her pocket, then stepped up closer to him so the other attendant couldn't hear her. "I *am* a friend, and I'll do what I can."

He smiled a little then as he held the door for her, then shut it firmly and walked away.

"You told him we'd help."

"Yes," Connor sighed. "I did."

"You are such an old softie. I'm beginning to wonder about the stories that are told of your prosecutorial days."

"What stories?"

"Some of them made you sound like a cross between an avenging angel and a hanging judge."

"Ouch," said Connor. "I didn't know my reputation was quite so colorful."

"Your conviction rate was higher than any other assistant. Your convictions were rarely ever overturned on appeal. You never played dirty, but you played hard. And some defense attorneys went straight to a plea bargain when they heard you were lead prosecutor."

"Do I have a fan club with a Web site or something?"

"No, but there's not exactly a shortage of information out there. You got a lot of press in those days. Besides, Benjamin and I talk about you on occasion."

"That's a scary thought."

"Shouldn't be. We both love you."

"Okay. Change of subject. I didn't want to get Luis's hopes up, but I also couldn't let him be completely miserable."

"You think he's right about the cops not being highly concerned over this murder."

"Don't know. Enrique isn't someone important, and I'm sorry to say that that's almost always a factor. Still, he's a Catholic priest, and Archbishop Johnston doesn't strike me as a mealymouthed kind of guy. If he doesn't think they're trying hard enough, I can almost guarantee he'll find a way to motivate them."

They left the downtown Laguna Beach area and picked up speed on the Pacific Coast Highway until they reached Jamboree Road and headed inland. Connor rested her hands on the center of the steering wheel and tapped out an intricate rhythm on the steering column with her fingertips.

"What?" said Laura.

"What-what?"

"You're tapping. That generally means you're impatient or your mind is racing about a hundred miles an hour."

Connor chuckled. "I think I'm getting too predictable. Must be time to change everything about my life…" She paused. "Except you."

"Glad to hear that I get an exception. And believe me, you're not that predictable. Sometimes you are positively eccentric. But even that endears me to you, makes me smile."

"So what you're saying is I have endearing eccentricities?"

Laura considered it for a moment. "Yes, I'd have to say you do."

"Such as? No, never mind. I'd probably be embarrassed to find out."

"Don't worry, they're my secret. Nothing that will find its way into a 'fan 'zine.'"

Connor shook her head. "Get real. Magazines are for rappers and semi-clad girl singers. My fans just write letters."

"I've seen those fat envelopes forwarded from your publisher. Don't tell me they're not all complimentary."

Connor snorted. "Half of them are from total wackos and nut jobs who want to…" she began ticking them off on her fingers, "(a) collaborate on my next book, (b) propose marriage. (c) propose something much less permanent than marriage, (d) complain that I don't know anything about the law and make all kinds of mistakes in my books, (e) Sue me because I stole the idea they had twenty years ago for a great book."

"And did you steal their ideas?" Laura asked, trying to keep a straight face.

"Of course. I've collected all of the high-school term papers, masters theses, doctoral dissertations, and rejected manuscripts of every citizen of the United States. I have combed through all fifty-two million of them, looking for inspiration because I have no original thoughts. I've also been accused of stealing ideas that people never actually put in writing. They only *thought* about them or told their old Aunt Minnie."

"So you're supposed to have gotten their idea by what—tuning in to the thought 'airwaves?'"

"Yep. Or beating it out of Aunt Minnie."

"And these people are serious?"

"Most of them are, oddly enough. I don't read much of that crap anymore, though. There's an editorial assistant who takes care of it. She does send me some of the funnier ones, of course, and all of the complimentary fan letters."

"I'll send you a fan letter."

"Complimenting my *writing*, I hope."

Laura laughed. "Maybe."

»——«

To Malcolm's surprise, Benjamin Hawthorne was waiting at the gate when he and Agent Franklin showed up for their flight with only minutes to spare. Benjamin smiled, introduced himself, and asked if he might have their tickets for a minute. Malcolm handed his over with a shrug, though Ayalla Franklin frowned before surrendering her ticket folder.

When Benjamin returned from the check-in desk, both folders had boarding passes with very low aisle numbers. "Hope you don't mind," he said, mostly to the FBI agent. "Since we're traveling together, it seemed silly to have seats scattered all over the plane."

She looked at her boarding pass. "This seat's in first class."

"Yes," said Benjamin. "It is."

"The Bureau doesn't authorize that kind of expense."

"The Bureau isn't paying for it," he said. "I am. Now, if you'll excuse me for a minute, I need to get something from the gift shop." He was gone before she could say anything.

"Does he always pull crap like this?" she asked Malcolm. Her tone was markedly cooler than it had been on the drive to the airport.

"I wouldn't call it crap, Agent Franklin. He wanted us all to be able to sit together, maybe compare notes if the flight's not crowded, and he also likes doing nice things for people. That's who he is. And he can afford it."

"I can't accept a gift like that. The fare must be hundreds of dollars more."

Malcolm swiveled in his seat and looked her square in the eye. "Or thousands. Look, could you get the chip off your shoulder? You'll never have a better friend than Benjamin Hawthorne, or know anyone with more integrity. So put a lid on the tight-ass FBI–rule book crap."

The airline desk attendant called for final boarding, and Benjamin appeared at their side. "My daughter's newest book," he said, holding out copies to both of them, with the enthusiasm of a father handing out celebratory cigars. "It's a long flight, and if we don't have the chance to talk, at least you can read or sleep." He grabbed his garment bag and briefcase from the chair beside Malcolm. "May as well get on board. We're the last ones, I think."

The flight didn't afford much opportunity to talk about Malleus Caelistis or Ricky Bell or the would-be terrorist threats. First class wasn't full, but there were people sprinkled about the forward cabin of the aircraft. The three travelers could each have a pair of seats to themselves and took advantage of the room to spread out. Malcolm started reading Connor's latest book because he wanted to. He assumed Agent Franklin was flipping through it because she was bored or didn't want to offend Senator Hawthorne. Malcolm expected to like the novel, and he did.

When he looked over, Agent Franklin, who had muttered something about crime fiction being contrived and inaccurate, appeared to be engrossed in spite of herself. Neither of them napped. Benjamin, after reading through a file from his briefcase, making a brief phone call, and eating his meal, went soundly to sleep.

Five and a half hours later, Malcolm allowed himself a brief sigh of relief when the flight attendant announced their imminent arrival at Orange County's John Wayne Airport. He didn't much like flying, though he hardly had reason to complain about the accommodations this time around. The plane descended smoothly through clear skies and touched down with a moderate thud on the runway. Malcolm, Benjamin, and Ayalla were among the first off the plane and they quickly descended to the baggage claim area. Malcolm spotted Connor and Laura. They were already moving toward him, having easily picked the towering D.C. cop out of the flow of passengers.

"Hey, big guy," said Connor, giving him a quick hug.

"Good to see you, Captain," Laura smiled up at him. "Benjamin's with you, isn't he?"

"How is it you know everything before I do? I didn't know he was going to be on this flight until he showed up at the airport."

"That's what those airplane phones are for," said Laura. "Ah, here he is."

Benjamin had stepped back to let an elderly woman go ahead of him. Ayalla had been forced to wait behind him. Now they approached the minireunion.

"Hi, sweetheart," Benjamin said, wrapping an arm around his daughter. "Missed you."

"Dad, it hasn't even been a week since we saw you in D.C."

"I'm old. Time passes slowly."

"Yeah, right. Do you guys have checked luggage?"

"Just have carry-ons," said Malcolm, suddenly acutely aware of Ayalla's presence. "Connor, Laura…this is Special Agent Ayalla Franklin. Agent Franklin, meet Connor Hawthorne and Laura Nez."

Agent Franklin shook hands with both of them, and all three women exchanged polite greetings, but Malcolm detected a definite cooling in the atmosphere. Connor's expression was neutral, but the muscles around her eyes and mouth had tightened slightly. He'd been worried about her reaction, although he hadn't discussed it with Benjamin. Connor did not think highly of some of the D.C.-based agents she'd worked with, and that relationship had soured significantly during the investigation into her former lover's murder. In the midst of her grief and anger, Connor had been forced to deal with a buzz-cut buttoned-down razor-creased misogynist of the first order—and also one of the worst examples of fed arrogance Malcolm had ever met. The agent had all but accused Connor of having Ariana killed. Had Malcolm not been present, Connor might well be serving time in prison—for murdering the agent.

Ayalla appeared at least as uncomfortable as Connor, and now that Malcolm thought of it, he hadn't mentioned to her that anyone was meeting them at the airport. And he hadn't had a chance to warn Connor in advance. *We're off to a great start,* he thought. *This can only get worse.*

Benjamin, who had a well-honed sense for impending difficulties, social or otherwise, slung his garment bag over his shoulder, slipped his arm around Connor's shoulders and started walking toward the exit. Laura kept pace with them. Malcolm followed about ten feet behind with Agent Franklin beside him.

"You didn't mention we'd be overrun with civilians," she said quietly through gritted teeth.

Malcolm slowed his pace to allow his three friends to move farther away. "You are welcome to conduct your investigation solo, Agent Franklin. I don't have to justify anything to you. Connor Hawthorne and Laura Nez are not only friends of mine, they're both experienced in criminal investigation and hold high-level security clearances—and by the way, they're smart as hell."

Ahead they saw Connor pull Laura close to her, an arm around her waist. The three of them walked in lockstep, Benjamin shortening his strides to match.

Malcolm glanced at Ayalla.

"Are those two, are they—"

"Are they what?"

"You know…a couple?"

"Yes, they are. You have any problem with that? I thought we'd already covered this ground in my office."

"That was about a past relationship. Apparently she's involved now with someone else. Seems strange if they have security clearances and…"

Malcolm stopped dead in his tracks so suddenly Ayalla was several steps ahead and had to turn back to face him.

"I may not have made myself entirely clear this morning. If you do not wish to work with us, or you have personal prejudices that would diminish your ability to act like a professional, then I suggest we part company here and now. I won't tolerate any bullshit on this particular subject."

She glowered at him for several seconds. "It so happens that based on profiles compiled at our behavioral science unit, such people tend to be higher-than-average security risks as well as potentially unstable."

"Such people?" The menace in Malcolm's voice was unmistakable. "That's what you think? That Connor and Laura are right out of some internal memo on aberrant behavior? Maybe you've been carrying that damn badge too long, or can't stop trying to be one of the boys of the Bureau, but starting right now, you drop that line of crap and start acting like a regular human being, or you're on your own out here. That means all you've got is your buddies at the field office in L.A. And how much do you suppose they know, compared to Benjamin, compared to the local cops, and, by the way, compared to Connor Hawthorne and Laura Nez?

"For starters," Malcolm went on, "Connor found the body of the priest who may have been offed by one of these terrorists. She's the one who recognized the name of Ricky Bell's little gang of fruit cakes…written in Latin for God's sake. She doesn't miss anything. And she's already set up a meeting for us with the archbishop who was the priest's boss and knows something about this group. So now's the moment to figure out which side your bread's buttered on, Agent Franklin."

He had to give her credit. She didn't flinch even when he got right in her face. But he could see the wheels turning. She knew if he dumped her right there at the airport she wasn't any farther ahead on the case than one of the local agents would be. If she was half as ambitious as he suspected, she would know she needed the inside track on this right from the get go.

"All right. I agree to your terms as long as you agree to note that I have reservations."

"Noted, Agent Franklin," Malcolm said icily, and started walking again. By now, his friends were out of sight. "By the way, if you're wondering about what Laura Nez brings to the team, she's done quite a bit of work for Benjamin over the past several years—very sensitive work."

"Yes?"

"She can fieldstrip, reassemble, and fire any weapon you've ever *seen,* and some you probably haven't. You probably would do well not to get on her bad side."

Ayalla walked silently, digesting this.

"And one more thing. She wouldn't actually need a *weapon* to kill you. So you might want to mind your manners."

This time, the agent seemed to pale ever so slightly. Malcolm suppressed a smile. He was jerking the woman's chain a little. What he'd said about Laura was patently true—she was highly proficient with all manner of small arms as well as a trained martial artist, but he'd left out the fact that she was also someone who would do everything in her power to avoid harming another human being. The fact that she *could* kill didn't mean she *would*—unless she were given no other choice.

»——«

"Do you honestly think there's anything here someone would kill for, Your Eminence?"

"Beatrice, I appreciate your respect, but please call me Father, and yes, I do think so, or I wouldn't be here right now and I certainly wouldn't be making you go through Enrique's things so soon."

"But what are exactly are we looking for?"

"Most likely something that's here in the office here, rather than in his room. I'll take a look in there before we leave, just to be sure there are no more notebooks or folders. For now, I only want to separate out his research notes and materials from the files and papers that have to do with church business. We'll put everything related to St. Mary's in this pile over here. The diocese will need all those records for the"—he stopped, the look on Beatrice's face choking off the rest of the sentence—"next pastor." He hadn't meant it to sound callous. God knew his heart ached at the loss of Enrique. But he couldn't allow himself the luxury of grief, at least not now.

"I'm sorry, child. I didn't mean—"

"I know, Father, I know," she whispered, and went back to sorting through the church ledgers and stacking them on a shelf as Johnston piled more files on the desk.

The archbishop couldn't have fully justified his beliefs, but he was convinced that Enrique had been murdered because of his inquiries into the Cult of Magdalene, and because of the documents he'd stolen from the Vatican archives. Johnston had further concluded that the murderer was connected to Malleus Caelistis, or at least someone wanted it to appear connected. The hammer used to commit the killing was a patently obvious clue, but the archbishop was troubled that it was simply *too* lacking in subtlety to be taken seriously. Was it no more than a red herring of sorts? Still, this was all he had to go on, and he was determined that Father Rosario's notes would not find their way into anyone's hands but his own. Even now, he felt a sense of imminent threat, as if he were fighting off a wave of malevolent anger directed toward him and even toward Beatrice.

He hadn't told Enrique's sister many details. She'd looked puzzled when he asked her if Enrique had received any threats or any strange correspondence. Beatrice was in and out of the rectory all the time and might have noticed a stranger visiting or a package large enough to attract attention. He'd asked the same question of Lucinda, who could only shake her head. "*No se*," she murmured softly in Spanish. "*No se*."

He carefully stacked Enrique's spiral notebooks, steno pads, and file folders into a cardboard box and peered into the old built-in cupboards one more time. He checked his watch. He'd asked Beatrice's two young friends to call on him at his office this evening. He'd promised Ms. Hawthorne a more detailed explanation of his reaction to the symbols and phrases she'd observed at the crime scene, and when he called her hotel, she'd accepted the invitation and added that she would be bringing a couple of friends. The archbishop hadn't been thrilled, but she assured him these were people who would be able to help, no matter what the problem might be.

Johnston hugged Beatrice and told her to go back to her upstairs and make sure Lucinda was all right. He suggested she take the elderly woman home with her for a until he could send his housekeeper Cecilia, who was Lucinda's sister, to take care of her. "I don't think it's good for her to be here alone, not after what's happened. For that matter, I don't think you should be alone either. Where is Luis?"

"I told him to go back to work before he loses his job."

The archbishop frowned. "I can't believe they'd fire him under the circumstances."

"Probably not, Father. I thought it would be better if he didn't have to be here, looking at his brother's things, you know."

Johnston held her away from him, a hand on each of her shoulders. "Don't treat him like a child. Yes, he's young, but he is a grown man, and he needs to be here as much as you do. So you don't have to always be his big sister. Sometimes a man needs to be a man. Do you understand me?"

"Yes," she said, her eyes filling with tears. "I can't help wanting to protect him."

"Maybe he needs to feel that he can protect you. Now, go along and

I'll be up in a moment. Tell Lucinda to pack a small bag, and I'll take you both to your apartment. My car's in the parking lot in the back. I'll put this box in the trunk and wait for you outside."

She walked up the stairs, and a few moments later he heard the murmur of voices from the kitchen. He pulled out the desk drawers one more time. He knew in his heart there had to be something else, something Enrique had not yet divulged. There'd been something unsaid between them, and Johnston had felt Enrique's tension. He only hoped that somewhere in these notes he would find a clue to what the young priest had been doing. *Playing with fire,* thought the archbishop. *But who else is worried about getting burned?*

»——«

Monsignor Johann Kursk ducked down in the driver's seat of his rental car as the headlights of the archbishop's Lincoln swept over his windshield. He'd expected him to turn right out of the driveway, toward the diocesan house in Rancho Manzanita. Instead, he'd turned left and aimed right toward Kursk's brown Ford Taurus. Fortunately, it was a nondescript car and he was out of sight before the Lincoln came abreast of him. He caught only a glimpse of passengers.

Good, he thought. Perhaps that means they are all gone, even the damn housekeeper. He'd seen various parishioners come and go earlier in the afternoon, and pleaded with God that he would be able to carry out his search-and-destroy mission before more time had passed. He wasn't worried about the cops. They were looking for clues to a murder. Kursk, on the other hand, was only interested in clues to a legendary object he wasn't even sure existed. For that matter, he didn't know what it was. Just what it could do. And what it could do, if the legends were only half-true, was positively unthinkable.

He waited an extra thirty minutes to be sure no one came back for something they'd forgotten, then got out of his car and walked across the street, briskly enough to avoid appearing to loiter, but slowly enough so as not to draw attention. He continued down the driveway next to the rectory. At the rear of the building, he looked around once more, then ducked out of the pool of light cast by the security lights on the build-ing into the shadow of the large dumpster. There was his target, an unsecured window leading into the basement. It would be a tight fit, but not impossible. And, chances were he would not have to come back out that way.

Kursk swung the horizontal window inward, pulled a small flashlight from his pocket, and swept the beam around the interior. It was a store-room, and to his delight there was a stack of boxes just under the window. He turned around so that he could slither feet-first on his stomach through the opening. His dangling feet finally detected the surface of the nearest box. He tested it gingerly with one foot. The platform felt solid. He stepped down with all his weight and reached into his coat pocket again for the light.

The particular cartons on which Monsignor Kursk stood were not filled with books, hymnals, sturdy reams of paper, or canned goods. They were instead packed very loosely with choir robes. These were quite nice robes (only slightly irregular factory seconds recently donated by a manufacturer in the Midwest), but not very useful to stand on, even in quantity. The boxes were certainly not solid enough to hold a grown man's weight. They crumpled and caved in just after the monsignor had fully let go of the windowsill. With a muffled screech he toppled backward. The light flew from his hand and smashed against the wall. His head connected with the basement floor at a brisk velocity. Since his skull was of less sturdy stuff than the thirty-year-old poured concrete, Monsignor Kursk went out, just like his little flashlight. The latter was pretty much beyond repair. Whether the former could be fixed was a question only God could answer. Unfortunately for the monsignor, there was no one there to consult the Creator on his behalf.

Chapter Thirteen

The last temptation is the greatest treason:
To do the right deed for the wrong reason.
—T.S. Eliot, *Murder in the Cathedral*

Small talk dwindled away to nothing, though it had hardly been scintillating to begin with. Benjamin was driving the full-size Buick sedan he'd rented at the airport so that they all could travel together if need be. Malcolm was happily ensconced in the front passenger seat where there was almost enough room for his legs. In the back sat Connor and Ayalla, with Laura between them, feeling somewhat like the keeper of the demilitarized zone. Earlier that evening, it had taken her half an hour to talk Connor out of taking separate cars.

"We'll be more comfortable if we take the convertible," Connor had insisted.

"Not if you're talking about roominess, as opposed to emotional comfort. Have you seen the size of that tank your father rented? I think he only did that so we could all fit."

"Yeah. He's not much for a big mushy ride, although I think Buicks and Crown Vics are near and dear to Malcolm's heart."

"You're evading the issue, sweetheart. What's up with you and the FBI lady? I thought you were actually going to snarl at her."

"Why wouldn't I? First, I can't believe Malcolm brought her out here without talking to us first. Second, I think FBI agents are generally arrogant jerks who've been brainwashed into group-think until they can't even formulate an original idea. Third, did you see the way she looked at us? If you'll turn on your homophobe detector, the needle should be just about off the scale!"

"Is that anything like a Geiger counter?" Laura asked with just the right mix of earnestness and teasing calculated to make Connor stop and wonder if her lover were serious. The pause gave Laura a chance to get a few more words in edgewise.

"To answer your objections, my wonderful ex-lawyer…first, Malcolm whispered to me at the airport, while we were waiting for their car, that he had no idea he'd be working with the woman on this case until she showed up at his office right as he was leaving for the airport. Second, I've had some bad experiences with FBI agents, but I've also encountered a few here and there who've been dedicated, smart, and do manage to have their own ideas about cases. So I try not to *generalize*." Connor started to open her mouth and Laura held up a hand. "Please, Counselor, let me finish the rebuttal. As to your third point, yes, I noticed she doesn't act very comfortable around us, but since when does that come as surprise? You've been 'out' most of your adult life, at least since you divorced your husband over twenty years ago, and so have I. We've met lots of people who judge us when they don't even know us. She's an FBI agent, Connor. They probably still can't help thinking of us queers as security risks."

"It still pisses me off."

"I know. But for now we're kind of stuck with her, and Benjamin wouldn't have set this all up if he didn't have a reason."

"Ah, yes. The serpentine workings of my father's mind—doesn't mean I have to like it."

"True. But refusing to ride with them makes us seem a tad childish, don't you think?"

"Probably."

"And we're both relatively grown up, aren't we?"

"Speak for yourself. Being a grown-up is highly overrated."

Laura knew she'd won when she saw the tiny crinkles around Connor's lips that presaged a smile. "Well, then you'll just have to fake it 'til you make it, girl." She laid her hands on Connor's shoulder. "You're one of the wisest women I've ever known, and I love you, you know that?"

"I don't know about the wise part, but I'm kinda getting convinced about the love part."

"Good. It's about time. Now let's go face the combined might of law enforcement as we know it."

They arrived at the archbishop's diocesan house just after eight-thirty. A young priest who looked barely old enough to shave led them to a conference room where he told them "His Eminence" was on the phone and would be with them shortly. He also offered them tea or coffee. Everyone opted for coffee, and within a few minutes the door swung open to admit a pleasant older woman pushing a tea cart. The archbishop was right on her heels.

"Just leave the cart, please, Cecilia. We'll help ourselves. Thank you." He ushered her out the door and closed it firmly before turning to face them. All five had remained standing since they arrived. The archbishop turned his attention to Connor. "I must say, Ms. Hawthorne, I don't know if I'm comfortable with…with so many people being involved with this. I'd hoped we might simply share some theories. But this has taken on a much more formal…um…atmosphere with the police being present and, I believe you said, an FBI agent."

Benjamin stepped forward, extending his hand. "Archbishop, I'm Benjamin Hawthorne, this is D.C. Police Captain Malcolm Jefferson and Special Agent Ayalla Franklin." The archbishop shook hands with each of them in turn as Benjamin continued. "I apologize for springing this on you with so little notice. But I've come to believe that there's some urgency to this situation. Could we sit down at least for a few minutes, and I'll explain why I think it's important that we work together? Once you've heard me out, then we'll honor whatever decision you make about sharing your knowledge with us."

Archbishop Johnston regarded Benjamin for several moments before shifting his gaze to the others, one by one.

"Let it never be said that I'm unreasonable," he replied. "Though I believe my aide says so quite often." He smiled, putting his guests a little more at ease. "Please help yourself to some coffee and be seated."

The archbishop took his chair at the head of the table. Benjamin sat to his right, with Connor and Laura next to him. Malcolm and Ayalla were on the priest's left. Everyone's eyes were on Benjamin.

"I was doing some research on Malleus Caelistis ab Deum for Captain Jefferson," he began. "This group's name came up in conjunction with a series of what were purported to be terrorist threats against the government. Some of them were somewhat vague and contained only general rather than specific threats, but in the past several months, the communications became more specific. The group claims to oppose the existence of nuclear power generating plants or, in the alternative, suspects these facilities of serving as fronts for military installations or weapons manufacturing centers."

The archbishop frowned and shook his head. "Your daughter mentioned some of this, but I can't honestly imagine how Malleus Caelistis, which, by the way, has been around for untold centuries, can have any connection with your group of so-called terrorists. It doesn't make any sense at all."

"I agree it seems unlikely. On the face of it, the only connection is the name, and I don't doubt that it might simply have been borrowed by some highly misguided, pseudoreligious splinter organization. But until we have a better understanding of the origins and history of the original Malleus Caelistis, we have no way of either confirming or discounting a connection between them and this current group."

"Senator..." the archbishop began.

"Please, Your Eminence, I appreciate the courtesy, but my Senate days are far behind me. 'Mister' is fine, and 'Benjamin' is even better."

"Very well then, Mr. Hawthorne...at least until we know each other a little better...Malleus Caelistis isn't recognized by the Roman church as a legitimate Catholic organization. Its membership has always been secret, though I suspect that throughout its existence it has included members of the Catholic clergy, even perhaps high-ranking ones. The group has been at the least an embarrassment and, at worst, a destructive and divisive influence in the church's history. There is an unspoken policy that any knowledge a priest has regarding Malleus Caelistis may not be disclosed to anyone outside the church. That limits how much I may divulge to you."

Benjamin listened patiently and considered the archbishop's words for a few moments before answering. "I believe I understand your concerns. In your shoes, I'd probably feel the same way. The problem is that I don't know if you can help us with our problem until I know a little more about the history of Malleus Caelistis and about Father Rosario's work. But if there is any possibility that the group's members are involved in his murder, I think it would be prudent to pursue that possibility, at least until it can be put to rest. Second, you have my personal assurance that nothing you say here will leave this room unless we have your express permission."

Benjamin felt, rather than saw, Agent Franklin sit up straighter and lean forward to voice her objections. He'd anticipated that she wouldn't happily agree to a gag order, but he wasn't about to let her interrupt the flow. He swiveled his head just enough to meet her eyes. His expression (not precisely threatening, but impossible to ignore), appeared to quell her objections instantly. He thought it another point in her favor that she could control her annoyance.

Archbishop Johnston sighed heavily. "I don't know any of you really," he said. "Of course I've heard of you, Mr. Hawthorne, and although I can't say I've read any of your daughter's books, I understand she's a former prosecutor and is well-respected. But...I don't know...the police...the FBI...it's all rather alien to me, I'm afraid."

"Most people aren't comfortable with the law personified, Your Eminence. You see, in theory, law enforcement is fine. But when we're confronted with the people who do the enforcement, the ones who carry guns, and ask rude questions, and investigate all manner of sordid human drama and outright violence, we start to feel as if we've stepped into something we'd rather have avoided. And we also get cranky about keeping our personal lives or professional secrets to ourselves. We get stressed and start circling the wagons. It's just human nature."

The archbishop looked at Benjamin with something akin to surprise and perhaps even relief on his face. "So maybe I'm not just a crotchety old fool after all?"

"I don't think any of us would dare even think it," said Benjamin with a little smile in his voice.

The priest laughed. "Of course you would. But sometimes that's just what I am. Funny thing is, you're right. I truly hate all the secrecy and cloak-and-dagger nonsense that goes on in certain parts of the church. But the minute I feel a little threatened by 'outsiders,'"—he held up his fingers to denote the quotation marks—"then I start hedging about confidentiality. But I'll take you at your word, Mr. Hawthorne, and since you vouch for the discretion of your friends, that will suffice for me as well. But I reserve the right to choose what I share. This is a long story. I hope you've got some time."

Benjamin smiled. "All the time in the world. Please treat us as your students. We're willing to listen and learn."

"All right then. We'll start with what little history is known, but to give you some background, keep in mind that there has been conflict among the followers of Jesus Christ since he walked among the people almost 2,000 years ago. Even the apostles couldn't agree on what Jesus said, or what the words actually meant. There were quite a few different versions of his life and his teachings, most of which were written down long after his death, in some cases as much as a century or more later. So the Scriptures that make up the New Testament as we know it today were not composed on the spot, so to speak. As a result, over the centuries the church, as well as every other religion on earth, has spent thousands of hours debating every passage, every phrase."

Connor raised her hand. Benjamin smiled. His daughter was obviously willing to accept the role of student if it would help their inquiries get on track.

"Archbishop, the Bible in its current form is the product of, shall we say, extensive editing, especially during the Middle Ages and again during the Renaissance?"

"It's gone through several major...transformations, although everyone involved liked to think of the process as clarification of holy teachings." His expression belied the earnest tone of voice. Clearly, the archbishop had his own reservations about church dogma. "Unfortunately, there was a tendency to completely discard any number of arguably authentic accounts of the life of Jesus, some of which may have been written contemporaneously, either while he was alive or very shortly after his death."

"Are you referring to the Gnostic Gospels, Archbishop?" asked Laura.

"In part," he answered. "There are also much older texts that could have formed part of the Old Testament but were omitted. But I think we need to focus on the New Testament because Malleus Caelistis dates from about the early sixth century C.E. and may have been created at least partly in opposition to Gnostic sects who had their own interpretation of the teachings of Jesus, some of which are…well, let's just say some directly contradict or call into question some of the teachings of the Catholic Church and most Christian churches in existence today."

"But aren't you talking about differences in theology, Archbishop?" countered Malcolm. "Why would these Malleus Caelistis people get so bent out of shape because a few heretic groups disagreed with them? Clearly, the power of the church prevailed in the long run."

"Back then, the church wasn't a cohesive body by any means. There was political wrangling and murder and intrigue…a whole sordid history that no one is particularly proud of. But I don't believe that era is representative of what the church would eventually become. It was centuries before the church that you see today actually came into existence. The foundations were laid by hard-line supporters of the Vatican's patron saints, Peter and Paul. They relied heavily on the translations, edited or otherwise, of Aramaic and Greek manuscripts, especially the letters written by Paul, that supported their concepts of Christ's teachings. They fervently believed that their version of the truth should never be challenged."

"What were they so afraid of?" Malcolm asked.

"Dissention. Evil. I can't say. But the church went to enormous lengths to try and destroy every copy of the various gospels it officially had declared to be heresies and lies. They were very effective in stamping out rival accounts."

"Until Nag Hammadi," said Connor.

The archbishop looked at her with newfound interest. "You know of the cache of ancient scrolls recovered near there in the mid twentieth century."

"Yes," she said. "The so-called Gnostic Gospels were among them."

"And numerous other documents, not all of which may have been cataloged, but some of which directly challenge and contradict what many Christian churches teach and what we believe."

"Such as?" asked Laura.

"It would take me days to explain all of the implications of the Nag Hammadi documents, even if I understood them myself, so let's focus on just one aspect of the so-called lost secret teachings. That also brings us the subject of Father Rosario." The old man stopped, crossed himself, and his lips moved in a brief, silent prayer. "He was fascinated with one of the Gnostic-inspired groups that is believed to have survived into the Middle Ages, perhaps a little longer. It was popularly known as the Cult of Magdalene."

"As in Mary Magdalene?" asked Laura.

"Yes," said the archbishop, rising to fill his coffee cup at the trolley.

"What does the 'Cult of Magdalene' have to do with Father Rosario?" asked Malcolm.

The archbishop resumed his place. "This is getting into the sticky areas. A faithful and obedient priest would not countenance such a discussion. But I, like Father Rosario, am a scholar. I try to take off my blinders at least once in a while. So I'll risk disobedience, especially since you appear to believe that his death is somehow related to the research he was doing.

"Simply stated, the Cult of Magdalene was founded by those who believed—and professed to be able to *prove*—that Mary Magdalene was not a whore, not a fallen woman of any kind, but was instead a full-fledged apostle of Jesus." He paused. "And they believe that Jesus accorded Mary equal status with that of his male followers."

"Hmm," said Connor.

"Yes, it's pretty unorthodox. There is also some belief that Jesus did not condone or teach celibacy as a requirement of priesthood, or that he necessarily even practiced it throughout his life."

"And that must have gone over big with the pope," said Laura.

Archbishop Johnston smiled. "During the first millennium, and even into the second, most popes had female companionship. The celibacy requirement sort of developed strength over the centuries. Saint Paul appears to have been the most resistant to female involvement in Christ's ministry."

"The team misogynist, in other words," added Connor.

"Some have judged him that way, although Peter may have been just as oppositional toward women. There's a passage in the Gnostic Gospels where Mary is said to have complained to Jesus about Peter and his efforts in trying to keep her from talking. In that account Jesus remonstrates his apostles, telling them he doesn't care about gender, only about the individual. In the heretical texts, Jesus reputedly welcomed the questions of any follower and taught all of them without bias."

"Sounds like a much friendlier theology," said Connor.

"Indeed, it appeared to be. And there are ideas espoused in the Nag Hammadi papers that paint a very different picture of what Jesus taught. I'm not altogether in disagreement with some of it, although I still seriously question the sources."

"You firmly believe in the authenticity of the New Testament then?" asked Connor.

The archbishop looked at her for several seconds, as if trying to decipher the motivation behind her question. But Connor's tone had been entirely neutral. If she was challenging him, it wasn't obvious.

"I believe, with perhaps a few exceptions, in the teachings of my church," he said. "They may have been anxious to obscure some of their more embarrassing history, but what socially significant organization or national government doesn't do just that when it seems necessary? I supported Father Rosario in his research because I believe it behooves us to continue to understand our history. That doesn't mean I would have supported him in publishing information that would inflict damage on the Mother Church. I frankly don't believe he would have gone that far."

"Someone may have thought he might," said Benjamin quietly.

"Not someone associated with the church. If there are criminals masquerading as religious fanatics, then they should be dealt with firmly and quickly. But I'm not convinced that is the case, unless someone has entirely misunderstood the spiritual roots of Malleus Caelistis. Father Rosario was not setting out to hurt anyone. He only wished to discern the truth. That is my interest as well."

"Even if the truth doesn't match your current beliefs, Archbishop?" Connor asked, and this time there was an edge to her tone. "It's been my experience that truth almost always depends on one's perspective."

Johnston sighed. "I won't argue the point with you, Ms. Hawthorne, because we don't have the time. I know what I believe, and I know how important the church is in the lives of hundreds of millions of people around the world. Whatever its faults—and there are many—its roots go back to the time of Jesus Christ, and there is a beauty and majesty in its rituals and catechism that a non-Catholic simply cannot comprehend. Some of the greatest mystics in the last 2,000 years have been Catholics."

"I meant no disrespect, Archbishop, but I imagine we may disagree on the value of dogma."

"Undoubtedly."

Benjamin cleared his throat. "Perhaps it would be best if we simply gather as much information as we can."

Johnston turned his gaze on Connor's father. "Yes, I suspect it would. Now, where was I?"

"You were talking about the Cult of Magdalene," said Laura.

"Yes, as I said, the Cult of Magdalene died out a very long time ago, literally stamped out of existence by the orthodox church. Father Rosario considered it part of history and made the cult the subject of his dissertation at seminary. I do know that he continued to look for materials about it. As far as I know, the last reference he found indicated that remnants of the cult had survived around the middle of the sixteenth century, possibly a little later."

Benjamin, who had been making a few notes as the archbishop spoke, raised his hand slightly. "Your Eminence, how does this relate to Malleus Caelistis?"

"I don't know that it does, but if you're looking for something that ties Father Rosario to Malleus Caelistis, this is the only thing I can think of. He may have stumbled onto something that could have been perceived as heresy according to strict interpretation of our Scriptures. You see, over the centuries, Malleus Caelistis priests were said to have been far less tolerant of heresy than even the church authorities. They were fanatics about protecting what they considered to be the legacy of Peter and Paul. Reputedly, they were ruthless. They may have systematically executed hundreds of people, and this is in addition to the various atrocities of the Inquisition, though I suspect some of the inquisitors were also members of Malleus Caelistis. It stands to reason that the Cult of Magdalene would have been a prime target for their doctrinal enforcement activities."

"And this 'enforcement' group exists today?" asked Malcolm.

"It may have survived in some form. At least that's what I understand. It simply isn't talked about. I don't know how members are recruited, or if there *is* any recruitment. For all I know, the last of the old hard-liners may have all died off."

"But there is the hammer," said Connor. "That was a little obvious."

"Connor explained to us that the literal translation of the full name is 'the Divine Hammer of God.'" Malcolm said. "But where did that come from? I've heard about fiery swords and spears and even slings in the Bible, but why a hammer?"

"It's found in the Old Testament," said the archbishop. He reached for a King James Bible that lay on the table, smiling briefly as he ran his hand over the cover. "Those old priests would be horrified to find a Protestant Bible in an archbishop's home, but it was a gift from a dear friend of mine." He flipped the pages until he found the passage he sought. "They considered heretics to be as intrinsically evil and dangerous as false prophets. So they found justification for their enforcement of orthodoxy in ancient words said to have been spoken by God himself. It's found in Jeremiah 23.

"'Is not my word like as a fire? saith the LORD; and like a *hammer* that breaketh the rock in pieces? Therefore, behold, I am against the prophets, saith the LORD, that steal my words every one from his neighbour. Behold, I am against the prophets, saith the LORD, that use their tongues, and say, He saith. Behold, I am against them that prophesy false dreams, saith the LORD, and do tell them, and cause my people to err by their lies, and by their lightness; yet I sent them not, nor commanded them: therefore they shall not profit this people at all, saith the LORD. And when this people, or the prophet, or a priest, shall ask thee, saying, What is the burden of the LORD? thou shalt then say unto them, What burden? I will even forsake you, saith the LORD. And as for the prophet, and the priest, and the people, that shall say, The burden of the LORD, I will even punish that man and his house.'" He closed the Bible. "The hammer for them was a symbol of God meting out punishment to false prophets."

Connor looked at him intently. "You say 'was,' Archbishop, as if they no longer exist."

"I'm not personally convinced they still exist as a group. But there could be someone who knows at least a little of their rituals and secrets, or heard some of the old stories."

"And may be trying to carry on their work by silencing Father Rosario for entertaining heretical ideas. But how would that person find out about the Father? How would he know what Father Rosario was researching? If the murderer is acting alone, he somehow zeroed in on one obscure Jesuit priest pursuing his personal search for the scriptural Holy Grail or Rosetta stone or however you want to characterize it. Doesn't that seem a little far-fetched in this day and age?"

"Who's to say what's in the mind of a man who would be capable of murdering a priest in his own church," said Johnston angrily. "Surely you've encountered insanity amongst the criminals you've prosecuted."

"Yes, I have, Archbishop. But insanity has many definitions. We have to ask ourselves if this crime, horrible as it is, is the work of one man who's latched on to an archaic tradition to justify his deeds, or is there a conspiracy of fanatics determined to silence theological dissent."

"That sounds exceedingly melodramatic, Ms. Hawthorne. Perhaps you've been too long ensconced in writing fiction."

Connor was about to reply when Benjamin leaned forward between them and interrupted. He was determined to keep the discussion on track, though the fireworks set off by an argument between his daughter and the sharp-tongued archbishop would have no doubt been entertaining at another time and place. "Your Eminence, please. Let's not spend our time debating the merits of theories we are only considering. I understand you are reluctant to suspect any member of the clergy of involvement in this. Personally, I'm not wild about the idea myself. But Connor's right. We have to consider it. How did this murderer come to choose Father Rosario? He wasn't, from what I understand, a high-profile priest. He hadn't been the subject of media coverage. His work in his parish was excellent but hardly newsworthy. His academic research would hardly have been known outside of a select few people. If the perpetrator is a cold-blooded killer, did someone point him at the priest? The answers may be unpleasant, but we have to ask."

Malcolm cleared his throat, drawing the attention of the others. "Maybe if we try looking just at the evidence we have."

Benjamin smiled. "Spoken like a true cop. Look to the evidence. Why don't you run down what you have?"

"I don't have a copy of the police reports on the homicide in Santa Ana, but I do have my notes on the crime scene based on Connor's observations and our old file on Richard Bell."

"This is the man who associates himself with Malleus Caelistis," said the archbishop.

"Yes, sir. We have a dossier on him going back about ten years. Before that, he's a complete blank. Until he committed a crime in the District, he was completely unknown to any state or federal agencies and had no criminal record we could find."

"So you don't really know who he is," said Johnston. "I assume that must not be his real name. It's virtually impossible to survive in the world without some kind of interaction with the government."

"That's generally the case. And, no, we can't be certain of anything about him, including his name, except that he was arrested in D.C., tried and convicted by Connor, and sentenced to a fourteen-year prison term. He was released on parole about three years ago after serving seven years of his sentence. He has an absolutely clean prison record and acted as a volunteer chaplain for the other inmates. Bell's nickname was the Preacher."

"And his connection with Malleus Caelistis?" asked Johnston.

"The pamphlets and materials found among his belongings, which he said he had written, all carried the name '*Malleus Caelistis ab Deum*,' or its English translation, 'Divine Hammer of God.' There was also a logo…

here's a copy of it," Malcolm handed the archbishop a sheet of paper. "As you can see, it's a fairly elaborate circle design in a Greek key pattern enclosing the picture of a hammer descending on a figure tied or chained to an inverted cross. And there's something sticking out of the chest of the figure. Hard to say what it is, but—are you all right, Archbishop?"

Johnston's face was almost white. "Where did you...but...you say this...this image was printed on materials in this man's possession?"

"Yes, sir," said Malcolm, "it was. And Connor said she saw something similar to it painted on the weapon found at the murder scene."

"But that's impossible," said Johnston, "utterly impossible."

"Why?" asked Benjamin, alarmed at the change in their host.

"Because there aren't a dozen men still alive in the world who have ever seen this symbol. Its use was forbidden more than a hundred years ago, and it only appeared in print once, on the cover and in the pages of a small hand-bound leather book."

"So then someone has found a copy of the book," said Connor. "That's the obvious answer."

"No! During the sixteenth century there were only twelve copies of it made, one for each member of the inner circle of Malleus Caelistis. When a member died, his copy was passed on to his replacement. Ten of those books were gathered one by one into the Vatican archives over the course of centuries and then destroyed by order of the Holy Father."

"You said there were twelve," countered Connor.

"Yes, I did." The archbishop suddenly looked much older than he had when they'd arrived. "One of them was buried with an old priest in New Orleans. When it came to light that he had insisted on taking it with him, so to speak, the church was opposed to exhuming him just to recover it. I have no doubt that it is still in his grave."

"And the twelfth copy," Connor persisted.

Archbishop Johnston looked at his hands for several moments before he finally replied. "I'm ashamed to say I fell victim to the historian's greed for knowledge. I had the book in my possession, and several days ago I showed it to Father Rosario. But I don't know where it is now. Tonight I opened my safe and the book was gone."

Chapter Fourteen

All spirits are enslaved which serve things evil.
—Percy Bysshe Shelley, *Prometheus Unbound*

Santa Ana, California

If Richard La Cloche, a.k.a. Ricky Bell, had known of the deep distress his personal crusade was causing Archbishop Johnston, he would have been thoroughly pleased. In his mind, priests who failed to uphold God's supreme laws were beneath contempt. On the other hand, the ones who held the line against sinners, heretics, and blasphemers were worthy of praise and honor. Ricky's ethics were uncomplicated: Whatever he chose to do was divinely inspired and therefore correct. The moral compass by which he evaluated others was also simple. Someone who agreed with him (and behaved according to Ricky's expectations) was good. Someone who did neither…was evil. The former he honored, the latter he punished, which was why the priest, Monsignor Kursk, was still alive.

Ricky had intended to search the offices of the dead blasphemer, Rosario, at the earliest possible moment, but he'd been delayed by the constant comings and goings at the rectory. When it finally was quiet enough, he'd been waiting near the building, letting a few more minutes tick by, when he saw a man slink down the driveway and force open the basement window. Ricky waited, interested to see what was going on. Naturally, he had no intention of being thwarted in his plans to rifle Rosario's office and burn anything that even hinted of blasphemy, but he could wait a few minutes and then follow the intruder.

He was close enough to hear a muffled cry, a tinkle of glass on metal, and a thud. He waited, suspecting the man had met up with someone inside, a night guard perhaps. But after several minutes of silence, he risked a peek through the window. All was dark. He used his light cautiously. The beam picked out the figure of the man on the floor and Ricky saw that he wore the Roman collar.

"Interesting," he muttered under his breath. "I wonder what he's after."

He lowered himself carefully through the window and dropped to the floor. Kneeling beside the priest, he first felt for a pulse. It was slow but relatively strong. Then he felt the man's pockets until he found a wallet and shuffled through it contents. He fingered the identity cards, particularly the one issued by the Vatican. *Monsignor Johann Kursk—I've seen that name. I believe we are on the same side, Father.* Ricky prided himself on having never forgotten a word he'd read, and he was meticulous in keeping up with postings of priests to various offices within the Roman curia. He knew Kursk's name from a list of priests attached to the Congregation for the Defense of Doctrine. And he'd gotten that list from someone who believed, as did Ricky, that desperate times called for desperate measures, the same individual who had identified Enrique Rosario as a heretic and false prophet. Ricky did not know his source's name or position or anything else about him, which was the only blot on an otherwise perfect association. Ricky didn't like being at a disadvantage. Fortunately, however, the source had rarely contacted him since the very first time twelve years ago, when he had first researched Malleus Caelistis and tripped someone's electronic intrusion alarm in cyberspace. Since then there had been E-mails, coded messages, and even a few telephone calls. But he had never been able to trace the author of the correspondence, or the location of the telephone from which he called.

He put the wallet back, tiptoed out of the basement, and searched until he found Rosario's office. To his annoyance, the office had obviously been partially cleared out. The only documents he found were church records, no research notes or materials, about the enemies of Malleus Caelistis. The instructions he'd received were frustratingly vague on the matter of what the priest might have had in his possession at the time of his death. And though Ricky rarely miscalculated, this time he had. He'd thought he would have ample time to search the church and the rectory once the priest was dead. He also hadn't counted on anyone opposing him in this effort. But having seen the tall figure of Archbishop Johnston placing cartons in the trunk of his car, Ricky put two and two together. What Ricky wanted, Johnston probably had.

Now, hours later, he waited impatiently in the shadows of the orange grove that surrounded the diocesan house. He'd already searched the trunk of the archbishop's car. It was empty. He'd have to go inside. A quick tour around the perimeter reassured him this would be an easy task. A number of doors and windows were unlocked, and if there was an alarm system, he could find no evidence of it. The housekeeper had departed in her car, though he made a mental note to keep an ear open for her return. She could well be a pious woman, and it would be sad, though not unforgivable, if he had to kill her.

He knew the archbishop had one or more visitors because there was another car, a rental, in the parking area beside the house. He crept around the building until he heard the murmur of voices and saw light slanting outward from a set of French doors. Ricky shifted position until he could peer through the doors without being seen. They were closed, and he couldn't quite make out what they were saying. He focused on each of the people at the table, one at a time. The archbishop he recognized. Beside him was a well-built man with salt-and-pepper hair and a dark suit that looked expensive and well-cut even from a distance. He was no cop. Next to him a woman with a full head of dark hair, pale skin—wait, it hardly seemed possible, but his prodigious memory supplied the name instantly—Connor Hawthorne, the heathen witch who'd sent him to prison. What was *she* doing here?

Ricky's chest felt tight and his palms began to sweat. He imagined for a moment that he might actually be experiencing fear. How could anyone have so quickly connected him to California? But the idea was ludicrous. Ricky was never afraid. He was only tense, excited, on a mission for God. If the woman was here because of him, so much the better. He owed her some payback.

He didn't recognize the woman next to Hawthorne. Looked Indian to him. He dismissed her. Definitely a heathen, even after all the work the good priests had done to show those godless savages the true path.

From his position, Ricky couldn't see the faces of the other two people on the archbishop's left. Very carefully, he stepped back and then moved in a slow arc that kept him out of the pool of light. Pressing close to the rough stucco wall, he peeked in again and breathed in sharply. This was beginning to seem like old-home week. The big black guy, the cop—hard not to remember him from ten years ago. He had interrogated Ricky and testified at the trial. Finishing him off would not be easy, but Ricky loved a challenge.

The black woman beside the cop was a stranger, but his instincts told him she was the law, maybe a regular cop, maybe something else. Didn't matter. All human beings were fragile; all of them could die, all of them except the chosen ones, the soldiers of the Lord...the wielders of the hammer. Ricky was thoroughly convinced of his own immortality, so much so that he saw no need to put it to the test. Besides, God would want him to be humble, to keep a low profile, at least until the great day came. Letting the enemy know that Ricky was impervious to their bullets would only complicate matters unnecessarily. And he surmised that at least two of the people in that room were probably carrying weapons.

Ricky heard a sound—no, it was *almost* a sound. It seemed to register in his head instead in his ears. He whipped his head around and peered into the shadows under the trees. Nothing moved. He waited. There...there it was again, oddly familiar...like the sounds the nuns' habits made as they'd walked the hallways of his old school. Ricky's heart beat faster still, and he backed away from the window. He'd hide in the gardening shed he'd seen on his first reconnoiter. He could see the windows from there, see when the lights went out. Then he'd make his move to retrieve whatever the archbishop had taken from the blasphemer's office at the rectory.

»——«

The physical outline of the old priest in his long black cassock coalesced from pieces of shadow and light, as if he'd reversed the process of melting into the dark. He'd let the intruder sense his presence just for an instant. It was necessary to prod him away from the house, though the old cleric didn't know precisely why. He'd simply learned to do as his intuition urged him. It told him the man peeking in the window was dangerous—the priest could see his aura swirled in raging reds and oranges with streaks of crackling light and solid darkness at the core. He waited until the stranger slunk off toward an outbuilding before getting a glimpse of the people in the room.

He was comforted. They were on the right track as far as he knew. The old priest, for all his extraordinary abilities, was not necessarily prescient. He was a mystic and a sworn servant of the truth. To many he would have seemed a magician, though they would have likely not understood the source of his "magic." He was exceedingly wise in the ways of humankind, but he still could not know for certain which of the people in that room would live and which would die. For tonight, he would guarantee their safety. But his heart told him that at least one of them might joyfully sit in the presence of the Mother and all the angels of creation before this chapter of the story came to an end.

»——«

"Archbishop, you're tired. We don't need to keep at this tonight. Perhaps we can meet again tomorrow." Benjamin was concerned. The priest's face still had very little color, even after the brandy he'd poured for himself.

"You're right. I am tired, but that isn't what's wrong, Mr. Hawthorne. The problem is that I wonder if my disobedience in keeping that forbidden book is what got Enrique killed. And that will be on my conscience for a very long time."

"You said yourself that he was obsessed with his research. And none of it had anything to do with Malleus Caelistis. Their opposition to the Cult of Magdalene was at most a collateral subject of study. So I think you're probably being too hard on yourself."

Johnston tried, but couldn't quite muster a smile. "Priests, particularly archbishops, have to be at least a little hard on themselves. Who else is there to keep them honest with themselves? But perhaps we should stop for the night. There is one thing I want to do, though, before you go. I've kept too much to myself thinking I could cope with the fallout from Father Rosario's death and still protect his family all by myself."

"You think Beatrice and Luis are at risk?" asked Laura.

"I don't know. But earlier today I went to Enrique's office and took all of his research and notes. I'm not up to explaining it all to you tonight, but I'd feel better if you took his files with you. Obviously, my safe is not secure."

"We'd be glad to safeguard the files, Archbishop," said Benjamin. "And I think we'd better go and let you get some rest."

The priest led them out of the conference room and to his office. Beside his desk were two cardboard boxes. Benjamin took one, Malcolm the other. Connor and Laura shook hands with the archbishop, and as Ayalla followed suit, he held her hand for a moment longer. "I know you had questions you wished to ask me, Agent Franklin, and I'll be happy to talk with you again. In the meantime, you have my blessing." He solemnly performed the ancient ritual of forming the sign of the cross. She looked flustered and said only, "Thank you, Your Eminence."

»——«

Ricky heard the car start, but his hiding place was not in a direct line of sight with the driveway. Thus, he didn't see the boxes the two men carried out and placed in the trunk of the rental. He waited half an hour until all the downstairs lights were turned off, then made his way quietly toward the back door he'd found unlocked on his first inspection. He was within a few feet of the entrance when he was stopped abruptly by something shoving against his chest. He jumped back, heart pounding, as his hand went to the pocket of his fatigue jacket for the switchblade he carried. The blade sprung from its sheath…but he was pointing it at nothing.

Ricky stood there panting slightly, straining to hear any sound. The light breeze in the orange trees, a lone bird call, his heart hammering in his chest. He put one foot forward and waited. Nothing. Calmer now, he moved again toward the door. This time he wasn't shoved, but he felt as if he'd walked into a wall—a soft, smothering wall of dense heat. It sucked the very air out of his lungs. Ricky fell to his knees, pressed against the invisible barrier until he thought he would suffocate. He tipped backward, rolling over on one shoulder until he was lying facedown on the grass. He lay there catching his breath, inhaling the aroma of greenness and earth. What the hell was going on? Some trick of Satan, the workings of a witch perhaps. He pulled himself to his knees. The dampness of the freshly watered lawn seeped through his pants, and his right hand felt hot and sticky. In the dim moonlight he saw that he was clutching his knife by its blade and it had sliced deeply into the skin of his palm. Blood dripped from the three-inch-long cut.

Furious now, he stared at the house. Rage boiled up inside him and he longed to crash through the flimsy door, tear apart the archbishop's sanctuary, then burn it to the ground with the old man inside. But he couldn't. Deep inside he knew that whatever thing or being protected the house was, at least on this night, stronger than he was. He cursed himself for his lack of faith, but he could not bring himself to try again. Knees trembling, he got to his feet and backed away several yards before circling the house. He had parked a quarter mile away, across the groves. Passing the archbishop's car, he contented himself with leaving a message—a long, bloody streak across the windshield.

»——«

"You didn't have much to say all evening," Malcolm said. He and Ayalla were sitting in a quiet corner of the lobby, having reached a tacit understanding that they would not visit each other's hotel rooms.

"It isn't as if I had a chance," she replied. "The senator made it pretty clear he was going to do the talking."

"I imagine he didn't want the old guy to get overwhelmed. I don't think the archbishop was too happy about you or me being involved."

"The only time people don't like having law enforcement involved is if they have something to hide," she snapped.

"I imagine that's the sort of thing Benjamin was afraid you'd say. Accusing people isn't always the best approach to gaining their cooperation."

"So now you're telling me how to do my job, too. What I can't figure out is why in the hell Hawthorne wanted me to come here in the first place."

"You wouldn't be here if he didn't respect your work. But that doesn't mean you're not a hothead, and he won't let that compromise an interview. You may find out you can learn something from him. I know I have."

"He's never been a cop. What could he teach you about police work?"

"Nothing, but I wasn't talking about that."

"So you mean he's slipped you some intelligence from time to time."

"He *has* done that when it was appropriate, but that's also not what I'm talking about."

"Then what the hell *are* you talking about? I'm tired. It's three o'clock in the morning Eastern time, and I need some sleep. So enough with the riddles and bullshit. I know you and the senator are great pals. You don't need to rub it in."

Malcolm shook his head. "You really are something, you know that? Why do you take everything I say as a challenge, as if I'm baiting you, when I'm not. The point I wanted to make is that among the things I've learned from Benjamin are patience and the necessity of avoiding assumptions that won't hold up in the long run."

"Patience isn't my strong suit. I believe that action speaks a lot louder than words. Bull sessions don't accomplish anything concrete."

"If you think Benjamin is some sort of armchair quarterback, you're sadly mistaken. He's seen more 'action' than you and I put together. But he knows when to act and when to analyze. So maybe that's what you can learn. We all know you're tough, and strong, and you've got guts.

You don't have to prove that. You wouldn't be in the FBI if you were what my mama used to call a 'delicate flower of femininity.'"

"Gee, thanks," she said wryly. "I assume that's some sort of compliment."

"Yes, it is. I personally have no time for women who act helpless on purpose—women who equate being feminine with being weak. That's crap."

Ayalla stared at him for several seconds. "Okay, so maybe I have been a little obnoxious. But I hate not knowing what's going on. I don't like mysteries, guesswork, excessive theorizing, and I especially don't like spooky stuff."

Malcolm grinned. "You, an FBI agent, and you don't like the *X-Files*?"

"Oh, please."

"Hey, I'm kidding…sort of. But I should warn you that spooky stuff sort of follows Connor and Laura around. Benjamin, too, lately. And these past couple of years I've seen a few things I wouldn't want to have explain to my superiors at the Metropolitan Police Department. So if you're really worried about things happening that are absolutely *not* covered in the FBI manual, you may want to hightail it back to D.C. right now."

"Why do I get the impression you're yanking my chain, Captain?"

"Probably because you think just about everyone is. And please, let's stick with 'Malcolm.'"

She sighed heavily. "All right then. But I'm still voting for a cut-and-dried murder case with one perpetrator who likes making hollow threats against the government, and peddles a good line of bullshit to make himself look important—straightforward, simple, end of story."

"Life's never simple, Agent Franklin."

"A girl can dream, can't she? And stop with the Agent Franklin thing." She stood up, put her leather bag over her shoulder, and looked at her watch. "I'd say 'see you in the morning' except it already is."

»—«

Monsignor Kursk was excruciatingly cold to the point of paralysis. For a moment, he considered that he was so cold and numb as to be dead. Then he heard the sound of a car horn blaring and voices that were quickly drowned out by the pounding bass and snarling lyrics of some teenager's rap music. If he was dead, clearly he'd missed his salvation and been sent straight to hell.

Slowly he did a personal inventory. Hands move? Good. Feet? Yes. Arms? Still working. Legs? Ditto. So far, so good—until he tried to sit up. Huge mistake. Blinding pain seared through his head. He thought his skull was going to explode. "Sweet Jesus," he mumbled, trying to steady himself. "What hit me?"

Gradually, he was able to focus on his surroundings. He took note of the open window, through which a little bit of illumination, presumably from a streetlamp, filtered. The events came back to him a piece at a time. He'd waited in the car, walked up the driveway, then tried to climb in through the window, but then what? Window? Climbing in? Everything was a blank. He shook his head—another mistake—and had a strong urge to vomit. But he truly hated throwing up, and the thought of how much that would disturb the equilibrium of his head made him clench his teeth hard.

He gently probed the back of his skull with his fingers. The swelling had already started. It felt about the size of an ostrich egg. He needed to get himself together and out of this damned basement. He'd sit quietly for a while until he felt better. He might even be able to—what was it?—yes, papers, the priest's papers. He was going to look for that…thing…the cardinal was so determined to have. It'd be nice if Kursk knew what the hell it was, but then monsignors don't question cardinals. That pretty much summed up life at the Vatican. There was a pecking order, and Kursk wasn't really as near the top as he liked to think.

Right now, though, even thinking hurt. He wanted to close his eyes, but he remembered something about not sleeping if you had concussion. Might never wake up. He would wait quietly, say a few prayers, since he was fairly sure that is what priests do when they're in trouble. Had the priesthood actually been his true calling, he might have been certain. But Kursk had become a priest for all the wrong reasons, none of them having to do with serving humankind.

The light was beginning to bother his eyes. Was that another symptom? Sensitivity to…light. What light? To his horror, the monsignor finally understood that the illumination did not come from any streetlamp. The sun was coming up outside. If he didn't get out of the basement soon, someone would find him there. He would be hard pressed to explain why (or how) he'd gotten in.

Praying fervently that he would not set off any alarms when he left the house, Kursk got to his feet very slowly, fighting once more the urge to regurgitate everything he'd ever eaten in his life, and opened the door leading into the hall. At the rear was a staircase. He climbed them like a ninety-year-old man with a heart condition, but finally made it to the kitchen. Thanking God that no one was there, he shuffled across the floor, turned the deadbolt, and opened the back door. The small parking area was empty. No cars, no people. It was only a few minutes past sunrise.

He closed the door behind him and made his way along the side of the rectory building. Just a few more minutes and he'd be safely away. He was already wondering if he should drive himself straight to the hospital or call a cab. Providence answered the question for him. His car, though still parked across the street, didn't look the same. It took his fuddled brain quite a few seconds to conclude that it probably wasn't very useful without its wheels…or its doors…or its hood.

Monsignor Kursk sat down on the curb and for the first time in his adult life considered crying.

A passing patrol car found the disheveled priest about a half hour later, and a police officer tried to unravel his tale of woe.

Chapter Fourteen

The dream is the small hidden door
in the deepest and most intimate sanctum of the soul,
which opens into that primeval cosmic night
that was soul long before there was a conscious ego
and will be soul far beyond what a conscious ego could ever reach.
—Carl Jung

A part of Laura's consciousness knew she was sound asleep in a hotel room in Laguna Beach, California. Her sleeping mind registered sounds—the surf, the gentle, steady breathing of her lover, even the faint drip of water from the bathroom tap—but simply stored them away for later reference. The awareness of where her physical body lay did not diminish the clarity and reality of her journey in the Dreamtime. Since childhood she'd been able to travel to that place between sleeping and waking, between the "real" and the "unreal," perhaps even between life and death. Laura's Grandmother Klah (whom Laura suspected spent more time on shamanic journeys in other realms than in her remote home on the Navajo reservation) had spoken of it as a place where one discovered that what you thought of as everyday reality was no more than an illusion.

Laura had not consciously visited the other realms of reality in many weeks. Part of her reluctance could be traced back to the events in England—the nightmarish assault on Connor, and Laura's own atavistic fears of what she had encountered—but some of it was simply the general avoidance of complications. They both were hungry for a few days or weeks of pure "normalcy" if indeed anyone could ever truly find such a state. Yet Laura suspected life wasn't going to cooperate. So it was that she did not resist the gentle but persistent summons. She let her soul self drift clear of the body, checking first to see that everything felt right. Instantly she was…elsewhere.

"*You resist, little one,*" *said the grandmother.*

"*Perhaps. But I haven't wanted to travel here.*"

"*Why?*"

"*Whenever you or Connor's grandmother are involved, everything goes crazy.*"

"*The workings of the Spirit are crazy?*"

Laura felt herself drifting slightly. Near her field of vision were clouds that sparkled against a dark backdrop. "*No, I didn't mean that exactly.*"

"*Good, because I'd hate to think I taught you to be disrespectful.*"

"*No, my grandmother. You taught me to see clearly and to treat all beings with respect.*"

"*You cannot avoid helping these people, you know.*"

"*What people?*"

Silence.

"*All right. You mean Beatrice and Luis and the archbishop.*"

"*No.*"

"*What do you mean, 'no'?*"

"*You always did tend to see things too narrowly, my child.*"

Laura relaxed into the embrace of the nothingness that was everything and considered. "*So there is more to this than simply the lives of the people I'm thinking of?*"

"*Yes. Better. But you will have to discover your role in all this. Yours and that of the one you love.*"

"*Do you suppose that just this once you could be less cryptic and more specific? Everything would go faster, and we might not end up risking our lives over it."*

"Must we go back and start all over with your lessons, child? Life, if you're talking about conscious existence, has a very fluid definition. This place of transition where we communicate after a fashion is hardly death, now is it? And I am not here to serve as your personal question-answering ancestor."

"It doesn't hurt to ask, though."

"True. But I taught you to be resourceful, not impudent. Continue with your journey, little one, and stay awake."

In the next instant, Laura was alone. She no longer felt comfortably cradled in the oneness with all that is. Thus she knew she had moved from the fullness of the Dreamtime to the level of human dreaming.

Before her lay a field of stubbly weeds and rocks and dirt—real, but not quite real—a painted landscape come to life, rendered in a monochromatic palette of grays. The sensation that the scene was familiar fought with her mind's assertion that she'd never been to this place before. Gradually, night sounds filtered into the dream—the low calls of nocturnal birds, mice or something larger scratching in the soil, the soft nickering of horses somewhere near. There was a hint of a barnyard in the air. She started to walk toward the sound of the horses. To her right she saw a small fountain. Beside it stood an obelisk topped by a stylized Celtic cross. Some part of her mind registered that the two objects were oddly placed, being so close together. The design of the cross was familiar. She stopped to study it and then registered the shadow it cast in the bright light of a full moon, just as she realized that her body was not casting any shadow at all.

A sense of urgency pulled her forward, away from the fountain and the obelisk. She turned, her heart beating faster, and immediately stumbled over an object lying in the dead grass. She bent down to see it, put her hand on a flat-topped rock, and felt tiny valleys and ridges forming a circular pattern she couldn't quite make out. She knelt, sure she would be able to decipher the markings in the moonlight, but in the way that dreams transport the dreamer in highly unpredictable ways, she slipped sideways as if the ground had tilted. She fought the sensation of falling as she reached for tufts of grass that should have been within easy reach.

Where there had been dirt there was now the implacable firmness of cold, smoothed stone. She was standing in an open air corridor, an arcade defined by columns and arches on one side and a blank wall along the other. Again the setting struck no chord of conscious memory and yet.... it did. In the dim recesses of the corridor, just at the limit of her sight, a shape moved. She peered into the shadows. A person dressed in black, a long coat—no, a priest's garb. Laura moved toward him, but he shrank from her as if in fear. The face of the priest was turned away. All she could see was a thatch of white hair glowing in the half-light.

Laura heard a sound behind her and turned. At first glance it was the same man. In a heartbeat, he had moved from one end of the corridor to the other. Yet his hair wasn't white. It was dark gray. His face tilted toward her; she perceived a countenance that, to her perception, was not entirely human. The pupils of the eyes were enormous and completely black, encircled in tiny flames. The mouth that opened, as if to speak, showed no teeth. Laura stared into the deliquescent void of its eyes, then tried to step back. But her feet were rooted to the stone. He moved closer. "What do you want here?" The sound emanated not from the empty mouth but from somewhere behind his eyes. "It isn't time yet."

"Time for what?" Laura heard her dream self ask.

"To take back what is mine, of course...reclaim what he took from me."

"I don't know what you're talking about. What is this place?"

"This place...this place is nowhere, you simpering little fool. There is no such thing as a 'place' when you're 2,000 years dead."

His laughter—screeching, tormented, and ugly—bounced off the cold, gray stones, echoing and re-echoing, feeding upon itself, amplified over and over until a hundred hideous strains of discordant fury pummeled her ears. Uncontrollable fear gripped Laura's heart. Fire shot up from the stones beneath her feet. She was surrounded by a vortex of flame that singed her skin and set her hair afire. She screamed.

"Laura! Wake up! Wake up!"

Strong hands clasped her shoulders. Laura started to struggle until she opened her eyes and looked into the taut, frightened face of her lover. She pulled Connor into a hard hug, then laid back on the pillow, her heart still going like a trip-hammer. "It's okay, sweetheart, it's okay. But for a minute there…anyway, I'm glad it's you."

Connor let out a burst of air. "Of course it's me. You were expecting someone else?"

"Not in this dimension."

Connor scowled. "You've been wandering again, haven't you?"

"Seemed like a good idea at the time."

"Didn't sound very good. You screamed. I'm still waiting for the front desk to call and ask who's doing what to whom up here."

"I was that loud?"

"Maybe it just seemed loud because I was lying right next to you. But you scared the hell of out me, darling."

"Sorry. But the problem wasn't in the Dreamtime. I talked to Grandmother Klah for a bit, and then I sort of fell back into the halfway place—you know, more like regular dreaming."

"Sounded more like a regular nightmare."

"It felt like one, too. But I'm all right now. I just need to get up and write this down."

Connor, who had grown accustomed to Laura's dream journalizing, and knew better than to continue talking and perhaps derail the dream memories, turned on the light and picked up a book from the bedside table. Laura went to the desk for a handful of hotel stationery and a pen and went out on the balcony in the moonlight where she wrote for almost half an hour, recording images, sensations, audible messages—everything she could think of.

When she stepped back into the room, Connor was still awake. "Want to talk about now?" she asked. "Or would you rather wait until morning. There's still time to get a little sleep before the sun comes up."

"I don't think I could sleep. But I hate keeping you up. You've been so tired lately."

"I'm just a little burned out from changing time zones so often. But I'm wide awake and actually I'm kind of curious. You haven't done that kind of dreaming in a while."

"True. Maybe I've been avoiding it. Grandmother Klah would have said 'neglecting' it."

"No doubt. Was she chiding you again?"

"Not really. But I got the impression she was feeling a little testy with me, as if I hadn't been paying enough attention to what's going on. Maybe we both need to take a closer look at all this."

"So come here tell me about it."

Laura would just have soon have waited until daylight. But here, with her head nestled on Connor's shoulder, she felt safe. She started slowly and bit by bit described the dream encounter with a man whose eyes burned.

»——«

"You will supply Mr. Holcomb with all the information he requires. You will cease your extracurricular activities, and avoid drawing attention to yourself."

San Peligro Nuclear Generating Station

He'd taken the damn thing out of his desk half a dozen times and reread it. There was no room to misinterpret the instruction. The first sentence also confirmed what Archibald had long suspected, that Holcomb was part of whatever dreadful conspiracy the Preacher and his stupid secret society had cooked up that involved the nuclear generating station. For about the hundredth time, he considered taking all the notes, the copies of E-mails—everything—to the authorities. But he quailed at the prospect of revealing his association with these people. He would certainly be disciplined, possibly terminated. Where else would he be able to work once he'd been identified as a security risk?

As if that weren't enough, as an added surety for his silence, the envelope had contained a full transcript of his last computer sex session with a woman identifying herself only as Lolita69. Archibald was too humiliated to read past the first few sentences. How could they have obtained it? He was never foolish enough to conduct personal business at the office. His computer encounters always took place in the wee hours of the morning while he was at home. Then it dawned on him that someone out there in cyberspace knew his various user names and must have been trolling for him, and that meant Lolita could have been just about anybody. He shuddered.

He heard a voice in the outer office and jammed the papers into his desk drawer. Holcomb flung the door open without knocking, then slammed it behind him.

"What are you doing here?" asked Sims, anger bubbling up inside him.

The security chief smirked. "Just reporting in, Mr. Sims," he said loudly enough for Archibald's secretary to hear. Then he moved closer to the desk, so close in fact that his massive thighs were pressed against the front edge. When he leaned over, Holcomb was only inches from the plant manager's face. "I've been thinking that I need to keep a closer watch on every secure area of the generating station 24-7—not just the perimeter and the office complex. My men will need complete night access to the main control room, all the subbasement levels, and the containment area."

"But w-why?" Archibald stammered. "The technicians on the day shift secure those areas. Only the two night technicians have any reason to be in the control room. No one needs to be in the subbasement except during maintenance, and we have radiation protocols in effect near the containment area. No unauthorized personnel are allowed near the core. Your job is securing against unauthorized access. And no individual person is permitted to have access to the entire plant."

"Except you."

"That's different."

Holcomb leaned even closer. "Not really. So, before you leave on Friday, send me an interoffice mail pouch with next week's duty schedule for all the technicians, the security door codes for the locations I've listed, and the installation diagrams for the laser-triggered alarm systems on the lower levels. Wouldn't want to trip them by accident, now would we?"

"You…but I don't see…"

This time Holcomb jabbed his meaty index finger into Archibald's chest.

"You don't have to see. You just have to do what you're told." He shoved the plant manager away from his desk so that Archibald went skimming backward in his five-wheeled executive chair and thudded into the file cabinet behind him. Holcomb slid open the desk drawer and pulled out the crumpled note and the transcript. "You like 'em young, Archie? Or just the ones who pretend they're young?" He threw the papers at Archibald, who reflexively clutched them to his chest. "You figure the big bosses will approve of having a computer sex addict and closet pedophile running this place?"

Sims said nothing.

"Nah. I don't think so either. Face it…you're a fuckin' loser, Archie, and a pathetic little prick. You coulda been a rich man if you weren't so stupid, but now you're gonna do what you're told and you're gonna do it all for free. I'll expect the pouch Friday."

Holcomb covered the ten feet to the door in about three strides. "Yes, sir, Mr. Sims," he said, his voice once again raised for theatrical effect. "I'll get right on that. Thanks for letting me know."

The door slammed behind him, and Archibald sat frozen to his chair. His heart thudded so hard in his chest, he was sure he must be going into cardiac arrest. At the moment, he would welcome a visit to a cardiac care unit—anything that would put him beyond the reach of Holcomb and his goons, not to mention the Preacher. He looked down at the papers in his hands and wondered how Holcomb had known where they were. Cold prickles inched up his spine to the back of his neck. Surveillance? Did Holcomb have a way of keeping tabs on him, even in his office?

Carefully he rolled his chair back to his desk, not daring to look up at the walls or the ceiling, or in any way indicate he suspected he was being watched. Holcomb might have made a strategic error. The more Archibald thought about it, the more he clung desperately to the idea that he actually was smarter than most people thought. The proof of that, however, lay in whether he could outwit Holcomb. He didn't know, but he might actually try…if, in the next forty-eight hours he could find any courage to go along with what his IQ dictated.

»——«

"What in God's name have you been up to?"

Kursk closed his eyes. The archbishop's voice reverberated painfully in his skull. He thought if he so much as opened his mouth he'd throw up all over the bed sheets.

"What were you doing at St. Mary of the Groves?"

The monsignor opened his eyes and licked his dry lips. "Could I..." His voice was no more than a croak. "Some water, please."

The archbishop impatiently grabbed the plastic cup with a straw protruding from the lid and handed it to the patient. Kursk sipped slowly and tried to look pathetic at the same time. Unfortunately for him, Johnston didn't look the least bit sympathetic. "I...um..."

"'Um'...what?!"

"I only wanted to protect the church's reputation, Your Eminence. I thought that if—"

"That if you could break into the rectory and rifle through Father Rosario's papers, you might find whatever it is you think you're looking for. Is that about right?"

"I didn't break in."

"The police officers said a basement window was jimmied."

"Not by me."

Johnston shook his head. "Don't lie to me, Monsignor, and don't lie to the police. You'll only make matters worse."

"What could be worse than what that damn priest was doing?" said Kursk, though he regretted his vehemence as another wave of nausea passed through him. "He was trying to destroy us."

Johnston's eyes narrowed. "Destroy whom?"

Kursk hesitated a beat or two. "The church, of course."

"I don't think that's what you meant at all."

"What else would I mean?"

The archbishop pulled up a chair and sat down beside the bed. Still, given his height, he could look Kursk in the eye. "You're going to tell me right now everything you know about Malleus Caelistis."

The monsignor felt his skin flush with heat. "I...that is, I don't know anything. Malleus Caelistis is ancient history. And you know the topic is not to be discussed."

"I'm not buying that forbidden subject crap, so don't bother trying. I've always suspected there might be Malleus Caelistis priests in the church, especially in the Congregation for the Defense of Doctrine. And it strikes me that you'd be the perfect foot soldier to help them keep tabs on everyone else. Face it, Kursk, you've got 'minion' written all over you. And I'm not leaving this room until you give me some straight answers."

The monsignor shuddered, whether in anger or fear he couldn't be sure. His poor head still pounded. He felt as if his skull might split wide open and scatter his brains all over the room. Briefly, he considered that might not be such a bad way to go. He'd be out of his misery and the archbishop would be on the receiving end of lots of gore. Kursk tried to get hold of himself. It was absurd to let the old man intimidate him—him! Johann Kursk, the scourge of the heretical theologian, the blasphemous cleric, or even simply the wrong-thinking layman. He had spent the last decade putting out the fires of potential destruction. Who was this insignificant American archbishop to question a member of the Congregation?

Just about the time Kursk had worked himself into a state of righteous indignation almost sufficient to offset his physical misery, Johnston grabbed the hospital-bed control box and stabbed the button to bring the monsignor's torso up higher. The sensation was worse than seasickness. The archbishop heard him gag and snatched a porcelain bowl from the nightstand and shoved it under the priest's chin. Nothing actually came up, although Kursk expected to see his internal organs in the bowl.

"I'm not feeling terribly charitable, Monsignor, so stop wasting my time. I want to know right now if these religious fascists had anything to do with Father Rosario's murder."

Kursk's eyes widened. "What are you saying? Some drug addict or thief kills a priest in his church and you blame an imaginary secret society? That's nothing but foolishness."

"This was no drug addict or thief." The archbishop drew a piece of paper from his pocket. "This design was painted on the murder weapon, at least on one of the murder weapons. One of the witnesses sketched it for me. It was on the hammer that someone used to drive a stake through the heart of an ordained Catholic priest!" He held the paper up in front of Kursk's face. "Recognize it?"

The monsignor stared at the crude drawing. It was not entirely accurate, but there was no mistaking its meaning. It depicted the secret seal and symbol of Malleus Caelistis. "I don't understand," he whispered. "That can't be. It can't be."

"So you admit you're part of this."

"No, I mean, we—that is…not murder. It just can't be."

"You've said that three times. Why can't it be?"

"I was only here to…to make him turn over his research. He stole something from the Vatican archives, but we…that is…the theft wasn't discovered until recently. But we didn't know exactly what was stolen. And then someone discovered that Rosario's father had been to Italy to the old monastery at Torini."

"So what? The man was a devout Catholic and he was *born* in Italy. Why shouldn't he visit the ruins of a church or an abbey? Why would you care?"

"Because," said Kursk, still struggling to make sense of the drawing. "He may have gone there to get something, something that Rosario wanted. That place is, or was, once connected with serious heresies."

"Hundreds of places would qualify as hotbeds of heresy, Kursk, especially if your coconspirators in Malleus Caelistis are the ones doing the thinking. What possible significance is there in one old deserted monastery?"

"It was confirmed long ago that Torini was a hiding place for one or more men who—"

"Who what?!"

"Who were not loyal to the Holy Father or to the church. They were traitors to the faith. They claimed to be descended from the original founders of the Cult of Magdalene. The cardinal believed there might be something hidden there to support this disgusting blasphemy the Magdalenes preached."

The archbishop stood up from his chair so abruptly it tipped over. The metallic clang ripped through Kursk's head. "So you're telling me that not only is Malleus Caelistis still around, but they're worried about someone spreading a bunch of nonsensical pseudohistory about the town prostitute becoming an apostle and writing down some other version of the Savior's life."

"There's more to it than that, and you are know full well some still seek the descendants."

Johnston was tempted to laugh out loud. "The descendants? You're buying into that garbage as well? That Christ had descendants? For God's sake, Kursk, that's nothing more than the ravings of misguided people. It isn't dangerous. Have you lost your mind?"

"It's more than dangerous if there are those who believe it." Kursk snarled. Then he blanched slightly. "But I didn't *say* that Malleus Caelistis was still around."

"Don't try backing out of it now, you fool. I saw the look on your face when I showed you this drawing. This isn't ancient history for you. Now how many people belong to this self-proclaimed God gestapo?"

"How dare you ridicule the faithful! Even if they do exist, they would only be doing what they were destined to do, sworn by God to do. Some people may still believe in divine duty and honor."

"This isn't Camelot, Monsignor, and you're no knight in shining armor, so spare me the righteous platitudes. No cause on earth justifies murdering a priest and defiling a church. Father Rosario was killed on sacred ground by a cold-blooded murderer. If he is among the members of this little group of yours, I promise you I will find him, and he'll pay the full penalty for what he's done."

"You're wrong," said Kursk. "We may have been zealous in protecting the truth of the church's teachings, but never—"

"'We?' So the lies begin to fail you?"

"I mean, that is to say, the Congregation…"

"Now you're saying that the Congregation for the Defense of Doctrine is involved with Malleus Caelistis? Dear God, don't tell me they're one and the same."

"Of course not!"

"Good, because even though many of those old farts annoy me, I can't believe they'd stoop this low. So which 'we' are you referring to?"

Kursk swallowed hard. "You don't understand. I can't talk about it. I'll only say that I have no knowledge of anyone who would murder a priest."

"More precisely, Monsignor, you *hope* no one amongst your cronies is capable of sacrilege of this order. But you don't really know, do you?

This would be a good time to think about it—and think hard. You *will* talk about it, either to me or to the police."

The door to the room swung open, admitting a tall, attractive woman in a white lab coat. "I'm Dr. Fielding," she said. "Sorry to interrupt, Father." She glanced at the archbishop. "But I need to examine Monsignor Kursk. We're still monitoring his recovery. That was a pretty nasty concussion."

Johnston started to say something to her, then turned to Kursk. "Give some thought to the matter, Monsignor. I'll be back this afternoon." He nodded to the physician. "Thank you, Doctor." The door closed behind him and Kursk let out a long sigh.

Dr. Fielding looked at him curiously. "Is there anything wrong, Monsignor?"

"Uh...no, nothing."

"Good. Because it's important you get a lot of rest." She checked his pupils with a small penlight, felt his pulse, and gently probed the lump on the back of his head. Kursk winced. "Sorry. I know that smarts." She made some notations on a clipboard. "I'll be able to give you something for the pain now. The X-rays and the MRI are clear, skull still intact, though there may be a hairline fracture. In any event, we still need to watch for swelling." She glanced at his intravenous line, tapped the bag. "You'll be getting some more fluids and maybe this evening some solid food."

"No rush on that," said Kursk, his stomach clenching at the mere thought of food. "Nor was he comfortable with the proximity of the woman. On his home turf at the Vatican, only *male* doctors treated priests.

The doctor smiled. "I know that's how you feel at the moment, but believe me, you'll be ravenously hungry before you know it. Even hospital food will taste good."

"I'll take your word for it."

"I'll be back this evening, Monsignor. In the meantime, get some rest."

She checked her watch for the third or fourth time and hustled out the door.

He lowered the top half of the bed a little and closed his eyes. He desperately wanted to go to sleep and forget everything that had happened in the last three days, but the awful reality pressed in against him from all sides. A priest was dead, brutally murdered. And Kursk had broken into the rectory. If the police started looking around for fingerprints, his were bound to show up. How was he going to explain it? And what would Cardinal de Marcos and Bishop Rinaldi and Bishop Kreitner have to say about this mess? They'd sent him here to muzzle a rebellious Jesuit, and it had turned into a nightmare.

Kursk heard the door open again. A male nurse in a white shirt, pants, and shoes came into the room, smiled at the monsignor, and began straightening the sheets and blanket. "Anything you need, sir?" asked the nurse. "More water, a light snack?"

"The doctor said I didn't have to eat until tonight."

"Oh. I suppose she knows best," said the man. "Here, let me adjust the bed a little and get those pillows straightened out."

Kursk sighed with pleasure. No one had plumped his bed pillows since he was a boy. He leaned forward, careful not to jar his head.

"All right, then. Just lie back gently." The nurse cradled his neck in one hand as Kursk relaxed back into his cocoon of starched white pillowcases. His eyes fluttered closed so that he didn't see the other pillow in the nurse's hand. He only felt it when it covered his face. The monsignor immediately began to struggle, but an enormous weight settled on his chest and his arms were pinned at his sides. He fought, writhing in agony, thrusting his torso against the weight, but he was helpless. His lungs screamed in agony, flashes of light in every color of the spectrum swirled behind his eyelids, and finally, after more than two full minutes, he ceased to struggle.

Only then did the nurse climb down off the bed, raise the priest's head to tuck the pillow underneath, and tidy the bedclothes. "Rest in peace, Father," he whispered and then slipped out of the room, down the stairs to the service entrance, and into a car waiting on the street behind the hospital.

"Did he say anything to the old man?" asked the driver.

"Not from what I heard," replied the male nurse. "But he would have opened his big mouth eventually. And the Preacher don't take kindly to loose lips."

"But that priest didn't know who we are," replied the driver. "He didn't know the Preacher either."

"Don't be so sure of that," said the nurse. "Let's get the fuck out of here. We're gonna be late as it is, and Holcomb says we got stuff to do at the plant."

Chapter Sixteen

A grave, wherever found,
preaches a short and pithy sermon to the soul.
—Nathaniel Hawthorne

"I'll have four eggs over easy, bacon, sausage, hash browns, whole wheat toast, and a short stack of buttermilk pancakes…and a large orange juice and coffee."

"Mid-morning snack?" said Connor.

Malcolm grinned. "Yep. The continental breakfast at *our* hotel wasn't enough to feed a fly."

"How do you *do* that? By all rights, you should weigh 500 pounds."

"Good thing I don't. My sister would have to spend a lot of time letting out my clothes. But on the plus side, the bad guys would be scared of me. Afraid I'd sit on them."

"I know plenty of bad guys who are scared of you just the way you are."

"I wonder if they have any fresh fruit?"

"You know we're having lunch in about two hours."

"I'll be ready by then," he said, reaching for the orange juice as soon as the glass hit the table. "So tell me what's going on. When you called this morning, you sounded kind of anxious."

"Thanks for coming. I'm surprised Super Agent Franklin didn't insist on tagging along."

"Special Agent."

"Whatever."

"She did ask if I was looking into anything specific, and I told her I was meeting you."

"And she didn't tail you here?"

"Connor, could you give it rest? I know the FBI is one of your least favorite agencies on the planet. But could you possibly keep in mind that not everyone who works for the bureau is a creep?"

"I can keep it in mind as a potential theory yet to be proven to my satisfaction."

"God, you're stubborn." The waitress appeared with his food. "You know what I love about breakfast, other than the usual ingredients?"

"What?"

"It's one of the fastest meals to come out of the kitchen." He nodded to the waitress. "Thanks, and could I have some more maple syrup, please?"

Connor watched him slather butter on his pancakes. "All right, I want some of that," she said, reaching with her fork.

"Help yourself," he grinned. "Now tell me what got you out of bed at the crack of dawn."

"Laura had a dream last night."

Malcolm put down his knife and sighed heavily. "Oh."

"'Oh,' what? How can anyone invest that much dismay in one syllable?"

"Practice."

"Well, don't get all bent out of shape yet. I haven't even told you about it."

"When you say Laura had a dream and you have that look on your face, it can only mean one thing. Events are bound to get weird, and the next stop is probably the Twilight Zone."

"Don't you think that's a little bit of an overstatement?" said Connor, frowning.

"No. Don't forget I was in England with you guys. I saw the world's strangest things there. And you and Laura were the head of the strange team."

174

"The strange team? Thanks a lot."

"Hey, no offense. I'm getting used to it. But at least I'm willing to admit that whatever is going on here with the priests and Malleus Caelistis and even Ricky Bell—all of it could end up stranger than fiction."

"I don't immediately jump to that conclusion."

"I know. You're too hardheaded, even after all you've been through. I, on the other hand, while not liking spooky, invisible crap, have made peace with the idea that there's some stuff I'll never understand. But that doesn't make it any less real. And if it's some of that evil shit you seem to run into occasionally, then whether I like it or not doesn't make it any less dangerous." He stuffed a forkful of hash browns into his mouth.

"Could you possibly be any more fatalistic?"

"Unh-uh." He swallowed. "So, tell me about the dream."

Connor related as many details as she could recall from Laura's account of the dream, both the communication with Grandmother Klah, and the frightening encounter with the not-quite-human being who claimed to have been dead for two millennia.

"I thought Gwendolyn taught you to ignore dead people. She said, and I'm quoting you, 'The dead who wander around near the earth plane are notoriously unenlightened and often highly annoying.'"

"That's what my grandmother said all right. But this guy didn't strike Laura as your average stiff from Middle America, if you know what I mean. He was definitely the menacing type."

"So we're talking someone or something that's dark or evil—or both."

Connor stared at her friend for several seconds. "It still amazes me when you say things like that. When I think about what a skeptic you've always been…"

"Still am," replied Malcolm after taking a long sip of his juice. "I don't take everything at face value. If you know how many quack psychics and fortune tellers we have just in the D.C. metro area, you'd be amazed. And just think how many there must be in California."

"I think that's a stereotype: Californians are flakier than the people in the rest of the country."

"Maybe, although I'm not so sure. For one thing, their cars are too clean."

"What?"

"Never mind."

"So what are we missing about Father Rosario's murder. If Laura's dream is any indication, Grandmother Klah seems to think that we're looking at the situation with tunnel vision. She hinted there's a lot more to it than we think."

"A lot more to it, as in 'weird' or as in 'conspiracy theory' stuff?"

"I don't know. But the creepazoid in Laura's dreams is hardly someone you'd run into on the street."

"You hope."

"I hope." Connor shivered involuntarily.

"My great aunt Josephine would say someone's walking over your grave."

"Let's not go there. Graves and graveyards don't rate high on my list of pleasant thoughts."

Malcolm thoughtfully chewed his last bite of pancake. "You said you always thought of me as a skeptic, so you're surprised when I don't get all annoyed about strange dreams and spooky manifestations. But I've learned to keep a foot in both camps, sort of. Some things I can explain, like plain old greed and fear and cruelty. I see those all the time, and I know how to deal with it. Cops arrest perps and put 'em in jail. But in the last three years or so, I've seen stuff I can't explain. Still, I think only a fool would ignore something or pretend it doesn't exist just because he can't explain it."

"There are scientists out there who insist there is a logical explanation for every phenomenon we experience," Connor reminded him.

"Then they haven't really seen what else is out there. And I have."

"Doesn't it scare you, though?"

"Sure. But we all get scared. I figure that instead of avoiding anything I'll just handle whatever comes up in one of two ways."

"And they are?"

"When we're working on the 'real world' stuff," Malcolm crooked his index fingers to indicate the quotes, "I'll do my cop thing with the badge and the gun and the authority to arrest people."

"And what about the other times, like in Glastonbury. Your badge and gun wouldn't have mattered one bit."

Malcolm grinned. "In those instances where sheer size, firepower, and the weight of the law have no effect...I'm just gonna hide behind you or Laura."

Connor burst out laughing, attracting the attention of the few other patrons in the restaurant. At that moment the cell phone clipped to her handbag let out a disconcerting chirp. "I can't figure out how to change the ringer tone," she said as Malcolm rolled his eyes at the foolish sound.

"Hello...Hi, Dad...No, what is it?...What the hell!...But what has he got to do with this?...No, that's okay. We're done here." She looked over at Malcolm's empty plates. "At least I don't think Malcolm is going to eat any more right now. Sure, I'll get Laura, and the three of us will meet you at the church."

Malcolm tapped her on the shoulder and pointed to the phone. She handed it to him.

"Benjamin, since I've got the car, why don't I swing by and pick up you and Ayalla. I'll call her now...About twenty minutes." He snapped the phone closed. "So what's going on?" He grabbed the check, threw down some money, and they headed for the lobby. Laura was already there waiting.

"I figured you'd want to leave right away," she said, swinging her small leather backpack over her shoulder. "Your father said we'd better meet him."

"Dad got a call a few minutes ago from Archbishop Johnston," Connor explained to Malcolm. "Some monsignor from Rome was apparently murdered earlier this morning, while he was a patient at a local hospital."

"He was killed *in* the hospital?"

"That's what the preliminary investigation indicates. And the reason he was in the hospital is that he says he got mugged right outside Father Rosario's church in Santa Ana."

"Does Johnston know him?" asked Malcolm.

"Yes, he does. He told Dad that this monsignor came to California specifically to complain about Father Rosario's historical research."

"Don't tell me. Malleus Caelistis rears its ugly head again."

"Could be. Dad obviously didn't want to go into much detail on the cell phone. We'll get more when we see him."

Malcolm headed down the sidewalk toward the street where he'd parked Benjamin's rental car. Laura waved at the car jockey as he trotted toward them. "You don't have the keys to our car in your cabinet," she explained. "We got back so late there was no one on duty. I parked it over by the wall so it wouldn't be in the way."

He reached for the keys in her hand. "No problem. I'll bring it up for you."

"We'll get it."

The young man smiled. "Oh, no, ma'am. It's my job to get the cars. The manager would kill me if I let guests wander around the lot."

"Lawsuits waiting to happen," smiled Connor.

He looked a little sheepish. "Something like that. Some people say you aren't a real Californian until you have a convertible, a therapist, a juice habit, and a lawsuit against someone."

The attendant dashed across the parking lot to where their convertible was parked. They saw him open the door, but he didn't get in right away. He finally leaned into the car, did something, then slid into the driver's seat. Still, he didn't start the car right away. Laura was about to head over to see what was wrong when the engine roared to life and he covered the 100 yards that separated them in record time. Laura came around to the driver's side and was startled by the young man's appearance. He looked ashen despite his dark, tanned complexion.

"What's wrong?" she asked.

"There was some stuff on the seat. I...um...put it in the litterbag."

"Stuff," Laura repeated, puzzled. "I didn't leave anything on the seat last night."

"Maybe someone's playing a joke or something." The attendant still looked nauseous.

Laura peered into the car, but all she could see was the white plastic bag. "What was it?"

"It was like, bones or something, and they were dirty. I brushed the seat off, but…" he looked down at his hands. "It's some weird kind of dirt—it sticks to you."

"Bones?" Laura looked over the roof of the car at Connor. "They must be something else. But why would someone put whatever it is in our car? Besides, I locked it last night."

"It was still locked, ma'am." He backed away from the car, still wiping his hands on his pants. "Like I said, maybe someone's idea of a joke. I gotta go."

"Wait," said Laura, fishing a five-dollar bill out of her pocket. "I'm sorry you had to deal with that."

He took the money almost reluctantly. "It's okay, I guess. I gotta go wash up before I get any more cars." He walked briskly around the corner of the hotel.

"What the hell was that all about?" said Connor, who had opened her door and was staring at the bag.

"I don't know." Laura sat in the driver's seat and picked up the bag gingerly to peek inside. "I can't see them very well, but they do look like bones." She carefully reached inside, trying not to touch the pieces of paper smeared with the fine black dust that had been all over the lot attendant's hands. She withdrew a small whitish object. "I'd say this could be a finger bone," she decided.

"Human anatomy another specialty you haven't mentioned?" said Connor.

"Just a couple of premed classes I took while I was enthralled with life drawing. I was sure if I could dissect the human body and see the insides, I would automatically be a brilliant artist."

"And?"

"You never see me doing any drawing, do you?"

"No."

"That's because I wasn't the least bit brilliant, and the labs for anatomy class weren't the least bit artistic. I barely managed not to toss my cookies. I ended up watching videos of dissections instead. So I'm fairly sure this is a metacarpal bone, but don't quote me."

"All right, Dr. Nez. But how about a theory on why we have a meta-carpal bone in our car?"

"Bones."

"What?"

"Bones, plural," she said, looking into the bag.

"All right, then. Do you have a theory about why we have human *bones* in our rental car?"

Laura scowled at the object held delicately between her fingers. "Nope. But I can't say it fills me with optimism."

"No way to tell how old they are."

"Not without my Tom Mix carbon-dating kit. Left that back home."

"Did you know you get a little sarcastic when you're scared?"

"Yep. And so do you, my love. That's probably the main reason we were attracted to each other—we do snide humor in the face of disaster."

A car horn sounded behind them, signifying that a new and impatient guest had arrived. Laura dropped the bone back in the bag and noticed with annoyance that despite her efforts, she'd gotten some of the black dirt on her wrist. She rubbed at it with her thumb. "Geez, the guy's right. This stuff is almost greasy. Hand me a tissue out of the glove box, will you?"

Connor obliged with a tissue as Laura put the car in gear and pulled to the end of the driveway. She stopped and scrubbed at her skin with the tissue. Most of it came off. "All right, we'd better get going." She looked both ways and turned left onto Pacific Coast Highway.

"I don't suppose we ought to call the police about this."

"We could end up standing around here all day while they decide whether to do a full crime-scene investigation, then figure out whether we're murder suspects or cannibals disguised as a prosperous lesbian couple. Besides, I don't think those bones are all that recent."

"Hunch?"

"Sort of. I get kind of an 'old vibe' of them."

" 'Old vibe'?" Connor repeated, raising an eyebrow. "That would be the scientific term?"

"That would be the Twilight Zone term."

"Okey-dokey, then. We'll just put these in the trunk and ask our associates what they think."

"Good. Then we'll be reporting it not only to the police in the person of Malcolm Jefferson but also to the feds, represented by Ms. Franklin. That way we've done the CYA routine without ending up in yet another police station."

Connor grimaced at the memory of her encounter with the charming Detective Consadine but held her tongue on the subject of federal agents. She switched gears. "So what is going on with this monsignor from Rome?"

»——«

Richard La Cloche had entirely abandoned the pseudonym Ricky Bell. He now carried complete identification (that would stand up to reasonable scrutiny) in the name of Father Francis Lemarteau, a Catholic priest from Louisiana. The soft Cajun accent he had trained out of himself—and rarely used intentionally—came in handy as one of Father Lemarteau's most engaging personal characteristics, along with the subtle gray at the temples of his dark-brown hair and the eyes so dark they reflected ambient light.

He watched with satisfaction as the two women sat in their car at the end of the hotel driveway. He imagined the fear and loathing his little message must have caused, and once again marveled that God had put this old enemy in his path so that all accounts could be settled. He didn't care about the long-haired one, but he already harbored nasty suspicions about what these two were to each other. They were staying in the same room, a room that was equipped only with one king-size bed. And a full night's work at his computer had netted him a sheaf of printouts with hundreds of details, large and small, of Connor Hawthorne's life. He knew her father was an ex-U.S. senator, and he'd learned from a photo caption in *The Washington Post* the full name of the tall black man who'd been at the archbishop's house—Malcolm Jefferson.

Finding where the Hawthorne witch was staying had been child's play. And people really thought their lives were private. He smiled. The bones had once belonged to the old voudun woman in New Orleans. And the black greasy powder, well, that was another surprise for the heathen sinners.

He fingered the cross around his neck. As Father Lemarteau, he preferred wearing the Roman collar. But there was no sense spooking his quarry this late in the game. They might be getting a little nervous around priests, and who could blame them? Except for the traitors, priests were, after all, the front line of true believers, the defenders of the true faith.

He saw the convertible move out. He started the engine of his rented Infiniti and pulled into traffic behind them. The luxury car was absurdly ostentatious, but he certainly didn't stand out in Laguna Beach, which was the point. Now that he knew his enemies, he would stay close to them when necessary. Connor Hawthorne and her little group of meddlers were no more than flimsy obstacles in his march toward Armageddon.

»——«

Their footsteps echoed in the silence of the church. At first the sanctuary appeared empty, but then Connor heard the murmur of voices and in the dim light picked out the heads and shoulders of four people sitting in the pews nearest the altar. She and Laura walked down the center aisle to where Benjamin, Malcolm, Ayalla, and Archbishop Johnston were seated.

Benjamin greeted them briefly, then said, "I asked the archbishop to hold off on telling us about what happened at the hospital early this morning so you could hear everything as well."

Connor and Laura slid in next to Benjamin. The archbishop stood up and faced them, his back to the altar. Connor found her eyes straying to the altar screen, a stunning example of the woodcarver's art; its gilded surfaces gleamed softly in the glow of dozens of votive candles set in metal racks. They flickered, row upon row, in muted remembrance of the dead, or in prayerful supplication for the blessings of Mother Mary.

"A short time ago, I got a call from the same detectives who are working on Father Rosario's murder. Monsignor Johann Kursk was smothered to death in his hospital room early this morning. As I already told Mr. Hawthorne, Kursk was sent from Rome. He is assigned to the Congregation for the Defense of Doctrine, and he brought letters from his superiors demanding that Father Rosario cease his research and turn over all of his materials and any artifacts he might have in his possession."

"Artifacts?" questioned Benjamin. "There weren't any objects in the boxes you gave us, only notes and some original historical documents."

"I don't know exactly what Kursk was fishing for," shrugged the archbishop. "And I don't think he did either. But the wording was specific about artifacts. Someone in Rome, probably Cardinal de Marcos, is convinced Enrique's father brought something back from his last trip to Italy, something his son may have sent him to find."

"If he did, presumably he got it through customs somehow," suggested Ayalla. "Did it have something to do with Malleus Caelistis?" Her voice startled Connor, who had been so intent on watching the archbishop and speculating as to whether he was withholding anything, she lost track of the people seated on either side of her.

"No," said the archbishop. "And I don't think we need to keep pursuing that particular avenue. If there is indeed something that the elder Rosario found, it might be connected to the Cult of Magdalene that we talked about. Enrique must have discovered more specific information than he shared with me, and perhaps he sent his father there, knowing that the Vatican would certainly keep track of Enrique's comings and goings."

"But what is it?" asked Malcolm.

"And where is it?" added Laura.

"I don't know the answer to either question, but let's back up for a minute. Monsignor Kursk tried to break into the rectory very early yesterday evening, just after dark."

"He admitted to breaking and entering?" Malcolm asked.

"No, he wouldn't admit it, the gutless wonder. And he would have succeeded in searching Father Rosario's office, except someone either hit him over the head, or he simply fell trying to get in through a window. The police responded quickly when a patrol car found Kursk sitting on the curb out front holding his head in his hands. Because of what happened to Enrique, they searched the church and the rectory and found a basement window jimmied open. Given Kursk's condition, they took his fingerprints and matched them to ones on the window and in the basement."

"Not a very smart burglar," said Malcolm.

"Not a very smart *anything*," growled the archbishop. "His only talent is—I should say *was*—intimidation and being an all-purpose snoop." He paused. "Forgive me for speaking ill of the dead."

"Did he find anything at the rectory?"

"I don't think so. By the time he got back outside, though, vandals or thieves had stripped his rental car, and he sat down on the curb trying to decide what to do. That's when the cops found him. They called me, and I went to see him this morning."

"Then what happened?" asked Connor.

"I had it out with him. He prevaricated in his usual way but kept tripping over his own story. I think he was simply being overzealous in trying to carry out the instructions from his superiors at the Vatican."

"What about Ricky Bell?" asked Ayalla.

"Who?"

"Ricky Bell, our suspect."

"Oh, yes, the one you believe has sent terrorist threats supposedly under the aegis of Malleus Caelistis. No, I didn't think to ask about that, and I still don't believe there's any connection with these deaths. Kursk seemed torn between being outraged and being terrified. But I don't know what he would be so scared of."

"Why wouldn't he be nervous if Malleus Caelistis is involved in this?" commented Benjamin. "He might have had good reason to be scared of them."

The archbishop turned on Benjamin. "First of all, as I've already told you, I don't believe Malleus Caelistis still exists in any recognizable form, and I certain don't believe anyone associated with our church is involved in the murder of Enrique Rosario. In fact, I choose not to lend any credence whatsoever to that theory. No matter how far right some of the Curia's politics may be, these are still *priests* we're talking about. They would not commit a murder, and they would not commit the ultimate sacrilege of butchering a fellow priest in his own church. That simply did *not* happen." Johnston's face was bright red.

Laura stood up and went to him. "Sir, I know you love your church, and that you honor the truth. But there may be some people who aren't willing to acknowledge a truth they don't like. It threatens them. And there also may be a few who are willing to do anything they believe necessary to protect something they cherish. Who knows what drives a particular human being at times? I doubt that even Catholic priests are immune to human temptation."

Johnston looked at her strangely for a moment, then patted her shoulder. "I'm sorry," he said, finally. "It's a little eerie that I said almost exactly those words to Enrique just a couple of days ago." He sighed. "There are times any man would just as soon put on blinders so he doesn't have to see unpleasant reminders of human nature, but I guess I don't have that luxury."

Laura smiled. "I have to say I don't share the notion that all humans are tempted to do bad things, Father. I don't believe we're all sinful by nature. But I do believe in the existence of evil. And some individuals are guided by evil. The most frightening occurrence of it, though, isn't when people kill out of greed and cruelty, but when they kill in the name of God."

Johnston met her eyes and nodded. "You are correct. That is the ultimate hypocrisy. But Kursk was adamant that murder would never be sanctioned by anyone in the church."

"And you believed him?" asked Laura, returning to her seat.

Archbishop Johnston closed his eyes and stared up toward the choir loft at the rear of the church. "Not entirely. I wanted to, but I can't be sure."

"So the cause of death was suffocation," said Malcolm.

"Yes, and it was a little sloppy. That Detective Consadine said a smart killer would have just slipped something into the IV line attached to Kursk. Instead the killer used a pillow and there may be lots of…what did they call it…?"

"Trace evidence," offered Ayalla.

"Yes."

"The killer couldn't have known for sure that Kursk would be hooked up to an IV," said Connor. "But he knew a pillow would make a handy weapon. It's quiet, and the odds are there's going to be at least a few in a hospital room."

"I suppose," said the archbishop, and his whole body seemed to sag slightly. "But as much as he annoyed me, I didn't want him dead. And I certainly don't understand exactly why all this is happening. That's why I called Mr. Hawthorne. I don't think the police have any concept of what might be involved."

"Have you told them about Malleus Caelistis?" asked Connor.

He took a deep breath, then exhaled noisily. "I couldn't do it. I tried, I considered it. I even think Consadine thought I was hiding something, and he's hardly the sharpest tool in the box—"

"Amen to that," said Connor.

The archbishop nodded at her and forced a small smile. "But something held me back. Besides, I didn't think he'd believe me anyway."

"It's best to follow your instincts," said Malcolm. "And maybe this guy isn't very trustworthy. Who knows? Laura and Connor didn't find Consadine very reassuring either."

"He isn't interested in anything unless it can help him close a case, one way or the other."

"So what's his theory on this?"

"From what I could tell, he's decided that whether or not Kursk tried to get into the rectory is irrelevant. He says the monsignor was assaulted by whoever vandalized the car and was too afraid to describe them. One of the attackers then decided to come to the hospital and finish the job so he couldn't identify them later on."

"And he doesn't see any connection with the murder of Father Rosario?" asked Malcolm, his face a study in disgust.

"No, according to the detective, that was a separate incident, an attempt to rob the church."

"And most thieves walk around with stakes and hand-painted wooden hammers," said Connor, sarcasm etched into the words, "in case they need to kill someone in an unusual and shocking fashion."

"I agree with Connor," said Ayalla, swiveling in her seat to face them. "The cop's obviously an idiot and isn't going to pursue any other leads."

Connor, surprised at the FBI agent's agreement with anything she had to say, cast a glance at Laura, who shrugged and scratched at the patch of dirt on the wrist she hadn't yet had time to wash.

Benjamin nodded. "Maybe we have the only leads worth pursuing. Question is, what are they?"

"Ricky Bell," said Ayalla. "Although the man is like a ghost. Hard to believe someone could move around without leaving a single trace, but he certainly appears to do just that."

"Why don't we head over to your field office?" said Malcolm. "I need to make some phone calls and check out a few things. From everything I've heard about the local detective, I don't think I'm going to get anywhere working with him."

"That's fine. And I'll get in touch with INS. Maybe it's worth checking out when Father Rosario's father went to Italy."

"Yes," said Connor, having made the decision to match courtesies with the FBI agent. "It would at least give us a time frame for when this elusive artifact might have come into the priest's possession."

"I want to focus on Enrique's research notes," said Benjamin. "I've only had time to glance through them. But I want to quickly catalog what's there. Archbishop, would you help me? You're much more conversant with his work."

"Yes, I'd be glad to. But right now I have some other business to attend to. There's the matter of Monsignor Kursk. I have some calls to make to his offices in Rome, and there's the time difference to consider. It's already early evening there."

"Of course. Call my hotel this evening. I suggest we all meet at some point and do some brainstorming. There's something about all this that seems—"

"Seems what, Dad?"

Benjamin frowned. "Preparatory," he finally said.

"Preparatory to what, Senator?" asked Ayalla.

"If I knew the answer to that," said Benjamin, "I'd sleep a lot better tonight."

»—«

Outside the church, they watched the archbishop get into his car and drive away. Malcolm and Ayalla would take the rental sedan to the FBI field office in Santa Ana. Connor and Laura offered to drop Benjamin at the hotel. He opened the trunk of the Buick to get the boxes of Enrique's research materials.

"You brought those *with* you?" Connor asked in surprise.

"Since two Catholic priests have died in the last few days, both of whom were connected to these papers, I decided to keep them close."

"But someone could easily have stolen them out of the car," said Ayalla.

Laura smiled. "If I know my sometime employer, he took precautions."

Ayalla frowned. "What, you mean a car alarm? These American rental sedans don't usually come with an alarm."

"True," said Benjamin, "which is why I always bring my own." He detached a pair of wires from the trunk latch. The wires ran into a long black plastic tube with large plastic circles at each end that looked somewhat like loudspeakers. He plucked the device from the trunk.

"How did you disarm it with just the standard trunk key?" asked the FBI agent.

Benjamin reached into his pocket and withdrew a small keypad. "Arming and disarming. And if anyone had messed with the lock at all, or even leaned hard against the car, it would have sounded like World War III around here. You wouldn't believe the volume."

"Most people don't pay much attention to car alarms," she said doubtfully. "Or even recorded warnings."

"You're right. But this produces the sound of automatic weapons fire. And it's extremely realistic. Besides, I'd only need thirty seconds or so to get outside. This little keypad vibrates the instant the alarm is set off—in the very unlikely event we didn't hear the loudspeakers."

Ayalla looked at him quizzically. "Do you always carry around gadgets like that?"

"Only when I think they might come in handy," Benjamin shrugged. "You never know when you might need to protect your transportation or secure a car trunk."

"Speaking of car trunks," said Connor. "We have something in ours that is right out of *Tales from the Crypt*. Someone left us a 'present' in our car last night."

Her father immediately turned serious. "What are you talking about?"

Malcolm bristled visibly. "Someone broke into your car?" And you didn't tell us."

"Chill, big guy," Connor smiled. "The least little thing happens, and you go all supercop on me."

Laura walked toward the convertible, parked behind the Buick. "I can't say for sure that someone broke in. I thought I locked the doors last night, but I was dead on my feet when we got in. The parking lot attendant found some stuff on the seat. She opened the trunk and removed the plastic bag they'd placed there earlier when they arrived at the church. Malcolm, Benjamin, and Ayalla huddled around her. "I did touch one of these briefly, but I think maybe you should just peek in. The black stuff doesn't want to come off your skin." She scrubbed her wrist against her jeans.

"What the hell are these?" said Malcolm.

"Near as I can tell, though I could be wrong, they're finger bones from a fairly small person."

"Finger bones? We're looking at another murder?"

Laura put her hand on his arm. "Not unless it's a very, very old unsolved case. The bones are dry, white, chalky, and very brittle. And I think they're pretty old."

"How old?" asked Ayalla.

"There's no way to be certain without testing," said Laura. "But I have a hunch these may have been around a long time."

"A hunch," said Ayalla, a hint of skepticism in her voice as she peered into the bag at the white fragments.

But Laura didn't appear to take offense. "Yep. Something tells me these were very significant to someone who saved them for a long time. But beyond that, I don't have anything scientific to back up my feelings."

Connor was prepared to fend off the FBI agent's derision. She opened her mouth, but then stopped. Instead of discounting Laura's theory, Ayalla appeared to be considering it. "Could be," she said. "Do you want me to send these to a government lab for analysis?"

Benjamin intervened. "I think we'd better sit on them for now. Yes, I'd like them analyzed, but let's face it, there's no federal case to tie these to. You'd be questioned about using resources without a reason."

"True," said Ayalla. "So far nothing has happened that's really in my jurisdiction. Still…"

"We'll get to it," said Benjamin. He opened a fat briefcase that lay in the trunk and pulled out a large heavy-duty plastic bag. Gingerly he eased the entire litterbag and its gruesome contents into the clear evidence container.

"And you also happen to carry around evidence bags," said Ayalla, raising one eyebrow.

"As I said, you never know what you'll need," smiled Benjamin. "If you and Laura don't mind, Connor, I'll hang onto these."

"Be my guest, Dad. I have no burning desire to keep bones in the glove compartment *or* the trunk."

Malcolm still looked frustrated. "Aren't we going to at least discuss what message someone is trying to send you?"

They all stared at each other for a moment until Laura spoke. "Connor and I talked about it on the way over. We assume, naturally, that it has something to do with the murder of Father Rosario, but what message? If someone wanted to communicate, this hasn't accomplished telling us much."

"Unless it's that they have a very macabre sense of humor," added Connor.

"Malcolm, I don't like this any more than you do, but I don't see what we can do about it at the moment." said Benjamin.

"At least if we could have them analyzed…"

"Which probably wouldn't tell us much of anything."

"All right. But I'd feel better if Connor and Laura stayed at our hotel."

"So you can keep an eye on us?" Laura smiled.

"Yes."

"The sentiment is much appreciated, Captain, but we'll be fine. If we need help, I'll send up a flare."

"Lot of good that'll do," he growled.

"You'd be amazed," she said, and hugged him.

They transferred the boxes from the Buick to the convertible. Benjamin tucked the evidence bag containing the bones into one of the boxes. Malcolm and Ayalla set off for the FBI office, and Laura and Connor headed for the Hilton to drop Benjamin off.

"Malcolm said you had a dream, Laura" said Benjamin as soon as they were all buckled in and Connor pulled the car out of the space.

"News travels fast," she said without turning to look at him.

"Malcolm mentioned it briefly on the way out of the church. Anything you want to tell me?"

"Sure. But I don't know if it has any particular significance."

"He said Grandmother Klah was in it."

"True."

"I like that old lady a lot," he said. "And not just because she saved my life forty years ago. So where is she?"

"Physically, I have no idea. Metaphysically, she's apparently been hanging out in the Dreamtime."

"She came to warn you about something?"

"Probably. Though she was as cryptic and maddening as ever."

Benjamin chuckled. "Talking with her is a challenge, but she never says anything unless there's a point to it."

"Would that the rest of the population would follow her example," added Connor. "If only every person in the world would know to shut off their mouths when their brains are in neutral."

"We all gotta babble sometimes, sweetheart," said Laura. "Even you."

"Never," laughed Connor. "Now tell him about the dream."

For the next few minutes, Laura went through the story again. Benjamin listened attentively, and Connor knew her father's habit of making precise mental notes. His facility for calling up details still astounded her.

"So we've got an unknown figure in the dream who was too far away to distinguish but didn't seem threatening. And then we have another figure, also dressed like a priest, who definitely did seem dangerous and spoke to you."

"And the part before that," Laura said, "might not be important, the image of standing in the field of stubble and weeds. But there was that feeling of familiarity."

Benjamin thought about it for a moment. "The colonnade you

described, with all archways and pillars. And perhaps a rural setting. Hmm."

"The only structures I can think of in this part of the country that might match that description are the old Catholic missions. They were often built in a traditional cloister design. Why don't you and Connor check out some of the missions around here?"

"How do we know it's one that's close by? That arcade could have been from a church in Europe."

He put a hand on Laura's shoulder. "Can you imagine for a moment that your grandmother would send you on a wild goose chase? If you were led into that dream image while you're here in California, then there has to be someplace here to which that image corresponds. Stands to reason. Grandmother Klah doesn't waste her time."

"Couldn't hurt to look," said Laura. "Next stop, a bookstore. We need a guide."

"I thought we already had one or two," said Connor, the corners of her mouth turning up.

Laura shrugged matter-of-factly. "Yes, we have several of the invisible kind. But they don't quite grasp the concept of freeways. They give great spiritual guidance but lousy directions."

"There are times when I'm not sure whether you're serious or you're kidding."

"That keeps the magic in our relationship, my love. I have to keep you guessing at least some of the time."

"Why's that?"

"You love a mystery."

"I don't know about that, but I do love you."

"Okay, okay Enough of the mushy stuff. There's a tough, insensitive macho male back here."

"Gee, Dad...macho? I haven't seen you spit tobacco or scratch yourself all day."

Laura burst out laughing. "That picture is so entirely absurd, I can't even picture it." Benjamin, though proven tough under fire, was an urbane and courteous gentleman unless circumstances required him to be otherwise.

"Hey," he said. "I can fit in with my more earthy brethren."

"I'm sure you could," said Connor with a grin. "But I'd just as soon you didn't practice on us."

"If you insist," he answered, his eyes twinkling. "And if you'll take a right at the next light, you can drop me off around back of the hotel. A little less public, I think."

"You think there's surveillance?"

"I have no idea, but I'd rather err on the side of caution. Besides, I thought I saw you checking your mirrors fairly often."

"Safe driving."

"Right."

Connor stopped the car and got out to let Benjamin exit the backseat. Then she popped the trunk and asked him if he wanted help carrying them inside.

"Nope, your old dad can make it."

She kissed him on the cheek. "I love you too, you know."

Connor quickly got back behind the wheel and after seeing Benjamin inside the door of the hotel, pulled away.

"He was right on the money," she said to Laura.

"About what?"

"I was checking the mirror, and I think someone was following us."

"Are they still?"

"I don't know, but I think we'll take some detours and see what happens."

"And then we'll search for the missions?"

"Then we'll search for *your* mission."

Chapter Seventeen

All mankind is of one Author, and is one volume;
when one man dies, one chapter is not torn out of the book,
but translated into a better language.
—John Donne

Benjamin laid aside the notebook and took off his glasses. His eyes were starting to burn from deciphering so much bad handwriting, but the reading had been fascinating enough that he hadn't even thought of taking a break. When he looked at the clock, it was late afternoon. The time had been well spent. He picked up the loose pages that he had put aside and read the first sheet again. These were harder to read than some of the other notes, if only because Father Rosario had clearly struggled with the translation as well as the original author's handwriting. In many cases he had been reluctant to settle on one word or another, and had left optional choices in brackets. But Benjamin understood that there were fine nuances to the art of translation that went well beyond the substitution of a word in one language for its corresponding word in another. Idiom, culture, and even slang had to be taken into account. He could not tell how closely Rosario had gotten to the true meaning because the originals from which he'd worked were not in the files.

Title: Personal journal entry of Father Jose Maria Canara,
Senior religious of Santa Maria de Los Angeles in 1792
Prelim. Trans. by E. Rosario

*I am troubled by the cardinal's letter. It seems I must have a
spy among the brothers here. There are one or two likely culprits
[translation?] who do not approve of the thoughts I express to
them and to the [natives? Aboriginals?] we teach here. Perhaps
I am too careless in revealing my true faith. Holy Mother guides
me in all that I am and do, but it is often difficult to disguise my
true [real, inner?] self. If I go too far, I will be called back to
Toledo, or worse. The thought of what happened in Spain still
makes cold my blood.*

*If I leave, I will miss these gentle people. Their beliefs are
not always in agreement with the church, yet I sense in them a
peaceful acceptance of other human beings that is no longer to
be found in our own doctrines. Sometimes I think they are
more amused by us than anything. Our customs are indeed
strange. But we so seldom try to see ourselves from another
view [angle?]. We do so many things out of habit, or simply
because we have made arbitrary decisions about what must be.
So we wear our long woolen robes even in this oppressive summer heat, and we do not stop our work, except for prayer, from
sunrise to sunset. There is almost no laughter here, at least
among the brothers. It is as if most of them actually believe that
to feel delight or simple joy [contentment?] would offend God.
Yet I believe that joyous laughter and even merriment are gifts
from God. The native people here celebrate with dancing and
singing, though it seems to me more like chanting. In fact, if the
brothers were to consider a comparison, their chants are not
entirely unlike our own, or those of the Benedictines, which I
once heard in a church in Barcelona.*

*I know in my heart these people were happier before we
came. Yet we convince ourselves they would have died without
our help. We consider that we have civilized them because we*

went to great lengths to make them stop wandering through the hills and settle in one spot. We pretend to encourage their independence, yet we teach them that to obey us and the soldiers is the same thing as obeying God. For Spain, our work is part of the process of claiming this land for the King. Small wonder that the salaries of the friars are paid from the funds set aside for war.

I don't believe these people would have died without us, though there are other threats to their sovereignty. And someday they will probably die at the hands of those who will fight to claim this land. So I must ask, even though we brought the word of God to those who did not know it, have we truly saved them? Is it better to be a civilized subject of the King or a free man? I find myself thinking, God forgive me, that at least they would have died in a state of natural happiness [innocence?], *even grace, if we had not come here.*

They once ignored us. But since their poverty has become so oppressive, they look to us for charity and my fellow monks insist that there be promises riding in the same wagon [conditions attached to the charity? strings?] *They would have the men, women, and children kneel and repent and—Mother God, turn away your sight from this shame—beg for the bread and grains we give them. It hurts my heart to the core when I see it. But if I refuse to follow the recommendations of our superiors, my days here will become even fewer.*

My friend in Barcelona wrote to me again. He is quite sure now…IT is lost to us, perhaps for all time to come. His search has been fraught with danger, yet he persisted. He traveled to Italy and says that he is sure the chain was broken. The successor appointed to [destined to] become the next keeper was killed on the road to his new post. My heart is heavy [leaden?] *with grief. If IT is lost, I think perhaps we are lost.*

Here, Father Rosario had written in the margin, "What is IT?" The word 'IT' was underscored heavily. He had clearly been frustrated by the old missionary's ambiguity, but Benjamin understood, as Father Rosario probably did also, that the author of the journal was highly reluctant to write down much that was specific.

When I was first initiated [why not ordained?] *by those who came before me, I was filled with wonder at the love and radiance of the upper* [higher?] *way. I have never lost completely my connection with the Holy Spirit that is in us all, and yet I stumble with fatigue and I wonder if it is all for nothing that we have kept the vows to carry it unto the children's children until two times a thousand years have passed...again it troubles me, for I know not what will become of us and all humans without that which was given to us in sacred covenant. I pray daily that the true words of the beloved teacher Immanuel, in the body of Yeshua, will see the light of dawn and penetrate the darkness in the hearts of men.* [Is he referring to Jesus Christ? Why 'in the body of'?]

I most assuredly will live until that day, though perhaps I will have returned by then and will be made aware of my lives by our Mother. No matter: The prophecy will be fulfilled by another who will come long after I have returned to the mind [consciousness?] *of God. Yet if the last keeper died, and IT has been lost for over a hundred years, what hope have we left?*

Still, I must believe that in all that has transpired there is the will and order of God. Somehow the words will be revealed, the lies will be uncovered, and the light of truth will shine. I have been told of the true teachings of Immanuel, though the true form of those words grow more uncertain with each generation. Unlike the church, which now holds sway and puts its written words in print [publishes?] *to all, we were sworn never to write down what we learned from the wisdom of Mother Mary and the apostle whose name is not spoken. We are taught that the day will come when the truest source will be revealed.*

Immanuel taught our ancestors that humankind would struggle with the burden imposed by false teachings. He said there would be founders of religions, and those religions would eventually be rife with falsehood and misunderstanding because

the Apostles themselves did not understand their teacher's words.
They heard what they wished to hear or believe. All but one. All
but one precious voice. Will it ever be heard again?

I grow tired, and the days at this time of year are so many
hours long that sleep is not sufficient. The morning bell finds
me hardly able to move my stiff limbs. Perhaps I am getting
old, after all.

Following entry, dated two weeks later:

Yesterday a young girl who sweeps the chapel of the Holy
Mother shyly asked me a question. She wanted to know if the
statue behind the altar was the same personage as the one
depicted in the carving she wore around her neck, hidden
beneath her cotton shift. I looked closely at the amulet. The fig-
ure was of a female deity of ample proportions and not covered
sufficiently for modesty. My first reaction was to remonstrate
with her for practicing idolatry. But I held back the words [kept
silent] and looked from the tiny figure to the carving of the
Holy Mother, and then to the shining face of the young girl.
Again, I looked at all three. And I did not chide the girl.
Instead, as no one was around to hear me and perhaps report
on my unseemly behavior, I looked at her and said, "They are
the same divine being, my child." She smiled such a beautiful
smile. I knew that I had given the answer that God would have
me give.

Benjamin laid aside the translation for a moment and rubbed his
eyes. He tried to imagine what life had been like for the troubled priest
who had lost his faith, if not in a Supreme Creator, then certainly in the
leaders of his own church. The risks he undertook were hardly incon-
sequential. If his journal had been discovered, for instance, he would
have faced certain disgrace, official censure, and even excommunication. What had prompted him to abandon the teachings drilled into
him by the often grim priestly instructors of his day?

Curious to see what became of the disenchanted friar, Benjamin returned to the document.

Last entry, dated four months later:

My work here is over, though it is not done. I wish I could continue, but it is not to be. The emissary of the cardinal arrived unexpectedly and said he is taking charge of Santa Maria. I can see that he is a man who does not bend. Already he has announced new rules of behavior for the brothers, who already work very hard, and, even worse, he has said our mission has received yet another grant of land from the King and native people will be required to tend and gather the new crops. He brought with him more soldiers, and I fear the punishments they may mete out to the innocents I so wanted to teach about the grace and goodness of the Holy One. Now they will only fear rather than love God.

My only solace in this time is the angel. She has come to me three times during my hours of quiet contemplation, and she has said that I must not lose faith. The truth is not lost but will come to light at the time it is prophesied. I asked the angel what would happen after that. She shook her head, and I felt a strange combining of hope and sadness in the aura that washed over me.

I have been told to return to Spain, and I pretended to acquiesce, to remain obedient to the church and to the king who defends our faith. But I have made a decision not to go back. There is nothing left for me there, and though my heart cries out at the melting away [dissolution] of my bond with the brothers here, I will cease from this day onward to be one of them. I will leave here before dawn and seek to dwell only as a common man. I will use my small skills in healing in the service of my fellow humans. From there, God will show me the way.

Tonight I saw the young girl who wears the image of female deity around her neck. She was walking down the road near the stables and carried a small bundle. Several other natives walked with her. She looked at me sadly. "We go north, Father," she said. "It will be better."

I asked her why. The weather has turned colder these past few days. I feared for their safety if they found no home before winter set in. She said, "The Lady, she told me to leave here...she has told you to go."

I did not know if she meant this last as a question. I sensed it was not, and she gazed at me as if I would understand...I did.

I will hide this private account away where it will probably never be found, at least not until the walls of this place have finally crumbled into dust. But this is the message given me by the angel, that I must leave my story behind. If someone else is meant to read it, then surely the hand of God will guide his steps.

—J.M.C.

Benjamin shivered. The last part still made the hairs stand up on the back of his neck. How had Enrique discovered this document? Had he somehow been guided to it? And, if so, why? Benjamin opened the other box. He was determined to make the pieces fit together into some sort of coherent picture, and he was just beginning to experience that oddly queasy sensation that usually meant he needed to hurry.

»—«

Richard La Cloche, now fully immersed in his role as Father Lemarteau, checked into the hotel where Benjamin Hawthorne, Malcolm Jefferson, and Ayalla Franklin were staying. He had considered the Laguna Beach hotel so he could keep better tabs on the two women, but, as he asked himself, why would a Catholic priest stay at an expensive beach-front inn? Since he could possibly seem out of place there, he rejected the notion. In all these years, he'd remained invisible by developing a keen instinct for what people noticed and what they didn't. A Hilton hotel, on the other hand, would be suitably anonymous and reasonably affordable for a clergyman.

He also had decided to go with clerical garb, at least part of the time. Another fact of human perception—people saw the black shirt and especially the Roman collar but rarely registered the features of the man who wore it. To them he appeared as a generic priest. Catholics usually addressed him, and would say "Hello, Father." Protestants, on the other hand, rarely spoke, but would have called him "Reverend." Either way, people just weren't that anxious to interact with a man of the cloth. He understood. Considering that the vast majority of them were unrepentant sinners, who could blame them for shying away from one of those who would someday judge them in a harsh light.

Father Lemarteau was anxious to test his new appearance on someone who had met him in the past, so he arranged a brief encounter with the big policeman who was apparently investigating Malleus Caelistis. No doubt some of the threats he'd sent to confuse the bureaucrats and obscure his true intentions had found their way to the man's desk and the cop had remembered his previous encounter with Ricky Bell. But the cop hardly noticed the priest who stood next to him on the hotel elevator.

Father Lemarteau was pleased with the way his plans were progressing. The only question that remained was the timing, and that had not yet been revealed to him. The dreams were more vivid with each passing day. The single voice that spoke to him was at once soothing and intimidating. Yet he felt no real fear. He knew that his destiny had brought him this far. As the son of a prostitute and a hypocrite preacher, his life should by all rights have been a short and tragic story. And yet he had not only survived unscathed but would emerge victorious. He would lead the way to the Apocalypse that even now hovered a few short days away. He trembled at the thought. He could hear the angel's voice, even now when he closed his eyes and let the sound of the ocean lull him. *"We are one and the same, you and I. We are the beginning and the end, the alpha and the omega. We are united in death and in life. You are me made flesh in the world. As I command, so shall it be done."*

He had only come to understand that voice in the last few years.

Before that, he was troubled by blackouts and confusion and even the tendency to plan poorly at times. Fortunately, God had delivered him from his human weakness and protected him from those who would have ruined his work and perhaps even deprived him of his freedom forever. Now the angel was with him constantly, and once, when in a dream he had looked into an old, scratched mirror, another face had looked back at him—a face with eyes black as coal, each pupil outlined in flickering tongues of fire. This was not only his angel, but his alter ego, his true self.

From that moment he had known that someday he would be freed from the shackles of human form once and for all. He would no longer be Richard La Cloche, or Ricky Bell, or even Father Francis Lemarteau. Instead, he would be in form and in power the archangel of all archangels. He himself would lead the Four Horsemen and scourge the sinners from their comfortable homes and playgrounds. He would sit at the right hand of the Father as they passed before him to receive final judgment. The Divine Hammer of God would fall on the anvil of this pathetic little planet. He was about to fire the first shot in a war that evil could not possibly win.

»—«

Ayalla returned to the small conference room where she'd left Malcolm poring over the file on Ricky Bell. It wasn't a thick one, which was highly unusual, given the ability of the FBI to gather reams of information on even the most innocuous and harmless individuals. The FBI's data-gathering efforts could be impressive when properly focused. All too often, however, the sheer amount of raw data received at Quantico and various other undisclosed locations around the country made its usefulness tenuous at best. Still, Ayalla had been unyielding in her requests for deep background probes on anything and everything related to Malleus Caelistis, Richard Bell, Father Rosario, his parents and siblings, and even Archbishop Johnston. On a hunch, she'd also asked for runs on the management and staff of the nearest nuclear generating station—San Peligro. If the threats weren't simply a smoke screen, she wanted to look for indications that someone inside the facility might have been compromised. The prompt response she got on all of her requests was a little surprising. She suspected Senator Hawthorne might have smoothed the way for her, but for some reason that suspicion only irritated her.

She dumped the armload of printouts on the conference table. "Here's what we've got so far," she said. Malcolm eyed the pile of paper none too enthusiastically.

"That could take us about a week to read through," he said.

"Just skim through it. More than half the stuff we come up with on people is mundane crap that doesn't tell us anything."

"Then why do it?" he asked.

"You know as well as I do. You cast as big a net as you can and see what swims into it. Besides, we aren't getting anywhere with this Bell character. Data-wise, he's a ghost. I'd almost be tempted to think he hatched somewhere."

"As a fully grown lunatic, maybe?"

"Who knows? He could be completely harmless, just another fringe nut job who has delusions of grandeur."

"I'm not disputing that he could be a zero as far as this is concerned, but it bothers the hell out of me that we can't find a trace of him before his arrest in Washington."

"He wouldn't be the first person who managed to fly under the radar. Look how many fugitive warrants, federal and state, that have been outstanding for years."

"Yes, but they have histories. We know who they are, where they were born, and at least some details of where they've spent parts of their lives. I don't like having to look for someone who's all smoke and mirrors."

"We have his fingerprints, Malcolm, and we also have mug shots. You're reading his prison record."

"But nothing about him makes sense. He pulls this stupid break-in and panics, but then he clams up. He doesn't help his public defender one bit and goes quietly off to jail where he turns into some sort of modern-day Elmer Gantry. He does the model prisoner routine, and then the day he's released he disappears and instantly violates the terms of his parole. He didn't have money, I.D., transportation—"

"What makes you think he didn't?" asked Ayalla. "He could have made lots of friends in prison. Maybe one of them got out before he did and set up a way for him to disappear. If he's persuasive enough to build a following—"

"Maybe," said Malcolm. "Chances are his friends wouldn't tell us a thing. But what are the odds Ricky also might have made an enemy or two?"

Ayalla stared at him for a moment. "I can't imagine a man in prison doesn't piss someone off."

"Exactly. So how about you get your computer geeks to find out first of all if anyone he served time with is still inside, and second, a list of the names of all the inmates on his cellblock, and third, a list with current addresses of all the inmates who served a sentence at the same time he was incarcerated."

Ayalla had been nodding and making notes but stopped abruptly. "I was with you there right up until the last part," she said. "But do you have any idea how big a group you're talking about? Bell was incarcerated for seven years. There must have been hundreds of prisoners in and out during that time."

"That's why I want the addresses. I want to see if any of them live in California."

"And what about the ones still in custody? How are we going to interview them?"

"I already sent one of my people out there. I told him to call me or Benjamin with anything he finds."

"Is this guy an ex-partner of yours?" she asked.

"No, but he was one of my guys when I headed up homicide. Name's Leon. He owes me one."

"How did you spring him from whatever's he doing now?"

"He's retired."

"Then they wouldn't let him interview prisoners."

"They did," said Malcolm with a smug grin. "Benjamin arranged it."

"What is it with that guy?" she muttered, realizing she'd said this at least half a dozen times either to Malcolm or to herself in the last few days.

"Why does that annoy you?" asked Malcolm, looking genuinely puzzled.

"I don't like it when people like that operate outside the system. It's like we have to play by the rules and they don't. Just because they're rich and—"

"So that's it."

"What's 'it'?"

"He's rich, so you assume he's always got an unfair advantage."

"Something like that," she answered defiantly. "He's a rich white guy and a politician. That doesn't exactly inspire my trust."

"Just like all us black folk are dumb thieving niggers when you come right down to it?"

"I'm not talking ignorant stereotypes, just facts. White people treated us like dirt for about 300 years in case you've forgotten. Or have you turned into some fucking Oreo just because the great Benjamin Hawthorne acts like your bosom buddy?"

Malcolm's fists clenched around the file he was holding, crushing a three-inch stack of paper into an accordion. His anger radiated across the room. Ayalla involuntarily found herself pushing back from the table. But he didn't get up and he took a deep breath before speaking. When he did, his voice was carefully modulated.

"I'm going to ignore that last part, because you don't know shit about me, or the fact that I grew up in the Deep South more than forty years ago. What I could tell you about the crappy way some people treated my family is enough to fill a book. But that doesn't matter right here and right now. I don't know what happened to you in your life that's got you so twisted up inside—"

"My life is none of your business!"

"You're right, it isn't. But your attitude damn sure is getting close to being my business. And the minute you start in on my friends, well, you'll end up right at the top of my personal shit list."

"Like I give a flying fuck what some asshole city cop thinks." She glared at him as the second hand on the big institutional clock bolted to the wall ticked off the seconds. His eyes didn't waver. Finally, she looked over his shoulder at the grimy white paint on the wall. "I'm sorry. That was uncalled for. But I don't *want* any favors from anyone. I don't *need* any favors. Especially not from a politician…or any politicians' friends. That kind of help always comes with strings—and a knife in the back."

The clock kept up its noisy timekeeping. Malcolm laid down the bundle of paper and tried to straighten it out. Suddenly, his head snapped up and he looked straight at Ayalla. "Your father was Daniel Franklin."

Her hand went involuntarily to a place over her heart. She didn't speak for several moments, and when she did, her voice was thick, as if she had to talk around an obstruction in her throat. "How did you know? Your friend, the senator, tell you that?"

"No." Malcolm's voice was more gentle now. "Although I imagine he knows. But he wouldn't have mentioned it to me or anyone else unless he thought it was relevant to this investigation. It popped into my head because I followed the case pretty closely. I was a young beat cop back then and a lot of us looked up to him."

"My father wasn't corrupt."

"I didn't say he was."

"Just about everyone else did, including the scum-sucking politicians who hung him out to dry when the scandal broke."

"So that's it. You hate them all because of what happened to your father?"

"Twenty years ago, about six months after my father was promoted to Deputy Chief, some congressman's daughter got totally stoned, probably on pot laced with a hallucinogenic, chased it with a six-pack of beer, and drove the motorcycle her daddy bought her right through a plate glass window of a restaurant in Georgetown. Naturally, she wasn't hurt except for a few cuts and bruises. But she injured three people and killed a man right in front of his wife and son. Dad went to the scene and some flunky from the Hill pulls him aside and lays down the law. This is going down as a mechanical failure of the motorcycle, or somebody in traffic cut her off. The girl isn't to be taken to the nearest hospital, but to a private clinic. The flunky says he has a private ambulance on the way. There aren't going to be any blood or breath tests.

"In other words," Malcolm said, "the congressman wanted a complete cover-up."

"Yep. Dad couldn't figure out how the flunky guy had gotten there so fast. He suspected maybe the father had someone watching his little brat of a daughter. Anyway, bottom line is, Deputy Chief Franklin didn't cooperate. He walked over and told the cops to put her in the paramedic's transport. He rode with her himself, and when they got to Georgetown Hospital's emergency room, he told the doctor he wanted blood samples immediately. He personally took custody of them and drove directly to the lab and waited hours for the results. No one knew where he was. Then he took the reports, faxed copies to the chief of police, the girl's father, as well as a friend of his at *The Washington Post*."

"He wouldn't back down, would he?"

"No, and the public was so outraged by what the girl had done that the prosecutor didn't have much choice except to charge her with vehicular manslaughter and a dozen other counts. Her daddy tried to pull every string he could, but she went to prison anyway."

Malcolm regarded her thoughtfully. "So your father made a serious enemy."

"The congressman waited almost a year. Then weird things started to happen. My dad would get phone calls in the middle of the night, and letters dropped in his mailbox at home. But there was never anyone on the phone, and the envelopes were always empty, just sheets of blank paper. Six months later, someone leaked a story that my father was taking bribes."

"And some resourceful person had supplied photos of a scumbag or two dropping off the envelopes at his house. Implied they were filled with money."

Ayalla's voice broke slightly, but she gripped the edge of the table with both hands and sucked in a deep breath. "It was a nightmare. A reporter discovered a secret bank account in the Bahamas in my mother's name. Neither one of my parents knew anything about it. Then a cop came forward and said my dad had admitted doctoring the blood tests on the congressman's daughter."

"Del Smith?"

"You knew him?"

"Knew *of* him. Saw his name in the papers. I didn't believe a word he said if only because a lot of us knew he was a bigot and as corrupt a cop as you'll ever find."

"Funny how everyone seemed to believe him, though—the prosecutor, the judge who granted search warrants, and the detectives—the white detectives…who swarmed all over everything trying to dig up evidence."

"But they never did charge your father."

"But he resigned in disgrace anyway. And the congressman's slimy lawyers had his darling daughter out of prison within three months."

"Based on the allegations that the blood tests were phony."

"It was just enough to cast doubt on the conviction, and an 'expert' testified that the accident could have been caused by the failure of some obscure part in the front forks of the bike."

"What happened to your dad?" Malcolm asked quietly. "I never heard anything else after that."

"He and my mother moved to Philadelphia. He worked for a security company for a while."

"And then?"

"He died four years later, when I was about to graduate from college. He had two heart attacks inside a month. The second one was massive."

"I'm sorry, Ayalla."

"So am I."

"Is that what makes you so angry all the time?"

She looked up at him in consternation. "I'm *not* angry all the time."

"Could have fooled me."

She half rose from her chair. "So now you're a psychologist? What the hell do you know about anything?"

"I know when people are pissed off at life," he said. "I know how I felt when a couple of bastards gunned down my wife in a bank and left me and my kids alone. I was pissed off at just about every person on the planet."

Her eyes widened. "I'm…I didn't know that."

"It was a long time ago. Just like it was a long time ago with your dad. Actually, I'd say you've done pretty well."

"All that's mattered to me is my career."

"What else was there?" he asked. "Personally, I was lucky. Connor kept me from eating my gun and then made sure I didn't end in prison for blowing away the assholes who did the robbery. Then I had my children to think of. My sister read me the riot act and told me to stop feeling sorry for myself and start being a father."

Ayalla thought about this for a minute. "Then you're lucky to have people like that in your life. My job is all I have. It's who I am. And every time I turn around I have to deal with some politically motivated bullshit. There's always some son of a bitch trying to cover his ass."

"So we're finally back to the starting point. You want to generalize, put all the people on the Hill in one big bag labeled 'schmucks.'"

"Works for me."

"You know as well as I do that we can't do our jobs if we judge people by a title, or their bank account, or their color. Personally, I think politics sucks. I think the deals and the accommodations and the plotting that goes on in those offices would probably make most of us sick. But not everyone who works there is automatically suspect. And I can personally vouch for the character of Benjamin Hawthorne," he paused, "for whatever that's worth."

She thought about this for a full minute. "I guess it's worth something."

"All I'm saying is that he didn't get where he is because he has money, or because he's willing to step on people. He's risked his life more times than you and me and every agent in this field office. He doesn't take shortcuts to feather his own nest, you understand me? But he'll do anything he has to do when it comes to protecting his country, his family, his friends, and people who need his help."

"In that order?" she asked

"Pretty much."

She sighed. "I'm a skeptic. You act like he's James Bond, Sir Galahad, and Santa Claus all wrapped up into one."

Malcolm was silent for a moment. "He's a good man, Ayalla. He's my friend. I'm asking you to take my word on it."

"I hardly know you," she retorted.

"You probably know me better than you realize. There's nothing hidden about me. Just what you see."

"I doubt that."

"No, I'm telling you like it is. I'm not a seriously deep person. I like life, and I like my job, and I do what I can to make things better. That's it. Nothing complex. So stop worrying that I'm going to somehow turn into a major asshole. Now do you suppose we can possibly declare a moratorium on arguing for the time being?"

"I suppose," she said, though her tone lacked conviction.

The ghost of a smile twitched across Malcolm's lips. "That's a start. How about if I take the files I sort of mutilated? I wonder if anyone here has an iron."

They said nothing for the next hour and a half as they sifted through the piles of paper. The disagreement and its somber aftermath had given way gradually to a relatively congenial silence between coworkers. Ayalla gave a sudden victory whoop. "We've got something."

"Got what?" asked Malcolm, a little startled by her outburst.

"Here," she said, brandishing a handful of printouts. "I had them do a separate run on secret societies and cults using the keywords 'Catholic,' 'hammer,' 'malleus,' and a few other combinations. And look at this"— she turned the paper around so Malcolm could see it—"'the Malleus Society.' " She put another sheet beside the first. "And here's a list of members, though it's tagged as a partial list, based on other data sources." She scanned down the columns of names. "Damn, there's a lot of people...all men, though."

"Is this where we shift to debating why men are generally scum?

"No, I thought that was already a given." Ayalla smiled to indicate that, this time at least, she was joking. "Though I have met a couple who threaten to change my mind."

Malcolm started to say something, stopped, then started again. "So let's split up the list and see if any names ring a bell."

"Is that a pun, Captain Jefferson?"

He thought about it for a brief moment until he caught her meaning. "Ouch, if I'd thought about it first, I'd have skipped it completely."

"Clichés aren't always evil. Besides, we can take it as an omen. With any luck we might find Richard Bell himself on one of these lists of known associates."

Malcolm nodded, already skimming over the sheets she'd handed him. He didn't find Richard Bell on any of his and went back to check more carefully. One of the names he did recognize, along with several other political figures sprinkled through the list, but he kept it to himself. No sensible man pours gasoline on a smoldering fire.

Chapter Eighteen

Mother is the name for God
in the lips and hearts of little children.
—William Makepeace Thackeray

"I hope this is the one we want," said Connor as the car jounced over the ruts in the dirt parking lot flanking the historic mission, Santa Maria de Los Angeles—St. Mary of the Angels. "I think I've seen all the missionary priest quarters, Spanish soldier paraphernalia, and eighteenth-century icons I care to see on this trip."

"Your complaint is sounding vaguely familiar," answered Laura. "I believe I was feeling the same way about the stone effigies and sarcophagi in the National Cathedral."

"Oh, yeah," Connor grinned ruefully. "I do seem to recall that you had your fill of cold stone and gilded altars."

"Just about. Somehow these little churches are a lot less intimidating."

"But not as cool as Gothic cathedrals."

"No, but definitely closer to the ground."

"I'm starting to think if we've seen one, we've seen 'em all," sighed Connor.

"I think you're crabby because you're hungry."

"Am I so predictable?" She jockeyed the car into a space and felt the front wheels fall into an especially large depression at the edge of the lot. The frame landed with a thunk. "That can't be good," she frowned, putting the convertible in reverse and slowly backing out of the hole, the tires spinning slightly. "I'd better get the front end looked at when we get back to a town."

Laura got out of the car and looked at the map they'd received from the park ranger posted at the entrance while Connor put the top up and tossed their bags into the trunk. "I'll bring the camera and leave everything else," she said.

Side by side they walked toward the path that led to the main grounds of the old mission. To one side of the path was an old adobe building housing a small gift shop, rest rooms and a miniscule "museum" with a diorama of the mission as it looked in its heyday. Laura studied it for several minutes. "I wonder how many out-of-town tourists who plan to visit this mission think it's close to L.A. because of its name."

"Probably most of them," Connor shrugged. "And how many them do you suppose actually make the connection between the movie capital of the country and the English translation of the name?"

"Having lived there, I'd say it's a stretch to think of L.A. and angels in the same context," replied Laura. "Now here," she said, gesturing to the miniature buildings on the model, "this is more of a place where angels would hang out." She pointed at the map on the wall. "The stables are farther along. Let's walk along the path that circles the pasture."

They both moved onto the tree-shaded dirt track and strolled toward the mission. "It's beautiful in here," said Laura. "Smell all that green-ness."

Connor smiled. "Before I met you, I would have insisted that it is impossible to smell a color. But you know what?"

"What?"

"If I could bottle green-ness for you, so you'd have a whiff whenever you wanted, I'd do it."

"I love you," said Laura, taking Connor's hand.

"And I adore you. Which, as far as I'm concerned, makes life damn near perfect."

"And what would make it completely perfect?" Laura asked, absent-mindedly rubbing her right wrist against the leg of her jeans.

"If people didn't go around killing each other, but I don't think we'll see an end to that any time soon." She looked down at Laura's hand. "You keep rubbing your wrist as if it itches."

"Do I?" She held up her hand and pulled back the sleeve of her jacket. "Hmm. Does look kind of red."

"And splotchy," added Connor, peering at the patch of roughened skin. "You must be allergic to something."

"The dark parts are where I couldn't get that weird greasy dirt off my skin."

"The stuff from the bones?" said Connor.

"Yeah, it behaves like some sort of colorfast dye. I think I'd have to remove several layers of skin to get it all off."

Connor frowned. "I wonder if that's what you're allergic to."

"Who knows?" Laura shrugged. "But let's worry about that later. I've got some cortisone cream back at the hotel. Hey, look at the horses." Through the trees, she could just see the head of one horse and the switching tail of another.

"They still keep some here," said Connor, reading from the brochure, "along with a few sheep and goats, turkeys, and a pig or two. Kids come out here on weekends and learn about farm animals."

"Certainly smells like farm animals," said Laura, wrinkling her nose. Then she stopped in her tracks.

"What?"

"The smell. It triggered a memory."

"Of what?"

"Of the dream. I could smell horses and that general barnyard odor."

"Ah, yes: eau de manure. So you think we've actually hit on the place you saw in your dream?"

"Maybe. Although a lot of these places probably keep some animals around. So I don't think it's proof positive. I just had one of those déjà vu moments."

"Smell is a powerful trigger for most people. Let's keep walking. Maybe we're on the right track."

They continued a little farther until the path opened up into more cleared space around the perimeter fence of a large pasture. Across the field they saw a rundown barn and stable yard. An old mare wandered up to the fence, likely in search of a handout, but neither of them had anything suitable for horses. "I don't think candy bars are on her diet," said Connor, stroking the gentle horse's neck.

Laura started to follow the fence line and Connor trailed along after her, still struck by the profound silence of the place. Not a hint of traffic noise, not even a human voice could they hear, even though there were several other cars in the parking lot. Laura had picked up the pace considerably and widened the gap between them. Soon she was into the trees on the other side of the pasture.

"Hey, wait up," shouted Connor. "I think my age is starting to show."

There was no answer, and a frisson of fear tingled through her chest. She took a deep breath and chided herself. "She just didn't hear you. Don't get carried away."

She hurried into the tree line and emerged only a few feet beyond onto another path. To her relief, she immediately saw Laura standing about fifty yards away, staring at a fountain that lay in the middle of a broad walkway laid in worn brick.

"Is that the fountain from your dream?" she asked when she was within a few feet of her lover.

At first Laura didn't answer and Connor repeated the question.

"I'm sorry. I was concentrating, trying to bring back the image. The shape is the same, although there was water coming out of it in the dream. But the obelisk should have been right beside it."

"Didn't you tell me that dreams usually aren't literal, even the really lucid ones?"

Laura sighed. "Yes, and that's true. I suppose I wanted to be sure—to be able to confirm that this was the spot."

"We don't know that it isn't. Let's keep looking around. Maybe you'll see something else that seems familiar. If we head up around that next bend we'll be in sight of the main buildings."

»——«

A few hundred yards away, Richard La Cloche refocused his compact but powerful binoculars on the two women beside the fountain. He almost wished he could read lips, but he would settle for keeping them under observation. He still didn't know precisely why they were here, why they were behaving like tourists. He doubted they had any real interest in Spanish colonial history or architecture. It was more likely that they were on the trail of something, perhaps a document or artifact Monsignor Kursk had hinted at in their phone conversation. He didn't have any details, though, since the files had been spirited away by the archbishop before he could lay his hands on them. If Kursk hadn't been so damned secretive about what the upper echelons of the Malleus Society, the inner circle known as Malleus Caelistis, were seeking, Richard could have focused on the prize instead of stumbling around blindly. He uttered an obscene imprecation under his breath. Kursk had been a fool. Richard was only mollified by the fact that the monsignor was dead and soon to be buried.

He peered through the binoculars again. The two women were moving toward the main buildings of the mission. He sighed. Surveillance was boring when the subjects didn't do anything. But he wouldn't entrust it to any of the brainless goons who gladly did his dirty work. If the Hawthorne woman and her Indian friend found whatever they were looking for, or even stumbled on something by accident, he intended to be there.

The timing was right. The days until the prophecy would be fulfilled were dwindling away. His opponents, the representatives of the evil one, were sure to resist their fate. But what could they do against a man armed with the power of the one true God? At least he had identified them, or most of them. It was not unlikely that the cop, the FBI agent, the two women, and Benjamin Hawthorne, had other allies. Certainly he could number the interfering archbishop among them. So far, though, he wasn't worried. How absurd to send women against him! It demonstrated the contempt in which these sinners held their creator. But that was about to change. The Divine Hammer of God would descend again and again until the minions of that cursed cult of evil and lies was battered into dust.

»——«

Connor swung around abruptly and looked off into the distance.

"What's the matter?" asked Laura, still studying the diagram of the mission layout.

"You know that funny feeling I get sometimes?"

"Could you be a little more specific? Since I've known you, I think we've categorized a couple of dozen varieties of 'funny feelings' we both get. Is this 'funny' as in something bad is going to happen, or funny as in 'Did you lock the car?'"

"Would you think I was crazy if I said I keep thinking someone's watching us?"

"Nope. I would believe you even if I hadn't had the same sensation myself."

"You, too? Why didn't you say something?"

"Because you're a worrier, sweetheart, and I try not to add extra reasons for you to worry beyond whatever we have right in front of us at any given moment."

"Are you saying I don't handle stress well?" said Connor, her light tone belied by the defiant set of her chin.

"You handle it extremely well. Besides, you know perfectly well I hate to bring things up unless I'm pretty sure. And this feeling I have isn't consistent."

"So maybe we're not being watched consistently."

"Score two points for logic," smiled Laura. "Although it doesn't make total sense. If someone wants to know what we're up to, then he…or she…would have to keep tabs on us all the time."

"If they know where we're staying, which, given the macabre offering left in our car, is likely, then they only have to follow us to see where we're going. Maybe if it's a mundane destination, they don't keep it up. Maybe it's only when we do something that might be threatening that they stick with us."

"Like visit this mission?"

"Or any mission," said Connor. "I've had this feeling all day."

"Me, too. But I tended to wonder if it wasn't because I've been so spooked by that dream." She followed Connor's gaze and swept the trees on the other side of the field. Even her sharp vision detected nothing, and then there was a momentary flash of light. "Wait, what was that?" The flash came again.

"I see it," said Connor.

"And I think I know what it is," Laura said grimly. "Two options. The lens of a riflescope or some binoculars."

"A riflescope?" Connor grabbed Laura's arm and pulled her behind a tree. "You just casually announce that?"

"Who's going to come out here with a sniper rifle and shoot us at a historic mission?"

"They didn't have a problem getting rid of Father Rosario."

"True."

"And they even killed one of their own, Kursk."

"We don't know without doubt that the killer of Father Rosario has anything to do with the monsignor's death," said Laura. "I think that might be a bit of a leap."

"I don't. As a matter of fact, I'm sure of it. Let's sit down over here for a minute." She moved cautiously across the clearing, keeping an eye peeled for another flash of reflected sunlight, and chose a bench on the other side of the fountain, out of the line of sight of the trees across the pasture.

"All right. Fact: Ricky Bell is associated with Malleus Caelistis."

"Maybe," Laura interrupted. "He could have stolen the name from something he read. That doesn't mean he's actually a member of the real group, or that there is a real group."

"True, but I think we're safe in formulating a working theory that there is such a group functioning somewhere. And I have a feeling that he would never have gotten away with using the name or their coat of arms, if you want to call it that, over a period of several years without them doing something about it. If they still exist, then they knew full well what our ex-con was up to and let it go on. I think he may have proved useful."

Laura pursed her lips and blew out a stream of air. "But I still don't quite understand what this stupid society hopes to accomplish. What do they hope to gain by running around silencing people like Father Rosario who are just asking questions, looking into history, fiddling with a few odd hypotheses?"

"It's more than that. Father Rosario was determined to find data that would support his belief that the Cult of Magdalene was more than just a few first century malcontents."

"But even if that kind of proof comes to light, what does it do besides piss off some curmudgeonly biblical scholars and knee-jerk conservative priests. You make it sound as if the revelation of something like that is dangerous."

"You think there's no danger in pissing off not only one of the world's biggest churches but a great big chunk of the world population? Father Rosario apparently was on the verge of uncovering information that might contradict some of the basic tenets of Christianity. People don't like it when you mess with their sacred cows."

"I thought that was the Hindus. Christians are allowed to *eat* cows."

Connor started to say something, then recognized the playful twinkle in her lover's eyes. "Okay, you're being a wiseass, so now you're condemned to hearing my entire scenario."

"Theorize away, my dear Holmes," said Laura.

"All right. We have Ricky Bell, who is apparently brighter than we thought, and perhaps a lot more organized, and is now completely off the radar. But he's continued to issue various and sundry threats, many of them keyed to demands that the world return to a conservative Christian (read: Catholic) mode of living where men are in charge and women shut the hell up. This ties in with the historical attempts of Malleus Caelistis to stamp out any sort of heresy."

"Meaning anything that claimed Christ was in favor of equality between the sexes, or taught principles the church doesn't like."

"Exactly. But even without knowing everyone's precise agenda, we can see that Ricky Bell would probably get off on belonging to a group with ancient roots going back centuries. If he happens to be a bit of a misogynist, which I think is likely, then he's right in tune with them."

"All right. But what if he's a self-styled Malleus groupie? Maybe he wasn't sanctioned by the official group. And we don't know for certain that Kursk was a member."

"All right. We can't absolutely nail down every piece of it. But bear with me a little more."

"Always, darling."

"Thank you. Now, we've got Ricky Bell, Malleus Caelistis, and possibly Monsignor Kursk. Of course, I don't know if Bell and Kursk actually knew each other. But their goals may coincide anyway."

"And who killed Kursk?"

Connor shook her head. "I don't know. If Kursk was part of Malleus, and he and his cronies were after Father Rosario, then we could point the finger at them for killing Enrique, although I still have a hard time believing that they would murder the man purely on ideological grounds. It's too extreme."

"But if Kursk was somehow involved, then why did he end up dead?"

"Maybe he wasn't tied in with Enrique's murder, but he knew who was. Or suspected who was behind it."

"That's possible. Maybe Kursk wasn't willing to condone murder. But—and I'm just playing devil's advocate here—if this Ricky Bell is possibly responsible for Father Rosario's death, then why is he playing all these stupid games? Sending threatening letters about taking over nuclear power plants? How much sense does that make? He only draws attention to himself. And, no one's seen hide nor hair of the man. He could be sitting in some crappy little apartment back East, churning out threat letters."

"True. But I've got a hunch. And I have no idea how his correspondence fits into all this, but somehow it does."

Laura smiled. "Your hunches are always good enough for me. But where do we go from here?"

"Let's take a look at the rest of this place. Maybe we'll find your obelisk lurking behind some tree."

»——«

Had he known he was the topic of their conversation, it would have pleased him, though he'd had a moment of doubt when both women appeared to be staring directly toward him. From then on he was careful to angle the binoculars so they wouldn't catch the sunlight. After a while they went back to talking.

He almost sensed their confusion and he reveled in it. But then no one really understood his grand designs, any more than they understood the real meaning of the prophecies. His would-be masters, the religious elite of Malleus Caelistis, were almost as ignorant as his enemies. And the rank-and-file morons of the Malleus Society were even more pathetic. But they had their uses. The financial support he'd drained off from their contributions over the past several years had been sufficient to finance his projects, including the one that would begin within a mere forty-eight hours, the one that would put fear into the hearts of the heretics and blasphemers. At the bottom of the heap were the hangers-on—the snivelers like Archibald Sims and the thickheaded muscle like Holcomb and his thugs—all pawns in a game of chess between good and evil. And everyone knew that except in the case of rare strategies, pawns were supremely expendable. Holcomb and his people would get their reward, just not the one they were expecting.

The two women disappeared around the side of the church that stood on the old mission grounds. He debated moving closer, then decided to wait. If they carried anything out with them, he would notice and they couldn't return to the parking lot without passing his observation post. Likewise he rejected the notion of searching the trunk of their car and going through their belongings. It wouldn't do to pique the curiosity of the park ranger on duty. Stupid mistakes were a thing of the past for Richard. So he waited, itchy from the underbrush, but extraordinarily satisfied with himself.

For a few seconds, he swung his binoculars ninety degrees to the west. The rounded domes of the San Peligro Nuclear Generating Station were barely visible over the crest of a hill only a mile away. He smiled. It was all so perfect.

»—«

"Connor, look! Over there by the altar. Isn't that the priest we saw in Washington? Father Angelico?"

Connor stared at the old man clad in a long black cassock gray with dust. "That does like the same man, but what would he be doing here?"

"I have no idea, but the hair's standing up on the back of my neck."

Connor squared her shoulders in anticipation. "Well, I'm not a big believer in coincidence, and I definitely don't like being spied on. So let's see what the padre has to say for himself."

She half expected him to disappear before they crossed the court-yard, but he turned and looked directly at them. As they approached, his wizened face crinkled into a smile. "*Buenos días, señoras.* It is a lovely day, is it not?"

"Father Angelico?" asked Connor.

"Why yes. How kind of you to remember."

"Then we did meet in Washington?"

"Most certainly. In the Bethlehem Chapel as I recall."

"Why are you here?" Connor asked abruptly.

The old priest looked a little taken aback at her tone. "I came to visit the missions of California. The roots of the church go deep here."

"I thought you were an Episcopal priest," said Laura.

"No. I was not ordained in that church," said the old man. "I took my vows as a Catholic."

"But I believe you said you were a visiting priest," countered Laura.

"Indeed. I am a priest, and I was visiting. I also spent time at the National Shrine of the Immaculate Conception in that city. I'm sorry, have I done something to offend you?"

Connor took a deep breath. "No. I apologize for my rudeness. There have been some unusual events in the area lately, and when we saw you here, we thought perhaps…" She was reluctant to finish the sentence.

"That I was following you," he finished for her.

"I realize now that it sounds absurd."

"Not at all. But I've learned a few things in my long life. One of them is that God doesn't make mistakes. We are always where we're supposed to be, whether we are conscious of our destinies or not."

"I don't know about that," said Laura. "There have been a few times when I've missed the boat, so to speak."

"Then you weren't meant to be on it," he answered gravely. "But the key is in remembering that everything is perfect just the way it is."

"Sometimes that isn't exactly easy, Father," said Connor, who was growing a little impatient with the unsolicited advice. "I think it depends on your perspective." She nodded politely. "Again, I'm sorry we behaved rudely to you. We'll get on with our tour and leave you to yours."

He inclined his head in response. "Of course. And rest assured I've taken no offense." He inclined his gaze at the old bell tower that rose above them. "I've always been fascinated by the magic of a church bell, you know. The bell was used to summon the worshipers to mass, or even to ring out a warning in times of danger. Yes, the tone of a church bell is always worth noting." He smiled at Laura and Connor. "Before you leave the mission, you'll want to see the murals. They're along the outer cloister on the other side of the chapel. And there's a path from there that leads through the old botanical gardens where the brothers used to grow their herbs and medicines."

"Thank you, Father," said Laura. "And goodbye."

"*Vaya con Dios.*" He smiled again. "And may the angels watch over you."

Laura and Connor turned away and headed toward the chapel. When Connor turned to look over her shoulder, the old man was gone. She stopped in her tracks and scanned the courtyard. "Where the hell did he go?"

Laura shook her head. "I don't think we want to delve too deeply into that question right now. But I'm beginning to have a few ideas."

"Like what?"

"I need to think about it a little. For now, let's just—" They had rounded the corner, and Laura was staring down the long outer corridor, lined along one side with columns and arches. "This is it! This is the place I dreamed about." She spun around. "At least I think it is. That end down there looks right, but this end doesn't. Still, it was a dream image. They aren't necessarily accurate." She walked slowly along the passage-way. "He said to look at the murals. He probably had a reason."

They examined the somewhat primitive artwork adorning the wall on their left. Rather than purely religious subjects, the images por-trayed life at the mission: peasants and brothers worked in the fields, ground flour in the mill, tended livestock. The last picture in the series, however, reverted to a religious theme. A tall dark-haired woman clad in flowing robes, her head encircled by a halo, bestowed her blessing on the kneeling peasants while the resident brothers of the mission stood to one side looking on. She towered over everyone in the picture. Animals lay quietly at her feet. Her right hand was raised, and in her left she held a small sphere from which protruded a Celtic cross.

"It almost feels as if she's holding the entire world in one hand," Laura whispered.

"But how does this artwork fit in here?" said Connor in an equally quiet voice. "I can't imagine eighteenth-century Catholic missionaries condoning an image like that."

"Like what? Maybe she's a version of Mary, like Our Lady of Guadalupe."

"I don't think so," said Connor. "She's too powerful. Her hands and arms look strong. She's taller than everyone else in the picture. And that orb she's holding, that's a symbol of authority. I can't imagine any painter of religious subjects from that era depicting a woman as a spiritual leader."

"Then if someone did paint it, why didn't the brothers or whoever just destroy it?"

"Beats me. I want a picture of this." She stepped back far enough to fit the whole panel into the viewfinder and snapped the shutter release. "What does the guidebook say about it?"

Laura riffled through the pages. "Let's step out in the light a minute. It's getting really dark in the shadows." Connor followed her through the archway and onto the brick path. After a minute or two, Laura looked at her, obviously baffled. "There's nothing in there about that scene. There are illustrations of every picture except that one. See, it ends with number twelve: the flock of sheep and the two little boys."

"All right, we'll start back at the beginning." Walking outside along the edge of the cloister, they reentered it at the location of the first scene in the mural. One by one, they counted each distinct scene. "Ten, eleven,…" Wait a minute, this can't be the last one, there's…" Connor stood frozen to the spot. The twelfth painting in line was of two little boys and about a dozen sheep. But there *were* no more paintings. Her stomach clenched. She stepped back and put her arm around Laura. "Tell me I'm not going completely insane," she said. "The scene with the woman. Where is it?"

Laura shook her head, her eyes wide with wonder. "Damned if I know. But I saw the same thing you did. And if it was there, then we may have a picture of it." She pointed at the camera slung around over Connor's shoulder.

"I'm not sure I even want to find out. But let's get out of here for now, before we see anything else that threatens my sanity."

"I think we should tackle the botanical gardens on the way out," suggested Laura.

"Why? Because the disappearing priest recommended it?"

"Of course. You have to admit, he didn't steer us wrong about seeing the mural."

Connor shook her head. "This just gets weirder and weirder, but somehow I don't think I'll ever have a totally normal life again, so we may as well forge ahead."

"Who's to say what's normal, my love?" asked Laura, noticing for the first time that a family of tourists had arrived in the corridor and the parents were staring at the two women. Connor's arm was still around Laura's waist. "I'm sure we don't need to solicit *their* opinion of what's normal. I bet we wouldn't even qualify."

Connor grinned, pecked Laura on the cheek, and gave the man and woman in his-and-hers matching Bermuda shorts a half-salute before the two of them continued to the door at the far end. The sign said BOTANICAL GARDENS.

"They'll be talking about that for weeks," laughed Laura.

"If they had an actual life," said Connor, "they wouldn't have to spend time worrying about whether or not we're those dangerous perverts they've heard about."

"I don't think they're wondering," Laura smiled. "I think they're pretty sure."

They stepped out onto the path. The shrubs grew densely here, all along the edges and several yards back from the walkway, which turned in gentle S-curves back and forth. Soon they were out of sight of the mission buildings.

"Maybe we should retrace our steps and go back the way we came in," said Connor. "I'm not up for any more surprises today."

"Too late, sweetheart." Laura pointed just head of them to a clump of bushes. From their midst rose a narrow dark-gray stone, an obelisk almost seven feet tall. They approached it cautiously. The path split in two, each arm circling the object. The sign at the base of the shrubs was titled LA LUMIÈRE DE SACRÉ MÈRE.

THIS MEDICINAL HERB WAS HIGHLY VALUED BY HEALERS FOR MANY CENTURIES, AS IT WAS PURPORTED TO CAUSE ALMOST MIRACULOUS CURES OF A VARIETY OF ILLNESSES. HOWEVER, IT FELL INTO DISREPUTE AFTER THE SPANISH INQUISITION, WHEN THE INQUISITORS BANNED ITS USE AND PUNISHED THOSE WHO GREW IT, APPARENTLY BECAUSE THE COMMON TRANSLATION OF THE FRENCH NAME—"THE LIGHT OF THE HOLY MOTHER"—WAS JUDGED TO BE OFFENSIVE TO CHRISTIAN TEACHING.

"Wonder why its name is in French," said Connor, "when all the others are in Latin."

Laura stared at the obelisk for several seconds, then closed her eyes. Connor remained silent, waiting. She listened intently for the sounds of anyone else who might be nearby. She half expected Father Angelico to pop out of a nearby shrub. But there were only the sounds of nature—birds, insects, a light breeze in the taller trees on the edge of the garden.

"Can't nail it down," said Laura. "Whatever it is I'm trying to visualize keeps slipping away from me."

"Maybe you're trying too hard. Let it go for now. We can come back tomorrow."

"You're right. I am trying too hard. And I know better. Grand-mother told me time and again that thinking about something isn't the same thing as simply being in the experience of it."

"That was very Zen of her, considering she's a Navajo. And I'll *think* about that later."

"You're incorrigible," Laura said with a smile. "Now where do you suppose the exit is?"

As it turned out, the path led immediately out of the garden once they'd passed the obelisk. They'd come farther than they would have guessed. Off to their left was the pasture, and they were halfway down the track to the parking lot.

"I don't quite see how we managed that," said Connor, estimating the distance they'd walked in the garden against the time it had taken them to reach the mission on their way in. "But given the context of the day, and our very own Rod Serling dressed like a priest, I'm going to ignore the question completely. And you were right. I *am* hungry."

As they left the mission grounds and pulled out onto the paved sur-face, Laura pointed at the odd shapes on the horizon, their outlines limned by the slanting rays of the sun. "What is that over there?"

Connor followed the direction of Laura's finger. "Nuclear power plant, I think. I've seen pictures of some that have those minaret-shaped domes."

"I think I don't like it that Father Rosario's favorite historic mission and one of Ricky Bell's declared targets are within sight of each other."

"We haven't established a connection between Bell and any of this."

"You're talking like a prosecuting attorney, sifting facts, deciding when the weight of evidence is enough."

"Old habits," Connor shrugged.

"But they aren't you," insisted Laura. "That's old stuff. The real you is growing beyond the hard and fast rules of 'what you see is what you get.'"

Connor smiled ruefully. "But I liked the old me. No conclusions without hard evidence. Give me facts, give me forensics, give me taped confessions. I liked that."

"I know you did, sweetheart, but do you really think you can go back?"

A long silence ensued as Connor sped up the on-ramp to the interstate. Laura waited patiently, knowing her lover would have to come the conclusion on her own. Every other person in Connor's life had weighed in with advice, even those who weren't precisely alive in the accepted sense. Laura would push only so far. So she waited.

"You're right. I can't go back to where I only see with the eyes of a cynic, comforting as it would be sometimes. I once thought the five senses were the final arbiter of what was and wasn't real, and I was wrong about that. I thought death was an absolute end...wrong about that, too. As far as God, well, the jury was out on that for a long time."

"And now it isn't?"

"No, the jury's back."

"And the verdict?"

"Innocent on all counts."

Laura chuckled. "What crimes would you have charged God with?"

"Flimflamming the innocent and ignorant public, making false promises, acting in an arbitrary manner, letting the good die young— all that kind of stuff."

"And you finally figured out the Creator didn't do all that?"

"I finally figured out that people do that, not God. We make of our souls and our selves what we choose. We also make God into what we think God should be. Just like these myrmidons who are apparently willing to murder priests because someone has them convinced that God wants it done."

"I never thought I'd hear you wax philosophic on the subject."

"This is all so much easier for you," said Connor. "I'm slow to change."

"True, but when you do, the results are highly gratifying." Laura put her hand on Connor's knee. "And I love you, no matter what." She paused a moment. "And so do a lot of other people, including Mrs. Broadhurst."

Connor smiled. "And where is my dear grandmother when I need her? She could probably shed some light on all this, but not a peep out of her since we left England."

"You said she wasn't too fond of visiting the United States."

"But she's running around on the astral planes now. What difference would geography make when you're there?"

"I don't know," Laura grinned. "Maybe she stays in the British section."

»——«

The only circumstance that spoiled Richard Bell's day was losing track of his quarry. It baffled him that they never appeared on the path leading back to the parking lot. He had already checked to be sure there was only one way out of the grounds. But as the day faded into dusk, he gave up and made his way back to his car. Their convertible was gone. He knew his attention hadn't wavered for the several minutes they would have been on the dirt track that circumvented the pasture. He was annoyed. Clearly, he had been given bad information, or the diagrams of the mission grounds were inaccurate.

A tiny yet insistent worry pierced his otherwise self-satisfied view of himself and his future. He pushed it away. If they'd found something at the mission, he would know soon enough. Yet he refused to believe that they had. Ever since Kursk had communicated some of the details of Father Rosario's research, Richard had been visiting the mission regularly. He'd seen every inch of the place, probed into every niche. There was nothing to be found. If there ever had been, then the priest had taken it away with him. And it must be in the boxes that the Hawthorne woman's father had taken into the hotel. That would have to be dealt with.

Richard opened his car door and tossed the binoculars in the back. Yes, he'd have to deal with Mr. Hawthorne before the appointed hour. And the others. Fortunately, he'd already begun with the Indian woman. One down…he counted on his fingers…five to go.

»——«

The elderly priest watched from the fringe of trees as the man got into his car. He frowned at the sight of the Roman collar. This was no man of the cloth. This was the same man he'd encountered outside the archbishop's residence, the same one who had clearly intended harm to whoever was in the house that night, just as he intended harm to the two women who'd been visiting the mission. Sensing the watcher's presence, the priest had allowed himself to be seen in order to send the women on another way out of the mission grounds. He'd also felt a sense of urgency that they understand more of what was at stake here. Thus, he'd manipulated reality a little so that they might be able to perceive the last painting in the mural. He was gratified that they were indeed sufficiently sensitive and conscious. They'd seen it, been puzzled by it, understood the anomalous images that the tourists, with their cluttered thoughts and narrow perspectives, would never even notice as they wandered by. Not even the volunteers and rangers who passed through that corridor every day had even seen what the priest liked to think of as the thirteenth image. To him, as to the others that had gone before, thirteen was a truly sacred number, the culmination of God's work: the mother, the thirteenth apostle.

He thought again about the young Indian woman. There was something about her, something that troubled him. She was undoubtedly one of the Old Ones who had returned to earth in these times of turmoil. Her light was strong. Yet wisps of darkness clung to her aura, as if the strands were eating their way into her essence. He would have to watch her carefully, for he sensed she would need his help before too long.

Many other questions troubled him as well. For all his wisdom and training, he could not see into the future any more than most humans. He understood, of course, that future events were fluid and depended entirely on the choices made by individuals. Yet once certain events had been set into motion, whether for good or evil, the prophecies were accurate, sometimes frighteningly so. The old priest had studied this conundrum from many different perspectives, finally coming to believe that because time itself was a human construct, all events, all manifestations actually existed in the same moment. All possible outcomes of human choices existed simultaneously. Thus, some extraordinarily sensitive beings had been able to move their awareness outside the usual boundaries of thought and perhaps sense the natural results of certain patterns of behavior, at least in a general way. And a number of them had believed in Armageddon.

Had God truly ordained that humankind would eventually destroy itself, or become so evil that they would invite God's wrath? The old priest did not believe that for a moment, any more than he believed, as did some sad and disappointed humans, that God "did" anything to this world or its inhabitants. But the fact remained that human beings were indeed capable of bringing about their own downfall, and given the sanctity of free will, the priest doubted God, or even the angels and archangels would do anything to stop it. Instead, it was up to him, and others like him.

His oldest mentor had once said to him, "Why are you here, brother?"

"To protect the teachings."

"You will do that, but that is not why you are here. Consider it again."

"I am here to serve God."

"Again, brother, that is true, but very broad. Look into your heart for the sense of what you are sent to do and to be."

They went back and forth as the priest devised one answer after another until finally the mentor took pity on him.

"You are here, brother, simply to be, to acknowledge divine guidance, to act as your spirit leads you. You are gifted with a knowledge you may not yet share with anyone on the earth plane."

"Why am I permitted this?" asked the priest humbly. "Why is it given to me that I shall live for so very long, and glide here and there in the shadows of plain reality?"

"You do not remember, but you were there when Mother-Father God sent the great teacher Immanuel to the people of the world. You were there to see the miracles and the tragedies, the light and the dark that swirled in his wake. You knew Mother Mary as well. You returned to a mortal body for some reason that only you can completely understand. But my heart tells me your task is even more important now than it was then."

The figure of the elderly priest melted into the trees once more. He would trouble himself no more with questions he could not yet answer. For now, he understood that he must not allow doubt or fear to cloud his judgment.

Chapter Nineteen

Those about her
From her shall read the perfect ways of honour.
—William Shakespeare, *King Henry VI, Part III*, act V, scene 2

Malcolm dialed Benjamin's extension from the lobby. "Ayalla and I are downstairs," he said. "We've got something." He listened for a few minutes. "All right, we'll wait down here." He turned to the FBI agent standing beside him. "He says apparently we're all on a roll, and we should head over to Laguna Beach and meet Connor and Laura at their hotel."

"He's found something in Father Rosario's files?"

"I imagine. He had that sound in his voice."

"What do you mean?"

"When he gets excited or thinks he's hot on the trail of something, he talks faster and kind of intense."

"I suppose we'll have to wait until we get to Laguna to find out what it is."

"Probably. He won't want to lay it out for us and then do it all over again for Connor and Laura. It's better if we do it together."

"I suppose," she shrugged. "Any chance dinner is in the offing?"

"We'll get room service or something."

They heard footsteps behind them. "And I'm buying," said Benjamin. "Steak or seafood, Malcolm?"

The big man thought about it for less than a second. "Probably both."

Benjamin grinned. "Do you know what I would give to be able to eat the way you do? So, is the car out front? I called Connor's cell phone. She said they'd be back in less than an hour. That was about forty-five minutes ago."

"We're good to go," said Malcolm, leading the way out of the lobby. "You want a hand with that?" He gestured to the cardboard file box Benjamin was carrying, along with a briefcase, the strap slung over his shoulder.

"Nope, I got it, thanks."

"Where's the rest of the stuff?"

"I sorted all the papers out and put what I think is important in this box. The rest of it was mostly photocopies of journal articles, and notes on different books in the field. Nothing original. Now in here, this is the good stuff. Would one of you drive? I have a couple more calls to make."

"Sure." Malcolm tossed the keys to Ayalla, who caught them neatly in one hand and went around to the driver's side and popped the door-lock button.

Once in the car, Benjamin placed the box on the seat next to him and reached into his briefcase for the satellite phone he used in lieu of the more common cell phone. The signal was virtually impossible to intercept and even if it were, the communications were thoroughly encrypted to a standard few analysts could even hope to break without the appropriate keys.

"Jeannine, it's Benjamin," he said after several moments waiting for the connection from ground to satellite to ground again. "I got your message. Anything surface?" He listened intently for several minutes, with only an occasional "right" or "yes" at his end. Ayalla, glancing into the rearview mirror, could see the smile spread across his face. "Excellent! You tell her she's a miracle worker, Jeannine. Let me know when you can send me the data....What? Sure. You call him and let me know what else he found. Oh, and would you get that photo array ready for distribution? Good. I think at least four images: the original and then the extrapolated ones. Thanks again." Benjamin switched off the phone. "Yes!" he exclaimed.

Malcolm said, "You sound like you won the lottery."

"Not quite, but we might be getting close. You remember that sting operation in Europe I told you about?"

"The one where the hacker's information was then stolen by someone else?"

"Yep, the very one. And I told you I'd put some people on finding out what happened to those elusive hard drives with all their potentially embarrassing information."

"You're not telling me they found something already?"

"Luck was on our side this time. One of our people in Italy had already figured out which bureaucrat's sticky fingers were involved. She's been keeping an eye on him ever since. I got in touch with her because I knew she was stationed in Italy, and when I filled her in on what I was looking for, she told me she was one step ahead and would let me know if she could find something specific."

"And she did?" asked Malcolm.

"Providence smiled on us, though the corrupt government minister wasn't quite so lucky. Two nights ago someone blew up the bureaucrat in his car right outside his front door. My agent—that is, she used to be one of mine—" Benjamin corrected himself, "used the confusion to slip in through a rear door and grab the hard drives out of a computer concealed behind a false panel she'd found on an earlier reconnaissance."

"Why didn't she grab the stuff before then?"

"No orders to do so. That kind of information can prove to be as dangerous as old dynamite. She knew better than to remove anything from his house without the proper sanctions."

Ayalla spoke up. "I thought the spy patrol could do whatever they wanted."

Benjamin shook his head. "Not always. Intelligence services do a lot of things that people probably wouldn't want to know about and in the long run aren't particularly ethical. But there's a clear chain of command, and agents are strongly discouraged from running off half-cocked into the field and making strategy decisions without input from their superiors."

"But she grabbed the hard drives?"

"In under a minute if I know her. She's good. And because I'd alerted her, she made this a priority. She deduced correctly that someone else was after the same thing and would probably be along shortly."

"So was she right about that?" asked Ayalla.

"She was only just out of the rear garden, with two hard drives tucked into her bag, when she spotted a sedan cruising up an alley behind the house. Two men got out and unceremoniously bashed in the gate. She couldn't make the plates on the car, but she was fairly sure it was a government vehicle. So she decided not to stick around any longer than necessary."

"And what's on those drives?" asked Ayalla, her impatience showing slightly.

"I'll know tonight. They arrived this morning via diplomatic pouch and one of the best computer geeks in the country is already at work on them. He has instructions to look for what I need first. Then he can sort through all the dirty little secrets that have gotten more than a few people rich and then dead."

"You get a lot done in a short period of time," said Ayalla, her tone a mixture of amazement and respect.

"Only when we're on the side of the angels."

"You think the bad guys never win?" she asked with more than a hint of skepticism.

"Of course they do," he said. "But you know the saying, 'What goes around, comes around.' My daughter told me about one of the laws of Celtic witchcraft. I don't know the exact words, but it expands on that theory. They say that whatever you do in this world will come back at you three-fold. Something to think about."

"Your daughter practices *witchcraft*?"

Malcolm laughed. "I don't think she'd like being called a witch exactly, but her grandmother knew a thing or two about stuff you wouldn't imagine on your strangest day. Why don't you ask Connor sometime? Maybe she'll explain it to you."

"Hmm, maybe." Ayalla looked more suspicious than convinced, but she held her tongue, wondering if she were surrounded by certifiable nut cases. But then again…

She let the thoughts recede as they swung into the driveway of the Laguna hotel where Laura and Connor were staying. A young man dashed up to the side of the car and opened the front and rear passenger doors. As Benjamin got out with his briefcase and box of files, the attendant asked if he needed help.

"No thanks, I've got it."

"You are Senator Hawthorne?" said the young man, looking first at Benjamin, "and your two friends from the police and the FBI?" His gaze swept over Malcolm and Ayalla.

"Yes, but have we met?" asked Benjamin.

"No, sir. But your daughter told me you would be coming and that you are helping to find whoever killed my brother, Enrique."

"Ah, you must be Luis." He extended his hand. "I'm surprised you are working again so soon. Connor said you were going to spend some time with your sister."

"I was, but we were making each a little crazy cooped up in the house together. She mostly sits and reads. And the manager called to tell me that the man who is supposed to work today called in sick. He has the flu or something and may not be back to work for a while."

"Well, it's a pleasure to meet you, Luis. And my deepest condolences for your loss. I didn't know your brother, but Archbishop Johnston spoke very highly of him."

"Thank you, sir." He moved around the car and slid into the driver's seat Ayalla had vacated. "You call downstairs, ma'am, when you are ready to leave, and I'll have your car in front."

"Thanks," said Ayalla. "I'm not sure how long we'll be."

»——«

"You don't look so good, sweetheart," said Connor, frowning at Laura's flushed face and unnaturally bright eyes.

"That make sense, since I don't feel so good either. But it's just a flu bug or something." She scratched at her wrist and Connor realized Laura had been doing that all day. She reached for Laura's hand and drew it closer. The inside of her wrist looked like a Martian landscape of red blotches and bumps. Red streaks radiated up her inner arm.

"Look at your wrist and your arm," Connor frowned. "This doesn't look like any flu symptom I've ever seen."

"And when did you complete your medical training?" countered Laura, a hint of annoyance in her tone. "It could also be some kind of allergic reaction." To Connor, she sounded positively peevish, highly unusual behavior for Laura.

"To what, though? And isn't this the spot where you kept trying to wash off that black powdery stuff that was all over the bones?"

Laura stared at her wrist. "Yep. I guess it is, but that doesn't mean there's a connection. And if there is, then maybe I'm allergic to something that was in it." She paused, a grin flitting over her features." Or maybe it's the ghost sickness. If my ancestors were around, they'd be quite sure that I'd been stricken with it for touching the remains of the dead." Her smile faded. "Then again, maybe they'd have a point."

"Let's not jump to any conclusions," said Connor, "especially of the woo-woo variety. You probably need some more of that cortisone cream. I'll get it."

"Can we hold off on that for a bit? All I really need is to lie down. My head is splitting."

A knock at the door startled them both. "God, are we jumpy or what?" She strode to the door and flung it open. "You made good time," she said to her father.

"The FBI drove," he explained, giving her a hug. Malcolm and Ayalla followed him into the living room of the two-room suite. "Where's your other half?"

"The question is, the better or the worse half?" said Laura from the door to the bedroom. She started across the room to greet them, then, to Connor's horror, Laura's knees appeared to buckle completely and she slumped to the carpet, knocking over a lamp as she went down.

"Oh, God," cried Connor, who was too far away to catch Laura as she went down. She rushed over to her lover's inert form, dropped to her knees, and cradled Laura's head in her lap. "Oh, God, what's wrong?" She patted Laura's cheeks. The skin was hot, far too hot. "She's burning up." Malcolm was beside her in an instant. He scooped the unconscious woman up as if she weighed no more than a child's doll and carried her into the bedroom with Benjamin, Ayalla, and Connor on his heels.

"How long has she been like this?" asked Malcolm, his hand pressed against Laura's cheek.

Connor, kneeling beside the bed, her hands clamped tight around one of Laura's said, "She seemed fine up until an hour or so ago. Then she said she had a headache, and I could tell her eyes had glazed look to them."

Benjamin, standing at the foot of the bed, was staring at Laura's arm. Her sleeve had been pushed up above the elbow when Malcolm carried her. "What is that?" he insisted. "On her arm?"

"She's been scratching at it since this morning. She was trying to wash that black stuff off her skin, the powdery residue from the bones. She said it didn't come off very easily." Connor looked at Laura's arm again. Was it only her imagination or had the inflamed streaks of red moved much farther toward the shoulder in only the last few minutes? "But she insisted it was only the flu."

Benjamin's head shot up. He stared at Connor without speaking.

"What is it, Dad? Dad?"

He focused on Connor. "You said a parking attendant was the person who first found the bones in you car. Did he touch them?"

"Yes, he moved them off the seat, but what does that have to do with—"

"Did he *touch* them?" Benjamin's tone was so fierce, Connor looked as if she'd be slapped.

"Yes, he had black splotches all over his hands."

Benjamin looked at Malcolm and Ayalla. "Didn't Luis say the other attendant called in sick, said he had the flu really bad?"

"Yes," said Malcolm, slowly, his eyes narrowing. "You don't think."

"I *do* think. I don't know how or what caused this, but Laura's in trouble and so is that kid, wherever he is."

At that moment, Laura's eyes fluttered open briefly, then closed. Her chest heaved, as if she were laboring to breathe.

"I don't understand," Connor said, her voice choking in her throat. "Just a few minutes ago, we were talking and...and..."

Benjamin barked, "We need an ambulance." He dashed into the living room, but Ayalla was already there, phone in hand. She stabbed "9" for an outside line and called 911.

"This is Special Agent Ayalla Franklin with the FBI. I'm at the Laguna Vista Inn, Room 327. I need an ambulance here immediately. The victim is unconscious and having difficulty breathing." She paused, listened. "Yes, this is extremely urgent and life-threatening. No...Yes, I will remain at the scene...stop talking about it and dispatch an ambulance—now!" She slammed down the phone. "Idiot!"

Benjamin said, "How long?"

"According to him, five to ten minutes. I'll go downstairs and wait for them."

"Ask Luis the name of the other parking attendant. We've got to get to him."

"Just what I was thinking." She started to go, then said. "Wrap a towel around her arm. If whatever she has is contagious..." She shook her head and left the thought unfinished.

Benjamin's face was grim. "Then Connor could be infected—all of us could be, and whoever that young man's been in contact with. But I don't want to start a panic. And if we get the CDC crawling all over us, or worse, slapping everyone in quarantine—" He scrubbed at his face. "Jesus, I can't believe this."

"Let Malcolm and Connor look after Laura," said Ayalla. "Maybe it's time you started throwing some weight around. Get us some help, some discreet and very quiet help."

"You're right," he said, scraping his fingers through his hair. "Jesus! If anything happened to Laura, I don't think Connor could stand to live. She almost gave up before, when Ariana died. And I'm selfish, too. My daughter is everything to me. If anything happened to her..."

Ayalla laid a hand on Benjamin's arm. "Stop thinking, and start doing. We'll figure this out."

The ex-senator looked her in the eye. "Yes, by God, we will." He reached for his case and the satellite phone and before he could dial,

Ayalla was already out the door. He heard her footsteps running down the hall. "Jeannine," he barked. "We need some help out here. Find Dr. Costanza Perelli. I don't care where she is or what she's doing. I want her here. Explain it could be a matter of life and death and everything about this top-secret. No leaks. No consultations with anyone else. She knows me, she'll understand."

"Who's that?" said Malcolm. He was standing in the doorway.

"She's one of the finest diagnosticians in the world. And she's also a consultant to the Centers for Disease Control in Atlanta. When they don't know what they're dealing with, or they stumble across some new set of symptoms, they call her in to have a look."

"You think whatever made Laura sick is some sort of communicable disease?" said Malcolm, moving toward Benjamin and lowering his voice. "If it is and we're not careful, we could put a lot of people at risk."

"I know. But if I call out the CDC people or even the locals, we could end up completely cut off, stuck in a quarantine. We'll just have to be careful and stay away from everyone until we know more."

"What about the ambulance attendants?"

"Get downstairs and tell Ayalla to cancel the ambulance right away. Tell the paramedics we decided not to wait and took our friend to the hospital ourselves. She can convince them—flash some badge, whatever. You're right. We can't expose any more unwitting people."

He punched some more numbers into his phone. "This is Benjamin Hawthorne. I need to speak with Harvey Flancher. Yes, I know it's late there, but get him for me right now. It's a priority-one situation." He waited, pacing the length of the room and back again. "Harvey. Sorry. But I need some information right now. Your ops people, they have a clinic out here on the coast, don't they?…Yes, I know it is, but I need it right now….No, it's not for me, it's for one of my people….Don't know yet, I've got an expert on the way….I'm sure it's a small facility, but if I know you, it's probably state-of-the-art….I know, Harvey, but I need this, and I promise I'll explain it later….Good. What's the address?…Got it…Would you mind calling them and giving them a heads-up?…Thanks, I owe you one…okay, I owe you several." He punched the disconnect button and walked back into the bedroom.

"Get Laura wrapped in a blanket and wrap some towels around her arm. Then we need to get her to the car without making a scene." He stepped back into the living room and dialed Malcolm's cell phone from memory. "Is there a back entrance we can use?" he asked.

"I'll find out. Ayalla's dealing with the paramedics. They aren't happy, but she's giving them a song and dance about national security. That woman's good in a pinch, I'll tell you."

"Glad to hear it because we're going to need her cooperation on this. She can't report any of this to her superiors—not yet."

"I'll make sure she understands that," said Malcolm. "Wait, here she comes."

"Tell her to get hold of Luis and the keys to our car. Also tell him to stay away from Connor and Laura's rental car. Get the keys to it. Don't tell him more than you have to but make sure he knows he's got to keep his mouth shut."

Malcolm disconnected and passed on the instructions. He started for the back of the hotel while Ayalla went quickly in search of Luis. Malcolm went out a rear door of the hotel and scanned the back of the building. He spotted a service entrance and yanked open the door which thankfully wasn't locked. Stepping quickly and hoping to avoid any employees, he explored the corridor to his right until he found the service elevator. He stepped inside and pushed the button for the third floor while dialing Ayalla's cell phone.

"There's a door at the rear," he said. "Just past the patio. We'll be coming out there. On the other side of the hotel is a short driveway they must use to make deliveries. Pull up there and we'll find you."

Malcolm pressed the stop button on the elevator, gratified that it wasn't hooked to an alarm bell, then ran down the hall to Connor and Laura's suite. The door was ajar and he continued through to the bed-room. Laura was wrapped in a blanket, and a streak of pain shot through his heart when he saw her looking so helpless. *Dear God,* he said silently, *don't let her die.*

"I found a back way out," he said. "I'll carry Laura. Let's go."

Connor was sitting on the bed next to Laura, and her face was rigid with pain and fear. "I'll carry her," she said.

Malcolm gently pulled her away. "You're strong, my friend, but not that strong." He lifted Laura effortlessly. "Besides, I've got experience with carrying damsels in distress, especially this one. Come on, we're going to the service elevator."

Connor grabbed her coat and her bag. Benjamin slung his case over his shoulder and tucked the box under his arm. Connor looked at him strangely but said nothing. Her father rarely did anything without a reason.

In less than two minutes, they were at the back door of the hotel. Benjamin pushed it open, looked out. There was no one nearby. He could see the headlights of a car splashed against the white walls of the beach cabanas to their left. "All right. I think that's Ayalla down there."

They half-ran along the walkway and instantly spotted Benjamin's rental car with Ayalla behind the wheel. She jumped out and swung open the doors. "You want to drive?" she asked Benjamin.

"No, I've got to get us directions to where we're going. Pop the trunk open."

"And where are we going?" she asked, reaching for the trunk release.

"A place that doesn't officially exist, and that means," he said, his eyes boring into hers, "you will have to forget you've ever heard about it." He went to the back of the car, deposited the box, and slammed the trunk shut.

She glared at his back for a moment as Connor and Malcolm settled Laura between them in the backseat.

"Come on!" said Malcolm. "Let's go!"

Ayalla reacted instantly and jumped into the driver's seat. Once Benjamin was in, she backed out quickly but carefully. All of them were too preoccupied to notice the black-clad figure in the shadows near the southern wall of the hotel, a figure that peered at them intently as the car passed.

"Which way?" Ayalla asked.

"Right. Down the coast."

Benjamin reached into his case and pulled out an ultra-slim laptop computer. Within seconds he had attached an interface cable to his satellite phone. The computer quickly dialed out to a computer in Benjamin's home office. Once the connection was established, he typed in instructions. A minute later, a map in vivid colors was displayed on the screen. Ayalla glanced over at it. A blinking red dot changed position and she instantly understood what he was doing.

"That's us, isn't it?" she asked. "On the screen. You're hooked up to a GPS system."

"Exactly. And we're going to find this place in record time." He looked at her. "It's a clinic of sorts, and it's completely secure. We'll be able to find out what's wrong with Laura and if there's a threat to anyone else who's been near her without bringing down the entire government bureaucracy on our heads and possibly starting a panic."

"And if it is contagious?"

"Then we'll contain it quickly, I promise."

In the backseat, Ayalla heard Connor's soft whispers. "It's all right, sweetheart. It's going to be all right. Please, hang on. You didn't leave me before, and you can't leave me now. You hear me? I love you, Laura. I love you."

Ayalla felt tears prickle at the back of her eyes, and their presence surprised her. But then, she thought, perhaps it came as no surprise that such raw emotion triggered the same in her. She'd avoided it after her father's death, avoided letting herself feel anything too deeply or becoming too dependent on anyone. That way, she was convinced, led to disaster. None of her handful of lovers had ever said anything remotely like that to her, not in all her life. And she had never been tempted to say it to any of them. She couldn't imagine what it would be like to care that much, to love that much, to be willing to give your life, your heart, and soul for someone you passionately adored. For years she'd been convinced that kind of love was the stuff of fairy tales and soap operas and sentimental movies. Yet there be could no doubt that Connor Hawthorne felt precisely that way about Laura Nez. It didn't make sense. Or maybe it did. Ayalla blinked once or twice and focused on the pavement in front of her, driving as fast as she dared without drawing the attention of a police officer.

"Another three miles," said Benjamin. "Then look for Brea Pacifica

Street on the left. I'll tell you when we get close." His eyes were glued to the screen. "How's she doing?" he asked in a soft voice.

"She's still having trouble breathing, Dad. And she doesn't respond to me at all."

"Hold on, honey. We'll be there in another twenty minutes or so."

Ayalla pressed her foot down on the accelerator. *To hell with the cops,* she thought. *I'll deal with them if I have to.*

Connor had fallen silent, but her mind was in turmoil. She tried to calm her panicked thoughts and reach out the way her Grandmother Broadhurst had taught her. She needed answers, she needed to know what was happening, and there was a chance that Gwendolyn could help her. But she couldn't find a calm center; she couldn't focus. All her swirling thoughts were unraveling in the face of the fear that coursed through her. She closed her eyes. *Grandmother, I need you.* But she heard nothing except the pounding of her own heart. Maybe this time she was truly on her own. But how could she summon the healer's magic? How could she do what she herself still did not fully understand?

Chapter Twenty

He appeared first to Mary Magdalene.
—Mark 16:9, The King James Bible

Richard La Cloche smashed his hand against the steering wheel again, though the maneuver had not proved successful thus far in making the engine of his car turn over. He was furious, a state in which he rarely found himself, for he took pride in his unshakable equanimity no matter the circumstances. Only on two occasions had he allowed himself to get out of control, and both had proved costly. The first was when he had killed the stupid priest, Father Brainard, in New Orleans. He should have been more careful to discover who the man's friends were. That would have saved him a trip to the police station and the distasteful scene with the sweaty cop whose only interrogation style consisted of accusations laced with obscenities. The second, of course, was the incident in Washington that had cost him seven years of his life. But in that instance he had come to the understanding that God had sent him there to teach and recruit. And it was there that a fellow prisoner had given him the one piece of information that had started him on his road to the ultimate salvation. The boy's mother had taken a bribe. She'd looked the other way and let a nuclear generating station be built atop a highly unstable fault line. The son didn't care what she'd done. He'd bragged about it. The money was paying for lawyers to appeal his second felony conviction. Apparently, he hadn't learned his lesson the first time around. But that bit of knowledge had seemed to Ricky like manna from heaven. The entire plan came to him in one brilliant flash of insight. And he'd spent every moment since then preparing.

Thus he could not fathom how God could allow something so mundane as car trouble to keep him from His appointed tasks.

He took a deep breath to steady himself. Where had they taken the Indian woman? Surely they were headed to a hospital. He'd already located every facility within a twenty-mile radius on his map and would be able to find her. But it would have been so much easier to have followed their car. He'd found a rare parking spot on the street only fifteen or twenty yards from the driveway of the hotel.

He'd noted the arrival of the two women in their convertible, and he'd seen the now familiar rental sedan pull in only minutes after he'd settled down to keep watch. He calculated that it was about time for the Indian woman to be showing signs of illness. Ricky had it on good authority that the progression would be swift and unpleasant. He was only puzzled that she had seemed all right when they got out of the car and talked to the Hispanic attendant in the parking lot. The kid had seemed vaguely familiar, but Ricky had filed it away for another time.

Not long after the other three went into the hotel, he saw the black woman come rushing out. Then an ambulance arrived. Ricky was pleased. Punishment was at hand. Then he was less pleased. The black woman talked with the paramedics. They shook their heads; she gestured and said something else. Finally, they shrugged and slammed their equipment back into the storage compartments of the rescue vehicle. They killed the flashing lights and drove off.

Ricky sat up in his seat, trying to figure out what was going on. Did the woman die already? Not possible. The timetable allowed for about twenty-four hours. Or so the old voudun woman had said. And even so, the paramedics would have taken her to the hospital anyway. There was no logical reason to call for help and then send it away. Or was there?

He slipped out of his car, after turning off the dome light, and went to stand at the corner of a building where he could observe the entire parking lot and both cars. The black woman was now talking with the parking attendant. She had what looked like a cell phone in her hand. She talked to the attendant again, then snatched something out of his hand and literally ran to the rental car in which she and her friends had just arrived. *Ah,* he thought. *They're going to drive her to the hospital themselves. But why?*

He watched the black woman turn down the alley that ran along the other side of the hotel. She was out of sight, but having already checked the place, he knew there was no other vehicle exit besides the circular driveway. He'd pick them up as they came out. Within minutes he saw the flash of brake lights as the car came out of the alley in reverse. Ricky reached for the ignition and turned it. Nothing happened, not even the grind of the starter motor. Just a click, and then silence.

He could only watch as the big Buick roared out of the parking lot. He heard the scrape of the tailpipe as the back end dipped hard at the end of the driveway. Within seconds, he could barely see its taillights. But pounding on the steering wheel was not getting him anywhere. After several minutes, he composed himself and picked up his cell phone to call the car rental company. The clerk apologized profusely to Father Lemarteau. They would have a tow truck there very shortly, and a representative would deliver a replacement vehicle within the hour. Would the Father care to wait in Laguna Beach, or accompany the tow truck driver to the garage?

Ricky considered his options. The fewer people he had to deal with the better. He instructed the clerk to have the car delivered to the Hilton and the keys left at the desk. When he disconnected, he stuffed the cell phone into the small black backpack he carried and removed from it a small pouch that contained a jacket made of a paper-like material that allowed the garment to be folded into a tiny parcel. He pulled the white insert out of his priest's collar and tucked it away. With the white jacket over his black shirt, now unbuttoned at the throat, and the backpack slung over his shoulder, he was no longer Father Lemarteau. No need for people to remember seeing a priest, and no need to involve himself with a cabdriver who would no doubt remember taking a fare all the way to Irvine. Better to use a more anonymous form of transportation.

He walked across the street and waited for the bus that would take him out of Laguna Beach and up the Pacific Coast Highway to Newport Beach and Fashion Island. There he could get a cab to the hotel. And the ride would give him time to think. His first order of business would be to identify the hospital where they'd taken the Indian woman. The other was to check on the parking lot attendant who had called in sick. Shame the boy had touched it. Ricky smiled as he remembered the old woman's raspy words: *La poussière noir, monsieur…c'est le mort d'enfer, l'incendie du diable:* "The black dust, sir…it's hell's death, the fire of the devil." He hoped the Indian woman was enjoying her just reward.

»——«

Archibald Sims had come to the reluctant conclusion that God had to be punishing him. Granted, he had never been much for letting religious matters intrude into his everyday life. He had always believed that religion was an odd obsession for some and, for him, a waste of a good Sunday. Even when he'd joined the damned Society, he had been more attracted to the idea of belonging to an elite group than to their avowed credo of defending the truth of God, the "real truth," naturally, as opposed to the lies and distortions spread through the world by blasphemers. The latter group, who were thus consigned to eternal punishment and damnation, consisted, as far as Archibald could tell, of the vast majority of the people on earth. The Society had determined, ostensibly by the correct interpretation of Holy Scripture, that all Buddhists, Hindus, Muslims, Jews, pagans, atheists, agnostics—and pretty much all the Protestants ever born—were bound for hell. Archibald hadn't been too alarmed by all this, for it seemed to him nothing more than pure demagoguery. He hadn't personally reached a conclusion about heaven and hell, or whether the world would somehow end in the fires of the Apocalypse. He admitted its possibility but had always been comforted by the idea of its being much too far in the future for him to worry about it. What he now feared was that the mission of the Society had perhaps ceased to be purely theoretical because the Preacher and his thugs were thinking of accelerating God's timetable.

He didn't quite see how the nuclear generating station figured into it, though. Taking over the station wasn't going to confer a lot of bargaining power on the person who pulled it off. Granted, no one wanted a meltdown of the core, but given the safety precautions and the first-class construction of the plant, they weren't looking at another Chernobyl. The only real risk was in how far any escaping radiation would be spread. That could be nasty for nearby areas, but even around the Russian site, fallout had spread over only about a twenty-mile radius. San Peligro sat in the middle of more than a hundred acres of government land. Depending on the wind direction and speed, even if radiation escaped, it would likely be dispersed over the ocean. So why was it so important, other than to assuage the Preacher's ego?

Archibald wondered if he should make his own preemptive strike: take the reactor off-line and drop the control rods into the core to stop the reaction completely. The move would be questioned at every level above him, but he could say he'd received a threatening phone call and taken precautions. They might think he'd overreacted, or worse, exceeded his authority, but at least Holcomb and his creeps wouldn't have much leverage if they were indeed intent on taking over the plant. Still, what the hell could they possibly accomplish? People like Holcomb (and the two guards who could be poster boys for a fund-raiser on behalf of botched lobotomies) had to be in this scheme, whatever it was, for money. And how could this end up producing money? Ransom? Would the plant's owners pay to keep it from being destroyed? Perhaps. The plant was fairly new. It had been built in response to the growing energy crisis in California, despite opposition from environmentalists, and it would still be years before it had paid for itself, so to speak.

But a ransom seemed absurd. The inside people would never get away with it. And Archibald knew who they were. *He knew who they were.* Instantly, that thought sent a shudder through him. What were the odds they'd leave him around to share that bit of information? If Holcomb were smart or at least cunning, he could make it look as if he and his guards had been overpowered. They could get away clean.

Not for the first time, Archibald thought very seriously about running away. He simply couldn't figure out where he would go, or how he'd get there. He thought he might go and buy a gun, but the idea scared him. What if he shot himself, or some innocent person, or the store that sold him a gun reported him to the authorities for looking nervous? Archibald had at least one outstanding skill and that was the ability to come up with the worst-case scenario. He'd absorbed that idea from the old books he'd read about the early days of the Atomic Energy Commission and the old Advisory Committee on Reactor Safeguards. They were gone now, replaced by the Nuclear Regulatory Commission and divisions of the Department of Energy. But the advisory committee had been the ones who devised a safety standard of imagining "the maximum credible accident" and then planning how to contain it. He liked that way of thinking, although the Committee's extreme caution had eventually been overridden by pressure to create more nuclear power plants.

So what was the maximum credible accident here? A complete meltdown of the core would be disastrous but not necessarily dangerous to human beings in the surrounding areas. Theoretically, leaking radiation would not escape the containment building. There was the possibility of the immeasurably hot core melting its way down through the floor beneath it and into the ground. This was what scientists once called the China Syndrome, a grimly humorous (if geographically inaccurate) prediction of where the melted core would end up if it kept on going through the earth and out the other side. But most experts believed that the mass of radiation would continue for no more than a hundred meters.

Archibald sighed heavily. He should get the reactor shut down within the next twenty-four hours. Tonight he had to leave the duty logs and security data for Holcomb. If Archibald came in tomorrow, perhaps he could beat Holcomb to the punch. On the other hand, maybe he should get as far away as possible and not look back.

»—«

The archbishop fumbled for the telephone, but once he had it in his hand, he only heard a dial tone. Maybe it hadn't rung at all. Perhaps he had only dreamed it. But there had been a bell, hadn't there?

He'd fallen asleep in the leather easy chair in his office, still waiting for more news from Benjamin Hawthorne, who had phoned at midnight to report that Laura Nez was desperately ill and the cause could not be determined. He did, however, explain about the bones that had been left for Laura and Connor to find. The archbishop's blood had run cold when he heard the story. But once he hung up, after asking the senator to keep him advised, the image of bones covered in black dust nagged at him. He tried to tease the old memory to the surface, but it stubbornly refused to materialize. It was in that frame of mind that he finally succumbed to having gone many days without adequate sleep.

He looked at his watch—four-thirty in the morning, and still no word. He closed his eyes again, willing himself to remember what he had been dreaming. They flew open again, however, at the sound of a voice.

"It isn't the dream you must remember, but the memory you possess."

The archbishop, his heart pounding, stared in the direction of the voice. Finally a form moved out from the darker shadows beside the tall bookcases.

"Who are you?"

"Some call me Father Angelico," said the old man as if it hardly mattered.

"How did you get in here?"

"That was not difficult. But we have no time for long explanations of matters you do not yet understand."

The archbishop started to argue, but something about the old man, garbed in a threadbare cassock, his hands folded in front of him, made him hold his tongue. A light shone in his eyes, a radiance such as the archbishop had never seen. He had never believed in auras, but this stranger certainly had one, and it was visible to the naked eye. For the first time in his long career as a cleric, Archbishop Johnston suspected that something both supernatural and wonderful was happening right before his eyes. More important, he knew he did not have to be afraid of this odd visitor, though his stomach clenched with a certain trepidation about what the old priest might say.

"Why are you here?" he asked.

The wizened old man smiled. "Good. You are willing to listen to your heart and not argue with the evidence of your eyes and ears. To answer your question, I am here because it is my duty to protect something, a relic of great value. I don't think you know where it is, but you may be able to help me anyway."

Archbishop Johnston frowned. "I don't know what relic you speak of."

The visitor came forward, though the archbishop could not quite identify the movement as walking. Instead, the man was in one instant across the room and in the next only a foot or two separated them. He released the top button of his cassock and pulled out a silver chain. At the end of the chain was a design, not unlike the design Father Rosario had shown him, and remarkably similar to the top of the cross that Enrique's sister had fashioned. It was undoubtedly the mark of the Cult of Magdalene.

"You recognize this, then," said the old man, though his tone conveyed a statement rather than question.

"I've seen something like it."

"And you know what it represents?"

"I think so. It's the symbol of a cult—that is, a group who held a particular belief about the truth of Mary Magdalene's role in the life of our Savior."

"And that role was?"

"To be honest, I don't know. I only know what I've been taught, what my church has taught for century upon century. I can't begin to imagine that it could all be wrong."

"That is good, Archbishop. You are, as you say, an honest man, and I respect that above all else. But your associate, Monsignor Kursk, he was not an honest man. He and his kind have tried always to destroy the truth. We have sought to preserve it."

An unpleasant thought flashed through Johnston's brain. "Did you kill him?"

"No. I am sworn to honor the life that only God can give. I can use my knowledge and skills to prevent others from doing harm, but to kill would be to forfeit my own life and start the cycle again from the beginning."

"What cycle?"

"I wish I had time to explain it all to you, Archbishop, for you are a wise man who would benefit greatly from what I could teach you. But there is not time. Suffice it to say that there is a wheel of life that turns and brings us step by step through the tests and challenges of mortal existence. We advance, we retreat, we live and we die, we are born to live again. We climb a ladder, a rung at a time."

"A ladder toward God?" asked Johnston. "Is that what you mean? Jacob's ladder in the Bible?"

The old priest smiled. "In a way. But the ladder and heaven and God...they are all right here." He gently tapped Johnston's chest. "But you must turn your thoughts to remembering. A man has loosed an ancient evil into the world and you have knowledge that can heal that evil, and heal those who are afflicted with it."

"Do you mean the Nez woman?" the archbishop asked, his tone sharper. "Because if you know what's wrong with her..."

"I do. But you have the answer also, and it is ordained that you will be the one to bring light into that particular darkness." The old cleric seemed to recede toward the shadows.

"Wait," the archbishop cried. "I don't know what it is I'm supposed to remember."

"Yes, you do, my son. You once said to a young priest that he was foolish to try so hard to understand the ways of the wicked, and he told you that only by understanding could he vanquish that which poisoned their hearts."

"But I don't know what you mean!" said the archbishop, rising from his chair.

It was too late. The visitor was gone.

"Damn, damn, damn!" he said with unbridled vehemence. "How do I help someone if I don't even know..." He took a deep breath, then another. *When in doubt, pray.*

An hour later, the archbishop snapped awake. Tiny tendrils of dawn light were visible in the fading night sky. The horizon glowed. And Archbishop Johnston had the answer in his mind the moment he awoke. Father Cameron Stark.

Two hours later he dialed the number Benjamin Hawthorne had

given him. "Senator," he said. "I think I know what's wrong with your friend, and I also think I know how to save her life."

»—«

He sat on a bench in the old botanical garden of the mission. Oddly, he felt tired. For years, his physical condition hadn't been of any particular concern. He knew how to maintain his body in a state of relative health, and even if by all rights he should have been dead a few decades ago, his spirit was sufficiently strong and his will focused enough, to keep him active and able to go about his business. But he felt, well, somewhat faded, as if his body's substance were no longer as dense as when he'd been born into the world. Sometimes he thought that if he held up a hand, he might see right through it, or if he looked into the mirror, only a dim outline of a man's face would stare back at him. A fanciful thought for a not very fanciful person.

He'd done what he could for the Nez woman. All these rules about intervention could be very trying to one's soul, he reflected. He was never sure he entirely understood them. Most of the time, people had to save themselves, learn their lessons the hard way. On a few occasions, the descendants of the Old Ones might intervene. But when in doubt, all he had to do was go into deep meditation and the answer would become clear, though not always welcome. So the archbishop would either remember, or he would not. And Laura Nez would live, or she would not. Still, even after such a long life, he was not too jaded to feel a pang of sadness that she might leave this world and the other young woman, the companion who clearly needed her. That companion would have to think quickly and remember well if she were to save her lover.

He looked around him as the encroaching day softly illuminated the trees, the rough walls of the mission, the shiny leaves of the plants that grew here so profusely, even though rain had fallen only rarely in the last few months. This garden, he thought, is truly blessed. And the more he looked about him, the more he began to wonder if perhaps Father Rosario had realized the same thing.

Chapter Twenty-One

The wrong of unshapely things is a wrong too great to be told;
I hunger to build them anew and sit on a green knoll apart,
With the earth and the sky and the water, remade, like a casket of gold;
For my dreams of your image that blossoms a rose in the deeps of my heart.
—William Butler Yeats, *The Lover Tells of the Rose in His Heart*

Connor perched on a chair beside the hospital bed. Around her the machines of medical science beeped and clicked and occasionally sighed. Her eyes were hot and puffy. She hadn't slept in twenty-four hours, but no one, not even her father, had been able to coax her away from Laura's side. She gripped the metal rail hard, squeezing until her knuckles were white. It was the only alternative to screaming her anger and frustration. She wanted to revile the God who could have let this happen. But she knew that wasn't how it worked. God created. Humans destroyed. Someone had done this to Laura. Someone had wanted to kill either or both of them, not caring one way or the other. If Connor had the person in her sights, she firmly believed she could throttle the bastard with her bare hands.

"Hold on, sweetheart. Please, hold on. I know you can fight this. You can do some of that magic your grandmother taught you. My dad has been trying to find her, but no one on the rez who has a phone knows where she is right now. I've even tried contacting her, you know, the other way, but I don't feel her presence anywhere. But I know she'll come." Connor stopped, realizing she was babbling, afraid to listen to the machines humming away in the silence, afraid to allow herself even for a moment to consider that Laura might not live. She leaned her head against the railing. *Please, God, don't take her away from me.*

»——«

"He said *what?*"

Benjamin was huddled with Malcolm in the hallway and he kept his voice down to avoid being heard by the trio of doctors outside the door to Laura's room. "Johnston said something about what I told him jogged his memory. He remembered a conversation he once had with a priest who works in New Orleans. He called the priest and described what happened to Laura—the black dust, the bones, and her symptoms. The guy knew what it was!"

"So what is it?"

"I don't know the scientific designation, but it's a biotoxin that can be absorbed through the skin."

"You mean like anthrax?"

"In a way. This powder is distilled from a plant that only grows in a few places in the world. Apparently just making it takes months and a whole lot of very arcane knowledge."

"One of the places it grows being New Orleans?"

"Yes."

"But how would some priest down there know about it?"

"He's studied the local beliefs and practices for years. He knows more about voodoo than anyone in the country."

"Voodoo? You've gotta be kidding me. No one believes in that stuff. And how would some poison like that end up here?"

"I don't know, but Johnston is convinced that this substance—he said it's called 'devil's fire' in English—is what infected Laura."

"But what do we do for her?" asked Malcolm, his voice tight with restrained emotion.

"The priest told Johnston that there is an antidote for it, but the plant that holds a cure is just about as rare as the plant that causes the sickness."

"Great, so how are we supposed to find it?"

"I'm not sure. I called Jeannine to start researching it. I need to go talk to Connor about this. You want to come with me?"

"You go ahead," said Malcolm. "I'd better find Ayalla and fill her in. I think she's in the lounge. She's gonna love this new idea. Voodoo. Good Lord!"

»——«

His inquiries had come up empty. Not one hospital near Laguna Beach had admitted the Indian woman. But why? Common sense dictated that they would have rushed her to an emergency room. He pondered it as he ironed his black shirt. Maybe she'd died. That possibility made him smile. Perhaps the potency was stronger than he'd anticipated. And just maybe they'd taken her to a local morgue. Though how they'd explain that was a mystery. He smiled. Dead or dying? Either way the meddlers were busy with their little crisis, and he could deal with them in good time. He would deal with God's enemies at his leisure. Right now there were more important matters that required his attention. Only two more days and the struggle would begin.

He opened up his laptop and reviewed the schematics once more. Holcomb had already placed explosive devices at all the locations Ricky had marked on a diagram, though he was too stupid to grasp the significance of the placements. Two would blast breaches in the system of pipes that carried coolant to the reactor. Two more were designed to go off within ten minutes of the first, thereby destroying the coolant backup system, which would have automatically come on line. Yet another device, this one smaller but equally important, would disable the mechanism that dropped the control rods into the core. Without the control rods in place, there was no way to slow down the reaction in the chamber. It would simply accelerate, more and more neutrons of uranium releasing and colliding. Fission. The splitting of the atom. He considered it man's most foolhardy attempt to play God. And now the nuclear reactor would go beyond critical mass to supercritical. And the meltdown would occur right on time.

Holcomb actually thought the bombs were part of a blackmail threat. *But,* Ricky mused, *would he have placed them at all if he'd known the truth? Probably not.* Holcomb, the guards, Archibald Sims, and all those who worked at San Peligro would go out of this world and straight into hell. But they'd already be glowing.

»——«

"I don't get it. This is some kind of poison. But why? And how the hell are we going to find an antidote?" Connor stood in the corner of the room farthest from Laura's bed. She didn't want Laura to be out of her sight, but she also didn't want her to overhear something that might make her subconscious give up hope.

"The priest in New Orleans knows what the antidote is called. Johnston told me over the phone and I wrote it down. I've already got Jeannine working on finding out where it grows, who might have it."

Connor took the scrap of paper from his hand. She stared at the scrawl and felt her heart catch in her throat. She looked up at her father, shock written all over her face.

"What is it?" he whispered fiercely.

"I know this plant," she said, "I can't believe it, but I've seen this name."

"Where? Here?"

"The mission, the place we visited this afternoon. There was a sign in the garden. And this is what it said." She held up the paper. "'*La lumière de sacré mère*': the light of the holy mother. Dad, this is the same plant. But what the hell do we do with it once we get it?"

"Johnston said his friend would explain more. Right now we've got to get to that mission." He dashed out into the hallway with Connor on his heels. Malcolm and Ayalla were standing about thirty feet down the corridor, startled to see father and daughter almost running. From the look on Malcolm's face it was clear that he thought the worst might have happened. But then he saw the eagerness on Connor's face and let himself breathe again.

"The antidote. We know where it is," Benjamin almost shouted.

"Jeannine already found it," said Malcolm. "Wow, that was—"

"Not, not Jeannine. Connor has seen it. She's seen the plant. It's growing at that old mission they went to today."

Malcolm's mouth dropped open.

Ayalla shook her head in disbelief, as if to say "No one is that lucky," but she didn't say it out loud. Being around this group was beyond weird at some moments, but she had no intention of questioning providence. Not right this minute anyway.

"The director here has a staff car with government plates and a flasher. You're going to need all the speed you can muster to get there and back."

"What's the time frame?" asked Malcolm.

Benjamin swallowed. He hadn't shared that with Connor. "It can be as little as twenty-four hours from exposure to…the end."

Connor had to grab the wall to steady herself. "But it's been almost that long already."

"I know, honey." Benjamin swept his daughter into his arms. "I know, but she's strong, and the priest said if her exposure was over a small area, she could have more time."

"How much more?"

"I don't know."

"Then let's go."

"You can't leave now," said Malcolm. "Ayalla and I will go."

"You won't be able to find it quickly enough. I know right where the plant is in the botanical garden. The best thing I can do for Laura is find that damn thing. And Dad's got to get instructions on how to use it."

Benjamin was already moving toward the director's office. "I'll get the keys to the car."

Ayalla looked uncertain. "Should I just stay here?"

Connor shook her head. "No. You drive better than my friend here. He tends to get overly emotional and wreck up cars. And besides, we may need some federal badge flashing to get what we need."

Ayalla nodded confidently. "You show me the way, and I'll show you how to fly low."

They ran down the hallway, caught up with Benjamin, who tossed them the keys. They were hurtling down the driveway in less than three minutes.

»——«

"It isn't time, you know."

"I hoped it wasn't, now I'm not so sure. But I'd hate to leave her."

"You know the difference between visiting here and moving in permanently, I hope."

"Yes, my grandmother."

"Good. I'd hate to think I hadn't taught you well enough to discern the difference between a twist of fate and a summons to the light."

"It feels close, though."

"The light?"

"Yes…no, I think it's the pain that feels closer."

"Good. Then you haven't let go of the cord that binds you to your body."

"I haven't. But it's hard to see."

"See with your heart and your spirit, my child."

"Connor's gone."

"Only because she wishes to save you. But her love is still around you like one of the blankets I used to weave for you. Feel its warmth and beauty. Let it sustain you until it is time."

"Why does death keep testing me, Grandmother?"

"Because you keep testing the boundaries of life. You're a warrior. Now sleep, my child, but be prepared to awaken from this dream."

»——«

True to her promise, Ayalla drove as if pursued by all the demons of hell. Malcolm had slapped the magnetic blue flasher on top of the car, and no one had dared interdict the dark sedan as it raced toward Santa Maria. The Saturday morning traffic was light, but where it bunched up, Ayalla threaded through the cars, used the shoulder of the road, and whipped across all the lanes and back again.

"Jesus, Ayalla. It won't help Laura if we demolish the car on the way."

Ayalla looked in the rearview mirror and caught Connor's eye. "Is he always such an old lady?"

Connor shook her head. "I didn't think so, but then again he has totaled his share of police units. He may be getting cautious in his old age." She tried to inject a note of lightness into her tone that she didn't actually feel.

Malcolm, one hand braced against the dashboard, harrumphed. "Old, hell! Do your worst, Special Agent."

Ayalla didn't say a word, just pressed down on the gas pedal. Connor could see the speedometer creeping up, to ninety, then one hundred. But she wasn't nervous. The way Ayalla handled the car reminded her of the first time she'd ridden with Laura and noticed how her hands controlled the car with a skill that was precise yet seemingly effortless. That described Ayalla's technique. Her fingers were wrapped around the wheel, but not in a death grip. She sat well back in her seat, her eyes flicking from the road to the rearview to the side mirror in an easy rhythm. The car never swerved abruptly. Even at high speed, the woman slipped through narrow spaces in the traffic as if they had the road to themselves. Connor sat back and tried to focus on the garden where they would find the plant that was somehow an antidote for the toxin that was killing Laura.

Laura dying. Her fists clenched. Anger surged through her. When she found who was responsible, she would—No. She had to stay calm, stay focused. The fury would have to wait.

"Is this the exit coming up?" Ayalla asked.

"Yes, then right at the bottom of the ramp." Connor was grateful for the daylight. She wasn't sure she could have found the mission in the dark, let alone a plant in the overgrown garden. Ayalla slowed only enough to be sure there was no oncoming traffic, then turned the sedan hard, allowing the back end to swing into a controlled skid. She corrected perfectly as she accelerated, and the car straightened out and surged forward without losing so much as a second.

"Nice turn," said Malcolm.

"Yeah. Didn't you tell me you'd heard the Feebs knew how to drive cars *and* shoot guns?"

"I'm sorry I ever doubted you," he said with evident sincerity. But he hadn't loosened his grip on the dash. "Don't tell me…you trained at Daytona."

"Stock cars," she said. "My father hated it, but I loved racing."

"You're serious, aren't you?"

"I never kid about cars," she said with a half smile. "Connor, we just passed a sign for the mission. Which side is it on?"

"The left, the second entrance. There's a little guardhouse. There was a park ranger there yesterday, but I don't think the place is supposed to be open yet."

Ayalla whipped into the driveway and stopped hard enough to send dust billowing around them. The entrance was blocked by a single crossbar across the one-lane drive. Her abrupt arrival attracted the attention of the ranger who had apparently been sitting in the guardhouse with his morning coffee. He stepped outside and strode toward the car.

"Hey, slow down. We don't open until nine."

Ayalla was already out of the car and heading right at him, her badge case open and held high in her left hand. "FBI, sir. We need access immediately. Please raise the barrier."

"What?" The man frowned at the badge, then looked back at Ayalla, then at the sedan, its light still flashing.

"I said this is urgent. I need you to raise the barrier so we can get by."

"The hell I will. I'm in charge here. What's going on? You think we got drug dealers and kidnappers hiding out? Or is this just some VIP tour in a big hurry?" He smirked ever so slightly, but it was enough to get a reaction.

"You are seriously pissing me off, sir. If you don't step aside and raise that barrier, you will regret the results when I have my boss call your boss. What do you suppose my boss is going to say?"

"Hey, I don't need to take any shit from you."

"No, he's not going to say that. He is going to say that because you did not cooperate with a federal law enforcement agent, I had to arrest and charge you with obstruction of a federal investigation."

"Like that's gonna happen."

Ayalla continued as if he hadn't spoken. "And by the time someone figures out you're not here, we'll have your sorry ass tucked away at a federal detention center. So don't give me attitude. You do your job. We'll do ours."

The ranger was so focused on Ayalla, he failed to notice the passenger door open. "Is there a problem, boss?" said a deep voice, booming in the relative silence. The ranger turned his head to identify the source, and his eyes came to rest on the formidable physique of Malcolm Jefferson, whose mere presence made the full-size sedan seem strangely smaller. He stood with his elbows resting on the roof.

"Boss?" said the ranger, his head swiveling back to Ayalla. "You're his boss?"

"Good help is hard to get," she said, then raised her voice so it would carry farther. "Everything's just fine here, isn't it Ranger…" She scrutinized his name badge. "Fiedler."

"Yes, ma'am. I, um…yeah, it's fine. I just don't understand what you'd want here."

Ayalla leaned closer and spoke in a conspiratorial whisper. "We have a suspect in custody who came here to your historic site yesterday specifically to hide a murder weapon. We've extracted a confession; however, it is urgent that we retrieve the weapon and have ballistics tests done on it. Time is of the essence, not to mention we don't want any civilians getting hurt, do we? Kid finds a gun, shoots someone?"

"No. No, of course not. If you'd only explained that right away, I wouldn't have…" The balance of his explanation was lost as Ayalla trotted back to the car.

"I could have handled that without you making an appearance," she said to Malcolm.

"I know. But I thought one peek at big, bad me might save us a minute or two."

"You're probably right. When necessary, you can flaunt your big, bad self anytime you want."

"What did you tell him we were looking for?" asked Connor.

"A murder weapon someone hid here yesterday.

Malcolm smiled at Ayalla. "I'm impressed. I didn't know how we were going to explain the plant thing."

The ranger raised the barrier, and Ayalla shot through it, leaving him in the dust with his mouth agape.

"Over there, park by that large clump of trees," said Connor. "There's a shortcut to the garden, if only I can find it. We stumbled across it by accident yesterday, and I know it isn't marked on the map. If we don't find it right away, we'll take the long way around on the other side of the mission."

»——«

"Archbishop, thank you for coming."

"I didn't figure I had much choice under the circumstances. You needed me. Of course it would be nice to know *where* I am. That car you sent had completely opaque windows in the back, and the driver kept the partition closed. It was a little disorienting."

"I'm sorry for that, but this installation is rather…um…"

"Say no more, Senator, I get the picture. You were the president's national security adviser at one time, weren't you?"

"Yes, I was."

"That explains your cloak-and-dagger methods. I assume you brought Miss Nez here because you didn't want to start a panic about a contagious disease."

"True."

"And you didn't want to lose control of the situation by involving a bunch of bureaucrats and possibly attracting the media."

"Also true. I have to compliment you on your perspicacity, sir."

"You don't generally get to be an archbishop in the Catholic Church if you're an idiot. And it helps if you recognize strategy when you see it. So let's get on the horn with Father Stark. He's standing by to explain to one of your technicians how to process this plant for its medicinal value. I didn't dare try to take down that information and relay it to you. I don't know a damn thing about science. I avoided it like the plague. Sorry," he said when he saw Benjamin's face tighten. "Poor choice of words."

264

"No, it's all right, Archbishop. Let's find an office and a phone."

Thirty minutes later, Benjamin and the archbishop were seated around a small conference table along with one of the doctors who staffed the facility, which existed to care for patients who were "guests" of one of the intelligence services, or agents who had been injured and required a secure medical clinic in which to recuperate.

Dr. Hu had barely been briefed on the situation, but he had examined Laura. His expression was grave as he reported his findings. "We'll have to put her on a ventilator within the next few hours. She's having difficulty breathing on her own, and even with the oxygen mask, her blood oxygen levels are falling. I've never seen any disease or infection work this fast. I hope this person you've contacted knows what he's talking about."

Benjamin said, "So do I, doctor. And I'm going to have to ask you to suspend your skepticism until you hear him out. I don't imagine you'll necessarily agree with his assessment of the situation, but in the last several hours, no one here has had any ideas of how to deal with this. And he does."

"But you say this man isn't a doctor?" asked Hu for the second time in an hour.

"No, he's a priest. But that may be just what we need. Archbishop, if you'd make the call please."

Johnston did as he was asked and within a minute had Father Stark on the line. He handed the receiver to Benjamin, who pressed the speaker button so that everyone could hear.

"Father Stark, I'm Benjamin Hawthorne. Also here is Dr. Hu. I know the archbishop has filled you in on what happened. He tells us that you believe you know the cause of my associate's illness and can tell us how to prepare an antidote."

The priest's voice, with a hint of Creole, came through clearly. "If the circumstances are as the archbishop described, I can be fairly sure that you're dealing with a nasty substance prepared by some old-time voudun from around these parts. I'm surprised really because I didn't think anyone even knew how to make it anymore. But then again, it could have been around for a while, and someone found it."

Dr. Hu spoke up. "They've told me this is some kind of biotoxin. Can you elaborate?"

"I'm not a doctor or a scientist, so I doubt I could explain it correctly. But I do know the effects. The substance, like anthrax for example, is absorbed through the skin. It initially causes a rash that itches like mad, then the site of exposure turns red and blisters. After that, the infection causes red streaks spreading over the body. There's also a very high fever, the victim loses consciousness, and within a relatively short period of time, say twenty-four to thirty-six hours, death occurs."

"And you say you learned this from voodoo practitioners—witch doctors?"

"In a way. Though they wouldn't appreciate either of those terms, I'm sure. Still, if this substance touched the woman, then *la lumière de sacré mère* may be the only hope. And since it was customary to deliver the poison along with a few human bones, I'd say the odds are pretty high that we're dealing with *l'incendie du diable*."

Dr. Hu shook his head, but Benjamin laid a hand on his arm. "Doctor, I know this probably goes against everything you learned in medical school, but please, I need you to help me, and help Laura."

The physician stared at his notebook for a moment, then cleared his throat. "All right, Father Stark, tell me what has to be done to transform the plant substance into a medicine. Do we need to distill it? Then inject it?"

"No," said the priest. "It's actually much simpler than that."

He began to explain, and Dr. Hu took careful notes. The priest was right, it was simple. He would need to grind the leaves and the roots into a paste. It had to be done by hand. No machinery could be involved. Dr. Hu started to question this requirement, then shook his head and kept writing as the priest explained how often they would apply the paste to the site of infection.

"I'll need to find a good old-fashioned mortar and pestle," said Hu. Before he left the room, though, he spoke directly to Benjamin. "Are you sure you're willing to take this risk? For all we know, the plant itself could be toxic."

"It's up to Connor," said Benjamin. "Laura's unconscious, and her only family I know of is out of reach. Connor would give her life for

Laura without a moment's hesitation. If she believes this is the only alternative we have, then I support her in that."

"But if we at least tested the plant to determine its composition."

"There isn't time for that, Doctor. You said yourself you have no idea why Laura is so ill, but you know she's dying."

Dr. Hu's face was grave. "Yes, I did say that. And in these past few hours, not one treatment we've tried has had any measurable effect. So I'll do as you ask, but I still believe it's too risky." He left the room, and Benjamin picked up the receiver.

"I guess you heard that, Father Stark. The good doctor isn't any too pleased with this idea."

"I know, sir. But I promise you I wouldn't even suggest this course of action if I didn't firmly believe that it's justified. If there were time, I would be just as eager to have the substance in the plant tested. For all I know, it may have some remarkable healing properties that could be of use in treating other illnesses. For now, though, I think we have to focus on your Miss Nez. My prayers are with her."

"Thank you, Father. I'll let you know what happens."

"Please do."

»—«

"Damn it, I can't find the spot where we came out of the garden!" Connor's voice was ragged with frustration and anxiety. "It's got to be nearby."

Malcolm grabbed her arm. "You said you got into the garden from the mission. Right? So let's go around the long way. It beats wasting any more time here. Maybe the exit is designed so that you can't see it from the outside. You see it only when you're actually in the garden."

Connor swore softly under her breath. "All right. But it's a hike."

Ayalla shrugged. "Then we'll run. You lead the way."

The three of them set off at a brisk pace, Malcolm bringing up the rear. Of the three of them, he was the least fond of running. It had been quite a few years since he'd had to chase down suspects through alleys and over fences. But he strove to keep up with the women. Ayalla was obviously in excellent physical shape. Even in the dressy flats she wore, she covered the ground in long, easy strides. Connor stayed in front, driven more by fear and frustration than anything else. She wasn't any more enthused about aerobic exercise than Malcolm, but like him, she would have run until she dropped if it would save Laura.

They sped past the outbuildings and around the perimeter of the pasture, where the horses and goats stood staring at them curiously. Dodging around the fountain where Connor and Laura had last seen Father Angelico, they pounded along the path and into the arcade, past the murals. Connor didn't pause to see if the mysteriously changing image was visible or not. Instead, she turned left and almost leaped the gate leading into the botanical garden. But good sense prevailed and she skidded to a stop and yanked it open. Ayalla was right behind her, Malcolm a few paces back and breathing hard. "Go on," he said, bending over to catch his wind. "I'll be right there."

Connor broke into a run again, heading for the center of the garden where the path split around the circular bed where the odd plant grew. She rounded a slight curve, and saw it, the leaves shimmering in the sunlight. "Thank you," she whispered. "Please let this be the right one." Slowing to a trot, she approached the plant and read the sign once more. LA LUMIÈRE DE SACRÉ MÈRE. Yes, this is what the priest in New Orleans had said. She prayed he was right.

"How much do we take?" asked Ayalla who was now standing beside her.

"I'm not sure, but we'll take plenty just in case. We need some of the root as well."

"I'll call Senator Hawthorne. Maybe he has a better idea of just what we need to bring back. May as well be sure we have it right." She whipped out her phone and dialed as Connor stepped closer to the plant. But as she reached out to grasp a low-hanging branch of the tall shrub, all the lights went out.

»——«

Benjamin sat by Laura's bed and gently held her hand. He didn't know if there was anything he could say that would encourage her to hold on to life until Connor returned and the antidote could be prepared. Dr. Hu had scavenged around until he found implements that would substitute for an old-fashioned mortar and pestle. An assistant had returned from a nearby health food store with the requested variety of herbal tea. Now there was little to do but wait, and Benjamin was not particularly good at inaction in the face of crisis. For the twentieth time at least, he wished for his mother-in-law, Gwendolyn Broadhurst, to be alive and well and sitting right here with him, instead of wandering about in the "other realms" as she called them. He'd been sad when she died, but comforted to finally understand there was something besides infinite emptiness beyond death. Despite that awareness, though, he wasn't prepared to surrender Laura to the next adventure, if indeed that is what it was.

He squeezed her hand gently. It was so hot. "Laura," he whispered. "You never have given up before. You've done some good work for me, kiddo, and there's a lot left to do. So don't get any ideas about leaving us all here to fend for ourselves. Okay? You went and fell in love with my daughter, and she loves you…so…" His voice broke slightly. "You can't leave now. You can't."

His cell phone beeped.

"Hawthorne," he said quietly. "Yes, Ayalla, what's going on there? Do you have it? Ayalla? Hello? Hello?"

He looked at the screen of his phone. It still indicated they were connected. He frowned and slipped the satellite phone out of his coat pocket. He dialed Ayalla's cell. Her voice mail came on instantly, indicating the line was busy. He put the cell phone back to his ear. Empty silence. *What the hell!* The last thing they needed was a breakdown in communications. "Hello?" he said again. This time he heard a roar of static and was disconnected completely.

»——«

Ayalla smacked her phone against her palm. "Oh, for crying out loud," she muttered, stabbing at the send key. In the next instant, she couldn't even see the phone, mere inches from her face. The sun, shining brightly in a brilliant blue sky a moment ago, was simply gone. There was no sky, and not even the faintest outline of a single object in the garden. Ayalla had never experienced darkness so complete. Her heart thudded in her chest. She started to move and stumbled over an uneven brick. All sense of up and down, here and there, was completely lost to her. Ayalla pushed down the panic rising in her throat.

"Connor!" she shouted. "Connor, where are you?"

"Here," came the muted reply. "I can't see anything."

"Stay put," said Ayalla. "I'll follow the sound of your voice." *This is absurd,* she thought. *Connor wasn't more than ten feet from me. Now it sounds as if she's a hundred yards away.* "Keep talking. I'm trying to get a fix on you."

"Over here," said Connor. "I'm close to the shrub. I still have my hand on it."

"I can't see the shrub, but I think I'm getting closer to you."

"Keep coming then. I can't see my hand in front of my face, so I don't know where you are. Hell, I don't know where *I* am."

Ayalla thought the last comment strange. They knew basically where they were. The absolute darkness was intensely weird, but they were still in the botanical garden at the mission. She took another step and, inexplicably, Connor's voice came from directly beside her. She reached out and touched fabric.

"Jesus!" Connor blurted out. "You startled me."

"Sorry."

"No, it's all right. I'm just scared."

"Me, too," said Ayalla, then marveled that she'd agreed. She'd never admitted to anyone before when she was scared. "But what's happening? It isn't this dark even during an eclipse."

"No, it isn't. But…" Connor stopped, abruptly aware that she could just see the vaguest outline of Ayalla's eyes. "Wait, I can see you a little, but only your eyes."

"I tend to blend in to a black background," said Ayalla dryly. "Great camouflage. You on the other hand would be much easier to shoot at if—"

She didn't finish the sentence. Another voice did. *"If you'd come here to do violence, which you didn't."*

Ayalla stared at Connor, quite sure the woman's lips had not moved. "What did you say?"

"Nothing," Connor whispered.

"Then who…?"

"I speak," said the disembodied voice. *"I speak because you are here to take something from me, and I desire that you be conscious of what you do."*

Ayalla shuddered slightly. "Is that the plant talking?"

"No," said Connor. "I don't think so."

"That isn't entirely correct," said the voice. *"In a sense, I certainly am the plant. But that is not all that I am."*

"Then who are you?" said Connor.

"Where are you?" added Ayalla at almost the same moment, her hand creeping toward the waist holster under her jacket.

"You do not need a weapon against me, Ayalla Franklin. It is within my power simply to wish you into another place or time, or cause you to feel that you cannot move, but I have no intention of doing so. Nor would I bring harm to either of you, or to your male friend who is wandering about in the dark somewhat confused. But I think we shall leave him to his searches for a few moments. It is to you two women I wish to speak."

"Why?" asked Connor.

"Because of who you are—a priestess and acolyte of the Holy Mother."

"I'm neither of those," Connor responded, her tone of voice growing angry. "And right now I have more important things to do than debate the supernatural with you, whatever you are."

"What you have to do is save your loved one. I am aware of this. But before you continue on your errand, we will have some thoughts together. Otherwise, the cure you seek will not heal the woman."

"What is this? Some sort of blackmail. If I don't listen to you, then you won't let me have the plant?"

They heard a soft rippling sound that could almost have been a low, gentle laughter. *"As a human, you think only in human terms. Do you think that an angel of the one true God of Creation would play at such games—would bargain with a human life at stake?"*

"An angel?" whispered Ayalla. "But that's not..."

"Not possible? I assure you it is. And I can also assure you that I only came here to help your friend, Connor, obtain what she needs to save the earthly life of the woman who is ill."

"But I have what I need right in front of me," said Connor in frustration. "Or at least I did until you turned out all the lights."

The darkness receded instantly, pushed to the edges of their vision by a dim yet potent light that emanated from the center of the plant they had sought.

"Is this better?"

"Yes, but why are you here at all?"

"If you do not understand what it is you are doing when you take pieces of this creation of Spirit, then it will avail you not."

Connor frowned. "What is it I have to understand? The priest said pieces of this plant will save my lover. That's all I need to know."

"What you know is only part of the truth. Just as the one who created the substance called upon the powers of darkness and fear to permeate it with death, so you must call upon the powers of Light to imbue this simple plant with life."

"What could I possibly do?"

"Be precisely who you are."

"Just who are you supposed to be?" Ayalla whispered to Connor.

"I don't know. It's got something to do with my grandmother. She was the descendant of Celtic priestesses. She had a—well, has a circle sort of, a group that calls themselves 'light workers.'"

"And you are her heir," said the voice. *"You have always had a destiny, whether or not you acknowledge it. And you chose that destiny before you were ever born."*

Connor stepped closer to the shrub. "I don't give a damn about my destiny right now. I'm sick of hearing about all this important work I have to do. That's your schtick, not mine. And I'm not going to stand here arguing with a goddamn bush."

"Then perhaps you'd rather talk to me in this form." A vaguely outlined

figure coalesced in pools of light, as if forming gradually from the ground up. Where the huge leafy plant had been, there was now only an amorphous shape. Gradually, wisps of light moved here and there until an almost-human body was discernible. Still, the being appeared several feet taller than any human, and was almost, but not quite transparent.

"Is this more acceptable?"

"What are…wait…where's the plant?" shouted Connor. "It's gone."

"No, it is not gone. I have simply used its sacred energies to manifest a form that would seem familiar to you."

Ayalla almost snorted. "Familiar to a lunatic on an LSD trip maybe."

"Artificially induced visions are not always particularly useful or accurate."

"And this is?" answered Ayalla.

"Knowledge can always be useful if combined with wisdom and love."

"We're running out of time," said Connor, her voice rough with emotion. "Please, I'm sorry if I insulted you, but I need those leaves and roots."

"Yes, you do. And I am far beyond the state of existence in which I would be insulted. That is a plaything for the human ego. I understand your need."

"Then help me! All I care about is saving Laura. She can't die. Do you hear me? She can't die!"

"And she won't if you listen carefully, both of you."

Both women stood, rooted to the ground, waiting.

"You must bless this plant from which you take live pieces. You must ask it to heal your loved one. You must honor its existence, for this is one of only seven such plants on your entire planet. It anchors far more than a bit of dirt. It anchors what's left of the Spirit of the Holy Mother to your planet."

Connor's shoulders sagged. "I don't even know how to do what you ask. I don't know the words or the spells or whatever they are."

"Do not sound so despairing, dear one. I will show you. Now listen." Instantly, the light emanating from the center of the presence reached out to embrace them both.

After several seconds passed, Connor's face brightened. Ayalla took a deep breath and sighed as if relaxing for the first time in days. Together, they knelt.

Connor spoke first. "We give you thanks, Holy Mother God, for our lives and for the lives of all who dwell on this planet."

"We seek your love and healing," Ayalla continued. "Your blessing on us and our errand of mercy."

"We are here in love, to act in love. Be with us now in the hour of our need," murmured Connor, her eyes tight shut, her face turned upward.

"Allow us to use this creation of Your divine mind in averting death," said Ayalla, her tone clear and firm.

"And so it is." Connor finished. They waited for a few moments, then stood.

The presence shifted and sparkled, and their eyes were drawn to what could almost be described as a human face floating in the center of the nimbus of light. *"I have looked into you, and although your minds are filled with confusion, your hearts are pure. You have been offered the ultimate love, and you have accepted it. Thus, your prayers are easily heard and easily made manifest in your world. We will share consciousness of each other again very soon, for you will be in need of a guardian angel before too long. Now take the gift and go swiftly."* The light winked out as if it had never been there and was instantly replaced by the sun's early-morning warmth.

"But I don't have…" Connor began, then looked down at her hands. She was holding seven leaves and three roots. They felt warm to her skin, as if they vibrated with life.

She looked from them to Ayalla, who stood mute, as if unable to comprehend any of what had happened. In the distance, they heard a shout, and within seconds Malcolm was racing up the brick pathway toward them.

"What happened?" he panted, skidding to a stop. "One second it was light, then it was pitch-dark, and in maybe thirty seconds it was light again."

"What do you mean, thirty seconds?" demanded Ayalla, finally finding her voice. "We must have been talking to that—whatever it was—for fifteen minutes. And where were you?"

Malcolm scowled. "I told you, it was only a matter of seconds. Talking to what?"

Connor smiled. "Time's irrelevant, isn't it? And they talk about the world standing still." She started toward the exit she and Laura had used the day before. "We'll explain later. We have to go."

Ayalla fell into step beside Malcolm as they trotted down the path. "You are not going to believe this," she said.

"You'd be surprised what I'd believe," he said with a grin. "And you'd be surprised at some of the things I've seen."

"Then we need to have a talk."

Malcolm looked at her closely. "You don't look too well."

"I think I'm having some kind of breakdown."

He laughed. "No, you're probably just having a breakthrough. But don't worry about it. I once thought I was having delusional episodes, too—you know, breaks with reality. Turned out my delusion was thinking I understood reality in the first place. We'd better pick up the pace."

Connor was almost at the car. They ran to join her, Ayalla jumped behind the wheel, started the car and was moving before they even had all the doors closed. They flew by the hapless park ranger with the lights flashing and the tires kicking up enormous dust clouds. When it finally dawned on him he probably should have gotten the plate number of the car, it was already a quarter of a mile away. He decided to keep the entire episode to himself.

Chapter Twenty-Two

And thence we came forth to rebehold the stars.
—Dante Alighieri, *Divine Comedy, Inferno*, xxxiv

Ricky Bell, in his guise of Father Lemarteau, was on his way to the mission of Santa Maria de Los Angeles just after midday. He was unaware that some of those whose movements he very much wanted to monitor had been there only hours before him. He'd sent the two goons Holcomb had hired to watch both the hotel in Laguna Beach, and the Hilton where the others were staying. So far, there'd been no sign of them. He had concluded that the Indian woman was either dying or dead and they had taken her to some private clinic outside the immediate area. He'd also decided that it didn't matter. With the Hawthornes and the FBI agent and the D.C. cop all busy trying to figure out what was wrong with her, they would not be meddling in his business. Even Rosario's former superior, the old archbishop, was nowhere to be found.

The latter circumstance had been a godsend. The archbishop's residence was empty when he arrived. Even the housekeeper was absent. He'd used the time well, searching through all of Johnston's files. At first he found nothing. Then he'd taken a crowbar to the beautiful antique mahogany partners desk and splintered the faces of the drawers—a crude but effective technique. He was determined to discover if the archbishop still retained any evidence of the existence of Malleus Caelistis. The book had already been removed from his safe by Johnston's young and naïve assistant, Father Grolsch, a newly drafted member of the Society who was not quite as incompetent as he pretended. He was, in fact, awed by the thought of protecting his faith from enemies of God. Stalwart and loyal though he appeared, Ricky doubted the priest would necessarily approve of some of Ricky's methods.

Ricky sat in the archbishop's leather chair and allowed himself the luxury of contemplating with justifiable pride the way in which his careful plans were coming together so artistically. He'd spoken to his one contact in Rome. It wasn't lost on him that the man at the other end was, as he put it, "extremely concerned" about the events in California. He went so far as to intimate that the leaders of Malleus Caelistis might need to distance themselves from Richard, despite his obvious loyalty. Ricky smiled at the thought. Simply because they assumed they had retrieved the last available copy of the secret book, they were ready to abandon him. He suspected also that they had become worried about who Richard really was. They knew less about him than even the U.S. authorities, who knew next to nothing.

To the Society, he was a source of information, almost all of which had proved accurate over the past several years. He had also proved valuable in delivering stern messages to other Society members who'd demonstrated a tendency to stray from obedience to doctrine. What they did not know was that Richard was a killer. Still, the murders of Enrique Rosario and Johann Kursk must have set someone to thinking. And the voice on the phone had sounded a little nervous. Ricky wanted to laugh out loud. They understood so little. Their minds were so preoccupied with minor setbacks and irrelevant deaths, they were unable to sense that their true champion was at hand. The one they had awaited, the one who would restore the church to its rightful place in the universe, had arrived and was prepared to join the battle against the godless ones. Yet they worried that someone might read their little book, or discover that Malleus Caelistis was alive and well. And why shouldn't it be?

Dumping the last of the contents of the archbishop's desk onto the work surface, Ricky pawed through the papers quickly. He was about to sweep it all to the floor with the rest of the mess he'd created when he saw the bit of old paper sticking out from between two file folders. He snatched it up and quickly unfolded it. The paper was not antique, but it was well worn. The creases were deep and the paper almost tore in two. Gently, as if sensing there was something here that was meant for him to find, Ricky smoothed it out on the desktop.

It was a diagram, much like a map, but of one specific location. He scanned the surface, looking for clues. All of the handwritten notations were faint and written in Spanish.

Ricky's only languages were English and that curious Cajun patois— a cousin to the French tongue—spoken in certain parts of Louisiana. He couldn't decipher much, nor was there any map legend to identify it. But the outlines of the buildings and roads were familiar to him. The previous day he'd looked at a colorful printed version of the very diagram. This was Santa Maria! But this hand-drawn map had features not shown on the park service handout. Here were various dotted lines leading toward one section of the mission grounds.

"Yes!" he said gleefully. It was yet another sign that he was the favored one, the chosen defender. Every item he needed was brought to him. Every obstacle was overcome with ease. And now here was the key for which he'd been searching. Whatever Rosario had hidden, and Ricky had long suspected that the priest had actually gotten hold of the one item the devotees of Malleus Caelistis feared most—the so-called proof that had been spoken of in prophecy, the root of the poisonous heresy sprung from the Cult of Magdalene. But for all his efforts, he still did not know exactly *what* it was. Now he would find out. Now he would prove himself beyond any doubt. He would put an end to the ragtag remnants of the Cult because he would destroy the one thing that kept them alive.

He folded the map carefully and placed it in his pocket. He had just removed his thin latex gloves when he heard the door creak. Standing in the entry was an older woman. Cecilia looked at him, then at the wreckage of his violent search, then back at him. Her confusion was palpable. She couldn't even imagine a scenario to explain what she was seeing.

Her beloved archbishop's office had been destroyed, and in the middle of it stood not a burglar or a crazed drug addict but a man wearing the Roman collar of a Catholic priest.

She stood frozen as he walked toward her. "How unfortunate for you," he said, and still she could not comprehend.

"What's happened here?" she finally managed. "Are you a friend of His Eminence? Is he all right?"

"He, I'm sorry to say, is alive and well."

"Oh, thank heaven…" she paused, as the full meaning of his reply seemed to hit home. "Did you say you're sorry?" She started to back away, but he put a hand on her shoulder.

"Just as I regret that you are here. As I said, how unfortunate. I had no quarrel with you." He put both hands around her throat and squeezed. She fought, her nails scraping at his wrists as she tried to break his grip. But she was too old and too inexperienced with this kind of violence. She didn't let her body go limp and try to pull him down. She didn't try to knee him in the groin. Instead, she pushed at his chest and then used up the final moments of life yanking at his arms with her weak and arthritic hands. The contest was horribly lopsided, and Cecilia was bound to lose. "Remember that you died for your Lord," he whispered, and let the body drop to his feet. He stepped over her and into the hallway. He had places to be.

»——«

Archbishop Johnston sat with Benjamin Hawthorne in a lounge just off the main corridor of the clinic. "Do you think this will accomplish anything?" he asked.

Benjamin, who had been on the phone a dozen times with his assistant, Jeannine, and a few others who were of help to him from time to time, shrugged. "I never ignore a hunch. First, it seems likely that those bones and the 'devil's fire' powder came from New Orleans or somewhere in the vicinity. At least your Father Stark seemed to believe that this stuff is the product of some pretty arcane knowledge common only to practitioners of voodoo."

"But voodoo didn't originate in that area," objected Johnston. "Evidence of those kinds of practices exists all over the world."

"Yes, that's true. But I started with the supposition that Richard Bell is involved in all this, including Enrique's murder. We sent an old friend of Malcolm's to the prison where Bell served his time. He managed to come up with two inmates who'd been in the same cellblock as Bell and were still incarcerated. One of them specifically said that Ricky sometimes spoke with a funny accent, and the other one claimed Ricky spoke French."

"Ah," said Johnston. "So you make the connection between voodoo and the possibility that this Bell character is Cajun. But couldn't he just as easily be French-Canadian?"

"He could. But why not start at home? If that doesn't work, I'll see about getting some cooperation from our neighbors to the north. I have a friend or two in the RCMP and on the police force in Montreal. But, for now, I've had Jeannine fax photos of Bell to every single police station in every parish in Louisiana."

"But if he hasn't been back there in years, no one there will recognize him. And you said he had no police record before going to prison."

"You're a hard one to convince, Father," said Benjamin with a smile. "But I like that. Shows you're a thinking man. And your objections are logical. If someone hasn't seen Bell in a long time, maybe twenty or thirty years, it's unlikely they'd recognize a picture from only nine or ten years ago. Right?"

Johnston nodded.

"So we tweak the images a little."

"Tweak?"

Benjamin opened his attaché case and pulled out several pieces of paper. He laid it in front of the archbishop. "Jeannine just faxed me this a little while ago. A couple of days ago, I asked her to get one of our local experts working on the mug shots of Bell. Ordinarily he works with the police creating age-advancing software on photos of missing children."

"You mean he's able to guess how they would look if they were older?"

"It's not really a guess. Aside from completely unrelated factors such as a disfiguring injury to the face, his results are remarkably accurate. In this case, though, I had him do renderings of Ricky Bell not only as he might look now, ten years after these photos were taken, but also asked him to *regress* the face."

"Make him younger?" questioned Johnston, studying the array of photos.

"Exactly. I asked for suggested images of Bell at the ages of twelve, fifteen, and twenty-one."

"You're right. This is remarkable. They look like the childhood pictures of this man." He tapped his finger on Bell's prison photo.

Benjamin turned the sheets over to the next array. "Of course, there's always a question of hairstyles and facial hair. Did he, as a kid, have a crew cut or let his hair grow long? Did he wear glasses? My expert has a database of hairstyles corresponding to particular years. As you can see, he's produced different versions, including one with glasses. Here's a rendering of Bell at twenty-one with long hair, then short hair, then with a beard."

"These look like different men entirely."

"Facial hair is the one feature most likely to confuse people when they try to identify someone. A beard, especially a full one, disguises so many identifiable features of the human face. But still there are the eyes. And our Mr. Bell has not only rather noticeable eyes but also a slight squint that might be habitual. Who knows? Maybe we'll get lucky with these." He put the photos away.

Johnston looked at him for a moment. "How do you do it?" he finally asked.

"Do what, Father?"

"Stay calm. Keep working away at this case, or whatever it is. Your daughter is right at the breaking point, waiting to see if Father Stark's preparation is going to work. I can see how much you love her. And I saw you when you came out of Miss Nez's room earlier. You looked for a moment like a man who is afraid he's about to lose everything in his life that matters. Yet you keep going. You must have made or received a dozen phone calls in the last two hours."

"I suppose I'd really rather pace," said Benjamin with a tired smile. "Or, more accurately, I'd rather go put my fist through a wall, or kick someone's teeth in, preferably1 the person who did this to Laura. I'd like to shout the roof down and smack people who don't agree with me. But indulging my frustration wouldn't help much, would it?"

"Might make you feel better," said the archbishop, "if you let off a little steam. Not that I'm recommending punching people or breaking your hand on a wall, but sometimes there's such a thing as too much control."

Benjamin scratched at the stubble on his cheeks. "You're probably right, but that's how I cope. Don't worry," he said, picking up his phone again, "when this is over, I'll make mincemeat out of the heavy bag in my exercise room."

"I'll join you," said Johnston. "Might do these old bones some good to get back in the ring."

"A fighter, eh? You might come in handy for something other than prayers."

Benjamin's satellite phone rang. He listened for several seconds, his expression somber. Finally he said, "Find out where the family lives and put together a list of everyone who came in contact." He paused again. "Yes. Do that, too. See what they might need in the way of support and make sure its available to them." He stabbed the OFF button.

"What is it?"

"The attendant who handled the bones. We finally tracked him down. He went to a hospital last night with the same symptoms as Laura, only worse."

"Then we can get the antidote to him as well."

"He died over an hour ago."

The archbishop paled. "Then there can't be much time left for Miss Nez."

"Exactly. I think I'll find out what's keeping Dr. Hu. He's had enough of whatever time we do have."

»——«

"You ever going to tell me exactly what went on in the garden? I couldn't make much sense of what she was saying. Connor was more interested in getting the plant to Dr. Hu than explaining what happened. You both looked like you'd seen a ghost—or several ghosts."

Ayalla frowned and leaned her head back against the smooth surface of the Naugahyde couch in the private lounge. "Ghost stories are for kids."

"Okay, then let me rephrase that. Your expressions reminded me of the way Connor looked one time she heard from her grandmother, Gwendolyn Broadhurst."

"What are you talking about? Her grandmother was scary?"

"No. Her grandmother was dead."

Ayalla stared at him for several seconds. "This is some kind of joke."

"Believe me, this is something I would never joke about. And even if I were tempted, I don't want to think what Gwendolyn might have in store for me."

"You said the woman is dead. Is everyone here absolutely nuts?"

"No, I don't think so."

"Well, whatever we saw, it wasn't a dead person."

"Then what was it?"

"She, or rather, it said…that it was an angel."

"Cool," said Malcolm without changing expression.

"Oh, God, you *are* all nuts."

"I assume that you saw this being or angel. What explanation has your logical mind come up with to explain the phenomenon?"

"I haven't any explanation. It could be a delusion, maybe induced by exposure to some sort of organic hallucinogenic present in the garden. It could be temporary insanity or mesmerism. Or it could be—"

"Exactly what you said in the first place," Malcolm interrupted. "An angel."

"Are you telling me you believe in angels? What do you think this is, television? You think Della Reese is just around the corner waiting to give me a good talking-to?"

"Hey, don't knock Tess. I like that show."

Ayalla sighed heavily. "Fortunately for us, then, we weren't visited by Andrew, Mr. Angel of Death."

"So you watch it, too."

"Maybe."

Malcolm sat next to her on the sofa. "Why do I get the impression you think believing in magic makes you seem weak?"

"Is that what you're calling this? Magic?"

"For want of a better word. Connor usually says 'woo-woo stuff' but that's 'cause she's a lot like you in some ways."

"What ways?"

"She likes having everything in her life under control. She wants to be able to understand everything that goes on. She wants rational explanations, but sometimes being rational just won't get the job done."

"That's absurd. Being rational is the only way to get the job done."

"Right. And was that approach helpful back there at the mission? Did you tell the angel—excuse me, the logically explainable phenomenon—that you weren't buying it?"

"Not exactly."

"Then what did you do? Try and shoot it?"

She flung up her hands. "Oh, right. Can't you be serious for ten minutes at a stretch? You have to go out of your way to make light of everything?"

"Only when I'm awake."

She stared at him. "Now you really can't be serious."

"You said, do I 'have to make light of everything?' And I'm taking you literally. If there's one thing I've learned it's that we have a choice. We can be on the side of the angels or we can be on the side of…" He paused.

Ayalla sat forward to look Malcolm in the eye. "Of what? That's really the question. It's one thing to believe in angels and the guys in white hats and all the other fairy tales, but who's the enemy?"

"It isn't that I don't know the difference," he said. "It's hard to explain. A while back, some friends of Connor's grandmother tried to explain it to me. They've been doing what they call "light work" for a long, long time. They talk about it as if they're defending something. When I asked them, they told me that everything is part of God. I didn't like that too much since I grew up believing in God versus the devil. Know what I mean?"

"I got the same line from my mother."

"So I always thought it was either one or the other. But the Carlisles, these people in England, they said that the idea of opposites is a human invention."

"Now you're trying to tell me there are no bad guys in the world. Where have you been all your life?"

He regarded her seriously. "Some of the same places you've been, I imagine. I've seen the shit people do to each other, so don't think I'm some sort of Pollyanna. What I'm trying to explain is that what we think of as evil isn't some separate force that operates because a fallen angel named Satan wants it to."

"Then where does evil come from, according to these friends of yours?"

This time Malcolm held her eyes with his own. "Us."

Ayalla shook her head, but before she could speak, he raised his hand to ask her patience. "Everything about God is good. At least that's what I believe. But humans have free will. We make choices. And some people make some really crappy ones. Just as there's an energy to love, there's an energy to fear. It accumulates; it changes things. Love changes the world, so why not fear?"

"I thought we were talking about evil."

"People allow evil into their lives because they're afraid. They learn to hate because they're afraid. And when they hate, they kill and maim and cause so much pain I sometimes can't even believe it. But I've seen too much of it with my own eyes not to accept that, basically, shit happens."

"And what you're saying then," Ayalla spoke slowly, as if formulating the theory as she went, "is that all that shit happening sort of accumulates, creates an evil force that threatens us." She shook her head. "Good God, now I'm starting to sound like Yoda."

"No, but you are sounding a little like Gwendolyn, or maybe Laura's Grandmother Klah."

"Doesn't anyone around here have a grand*father*?"

"Presumably," said Malcolm, raising an eyebrow. "But to get back to the point of all this, let me ask you something."

"What?'

"Did you believe in whatever you saw…at least while you were seeing it?" He waited patiently for her answer. It was more than a full minute before she spoke.

"Yes, I think I did."

"And did you listen to whatever the angel said?"

"Yes."

"What did it ask you to do?"

"To show respect for the plant. And to pray, to give thanks."

"And did you do that?"

"Yes."

"Why?"

"Because I didn't have any choice."

"Of course you did. You don't strike me as the kind of person who does much she doesn't want to. So I figure you went along for one of two reasons—you were afraid not to, or it seemed right at the time. Which is it?"

"I'd be lying if I said I wasn't afraid, but…"

"But what?"

"The fear went away. All I felt was calm, peaceful. Doesn't make a lot of sense, does it?"

Malcolm smiled, and Ayalla noticed for the first time how it lit up his entire face. "Why not? If we get to latch on to a little piece of heaven, I'd hope we'd feel calm and peaceful."

"I'm not too keen on the idea," she said. "I've got no quarrel with God, but I don't necessarily want Him right up close, know what I mean?"

"Grandmother Klah told us that the Great Spirit is inside everyone, whether we like it or not."

Ayalla shivered. "I'll have to think about it."

"And are you sure you want to keep thinking about God as a 'him'?"

She sighed deeply and heaved herself off the couch. "I don't know. I don't even *want* to know. I came out here to find one stupid would-be terrorist, and now I'm surrounded by New Age crap and voodoo poisons, and you and your pals with your little Luke Skywalker club. So do me a favor and leave me out of it." Ayalla stalked away.

Malcolm watched her out of sight. He'd thought maybe they were making progress. But on the other hand, what did he know? He did wish he could ask Connor about what happened at the mission, but he knew she couldn't think of anything but Laura right now, and he didn't blame her one bit. He decided to find Benjamin. A little regular police work might take his mind off the thought of losing one of his best friends.

»——«

"Dr. Hu, please, just get on with it."

He made that sound with his tongue, a sibilant *tsk-tsk* that he'd been emitting for the past hour while the plant's leaves and roots had been carefully mashed, ground up, and pureed, so to speak. Connor had insisted on staying with every step of the process, and if anyone saw her lips move periodically in some sort of silent supplication, no one said a word about it.

"I still don't have much confidence that this will work, Miss Hawthorne," he said.

"I have enough confidence for both of us, Doctor. So, please, let's proceed."

He took the bowl from his assistant, along with a tongue depressor he intended to use to apply the paste. "According to Father Stark, it should be applied at the original site of infection," he said. "I suppose we'll begin with the wrist." He scooped up a bit of the dark-green substance and hesitated.

"No, not that way," said Connor. She took the bowl from him and scraped the stick clean before dropping it on the floor. "This is the way." She reached into the bowl and scooped up a clump of the antidote in her hand. With her other hand she took Laura's wrist and turned it so that the inside faced her. Then she carefully began smearing the green mixture over the skin. She didn't know why she knew that it must be applied by hand, or why she knew that her love for Laura was somehow mixed in with the pulverized plant. But she did know it. She continued to spread it over her lover's burning skin, moving up her arm where the infection had spread. Then she gently tugged at the neck of the hospital gown and pulled it down to just above the rise of Laura's breasts. There, too, on her chest were the angry welts left by the poison moving through her body. Once they were all thoroughly covered, Connor sat the bowl on the stand beside the bed and wiped her hands on a towel.

"Now we'll wait," she said and slid a chair closer to the bed. "We'll have to wait." She turned to Dr. Hu. "If you don't mind, I'd rather be alone with her."

The doctor and his assistant left the room quietly.

For a long time, Connor sat quietly, all of her attention focused on Laura's countenance. She felt she would know when the antidote had truly begun to work because she would see it in her lover's face—a quiver of the eyelids, a twitch of her lips—anything, any sign that she would return from wherever her soul wandered. After thirty minutes, her eyelids felt so heavy she put her cheek down on the edge of the bed and her hand on Laura's leg because she needed to maintain the connection between them.

When she lifted her head again, an hour had passed. She leaped to her feet and leaned over Laura, unable to believe she could have been so irresponsible as to fall asleep. Was there any change? She couldn't be sure, yet she thought Laura's breathing seemed easier, or else she wanted to believe it was. She glanced at the preparation she'd smeared over Laura's arm and chest, and did a double take. The mixture had dried, which seemed reasonable, but it was no shade of green or anything remotely close to it. The dried substance was glistening white with threads of black and gray running through it like vivid varicose veins under a translucent, porcelain skin. Even as she watched she could swear the veins were expanding and contracting, as if something flowed through them.

She took Laura's hand, and as she did, a piece of the dried paste fell away from Laura's wrist. *Don't let it touch your skin,* said a voice in her head. Quickly, Connor grabbed a steel emesis basin and a rubber glove from a dispenser on the wall. Gingerly she plucked the bit of dried-out remedy from the sheet and dropped it into the basin. She didn't like that the fragment continued to pulsate, but she ignored it and waited for more pieces to detach themselves from Laura. One by one, they did.

Connor collected each one and deposited it in the basin. With each section, more of Laura's skin was revealed. Connor peered at the spots where the black powder had seemed to eat into Laura's wrist. The skin was a healthy pink and completely unblemished! Connor's heart suddenly felt too big for her chest, too big to even fit in the room. She was almost giddy with relief, but didn't dare let herself relax quite yet. It wasn't exactly in her nature to accept good fortune until she was quite sure no one would snatch it away from her. She didn't always like being a skeptic, but it was home.

She heard a sound behind her and whirled around. Benjamin, Ayalla, and Malcolm stood just inside the door. All of their faces asked the same question. Connor motioned them to come closer.

"Look at this," she said softly. "The plant paste I put on has dried up, and it's detaching itself from Laura's skin." She pointed at a section as it dropped to the sheet. "I don't think we're supposed to touch it now," she explained as she used the glove to retrieve it. "I don't know how it worked, but the pieces that have fallen away are almost breathing. It's as if the plant sucked the poison right out."

"I'll hold the basin," said Benjamin, "and you can put gloves on both hands." Ayalla and Malcolm looked over his shoulder at the growing pile of discarded fragments.

"What the hell *is* that?" Ayalla murmured. "The leaves we collected were dark green, the roots were brown, and this is—"

"Just plain weird," Malcolm shrugged. "But look at her arm."

Connor had worked her way up to Laura's shoulder and was beginning to probe the pieces of the dried paste on Laura's chest to see if they were loose. Gradually, the edges curled up as if the skin on which they lay was actively rejecting the foreign substance. Connor quickly began to collect the pieces and add them to the basin. Within minutes, every last fragment had been removed. Underneath, Laura's skin looked perfectly normal.

"What do we do with this?" asked Benjamin, frowning at the mass, which had begun to give off a putrid stench. He carried it away from the bed and looked at it in the light from the window.

Connor and the others joined him. She wrinkled her nose. "Ick.

Thank God it didn't smell like that when I put it on Laura."

"I think it's getting worse," said Benjamin. "But I have a feeling that putting in the garbage would be like dumping toxic waste."

"It has to be buried, and Ayalla knows what to do," said Connor.

"No, I don't," the FBI agent retorted. "Why should I know what…." But she didn't finish the sentence. For the briefest moment, Malcolm could have sworn he saw her expression go completely slack. But then she was herself, and he dismissed the idea. "We need to bury it in the ground and…um…say a prayer," she said, though her expression was slightly doubtful. "And we need to do it right away"—she tugged at Benjamin's arm—"like *right* now."

Benjamin's attention swung back and forth between the basin and Laura's face. He clearly didn't want to leave, but Ayalla's sense of urgency dissolved his indecision. "All right, let's go." He patted Connor's shoulder. "We'll be back soon. You and Malcolm stay here and keep an eye on Laura."

He was about to pick up a towel to cover the basin when they were all startled by a new voice.

"If you're supposed to be keeping an eye on me, what are you all doing over there?"

Connor spun around and thought her heart couldn't possibly contain the surge of pure joy that coursed through her. "Oh, God," she said, rushing to the bed. "You're awake, you're okay. Oh, God! Yes!" She had hold of Laura's hand and was squeezing it between her palms. Connor closed her eyes. "Thank you, thank you, thank you!"

"If you'd get all these wires and tubes out of the way, maybe I could have a real hug," said Laura. "Otherwise, darling, I think you're going to break several bones in my hand."

"Oh, I'm sorry. It's just that…I can't believe it worked so fast."

"What worked?" She paused. "And what's that smell? Good Lord, I hope it's not me."

"No," said Benjamin. "We're just about to take care of that problem. And then we'll be back…in a while." His nod cued Ayalla and Malcolm to head for the door. Malcolm stopped beside the bed.

"Damn good to see ya, girl," he said.

"I like that ugly mug of yours, too," she smiled. "But I'm hoping some-one's going to tell me why you're all so inordinately happy to see me."

"I'll let Connor explain that," he answered. "See you in a while." They all left the room quickly, and Malcolm pulled the door shut behind them.

"And why are you looking at me like that?" Laura said softly, her eyes fixed on Connor's face.

"I was afraid I was going to lose you, for good," said Connor, swallowing against the tightness in her throat. "And to hell with the wires and tubes." She scooted onto the bed and helped Laura sit up. Then she wrapped her arms around Laura's upper body and held her tight. "I love you," she whispered. "God, how I love you."

Laura hugged her back. "I've never doubted it for a minute, sweetheart, but what made you think I'd ever leave you here all by yourself?"

"You almost did," said Connor, her tears trickling down onto Laura's hospital gown. "That stuff that was in our car…the bones were coated in some sort of toxin. No one here had any idea what to do about it."

"No vaccine, I take it," said Laura, when Connor finally relaxed her grip and let Laura lean back against the pillows.

"They couldn't even isolate the cause."

"But I'm still alive and"—she looked down at her wrist—"my skin is back to normal. So unless you shipped me to Lourdes via light beam for a quick miracle cure, how did I get so lucky?"

"This part's a little odd," said Connor, "and it'll take a while to explain." She grinned at Laura. "Do you know how many hours it's been since I kissed you."

"At least as many hours since I've brushed my teeth," answered Laura, giving Connor a chaste peck on the cheek. "So the good stuff's gonna have to wait."

"Not that long," said Connor. She jumped off the bed and yanked open a drawer in the bedside stand. "Aha!" She whipped out a hospital toothbrush and tiny toothpaste tube wrapped in cellophane, and handed it to Laura. "And we need water," she grabbed the pitcher. "And a basin…check. Okay, you're all set." She stood there grinning.

Laura laughed. "A little anxious, sweetheart?"

"So brush already."

"You really want to kiss me that much?"

"You have no idea."

"Oh, I think I do." She applied toothpaste to the brush. "Why don't you see if that door has a lock."

»——«

Father Grolsch was not a courageous man. Yes, he had robbed his superior's safe of the precious book, but only at a time when there was almost no possibility whatsoever of being caught in the act. And as many times as he'd wished to give the archbishop a piece of his mind, Grolsch was never greatly tempted to actually do it.

The last couple of days, he'd pleaded gastric distress as a reason to be absent from his duties. Although he didn't care to dwell on the various possibilities, he knew something was going on—something bad, perhaps even related to his theft. But how could his actions that had seemed so justifiable at the time now seem so potentially damaging to his career? First, Father Rosario had been killed, now Monsignor Kursk (who had assured Grolsch privately that his loyalty would be duly rewarded in time) was dead. Father Grolsch was quite frankly terrified.

The day before, when he finally came to work, Cecilia told him about the people who had come the previous evening to the residence to see the archbishop. She whispered that one was from the FBI and another was a police officer. Grolsch had quickly excused himself and raced to a bathroom to lose his breakfast.

This afternoon he'd tried to stay away, but curiosity overcame his dread, and no one was answering the phone. He was nauseous again when he saw the archbishop's car in the lot as well as Cecilia's, but he was determined to act as if he were supremely unaware of any events beyond the day-to-day business of the archdiocese.

He entered through the back door and walked through the utility room and then the kitchen. He saw Cecilia's purse and coat draped over a chair. That struck him as unusual because she was an absolute stickler for tidiness. She always hung her coat and hat in the cupboard next to the stairs. He continued through to the hallway and hesitated for another moment. *Just get it over with,* he chided himself. *The archbishop doesn't know anything...God knows I probably look sick enough to convince him...so what if he gives me guff for not showing up this morning...a little lecture won't kill me.*

Father Grolsch was right about one thing; a lecture wouldn't have been much of a risk to his health, but the sight he beheld when he swung open the door to the archbishop's office just about gave him a heart attack. Amidst a wreckage of furniture, china, books, and papers lay the still body of the archbishop's housekeeper. Grolsch stood rooted to the spot, afraid to leave, afraid to step inside. As he stared at Cecilia's body, some little voice in his head was prodding him to go to her, touch her wrist, her throat, see if she could be saved. But he couldn't. Instead he backed away, bile burning in his throat.

He couldn't take his eyes off her—so still, so white, her hands folded serenely on her chest. He stopped and the details finally registered. Cecilia was not sprawled in death, but rather laid out carefully, her sweater buttoned, her skirt demurely tucked around her legs, her feet together. *Oh, God,* he thought, *who would have done that? What if he's still here?* He turned and fled to the safety of his car and the cell phone he kept for emergencies.

So stunned was Father Grolsch that he never noticed the elderly priest in a long, old-fashioned cassock who knelt in a corner of the room. The old cleric's sorrow was great, and a potent fury at the cold-blooded murder of this harmless and pious woman threatened to overwhelm him. Evil had taken another life, and he might have prevented it had he come here sooner instead of wandering the grounds of the mission looking for something he might never find. Had he become so obsessed with finding the sacred object, that holy of holies, that he did not hear the summons of the angels when he was needed? Or had it simply been her time? His fists clenched, but he slowly relaxed them. This was not the path. The old priest stilled his raging thoughts and refused to surrender to either despair or hatred. He could not let himself lose contact with the One.

Earlier, he had respectfully arranged the poor woman's body and said the words that needed to be said. Now he prayed for her soul's easy passage to the other dimensions. He was aware of the young man who came into the room and saw that it was time to leave. Others would come now to take care of the dead. He must take care of the living.

»—«

Malcolm, Ayalla, and Benjamin stood silently beside the small patch of freshly turned earth. "Is that all, do you think?" asked Malcolm.

Ayalla, who had been silently mouthing the words of a prayer that kept running through her head, nodded. "As far as I know, but at the moment I don't feel like I know jack shit about anything."

"I feel that way most days," said Malcolm.

"Me, too," added Benjamin. "I think the trick is not to let that keep us from doing what we need to do."

"And what do we need to do?" she asked.

"Put a stop to whoever is behind the killing and the terrorist threats."

"You've decided they're one and the same?"

"I'm not completely convinced, but right now it's all we have." He went on to explain what he'd done in initiating a photo canvas of New Orleans area law enforcement.

Ayalla immediately pounced on the weak aspect of the strategy. "So let's say someone recognizes him from way back. How does that help us nail him right *now*?"

"It's a long shot," admitted Benjamin. "But if I've learned anything in all these years of tracking down bad guys, it's that the more you know about them, about who they are and what they've done, the better chance you have of anticipating what they'll do now."

"You sound a little like those behavioral analyst geeks we have down at Quantico," she shook her heard. "But every now and then they come up with something, so I guess it's worth a shot. But I think we have to follow up on the leads we found in the computer runs I did at the field office."

"We brought the lists of names associated with the Malleus Society. I'll get my briefcase," said Malcolm.

"I'll call in," Ayalla told them. "I want to see if they've completed the list of known associates of Ricky Bell. Is there a number where they can fax it?"

Benjamin thought about that. "This clinic needs to keep a low profile. Ask your people to fax the information to my office in Washington. I'll have Jeannine send it to us here."

"Okay. But it won't be as legible once it's been faxed twice."

"A risk we'll have to take in the interests of security," he said with a smile. "And you know what? I'm amazingly hungry. Let's include food in our plan."

They walked through the underbrush behind the clinic building and reentered through a back door. Dr. Hu was standing in the hallway outside Laura's room. He turned to them, his face a study in bewilderment. "I wanted to check on Miss Nez," he explained. "The nurse told me that all of her vital signs on the monitors at the nurses' station were back to normal after you left the room, but then they ceased recording at all. But there were no alarms. Now the door is locked!"

Benjamin fought to suppress a smile. Laura must be feeling much, much better. "Everything's under control, doctor. The antidote worked more quickly than we could have possibly hoped and once we determined she was all right, Laura asked for some privacy."

Dr. Hu looked around. "But where is Miss Hawthorne?"

"She was needed urgently," replied Benjamin with the same neutral expression. "I'm sure you'll be able to talk with her later. Now, let me explain to you what happened." He put his arm on the doctor's shoulder and steered him down the corridor with Malcolm and Ayalla following in their wake.

"You don't suppose they're…you know?" asked Ayalla, glancing over her shoulder at the door of the room.

"I have no idea," answered Malcolm primly. "But whatever it is, I'm sure they're pretty damn happy."

"But we're right in the middle of a crisis," she insisted. "This lunatic could be planning almost anything. This isn't the time to be messing around—not when all hell could break loose at any moment."

"Personally, I can't think of a better time." He turned into the lounge and picked up his briefcase. "So while they're celebrating being alive, why don't we figure out how to keep any more people from ending up dead?"

Someone near them cleared his throat. Malcolm and Ayalla realized Archbishop Johnston was sitting in a chair in the corner, his right hand clutching his cell phone. The expression on his face was bleak as a gray winter's day. "There's already been another killing," he said, his voice taut with anger. "That was my assistant, Father Grolsch. He returned to the residence a half hour ago. My housekeeper, Cecilia, is dead. And the house has been torn apart."

"Someone searched it?" asked Malcolm.

"Apparently so."

"She must have surprised whoever it was," Ayalla said. "He, or they, killed her because she was a witness."

Tears glistened in the old man's eyes. "She was a good soul. She was a joy to have around, and she was my friend." Johnston looked out the window. "First Enrique, then that fool Kursk—and the poor boy from the hotel." He stood up and straightened his shoulders. "We have to find out who did this. I want them stopped. I want them punished. God forgive me, but I want them to burn in hell," he paused, "even if I have to send them there myself."

"I understand, Archbishop," said Malcolm softly.

"No, Mr. Jefferson, I don't think you do." He took a deep breath. "Where is Mr. Hawthorne? I need to get back to my home and pick up my own car. Cecilia's sister will be needing me."

"I'll find him," offered Malcolm. "Right away."

"Archbishop?" said Ayalla, as Malcolm left the room. "Was there anything at your house to find?"

"What do you mean?"

"Was there anything related to this case, to the Malleus people, or to Father Rosario's research?"

He thought about it. "I don't think so. I gave Senator Hawthorne the files."

"But was there anything else? Something that might not have been in the files?" she pressed, seeing a flicker of doubt in his eyes.

"No," he said finally. "Nothing."

Ayalla sensed he wasn't telling the truth, but at that moment Benjamin appeared to show the archbishop to a car waiting to take him back. She let it drop, mostly because he was so distraught, but she would certainly bring it up again later. Her instincts told her he was hiding something, and she was in no mood for any more secrets, supernatural or otherwise.

Chapter Twenty-Three

Evil can never be undone, but only purged and redeemed.
—Dorothy L. Sayers

Dawn. The second-to-last sunrise before he would finally hear the voices of the damned as they perished. He laughed loud and long, and the sound rose on the morning wind. A hundred yards down the shore, a lone jogger stopped and peered at the sky wondering what sort of seabird could produce so ugly a noise. Ahead of him, he spied a black-clad figure standing at the water's edge. The noise came again, harsh and hysterical. The jogger reversed his course and doubled his pace. The sand sprayed behind him as he dug hard. Without knowing why, he wanted to be far from here.

Richard Bell turned toward the hills behind him and stretched out his hands to the eastern horizon, marveling at the way he could block out the sun itself with only one hand. The symbolism of this simple act dazzled him. The power he possessed was limitless because God was limitless. Tomorrow was the first step. And while the bureaucrats fumed and the people screamed in fear, he would make his way northward, quickly, quietly. Another disaster, another weakness exploited.

He breathed deeply, sucking the salt air into his lungs. Once upon a time God had covered the face of the earth with water, and wiped out the travesty that humankind had become. Now God would bring fire.

»——«

"What do we really know of this man?" asked Cardinal de Marcos. "And I don't want any of your usual temporizing."

Bishop Rinaldi cleared his throat. "He contacted us a few years ago and claimed to be an initiate."

"Claimed to be? You confirmed this assertion, I take it."

"We couldn't do so with complete certainty—that is, his sponsor was deceased by the time we received the communication."

"You never *spoke* to the priest who was supposed to have recruited and trained this man?"

"The good father was deceased."

"Where was the man trained?"

"In New Orleans."

The cardinal froze, staring at Rinaldi. "Not the one who had the… book…when he died?"

Rinaldi swallowed hard. "Yes, sir. That was the same priest."

"But the book was buried with him, correct?"

"As far as we know. It wasn't found among his possessions."

"You fool! This man should have been suspect from the moment he contacted us and claimed the dead priest as his sponsor."

"But he knew all the pertinent information, sir. He knew the passwords, well beyond those of the outer circles—"

"Which he could have learned from the book!"

"The text is in *Latin*, sir."

"And so you naturally assume that his claim to membership is legitimate because he's intelligent enough to translate a language that every Catholic school student is taught?"

"His contact seemed so provident. We needed someone in the United States, sir. And he gave every indication of being fully…er…aware."

"What I *now* want to know is whether this so-called initiate, the man whom you have designated in the ledger as R. La Cloche, is a convicted criminal and would-be terrorist."

"What!" Rinaldi blanched and began to sputter. "He's…I mean, no that isn't possible…that would be far beyond what we've asked him to do."

"Which is what?"

"Keep track of Father Rosario, the priest in California who—"

"I *know* what he was doing, Rinaldi. I sent the letter along with Monsignor Kursk as you will recall."

"La Cloche promised to make sure that Rosario didn't publicize anything about the Cult."

"And Rosario is dead. You don't find that the least bit coincidental, or disturbing?"

"American cities are extremely dangerous. Even priests are not immune from the violence of thieves and drug addicts."

The cardinal raised an eyebrow. "And I suppose those same vicious thieves attacked Monsignor Kursk in his hospital room and smothered him to death for his watch and ring?"

Rinaldi couldn't look his superior in the eye. "No, that doesn't appear to be likely, but I still don't think we need assume that anyone associated with us is involved."

"Then let me educate you, my dear bishop. I have my own sources of information, a fortunate situation as it turns out, since your sources are highly questionable. Mine tell me that the American FBI is interested in a man who has made threats against military installations and nuclear power facilities. This individual is also a convicted criminal who was sentenced to several years in one of their prisons. While there he recruited a handful of other criminals to join a religious society."

Rinaldi's face was dead white. "But—"

"*Don't* interrupt me." The cardinal continued his summary without benefit of notes. "This man circulated pamphlets, some of which bore a symbol strongly resembling this…" The cardinal drew out a paper from his top desk drawer and turned it to face the bishop, who recoiled at the sight.

"Malleus Caelistis," he whispered.

"*Never* speak those words within these walls," the cardinal hissed.

"I'm sorry, sir. I don't understand how an initiate could reveal—"

"Because he's *not* an initiate, you cretinous moron! He's an impostor and he's used you to feed him information to support his delusion. Don't you see it? La Cloche means *bell* in French. The suspect's name is Richard *Bell*. It doesn't take a lot of imagination to conclude that he is very likely the one who murdered Rosario and probably Kursk."

"B-b-but how can you assume that someone who supports us is guilty of murder?"

"Because, unlike you, I have made it a point to get the bottom of this. And I discovered a little known piece of information about the murder of Father Rosario. Thank God we have loyal supporters almost everywhere, people who provide answers without asking questions. That's why our public face is in the guise of the Malleus *Society*. It's nothing more than a—what do the Americans call it?—a booster club for staunchly conservative members of the church. Still, it is useful. I learned that Rosario died from a stake driven through his chest with a wooden mallet. And what do you suppose was written on that mallet, my dear bishop?"

"I don't…I don't know."

"Ah, yes. Your English is somewhat limited, is it not? Then let me help you. A mallet may also be considered a *hammer*. Does that clear it up for you?"

"Oh, God."

"You'll have to do better than that. Do you realize what is at stake here? Do you have any idea of how this may damage our cause? We have worked for decades to gather support. And we are so close. The Holy Father cannot live for much longer. Everything is in place. The votes have been orchestrated. And once the white smoke is seen, I will lead our Mother Church back to the true path." He paused and glared at Rinaldi. "But all that is in jeopardy if a hint of scandal touches us."

Rinaldi had closed his eyes, and his lips moved in silence.

"Praying isn't going to help us much right now. Later, you can get on your knees and beg forgiveness from the Lord, but we need to act as decisively as possible. There is also another potential problem."

Rinaldi, whose mind was reeling from the implications of all that the cardinal had told him, couldn't imagine how the situation could get any worse. "What is that, sir?"

"The information we suspected was being concealed by Signore Travertini has been retrieved from his home."

"But surely that is good news! He can no longer threaten us."

"It would be welcome news if we or our friends had been the ones to do the retrieving."

"Then who has it?" said Rinaldi with a growing sense of unavoidable doom. They'd long debated what might be in those computer files that one of Bishop Kreitner's assistants had been foolish enough to keep on a computer that accessed the Internet. He swore they were encrypted and consisted only of a few memos and a brief history he was writing. The cardinal assumed the files probably contained much more and that the fallout would be much worse.

"No idea, really," said de Marcos. "But I suspect it was someone from American intelligence. Though in all honesty it could have been just about anyone's intelligence service. The information was probably in a diplomatic pouch to Washington or London or Berlin the very next day."

"And everything was gone?"

"Must I keep repeating myself? Yes, *gone*. The storage devices— whatever you call them—had been removed from the computers in question. Whatever those damnable computer hackers got from our network is now in someone else's hands. That young idiot of Kreitner's may have ruined us all."

The phone on the desk buzzed twice. Rinaldi rose to answer it, but de Marcos waved him away and picked up the receiver. "Yes, this is he." He listened for a moment. "Who are you again?…Ah, yes, I recall your name. Now what is so urgent you insisted on being put through?"

For the next minute and a half, the cardinal did not speak. He listened, and Rinaldi, terrified by the flush of anger that spread over his superior's face, wanted desperately to run out of the office and not stop running until he'd crossed the border into Switzerland. But he doubted his quivering legs would get him as far as the door. Besides, where was there to go for a Catholic bishop attached to the Vatican? He had no skills other than that of a pampered minor bureaucrat.

"Thank you for informing me so promptly, Father," said de Marcos. "And please keep this entirely to yourself. I suggest a silent retreat of prayer and fasting would be in order. There are monasteries in your area that would be ideal for the purpose." He hung up the phone, and Rinaldi could swear the cardinal's hands were trembling.

"Sir?"

"That was Father Grolsch. I believe you know him. He told me you commissioned him to retrieve something from Archbishop Johnston's wall safe. Is that true?"

"It was the last known copy of…of the book."

"Yes. You said it had been found and turned over to us."

"It was," Rinaldi said, his tone whining with defensiveness. "I got it back, didn't I?"

"Yes. And how did you happen to communicate these instructions to Father Grolsch?"

"After we heard rumors that Johnston had it, I…um…"

"Ye-e-s?"

"I contacted La Cloche."

"So you alerted him that the archbishop might be in opposition to us, might be an enemy of our cause."

Rinaldi almost choked. "You don't mean something's happened to Johnston?"

"No, but that may only be a lucky turn of events. Father Grolsch informs me that yesterday he reported to his duties at the diocese residence and the house had been ransacked. Sadly, the archbishop's housekeeper had been strangled to death, perhaps because she came upon the person doing the ransacking. And do you have an educated guess about who that person might be?" The cardinal's voice fairly dripped with sarcasm.

"Well, I don't like to think so, but could it be La Cloche?"

"A reasonable, if somewhat tardy, conclusion."

"But we are not responsible. We did not tell this man to kill priests and women—and whatever else he is doing."

"You're a weasel, Rinaldi. You know that? A weasel."

"But I'm only pointing out—I mean, perhaps he was only doing what he believed was right."

"*God* will finally punish the heretics and blasphemers! You know full well that we long ago ceased to function as judges and executioners. For over a hundred and fifty years our only oath has been to follow the true path and protect the naïve from false prophets and the lies of the weak and sinful. Yes, I wanted the Cult stamped out once and for all, but only by destroying their damned artifacts and discrediting their renegade priests. We wanted to kill their *knowledge*, Rinaldi."

"But surely that isn't all we must do. What of the"—he leaned closer and whispered—"the descendants?"

The cardinal snorted. "Even you have fallen prey to that stupid legend. I'll tell you for the last time, Rinaldi, there *are no* descendants of our Lord Jesus Christ. To even give voice to such an absurd theory is the worst of heresies."

"But there have been so many indications that—"

"I said, *no!*" the cardinal roared. "You will not broach the subject again. And you will certainly not use it as an excuse for turning this maniac loose on members of our clergy."

"But everything was getting away from us. When we finally realized what Rosario had done, we tried the direct approach. We sent Kursk."

"That didn't turn out well, did it?"

"No, but what else could we have done?"

The cardinal leaned back in his chair. "I'd still like to know who else helped that arrogant young priest when he stole from the archives. I've always believed Cardinal Fitzhugh had to be involved, but there was so little real proof."

"He had some loyal followers, sir."

"Obviously. But we are blessed that he is gone now and has taken all that Celtic mythology garbage with him. The man almost qualified as a pagan!"

"Yes, sir."

Now de Marcos focused once more on his sniveling assistant. "You will do nothing, except report directly to me if you have further contact from La Cloche. For that matter, if he uses the telephone, try to encourage him to speak to me. Intimate that I am pleased with what he's done."

"Pleased? But you just said—"

"*Pretend*, you idiot! If he calls instead of sending a message, then tell him I want to speak with him."

"Yes, sir. But what if he doesn't call? It has been months at a time between contacts in the past."

"I've thought of that, too. A friend has agreed to help us with this problem. He's attached to the Italian embassy in Washington. He's already on his way to California."

"But what can he do that the local authorities cannot? If they suspect him and can't find where he is, then…" Rinaldi trailed off, confused.

"They will find him eventually. I understand that it isn't just the FBI and the police who are searching. This incident has drawn the attention of a very important man who was once a U.S. senator and served as a security adviser to a U.S. president. This Hawthorne won't let La Cloche slip through his fingers."

"But if the Americans find La Cloche, he might tell them everything. He might even claim that he was acting on our instructions."

"Yes, indeed he might. That is why I thought it wise to have someone of our own in place. He has contacts that will prove useful."

"But what can he *do*?"

"You are filled with 'buts,' Rinaldi. Have you no other word in your vocabulary with which to begin a sentence? This man can do whatever needs to be done. I have made it clear to him that La Cloche, or whatever his name is, *cannot* be apprehended by the American authorities."

"But…" Rinaldi corrected himself. "And how will he accomplish this? Surely you can't contemplate bringing him back to Italy."

"Of course not. I guarantee you that if our friend does his job, Signore La Cloche will not live to bring harm to us."

Rinaldi's eyes widened. "Does that mean you told him…that is…he is instructed to kill La Cloche?"

"He murdered two priests and a harmless woman. And that's just what we *know* about. Do you supposed he isn't insane enough to have killed before?"

"But…er…still, you said only a moment ago that we weren't judges and executioners."

"Not as a rule. Yet sometimes we truly have no choice, Rinaldi. I'm praying that the hand of God will guide our friend to his quarry and that he will not falter in his purpose. Now leave me."

Rinaldi levered himself up out of the chair, barely willing to trust his quivering legs to carry him to the door. He was halfway there when he turned back.

"Sir?"

"What is it?"

"Do you think La Cloche has the artifact?'

Cardinal de Marcos expelled a huge sigh. "If he does, our friend will retrieve it. If he doesn't, then pray that it stays lost for another few centuries."

»——«

"I wasn't entirely truthful with you," said Archbishop Johnston, looking first at Ayalla, then Malcolm and Benjamin.

"About what?" said Ayalla, though she had a pretty good idea. The three of them had agreed to meet the archbishop at St. Mary of the Groves early in the evening. Connor had chosen to stay behind at the hospital with Laura, whose recovery was so rapid she expected to be out of the clinic within a few hours.

They'd arrived to find Johnston standing on the steps of the church, looking up at the façade. He led them around the corner of the church and into the rectory. Father Rosario's housekeeper, Lucinda, her face stony with grief over the loss of her sister, Cecilia, brought them tea, then retired to her kitchen.

"I told you that I didn't have any of Father Rosario's papers left in my possession after I gave the files to Mr. Hawthorne. But," he paused, "there was one thing. I didn't really believe it was all that important, but now I wonder if that's what the thief was after, if that's why Cecilia…" He cleared his throat several times and his three visitors waited patiently for him to regain his composure.

"She was a wonderful woman—kind, devout, always worrying about me, much the way Lucinda worried about Enrique. I don't know how she's going to cope. She was devastated when Enrique was killed. And now this. That poor woman. I have to find a place for her. Perhaps she'll come to the diocese residence for a while. But," he sighed. "I'm avoiding the issue now, aren't I?"

"There's a lot going on around us," said Benjamin gently.

"Yes, and I can't help but believe that had I acted differently, then perhaps at least some of this tragedy could have been avoided."

"Hindsight is tempting," said Ayalla. "But it doesn't change anything."

Johnston regarded her somberly for a moment. "You're quite right. Unless one believes in the science fiction of time travel, I suppose one is forced to accept that what's done is done. Still, there is the matter of pondering the choices one has made." He stood up and went to stand by the window. A rare day of rain in Orange County had turned the sidewalk pavement a drab, muddy brown and deposited a smattering of droplets over the windows of the rectory. "I made a copy of something Enrique showed me. I never told him I did, and I've kept it for months."

"What was it?" asked Ayalla simply, endeavoring to disguise her growing impatience.

"A map, or a diagram really. His was a copy of an original, fairly modern rendering, and mine was a reduced facsimile of his that I had done at a copying place. The map showed the building and grounds of an old mission not far from here."

"Santa Maria de Los Angeles," Ayalla said with a complete certainty that surprised her.

"Why, yes," said the archbishop, turning from the window to face her. "But how did you know?"

"Just makes sense. It's one of the only consistent connections running through everything that's happened. Father Rosario went there, Connor and Laura went there because..." She stopped and pursed her lips.

"What?"

"Um, Malcolm told me that they went there because Laura, um, dreamed about a place that looked like it. They'd visited two or three other places before they found Santa Maria and Laura said that was it. Then, when we needed the antidote, that's where the plant was."

The archbishop's eyes widened. "That's right. I hadn't thought of it until now, but the place you described is marked on that diagram, in the old botanical gardens. At least I think it is. I can't say I remember most of the details."

"What was the purpose of the map?" asked Malcolm.

"Enrique had a theory about this particular mission and, as Mr. Hawthorne already knows since he's studied Enrique's notes, he found some letters or journal material written by a missionary who once served there. Those letters alluded to the Cult of Magdalene. So Enrique was quite certain there were other clues to be found and he'd begun to map out his explorations of the grounds and the buildings. Plus there were markings I couldn't quite decipher. I had it hidden amongst some other papers because I thought I would study it again. In any event, my copy of it is gone, and the original wasn't in the papers I took from Enrique's office."

His last sentence reverberated in the silence. Ayalla sat with her chin resting on one hand, a scowl creasing her forehead. Malcolm shook his head. Benjamin was the only one among them to display no emotion whatsoever. He regarded the archbishop thoughtfully. "The map isn't really the problem, though."

"Why do you say that?

"I found Enrique's diagram."

"But that's not possible. I looked for it."

"Let's just say I've had experience looking for things that aren't easy to find. In this case, it was between the cardboard and plastic cover of a three-ring binder. There was a slight bulge that caught my eye. But there's more to add to this story, isn't there?"

"What do you mean?"

"Don't forget that I've read all those files you gave me. I can't imagine that you didn't peruse them just as carefully as I did, if not more so. I have to ask—what about the artifact that you suspect Enrique's father brought back from Italy? I can't help but notice that you haven't mentioned it at all."

Ayalla detected the tightening of the archbishop's jaw. He was either angry or frightened...or both. "Yes," she said. "If we're right, and the Malleus Society is involved in these murders, then their goal may be ensuring the silence of all those who know something about Enrique Rosario's work."

"And his work was focused on the Cult of Magdalene," added Benjamin. "He believed he'd found proof that they still exist and they still guard some sort of secret that the Catholic Church in particular finds highly threatening. I have to tell you, sir," he continued, leaning slightly forward in his chair, "I think the facts we have lead us to only one conclusion." He gestured toward Ayalla. "Agent Franklin, will you fill us in on what you've learned so far?"

She opened the briefcase she'd brought from the car and opened a thick file folder. "This afternoon I had documents faxed to me from Washington. The Malleus Society is a worldwide organization, but there is very little public information available. Still, since they operate with such secrecy, their activities have from time to time drawn the attention of investigators with various branches of different governments. However, since they describe themselves as a quasireligious educational organization, various laws passed over the past couple of decades have generally shielded them from excessive official scrutiny. Also, we have very few reports on record of any investigator infiltrating their ranks or learning much about their activities and their purpose."

"Are they associated with Malleus Caelistis, or not?" asked the archbishop.

"We believe they are," said Ayalla. She slipped a piece of paper out of the folder. One disenchanted member of the Society shared some information with an agent back in the 1980s. Most of the data gathered was deemed unimportant and generally speculative, but the man did provide a written account of local meetings, the so-called credo of the group, and, perhaps most interesting, a drawing of their organizational logo. The agent filed everything away. Later it was transferred to electronic storage. In the tradition of J. Edgar, we never throw anything away that might someday prove useful." She handed the sheet to Malcolm who, being closest to the archbishop, passed it on to him.

He studied it for a few moments. "It isn't exactly like the crest of

Malleus Caelistis," he said, though obviously his heart wasn't in the argument. Ayalla sensed he was making it only for the sake of something to say.

"Not precisely, but I think it's close enough."

"It is," he finally said. "I think they are the same, even though Malleus Caelistis is the older and more secretive group." He dropped the paper on the coffee table and sat down heavily in an armchair. To Ayalla, he looked and spoke like a man who'd aged twenty years in only a few days.

"What haven't you shared with us?" said Benjamin, his voice soft yet insistent.

"I told you I saw Kursk before he died. He was nervous, and the more I badgered him, the more he tangled himself up in lies. He all but admitted that he, as well as perhaps some individuals who are part of the Roman Curia are members of Malleus Caelistis." He stopped and met Benjamin's eyes, refusing to flinch from the silent accusation he saw there. "For most of my adult life, I've served my church. I've lived my life knowing that I have a duty to God and to my faith. At first, I had to believe that all this spying on Enrique and suppressing his work was simply the work of a handful of overzealous and dogmatic theologians, not some sort of bizarre conspiracy. I couldn't bring myself to accept that there was much more to it. Even after I saw Kursk in the hospital, my mind refused to follow that path of suspicion." He took a deep breath. "I'm sorry. I should have been honest with you about everything Monsignor Kursk said—and about Enrique's map. I can't help but wonder if some of this might have been prevented."

"If you're blaming yourself for Cecilia's death, don't," said Benjamin matter-of-factly. "And don't give up completely on your church. No organization in the world is without its loose cannons. But I am glad you chose to come clean. Makes trusting you a great deal easier."

"Trusting me?" the archbishop echoed, looking slightly puzzled. "You mean you already knew I wasn't telling you the whole truth?"

Benjamin shrugged. "Cardinal Juan Emilio de Marcos, Bishop Ferremo Rinaldi, Bishop Ernst Kreitner. Do those names mean anything to you?"

"Well, yes. They signed the letters that Kursk brought. Is that where you found their names?"

"I'm afraid not," said Benjamin. "I guess now that we've heard from the FBI," he nodded to Ayalla, "it's my turn for a little show-and-tell."

"A couple hours ago, I received a preliminary report from my people in Washington on the contents of some computer hard drives that were liberated from their former resting place in the home of a would-be blackmailer. There's enough data that we could analyze it for months, but I asked for a specific search. Those three names I just mentioned, they are among the leadership of a very well-financed and powerful group of ultraconservative Catholics. The secular arm of this group, the Malleus Society, which comprises most of the membership, is insulated from the true believers who control the parent organization. That upper echelon, in contrast, is an extremely small brotherhood in which membership is reputedly restricted to Catholic clergy. On rare occasions, a new member is recruited and initiated into the 'mysteries' of '*Malleus Caelistis ab Deum*.'" He eyed the archbishop. "I'm sorry, but I am convinced that certain members of the Roman curia are fully initiated members of this group."

"But that's…even if you are right, there have always been disagreements, schisms between the progressive leadership and those who wish to maintain the status quo or even roll back the changes that were effected by Vatican II. But simply because these reactionary priests have taken on the mantle of an old heretic-burning brotherhood doesn't mean their intentions are sinister."

"No, but I've done a little background research. This de Marcos is heavily favored to ascend to the throne of St. Peter when the current pope dies. If the stolen information is even partially accurate, he's been busily consolidating his position and bolstering his support for years now."

"Again," answered the archbishop, "I never claimed that the cardinals and everyone posted to the Vatican are all angels. It's a bureaucracy. Politics is just as common there as it is here."

"Exactly," answered Benjamin, "and scandals are to be avoided, especially if you happen to be a man who seeks one of the most powerful and high-profile positions in the world."

"Then why would de Marcos be involved in any of this?"

"I'm not saying he would. But I am saying that he's used this organization for his own purposes for a very long time. And now that he is close to a goal I assume he's cherished all along, what might he be compelled to do if everything he holds dear, starting with the Catholic Church, was in jeopardy?"

"I don't know, but I still cannot believe that a prince of the church would resort to murder, let alone the murder of a fellow priest."

"You may be absolutely right, sir, but we need to keep an open mind. I'm not sure how important it is for us to fully understand the cardinal's motives right now, and he is thousands of miles away…I've checked. But the death of your housekeeper almost certainly indicates that the same person is involved in all three murders."

"But who?" asked the archbishop, his voice barely above a whisper.

Malcolm's deep voice startled the old man. "Richard Bell."

"Not that convict you've been talking about! I can't imagine how he could have any valid connection with the Malleus Society, let alone Malleus Caelistis itself. Surely he's simply deluded himself into thinking he's some sort of—"

"Avenging angel," said Ayalla.

"He's definitely no angel," added Malcolm. "But tonight we know a lot more about him than we did before. Thanks to Benjamin's idea of creating age regression and progression photos of Bell, and his hunch that Bell could be the one who left the toxic powder in Laura and Connor's car, we may know his real name. He pulled a grainy fax out of his pocket and handed it across the table to Benjamin. "Sorry for the wrinkles in that," he apologized.

"But who is he?" demanded the archbishop.

"Richard Renard La Cloche, born in New Orleans, Louisiana, in 1960. Placed in a Catholic-sponsored orphanage and raised by nuns until he left at the age of fifteen. The only reason we know anything about him at all is because of a police detective down there who is about two months shy of retirement, but still makes a point of keeping up with incoming alerts and bulletins. He spotted Bell, that is La Cloche, almost immediately. He called the contact number in Washington, and I called him back a little while ago."

"What could he tell you?"

"He hasn't seen La Cloche in more than twenty years."

"Then that doesn't help us at all," said the archbishop.

"Maybe, maybe not," said Malcolm, "but knowing everything you can about a suspect is always an advantage. The interesting thing is that this cop, Henri Duchamps, always believed Ricky was bad news. Seems the kid had a lot of people conned into thinking he was a model citizen, maybe even a candidate for the priesthood someday, but Duchamps said Ricky was just plain evil. He actually suspected the kid of having pushed a Catholic priest over a choir stall railing. The priest died instantly. But it could also have been an accident, and Duchamps couldn't prove otherwise. He sweated La Cloche about it and about a lot of thefts from churches in the area, but he said the kid just sat there staring at him with this little grin like he knew no one could touch him. Said it gave him the creepy crawlies. Then, a year or so later, the woman who was listed as La Cloche's mother on his birth certificate ended up dead—murdered."

"That's beginning to sound like our Mr. Bell," said Ayalla. "And did Duchamps have any opinion about the voodoo powder?"

"Sure did. He knew exactly what I was talking about. He's from a fifth-generation Louisiana family. He got so riled up when I told him about what happened to Laura, he wanted to fly out here and be in on catching La Cloche."

"I take it you dissuaded him," said Benjamin with a smile.

"Yeah. I don't think his boss would spring him to go chasing after a murder suspect who isn't actually a suspect, except where Duchamps is concerned."

"Good," said Benjamin, rubbing his hands together. "Now we're getting somewhere."

The archbishop frowned. "Where?"

"We've fulfilled the first rule of war—know your enemy," answered Benjamin. "Everything we've put together paints a general picture. We have Ricky Bell, whose real name is Richard La Cloche. He's extremely intelligent and likely a sociopath. If he indeed was responsible for killing the priest in New Orleans as well as his birth mother, then it appears likely he has some internal justification for killing anyone who opposes him or seems to pose a threat to whatever cause he believes in."

"And if he was raised by Catholic clergy," said the archbishop, "then he may be predisposed to do whatever he thinks is appropriate to defend the Catholic faith." He slapped his hand on the arm of the chair. "And remember what I said about the book of Malleus Caelistis? The only other copy was buried with the priest who owned it. That was in New Orleans!"

"Then he has the book," said Ayalla. "And that's where he got all this artwork and the idea to track down the Cult of Magdalene. I've seen some profiles of people like this. He needed a cause and he found it. But he didn't absorb the moral strictures against playing God. I'd be willing to bet that, like most true sociopathic personalities, he believes everything he does is absolutely justified."

"But even if what you say is true," argued the archbishop, "how can you possibly associate this clearly insane criminal mind with individuals who serve in the church, no matter how misguided they might be?"

"Maybe they don't know how misguided *he* is," suggested Malcolm. "What if he's some sort of, I don't know, renegade member of the secret society, or maybe not even a real member. This all may be part of his delusion."

"Except that if he's responsible for these murders," Ayalla reminded him, "he also showed up here at exactly the same time as Monsignor Kursk. And he appears to be looking for just what Kursk wanted— Father Rosario's research and this artifact. That tells me that someone told La Cloche what to look for."

Malcolm nodded in agreement. "You're right. There has to be some sort of connection, but," he added, looking at Johnston, "I don't think we need to leap to the conclusion that he's acting under specific orders from someone in Malleus Caelistis or someone in the Vatican. Kursk may have asked him to do a little B-and-E job at St. Mary of the Groves, and La Cloche took it upon himself to kill Father Rosario."

"Forgive me if I don't follow all of your logic," said Johnston. "But could someone explain how any of this helps us find this man and put him behind bars? And what has it to do with these threats against nuclear plants you told me about?"

"I was saving the best for last," said Benjamin. "I can't predict what is going through La Cloche's mind right now, or why he's got it in for nuclear generating stations, but he does. So I began with the assumption that he's been working on his plan, whatever it is, for some time now, probably since prison. Word is he proselytized all the time, got a real tight circle of allies in place, all in the name of religion. I reasoned that he would be using some of those people in the future. So I authorized some huge data runs these past couple of days, and cross-checked names of La Cloche's associates when he was in prison, when he was still Ricky Bell: nickname, the Preacher."

Malcolm glanced at Ayalla and had to smile. She was clearly impressed with Benjamin's ability and intellect. He didn't know if she'd ever admit it, however. He nodded at his old friend. "So now you're going to tell me that somewhere in all this, you found a connection between Bell, or La Cloche, and someone here in California."

"Got it in one, Captain Jefferson. Granted, we only have one name for a lead, but that may be all we need." He snapped open his own briefcase and passed a thin handful of paper to his right, to Malcolm. "On top is a mug shot of Bradley Holcomb. He was on La Cloche's cellblock. And, sadly for Mr. Holcomb, he's already added to the recidivism statistics and checked into San Pedro State Prison right here in California."

"Then he can't be our guy," said Malcolm.

"Nope. But the reason I show you his picture is because he is one of a pair of twins, identical twins. His brother, Peter, has no criminal record, however, I tend to believe that the apple doesn't fall too far from the tree. I haven't gotten hold of the visitor logs yet from the prison, but I suspect that the sibling on the outside has been a frequent visitor to the one on the inside."

"But the brother could be the Dr. Jekyll half of the set," said Malcolm. "What's to say he's not a law-abiding citizen?"

"Nothing, except for one interesting point. Peter Holcomb has a sealed juvenile record. That's fortunate for his choice of career."

"Why?" asked Ayalla.

"A felony conviction would have likely prevented him from getting his current job."

"Which is?" prodded Malcolm. "Come on. Don't play with us."

"Sorry. I guess I'm guilty of the sin of inordinate pride in my deductive abilities. But this exceeded my wildest hopes. Peter Holcomb is employed as chief of security guard at San Peligro Nuclear Generating Plant."

"Wait a second," said Ayalla. "That plant isn't far from here. As a matter of fact—"

"It's within sight of the Santa Maria mission," Benjamin finished.

Ayalla felt a cold surge of fear and excitement in her belly. "That must be it then. If he actually does have a target, then that's it." She paused and another thought lit up her eyes. "Somehow he thinks carrying out his threat aligns perfectly with his campaign against Father Rosario. For him, this is all tied together."

Archbishop Johnston, who'd sat quietly during the rapid-fire exchange of ideas and information between people who were clearly professionals, almost timidly raised his hand.

"If he really is going to try and destroy a nuclear power facility, thousands of people, maybe tens of thousands, could die. Why would he do that?"

Benjamin started to speak, then inclined his head toward Ayalla, inviting her to formulate the possible theory. She stared at some fixed point in the distance. "Because he's going to punish the world for its sins," she said. "That may sound a little melodramatic, but I have a hunch our Mr. La Cloche is a sucker for melodrama."

"Problem is," added Malcolm, "he wrote the script for this one, and we don't have a copy."

"Then I guess it's time to start improvising." Benjamin picked up the papers on the coffee table and tucked them into his briefcase. "I'm going to pick up Connor and Laura and fill them in. There's not much more we can do tonight. I suggest we all meet in the morning at our hotel." He stood. "You, too, if you would, Archbishop Johnston. I have a feeling your area of expertise is still going to come in handy."

"Thank you, Mr. Hawthorne. I'll be there. Now, if you'll excuse me, I need to spend some time in prayer with Lucinda."

The other three watched him walk stiffly out of the room and down the hall.

"I think this is just about killing him," said Malcolm softly.

"I wish he could keep all his illusions," said Ayalla. "But no one gets that luxury anymore."

"Spoken like a true cynic," replied Malcolm.

"Spoken like a realist," she retorted.

"How about we just have a truce," said Benjamin. "Now let's get out of here. I want to take another look at that map of Enrique's."

»——«

The elderly priest stayed in the shadows and gently pulled his awareness back into his energy field. It was an old but effective technique—the ability to project his mind (as well as the senses that fed it information) into an adjacent space, as long as it was within his line of sight and not too distant physically. Conveniently for him, the group of people had stayed together in one room that faced on the street. The old priest's method of eavesdropping, however inexplicable to most people, had worked to perfection. In the space of only an hour or so, many of his questions had been answered. He had a stronger sense of what he must do, yet he still waited patiently for the divine guidance that was his birthright. It would come, and he would act. And then he would go home.

»——«

"Now," he said. "Not later."

"But it isn't time for the shift change," Holcomb complained, his breath rasping into the telephone. He was starting to have some serious doubts about the Preacher's plans, but he was reluctant to appear disobedient. There was something about the man that made even the brash, arrogant security guard a little bit afraid. He was relieved that they rarely met face-to-face. The Preacher's eyes—dark, cold, and empty—gave Holcomb the willies.

"You can start setting the charges anyway. No one will question what you're doing as long as you're subtle. You can do that, right? Be subtle?"

"Yes, sir. Of course."

"And leave those two morons you hired to guard the B3 access door. I don't want anyone going through there."

Holcomb's brow creased in puzzlement. "No one ever goes there. They only put a door there in case anyone ever needed to get to the containment vessels from underneath. The guy who was here before me once said there were some caves down there, but I've never looked."

"Are you questioning my judgment?"

"No sir, not at all."

"Good, then get started. I want everything in place before dawn. And make sure that access door is unlocked."

Chapter Twenty-Four

And now I see with eye serene,
The very pulse of the machine;
A being breathing thoughtful breath,
A traveller betwixt life and death;
The reason firm, the temperate will,
Endurance, foresight, strength, and skill;
A perfect woman, nobly planned,
To warn, to comfort, and command;
And yet a spirit still, and bright,
With something of angelic light.
—William Wordsworth, *She Was a Phantom of Delight*

"You sure you're okay?" Connor asked, as she put her arm around Laura's waist and started down the corridor to their room. "It wouldn't have hurt to stay in the clinic until tomorrow."

"You can only say that because you weren't wearing a backless paper-blend nightie."

"I thought you looked kind of cute in that, actually, though if you'd worn it the other way around…"

"You're an incurable letch, you know that? And much as I love you, could I try walking all by myself? I've been doing it since I was about eight months old."

"You did not."

"Absolutely. I was precocious."

"You were probably just too damned independent to stay put."

"That, too. So I'm ready to solo."

Connor let go but stayed close as they covered the last few yards to their room, and she slid the plastic rectangle into the electronic lock. Before she opened it, though, she peered at the upper part of the door frame where it sealed against the door. Laura eyed her with some amusement.

"Don't tell me you did the strand of hair thing," she said. "That's so James Bond."

Connor shrugged. "If it's good enough for 007, it's good enough for me. And, as you will see," she continued, pointing to a wispy fine strand tucked into the door frame, "my little unauthorized entry detector worked fine."

"And what if the maid had been here?"

"I put it up there when I came back to change earlier, and, you will note the careful placement of the DO NOT DISTURB sign."

"Okay, I give. You're good."

"I'm only a pale imitation of spies like you," said Connor.

"In more ways than one, sweetheart." She held her hand next to her lover's arm. "You need to get out in the sun more."

"Like I've had a lot of time to lie on the beach." She pushed the door open and they stepped inside. Connor looked around to confirm that everything was as she left it.

"Are there more traps in here for the unwary burglar?" asked Laura.

"Not really, except for the anaconda in the bathtub."

"Then I hope it doesn't mind sharing because I need a long, hot, preferably bubbly bath."

"Your wish is my command," smiled Connor. "I'll run the bath. You get undressed."

Laura caught her by the arm as she turned away.

"Why don't you do both?"

Connor grinned. "No problem. As a matter of fact, you could expand your wish list if you'd like."

"Hmm, let me see what I can come up with."

»—«

Father Lemarteau removed the white insert from his black shirt collar and popped open the top button, once more settling into his true self, Richard Renard La Cloche, the man who would change the future of the world within a matter of hours. That thought made him giddy, almost nauseous, with delight.

Seated at the desk in his Spartan but serviceable hotel room, he unfolded and smoothed out the map he'd taken from Archbishop Johnston. He was less puzzled by some of the markings than the old man had been, simply because he'd done his research. The mission, like the nuclear generating station not far away, sat atop a somewhat unusual geological feature that had been formed when the world was much younger. Torrents of hot lava had erupted through the Cueva Antigua fault once upon a time, and due to a curious correlation of natural phenomena, some of the large lava tubes had hardened into twisting tunnels beneath the surface as the sea water rushed in behind the receding lava.

He saw that Enrique Rosario had probably discovered one of the best kept secrets of Santa Maria de Los Angeles—the tunnels. A faint dotted line followed a meandering course toward the San Peligro Nuclear Generating Station. La Cloche suspected that indigenous peoples had known of the tunnels for centuries before the missionaries came, and no doubt one of them had revealed the hidden passageways. He himself had managed to find only one entrance, tucked away in a dense grove of trees on the northern edge of the mission grounds. He had followed it long enough to ascertain that it must connect with the small cave system beneath the nuclear plant. The actual physical connection between the generating station and the mission was, to him, irrefutable proof that divine destiny was guiding his hand in all that he undertook.

A few moments later he looked at his watch and was disturbed to see that he had been sitting at the table for more than an hour. Surely he hadn't fallen asleep! He'd been looking at the map, tracing the other lines, wondering if they represented more tunnels or were merely notations of the priest's search around the grounds. But not for an hour! He rubbed his eyes and checked the watch again, then compared it to the digital clock across the room. They were within a minute of each other. Odd that he would nap, for he wasn't particularly tired. In fact, he'd never felt better in his life. His mind was clear, his vision razor-sharp. Every muscle in his body felt poised to spring into action. Still, he would rest a short while, because tomorrow he might need to call on every resource he had to do the work of the Lord.

»——«

It was an hour or so before dawn when Benjamin stretched his arms overhead and took a deep breath. He'd been at it for hours, running through Father Rosario's files again before settling down to study the map he'd found secreted in a binder. As he traced the various lines drawn on it, something about the pattern of dots and dashes nagged at him. Powering up his laptop, he connected with his home system and began accessing topographical and geological data for the area. He made notes of some of the features that stood out, then switched to another server to access some very different information. He specifically wanted to look at the history of the approval and construction of the San Peligro nuclear station. He searched the online records using an array of keywords such as geological, bedrock, fault, earthquake, and phrases such as "risk factors." He felt as if his eyes would slam shut when yet another search returned the results and be began to scan down the list of excerpts. Something jumped out. Benjamin clicked on the link to access the indicated portion of the hearing records, and as he read, piece after horrifying piece of what must have been taking shape in the mind of Richard La Cloche became clear. "Oh, God," he breathed. "he can't possibly want to…" But in his heart, he knew that was precisely what La Cloche wanted to do. He would somehow initiate a full-scale geological event, with the nuclear generating station right in the middle of it. Benjamin couldn't begin to guess at the final results, but a quick scan of information available on the safeguards in nuclear power plants gave him a few ideas as to how the most possible damage could be done. He had no doubt that La Cloche knew all this and much more.

He consulted his watch. It was barely after seven A.M. on the East Coast, too early to reach the people he needed to consult. He'd give it another hour, time for a quick shower and shave and a change of clothes. After that and a pot of coffee, he'd feel almost human again. He reached for the map to refold it when it slid across the slick surface of the table. As it did, the lines drawn on the diagram appeared for an instant to actually move, and it was then that Benjamin finally understood what some of them were. He grabbed the paper and leaned over it.

"Well, I'll be damned!" he muttered. "Our intrepid Father Rosario was a very clever man." He snatched up a pencil and pad and began to test his theory. Letters, then words emerged under his pencil. He had to laugh. "Dots and dashes…Morse code…hiding right there in plain sight. I bet when he was a kid he had a secret decoder ring."

»—«

The dream came again. But there were new aspects to it. Laura stood in the corridor again. This time, though, she could clearly make out the murals painted along the walls. The last mural, the one that had inexplicably changed from one moment to the next when she and Connor had looked at it, appeared to float out in front of the surface of the stone, as if it existed in three-dimensional space. The figure of the dark-haired woman in long robes occupied the foreground. Her halo gleamed bright in the darkness. Laura moved closer and instantly found that the saint, or perhaps priestess, was looking right at her. For a moment she extended the sphere that supported a stylized Celtic cross toward Laura and more light flowed from it. The symbols carved on the sphere and the circular part of the cross burned fiery bright. Yet Laura was not afraid. She knew they were the same as the ones on Connor's cross, and that thought gave her courage.

The figure grew in size and appeared much as Laura had imagined a high-tech hologram might—almost but not quite solid. The hand bearing the cross beckoned her closer. She felt fear squeeze her heart, but slowly moved forward.

Instantly, something grabbed her from behind. She whirled around, moving instinctively into a martial arts defensive posture. There he was, the one with the empty eyes, the one who had invaded her other dream and drawn her into a fiery circle. He reached for her again, and once more her feet did not obey the command to move, or run, or fight.

"You came back. But you should have stayed dead. Now you experience the worst of both worlds," he laughed. *"To be alive and yet without will, without strength, powerless to obey anything but the voice of evil. You'll spend eternity in hell. How perfect."*

"No," Laura shouted. *"No!"*

"Who are you to refuse me? I've been punished for too long, and have grown stronger from the pain. You cannot leave this plane unless I release you from it, and I won't."

Her chest heaving, Laura fought to move her legs, her feet. He grinned his empty mouth at her. She looked away, over his shoulder, and in that moment saw another figure, the same man she'd seen before in her dream, an old bent priest in a worn cassock. He gestured to her, and she heard the words in her mind. *"Look away from him. He is a tormented soul. Ask the mother to protect you. All you need do is ask."*

Laura closed her eyes and centered her thoughts on one thing—the light of the scepter and cross held by the lady in the painting. *"Mother God,"* she whispered, *"deliver me from this evil. Deliver me from fear."* She opened her eyes.

The wraith in front of her reacted as if he'd been slapped. *"You would call on a whore to save you?"*

Laura looked over his shoulder again, focusing on the elderly white-haired priest who still waited patiently. In her head, she could just make out a voice very much like her grandmother's prompting her with the right words. She repeated them, her strength growing with each word. *"I call on the Great Spirit. I call on the Divine Mother of all life. And She is with me."*

Around her the paving stones began to glow with a warm light. No fire, only the embrace of something far greater than she could comprehend. The light seeped across the rough faces of the stones, ever closer to the hollow-eyed demon who snarled with rage, still reaching for Laura, yet unable to cross the pools of light that now lay between them. For a brief instant, his face looked almost completely human.

"She can't save you," he screamed. "She isn't real. She tricked me once, and this is what I became. I didn't finish the work God gave me. And she mocks me. She will mock me until I destroy every soul that feeds her and keeps her alive."

The intensity of the light fanned outward even farther. He shrank again. Laura saw that the ancient cleric was gone. Instinct told her it was because she no longer needed his protection. She was fully in the center of her Self now, fully aware of the power of the Essence of Life that flowed through her body, her spirit. Colored lights spun within her. She sensed movement beside her and felt a brush against her arm, the caress of what felt like downy soft feathers. She heard the rustle of wings.

"No!" he screamed and then he fled into the darkness beyond.

Laura turned her heard, wanting desperately to see the being whom she could feel beside her. But the light from beneath her feet had blazed into a brightness that almost blinded her. Thus she heard but could not see.

"Thank you for asking us to be with you," came the voice, neither male nor female, neither loud nor soft. But its quality brought tears of indescribable relief and joy to her eyes. "When it is time for us to one day return to your world and be visible to the Creator's children, you will be among those who see us first. Now, you must go peacefully back to your Dreamtime and from there to the awareness of your human life."

"But wait," cried Laura. "Can you tell me what's truly happening there, in my human world? I don't really understand what's going on, and I'm afraid that a lot of people are going to get hurt."

"That might well happen," said the gentle voice. "Or it might not. You will have a role to play in deciding which illusion comes to pass, but whichever it is, you must accept it and act according to your heart."

"We need your help."

"We will always be within the sound of your voice."

"You mean I can call you to me?"

"Your heart can call to us, and your spirit can join with us. But the rest depends on you." She heard once more the whisper of wings in the air, and around her the light receded to a soft glow. She ached to go with that voice, to listen to the music lingering between the words.

In that moment, a different voice sounded inside her head. *"Go back, child. I think you've had enough excitement for one trip to the threshold."*

"What threshold, Grandmother?"

"Some call it heaven, some call it Nirvana, and I like to call it home. Now go!"

»——«

"Off somewhere adventuring again, my love?" Connor's voice was soft and reassuring.

Laura opened her eyes and blinked against the light from the windows. "Don't tell me it's morning already," she grumbled. "I don't feel like I've even been to sleep."

"You were doing a pretty good imitation of a sleeping person, except for the occasional murmur I couldn't quite make out. I was about to wake you at one point because you seemed frightened. But then you got this incredibly serene look on your face, and I didn't want to spoil the experience, whatever it was."

Laura rubbed her eyes and sat up, propping herself against the headboard. "You might think I'm finally over the edge, but I think I met an angel."

One of Connor's remarkably expressive eyebrows reached its highest elevation. "Hmm. An angel? This angel have a name?"

"Not that she…he, well, maybe 'it' mentioned."

"So we're not talking major league—Uriel, Gabriel, Rafael, Michael—one of the top executives, so to speak."

"You're not taking this very seriously."

"I'm sorry. I *do* take it seriously, but anytime we start talking about, you know, this invisible stuff, it makes me a little queasy. So I turn into a wiseass."

Laura smiled and tugged Connor's arm. "So, you're my favorite wiseass. Give me a hug."

After several moments of comforting closeness, Connor pulled away. "I suppose you have some message to deliver from your angelic messenger."

"Nothing startling," said Laura, closing her eyes to bring to mind the image of her dream travel. "But the presence was comforting, protective, which was especially good because I ran into that same demonic personality from my last dream visitation. What nags at me is that he seems vaguely familiar, as if I should know him, and yet his face isn't the least bit familiar." She shrugged. "Maybe it'll come to me. Now how about breakfast?"

"Whenever you're ready. We're due to meet the others at their hotel in about an hour and a half. I talked to Dad, and he sounded as if he had a lot tell us. What do you want to eat?"

"A breakfast burrito smothered in green chile sauce."

"In Laguna Beach?"

Laura sighed. "I know. It'll have to wait. I wonder if they actually prohibit shipping Hatch green chile out of New Mexico."

"Sorry, sweetheart. How about we plan on breakfast at the Pantry in Santa Fe one week from today?"

"Assuming everything goes okay here, then you're on."

Connor frowned. "You have a bad feeling about all this, don't you?"

"Kind of. But I know it isn't hopeless, so no sense in getting worried in advance."

"I agree. Let's hear what the rest of our little group has to tell us and then we'll figure out what to do. I'm thinking maybe we should let it go, leave town and let someone else worry about Ricky Bell, and solving the murders. That's their job."

"Since when, Ms. Stubborn-as-a-Mule Hawthorne, did you ever quit an investigation?"

"I haven't, at least not as a rule." Connor walked to the window and looked at the sea beginning to sparkle in the morning light. "But I'm not a prosecutor anymore. I don't *have* a legal and moral responsibility to bring criminals to trial. There are plenty of people whose job it is."

"Your father isn't officially responsible either," Laura countered, "but he keeps right on doing what needs doing."

"That his choice."

"And after everything we learned in England, you're saying you choose not to be involved, not to care."

"I do care! But why does it have to be us? Why does it have to be *you*?"

Laura joined Connor, and they stood side by side staring at the ocean. "Is that it? You're afraid something will happen to *me*? You're willing to abandon that sizzling zeal you have for seeing justice done, simply because it's dangerous for *me*? Forgive me if I'm not particularly flattered."

"What?"

"There may be women in the world, maybe a lot of them, who would be gratified to have their mate change completely, just for the sake of love. I'm not one of them. I love *you*—the Connor Hawthorne who is willing to take big risks for what's right, willing to go toe-to-toe with the bad guys. Why do you think I'd want you to stop being *you*?"

"I only meant that I keep getting you into these situations where you could get hurt. For God's sake, you could have died from that voodoo crap!" Connor appeared to be avoiding tears only by the greatest effort of will.

"*You* 'keep getting me into'? I'm sorry, I wasn't aware that I was following you around like some sort of faithful sidekick. Are we doing the 'call me Tonto' thing?"

Connor looked at her in wide-eyed surprise. "No, I would never…I mean that would be awful…I'd never say…"

Laura smiled and put her fingers gently against Connor's lips. "I was only trying to get your attention, not accuse you of political incorrectness." She moved her hand to Connor's cheek. "You are one of the kindest people I've ever known, as well as one of the bravest. So would you stop worrying about me, and just keep on being the woman I adore?"

"I'm doing that knight-on-the-white-charger thing again, aren't I?"

"Kind of, and I'm not saying I don't ever want you to rescue me if I need it. This is one damsel who knows how to yell for help. But don't borrow trouble. Don't start making decisions based on whether I might be at risk. Okay?"

Connor sighed. "Okay."

"And don't forget, in some circles I'm considered to be a fairly daunting opponent."

"That's true. I'm extremely glad you're on my side."

"Always, my love." Laura hugged Connor.

"Did we just have our first official fight?"

"No. But we are having our first actual making-up."

»——«

Shortly after ten A.M., the six people who stood the best chance of thwarting the plans of a man bent on destruction, gathered around the conference table in Benjamin's suite. Of all of them, Archbishop Johnston looked in the worst shape physically and emotionally. Gone were the ready smile and the easy self-confidence of a man in authority. The lines in his face appeared to have deepened in only a matter of days. Where once he had surveyed the people around him with the sharp eyes of a would-be gladiator, he now gazed at them as if he couldn't quite focus. Benjamin was troubled by the man's appearance, but knew there was nothing he could do about it at the moment. The information Benjamin had uncovered during the long hours of the night must be weighed and acted on…immediately.

"We have two distinct issues," he began, once everyone had been seated. "First, and most critical, is that I believe Richard La Cloche, alias Richard Bell, is here in the vicinity and plans to make some sort of move on the San Peligro Nuclear Generating Station. Somehow this is tied in with his membership, or perhaps," he continued in deference to the archbishop, "what he believes is his membership in the Malleus Society."

Connor leaned forward in her chair. "I know I missed the meeting last night. Could you quickly fill us in on what all of you have discovered?

Malcolm mentioned that you and Ayalla and some of his own sources all came up with some of the pieces of this."

Benjamin swiftly summarized the data they'd gathered and shared the previous evening during their meeting at the rectory of St. Mary of the Groves.

"Have you given Washington a heads-up," asked Laura, "to put the plant on alert?"

"I discussed it with some people there. The problem arises that the alert would go directly to someone we suspect has ties with La Cloche through a mutual acquaintance. The head of security, Peter Holcomb, has a brother who served time with La Cloche. For all we know, Holcomb could be in this up to his neck, assuming there's a financial motive for the threats."

"You mean some sort of blackmail?" asked Ayalla.

"Yes. You see, there are a lot of fanatics in the world, but in order to carry out their delusional missions, they are often smart enough to recruit help with the promise of money. In this case, even if La Cloche is convinced he's on a holy crusade of some sort, he's smart enough to realize that a lot of men are motivated by personal gain. Holcomb could be his man on the inside."

"Do you really think this creep believes what he's doing is righteous?" asked Malcolm.

"I don't know. I think he's a dangerous mix of intelligence and insanity. He may have latched onto the ultraconservative goals of some group like the Malleus Society, or been enamored of its age-old ties with the Inquisition. Granted, we're only guessing at his pathology, but their drive to maintain a particular form of Christianity may have fed into his delusion. He wants to justify the crimes he's committed. What better way than claiming the ultimate reason."

"God made me do it," said Ayalla.

"Exactly. I tend to agree with the archbishop when he says that no one at the Vatican would condone the murder of a priest. That doesn't mean that other self-styled hammer-of-God types would have the same scruples. People can talk themselves into just about anything."

"Group mentality is dangerous," said Malcolm. "Look at the cults that have sprouted up everywhere in this country."

"One man's cult is another man's religion," Benjamin shook his head. "We can't really generalize. The only factor we need to consider is the potential for violence. In this case, the potential is pretty high, but it's one man we're talking about, not an entire group."

"One man who bought into a boatload of crap this group was peddling about Christianity," snapped Ayalla.

"Crap it may well be," said Benjamin mildly. "It doesn't exactly require a leap of imagination to reach the conclusion that the Catholic Church has fought for centuries to preserve its own version of history. But I don't think now is the right time for a philosophical debate."

"You're right," Ayalla conceded. "Let's move on. You said that La Cloche might have some sort of blackmail scheme in mind, or at least he may have told his associates that's what it was."

"Right."

"But how could anyone believe they'd get away with it? If they take over the plant, they'll be immediately cut off from the outside world. They don't have a snowball's chance in hell. All we'd have to do is wait them out. They're not going to cause a meltdown while they're inside."

"Sound reasoning," replied Benjamin. "Except for one new piece of the puzzle I discovered last night." He reached into his briefcase and removed the copy of Father Rosario's map. "I could be wrong about this, but all the checking I've done indicates that there is probably a series of naturally formed tunnels or passageways beneath San Peligro. They may have been enhanced by human hands, I don't know. But if you look at this map, you'll notice one particular type of marking that Enrique used in these two areas—a solid double line meandering away from the mission and toward the nuclear plant. I think they represent tunnels."

"What about the other lines?" asked Connor, leaning over the map as it was passed to her. "These dotted ones?"

Benjamin almost smiled. "That's where we come to the second issue I mentioned. Enrique was a very clever man. I wish I'd had the chance to know him personally." He fixed his gaze on the archbishop, who nodded slowly, sorrowfully.

"It finally occurred to me a few hours ago that there was a pattern to those dotted lines, the way they alternate with longer dashes."

"Morse code!" Ayalla exclaimed. She now had the map in front of her.

"You're a lot quicker than I am, Agent Franklin. I stared at the damn thing half the night before it hit me."

"Did you have a chance to translate it?" she asked.

"Yes, although some of it didn't quite seem right. But then he may have been using it as a personal code and not necessarily remembered all the letters of the Morse system with complete accuracy." He looked at the archbishop again. "Enrique did send his father to Italy to retrieve something. And he hid it at the mission. I think it's the artifact that Kursk was so anxious to find."

"But what *is* it?" said Johnston with unconcealed anger. "What could be so damned important that it got Enrique killed—and Cecilia and Kursk?"

"And the young man from our hotel," added Laura. "He died simply because we were staying there." The muscles in her jaw clenched.

"But if we assume the person who left the 'devil's fire' in your car is La Cloche, that had nothing to do with the artifact, really. He must have identified you and Connor and probably all of us as threatening to his plans. I'm not saying he doesn't know about the artifact. He may simply suspect its existence."

"You still haven't said what it is, though," said Malcolm.

"I still don't know. Father Rosario wasn't foolish enough to put that on paper, and since he probably knew what it is, there would be no point in risking someone else discovering a written record. Still, there were a few cryptic notations here and there throughout his research. I tried to synthesize them." He stopped and gulped his coffee. "Basically, there is the question of whether Mary Magdalene was indeed an apostle who was taught by Jesus. Then there are additional possibilities—that she was the wife of Jesus or of Jesus' brother, James."

"He had a brother?" Ayalla frowned.

"There is some evidence that lends credence to that," said Benjamin. "And there is also the question of whether she may have had children who might be the descendants of Jesus. But I'm no scholar. Better men than I have debated these issues for years."

"The operative word being 'men,' Ayalla retorted. "I've found their discussions often reach the same conclusions when it comes to women and their place in the church. What I want to know is how this is getting us any closer to catching that son of a bitch La Cloche."

"Are you by any chance Catholic?" asked Malcolm.

"Recovering Catholic, if you must know."

"Ah, that explains it."

"Explains what?" she demanded, as if spoiling for an argument.

Malcolm lifted his hands in mock surrender. "Nothing. I only meant that it explains some of why you're so pissed off about this."

"I am not pissed off that he is a misogynist hiding behind religion. If that were grounds for condemning someone, I'd have half the Catholic clergy and a whole lot of born-again Christians in my sights. I am, however, pissed off that he's killing people and threatening to do a lot of collateral damage. Are we clear on that?"

"Yes, ma'am," said Malcolm, looking to Benjamin in a mute appeal for support.

"Ayalla's right. We have to move on and worry about the artifact later."

"What do you propose, Dad? If we can't alert security at the plant, and we don't know for sure if Holcomb is involved, how are we going to accomplish anything useful?"

"Fortunately, we have options. Our first advantage is the presence of Agent Franklin. She's federal law enforcement, which means she has enough authority to get inside San Peligro without making a big fuss about it. If Holcomb is involved, that will make him nervous, but he can't make a move on her since he'd bring down the whole FBI on the place if anything happened while she was there. So I'd like you, Ayalla, to pay a call on the manager of the plant," he consulted his notes, "Archibald Sims. Sound him out carefully. See if he's got any idea that something's going on."

"What about me?" said Malcolm. "Why don't I go with her?"

Benjamin thought about it. "All right. That's probably not a bad idea. But don't start flashing your badge unless Holcomb demands I.D. Try to get in on the strength of Ayalla's FBI identification. If he knows all about La Cloche's prison time, then he may also know that the arrest was in Washington. Having a D.C. cop on his doorstep might make him so hinky he does something really stupid."

"As for Connor and Laura, I'd like you two to head back to the mission and take this copy of the map I made. See if you can find the two entrances to underground passageways that I marked in blue. They may not be there, but I think we're going to have to be aware that La Cloche may have found at least one of these tunnels, and his plan involves using it to move between the generating station and the mission grounds. For all we know, that's his getaway plan. We need to cover those."

"What are you going to do, Benjamin," asked Laura, "now that we've got *our* marching orders?"

"I'm going to have a talk with the archbishop," he said. "We'll be meeting you at the mission shortly, but I have to stop at John Wayne airport and pick something up."

"Jeannine sending you extra vitamins?" asked Connor with a smile, alluding to his assistant's penchant for sending him herbal restoratives while he was traveling since, oddly enough, he never seemed to remember to put them in his suitcase.

"Probably, but there are some other things we might need."

He didn't elaborate, and only Ayalla looked as if she wanted to know the details. Malcolm, Connor, and Laura merely shrugged, trusting, as always, that Benjamin did almost nothing in life without a good reason. The archbishop appeared to be ignoring them all.

Malcolm and Ayalla were both clearly relieved to be doing some actual police work. They nearly raced each other to the door. Benjamin suspected they would argue over who would drive. He also suspected Ayalla would win.

"Be careful," he said to Connor, then Laura. He hugged them both. "Stay in touch and call me as soon as you find one of the entrances. We need to secure them as soon as possible."

"Aye, aye, Cap'n," Connor smiled, and gave her father a quick peck on the cheek. "We'll be in touch."

In seconds they were gone and the door closed behind them. Benjamin took a deep breath, his eyes fixed on the spot where'd they'd just been.

"You worry about your daughter," the archbishop said quietly.

"Yes, always. And Laura, too."

"Then why send them out to the mission alone? If La Cloche is nearby, he won't hesitate to try and kill them."

"They have each other. Don't let Laura's slight build and good looks deceive you into thinking she isn't tough as nails. And Connor stopped being a little girl a long time ago. She's a smart, independent woman. If I tried treating her as anything less, we wouldn't be friends."

"I didn't know parents and children were often friends."

"Only if they're very lucky."

»——«

He still clung to a slim hope that he'd found one of them, one of the women whose parentage could be traced back 2,000 years. But in all his time of service, not one possibility had been proven. Neither a descendant nor a reincarnation of the Holy Mother had been ever been identified beyond doubt. Yes, there had been false alarms, and without doubt he had come to know many remarkable beings as a result of his search and his lifelong vocation. Yet he yearned to finally meet the one who would come again. He was not alone in his longing for the return of a Messiah who would finally teach human beings to live in peace, but he was one of only a handful who knew that their modern-day savior would appear in the world as a woman. She would restore the balance. She would correct the twisted words that had been written, and reframe the teachings of Jesus, Buddha, and Mohammed in ways that all people could embrace and understand.

The elderly priest's greatest fear was that he, one of a long succession of sworn servants of the Mother-Father God, would not find Her in time, would not be able to protect Her from those who could not tolerate the dissolution of all they had built. They were invested in their dogma, their institutions, even their buildings. They would resist the advent of a complete and ecumenical peace on the planet by proclaiming Her a tool of evil, and they would destroy Her.

For the second time in as many days, he felt very old, older indeed than even the eldest of his sisters and brothers who had lived phenomenally long lives during their walk on earth. He considered that it might be time to go. But he would not relinquish his responsibilities before his own successor had arrived. He remained cautious, wary of every disturbance in the field of sacred energy, for he was determined that he would not fall victim to the circumstances that had trapped Brother Gandolfo centuries before. He said a brief prayer for the soul of the man who had found himself near death without hope of passing on the precious relic to trusted hands. And he had hidden it so well and fled so far into the other dimensions of reality that none of his sisters and brothers, living or dead, could discover what he had done—until now that is.

In the deep stillness of night, the old priest had carefully read all of Father Rosario's notes. He'd discovered the chilling report of the young monk who'd known of Brother Gandolfo's death. It was a relief to know, finally, yet a frustration to think that he'd been so close to recovering the relic and yet had failed. He'd even tried to contact Rosario, but the man's consciousness was as yet too limited to admit the fullness of creation. His soul wandered, content yet confused, and could not hear the communications of others. In fact, he thought himself alone in a lovely garden. It might be another dozen more lifetimes come and gone before the one who had called himself Enrique Rosario would discover the garden was filled with others.

Perhaps it was time to walk for a while. This earthly garden with its fragrant jasmine and India hawthorne soothed his troubled thoughts, although from time to time, as he passed over a particular spot here and there, he could feel the resonance of a long-ago tragedy—a death, a punishment, a cry for help. Yet these echoes did not prevent him from breathing in the holy energy of Mother Earth. He gazed at the walls of the old mission church and wondered if it would still be standing in another 200 years. Then came a flash of images through his mind, a painful precognition. He saw the mission buildings shudder and crumble as the ground rose up beneath them. Fire burst from cracks in the earth. In the distance a blinding burst of light exploded across the horizon. He heard screams of pain, anger, terror.

"No," he prayed. "Let this not be so."

Like others who understood some of the workings of the universe, he knew this vision was only a possibility. At each point along what humans perceived as a linear time line, infinite choices resulted in infinite outcomes. But that was not entirely a comfort to him. In at least one of the those outcomes, one of those parallel dimensions of reality, this single act of insane zealotry would set off a chain reaction of not only geological disasters but also human atrocities. The results would be of such horrifying magnitude that the Biblical stories of Armageddon would pale in comparison.

He breathed deeply and repeated his own mantra, the one that grounded him in *this* reality at *this* time. Here lay his responsibilities.

Chapter Twenty-Five

And yet be patient. Our Playwright may show
In some fifth Act what this wild Drama means.
—Alfred Lord Tennyson, *The Play*

"I don't understand why you're here," Holcomb protested. "We got the memo about the threats. I put on some extra guards. Nothing's happened. What's the big deal?"

Ayalla noted with interest the sweat that had begun to trickle down Holcomb's sideburns within moments of their arrival in his office. His hands were a little twitchy, and he'd been unable to stay relaxed in his chair. He'd spent the last minute standing by the window, arms crossed, expression defiant. *Yes,* she thought, *there's something going on here.*

"We're not questioning your actions," she replied mildly. "We simply want to speak with Mr. Sims, the plant manager. For some reason we were kept waiting for over an hour and a half and then shown here—to *your* office."

"Security matters are my responsibility," he barked, but even his aggression lacked conviction. Malcolm remained silent. They'd agreed Ayalla would do most of the talking since they were there on her authority. He contented himself with staring at Holcomb, his expression one of general cynicism and barely disguised contempt. Ayalla, with only a glance at her companion, decided this look alone was enough to unnerve almost anyone, particularly if he had something to hide. Little wonder that Holcomb's eyes kept veering toward Malcolm and then just as quickly back to Ayalla.

"It's my understanding that every facet of plant operations is the manager's responsibility."

"Oh, well, Sims, that is, Mr. Sims...he...uh...leaves that stuff pretty much to me. He doesn't really know squat about security. Kind of an egghead, you know. Techno-geek. He knows to leave that kind of thing to us professionals." Holcomb mustered a weak smile, but his feeble attempt at a "we're all brothers behind the badge" plopped into the silence and was received with the sort of enthusiasm that would be accorded a noxious fart. He stared unhappily at the two visitors.

"Well, then Mr. Holcomb, perhaps you'd like to bring us up to speed on the state of your security here. Then we'll go and see Mr. Sims."

»——«

Archibald, unaware that official visitors awaited him, had ventured down to the lowest level. He'd scraped up whatever small bits of courage still lived in him and decided he must see for himself whether anything really bad was going on in his plant. Of course, he had no idea what something "bad" might look like. He couldn't fathom what Holcomb and the Preacher were up to. He only knew that it couldn't possibly be good—not for him, not for anyone. He'd walked slowly through the control room on his way down, noting that most of the technicians were surprised to see him. Had it been that long since he'd made the standard inspection tour?

Everyone looked up, but they kept doing their jobs, which in most cases required only monitoring the vast array of gauges, indicators, LED meters, and warning lights. He thought it overkill in some ways. They had lights that warned of the failure of warning lights whose purpose was to warn of the need to replace a bulb for a warning light. And even if no one happened to be looking at one of the more relevant cautionary lights, each system was programmed to activate eardrum-shattering, bone-vibrating Klaxon horns mounted on walls throughout the complex. And yes, there were backups for those as well. On the other hand, he decided, how many backups were really enough when you considered that just beneath them, albeit enclosed behind thick layers of concrete and steel, lay enough radiation to kill them all within days if they ever were directly exposed?

A few technicians circulated from one monitoring station to another, dutifully marking their hourly checklists. But Sims sensed that no one cared whether he was there or not. Their routines remained the same, and he had hardly garnered a reputation for toughness as a manager.

Glancing over the main display panel one more time and finding everything in order, he continued out the other door to the control room and took the elevator down to the lowest level. No one visited there often. It had only been constructed as an access for possible repairs to piping that ran beneath the containment structure, the system of plumbing that carried the coolant to control the reactor. Thus Sims, who expected to find himself alone, was unpleasantly surprised to come face to face with one of Holcomb's scrungy-looking guards. Leonard Zemecka sat on a chair in the corridor, a few feet to the left of an access door, though it was built more in the shape of a hatch on a submarine and locked by means of a wheel set into the middle. Sims had a vague recollection that there was one secured entry to the underground terrain beneath the plant, also included in the plans to provide emergency access. As far as he knew it led into a short, narrow corridor carved out of the rock and dirt and running about thirty feet along one side of the very bottom of the containment structure. What he couldn't figure out was why on earth Holcomb would have someone down here guarding an access door to a passage that led nowhere.

Zemecka smirked at Sims and didn't bother to get up. "Hey, Archie, how's it hangin'?"

Archibald bristled, still determined to preserve his dignity, if nothing else. "I'll thank you to display some courtesy while you're on this job," he said. "And I'd like to know what you're doing down here."

"Orders," the man grunted, still smirking.

I'd like to wipe that expression right off his face, thought Sims, *but he'd probably break my arm.* "Whose orders?"

"The boss."

The guard was playing with him. "At this station, I'm the boss. I take it you are referring to security chief Holcomb?"

"Like I said—the boss." He stared at Sims, as if daring him to contradict.

"There's no reason to have a guard on this level. It's a waste of resources."

"So take it up with him."

"I'm taking it up with you. I'm ordering you to report back to the duty station at the gate until further notice."

Zemecka stood up, and Sims stepped back. "Look here, you little prick, I don't take orders from nobody but Holcomb. And he said don't leave this spot. So I stay here—got it?" His face was inches away from Archibald, who was close enough to smell the hot, sour breath of a man with a hangover and a heavy smoking habit. "Now, why don't you trot your ass back upstairs and hide in your office?"

Whether or not Sims would have slunk away ignominiously or finally taken a stand on his own behalf was destined to remain undecided, for in that moment the guard's walkie-talkie emitted a series of beeps. The guard backed away from Sims and put the earpiece for the radio into his ear, effectively preventing Sims from hearing what was being said. The guard's empty eyes stayed fixed on the plant manager while he listened. After fifteen or twenty seconds that stretched into years for Archibald, the guard pressed the SEND key on his shoulder mike. "Will do," was all he said."

"What was that about?" asked Sims. "Is there a problem?"

"Not one I can't solve," the guard grinned. He moved fast for a slovenly, out-of-shape guy who was perpetually hung over. In a heartbeat he had spun Sims around and pinned one arm behind his back.

"What the hell are you doing?" the plant manager sputtered. "Let go of me."

"Sure thing, *Mister* Sims," Zemecka hissed in his ear. "Right this way."

With one hand he twisted his prisoner's arm even higher, and with the other he spun the wheel on the metal hatch and swung it open. He half-lifted, have shoved Sims over the threshold and into the semidarkness beyond. Sims landed facedown in dirt, and before he could recover himself, the hatch closed with a thump behind him. In the dim illumination of the yellow safety lights, he saw the crossed steel bars rotate the four bolts into their sockets. Then he heard a muffled clank from the inside corridor. Sims stumbled to the door and tried to turn the wheel on his side, but it wouldn't budge. He gradually figured out that the guard had slid something into the spokes of the wheel to keep it from turning. He stood there panting, tasting blood on his tongue from where he'd bitten his cheek when he fell.

His mind was sluggish, but as he turned and stared at the passageway, an awful sensation crept into his stomach. He dropped to his knees and threw up in the dirt. Whatever the Preacher had in mind, it was too late to stop him. Archibald knew he was going to die and even allowed himself to wonder if perhaps he deserved his fate.

»——«

Ayalla and Malcolm couldn't have been more surprised when Holcomb slammed the door in their faces and locked it. Yes, they knew he was probably dirty. He'd been nervous and obstructionist since they walked into his office. He'd lost all the color in his face when Ayalla had broached the topic of Holcomb's brother and his relationship with a man named Ricky Bell, also known as the Preacher, also known as Richard La Cloche. The security chief had hemmed and hawed about it, insisting that his brother was a no-good bum with whom he had nothing to do. Hadn't seen him in months.

The next blow to the man's confidence came when Ayalla asked why the station's personnel roster included two men with criminal records. He insisted he had no idea, but it was a weak defense. All security personnel were required by regulation to undergo stringent background investigations prior to hiring. Ayalla asked to see the results of those checks. Malcolm added, "And then you can escort us to the plant manager's office. We're anxious to have a talk with him."

"I'll get the files," said Holcomb, and despite his sweaty trepidation, they didn't expect he'd be stupid enough to panic and run. Malcolm had only begun to rise from his chair when Holcomb announced that the files were in the outer office under lock and key. Malcolm had every intention of going with him to make sure he actually found the files, but he was several feet away when Holcomb opened the door, slipped through, then slammed it shut. Ayalla and Malcolm heard the deadbolt slide home. Unfortunately, the lock was keyed on both sides. They heard Holcomb's voice on the other side, receding in the distance.

"He's on the radio with someone," said Ayalla. "Probably his two cronies. We need to get out of here."

"If this were the movies, you could shoot the lock off," said Malcolm, who wasn't carrying a gun since the paperwork to do so in California was more trouble than it was worth.

"Yes, and then we dodge the ricochets, or wait for a scream from the secretary out there letting us know she's hit."

"How about something more old-fashioned?"

She eyed the door. "Like breaking down the door. If you're talking old-fashioned, I'd say that real wood qualifies."

"Yeah, but I'm kinda pissed off. I hate being locked up anywhere."

"Go for it, big guy." She stood aside smugly and watched Malcolm challenge the door to a test of strength. He charged. It was a tie. The wood cracked slightly, but from his grimace of pain, Ayalla wondered if the sound had come from his shoulder. "You sure you want to do this?" she said. "We can call for backup from here."

"And sit here twiddling our thumbs 'til some of your pals come and unlock the door? How stupid will that look?"

"Pretty stupid. Okay, give it another try."

He rammed against the door again, and this time the wood in the inset panels split. Malcolm backed up, rubbing his shoulder. "This is another one of those things that looks easier in the movies."

"But it's an honorable pursuit for manly men," said Ayalla, a rare and wryly amused expression fighting with grim seriousness for possession of her face.

"Thanks. On top of pain I get ridicule."

"Just an appreciation of your blatant masculinity."

"We're going to discuss this later."

"Assuming there is a later. Have you forgotten we're trapped inside a nuclear generating station that some deluded psychopath may be planning to blow up?"

"No."

"Then try, try again."

"Fine," he said a little too pompously. "This one ought to do it."

Fortunately or unfortunately, Malcolm was spared from the potential embarrassment of failure. Just as he prepared to launch a mighty assault on the door, they heard the snick of the tumblers and the bolt sliding back. Ayalla yanked the door open hard.

Malcolm must have looked rather frightening to the timid young woman who stood there, key in hand, as he tried to stop his momentum from carrying him right into her. Holcomb's secretary took one look at him and fainted.

Ayalla quickly bent over her. "I think you scared her to death."

"Not possible."

"You're right. There's a pulse. Pick her up and put her on the couch in the office. We've got to find Holcomb and the plant manager before some really bad shit hits the fan."

»——«

Richard La Cloche heard an odd sound as he carefully made his way through the tunnel, almost like someone moaning. The echoes in the tunnel made it hard to distinguish, but as he came closer the sound took on more form. Someone was talking, first angrily, then in a whine. There were thuds periodically. He moved even more softly and extinguished the powerful light he carried. Who the hell was down here?

Peering around the corner, he was both puzzled and relieved. It was the idiot Sims, who posed no threat at all as far as La Cloche was concerned. But why was he in the crawl space (the height of which belied the term), and why was he banging on the access door? La Cloche considered it for a few moments, and wished that his radio would work from this location. But the shielding around the lower part of the containment structure blocked out most communications. He'd planned on stepping into the interior corridor before communicating with Holcomb. Now it appeared that Sims was locked out. That meant La Cloche was also at the same disadvantage. Still, he believed Holcomb would keep to the schedule and a guard would be posted on the other side of the door. Once he shut Sims up, he could communicate his presence to the guard, who would open the door. Simple as that. He put down the flashlight and the backpack he had slung over his shoulder. It was time.

»——«

Malcolm and Ayalla ran down the corridor leading to the control room of the facility. A guard held up his hand to stop them, but Ayalla slammed him against the wall and held her badge inches from his nose while she checked his name tag. They had to be on the lookout for the two guards they knew were Holcomb's accomplices—and hope to God they could trust the other security people.

"FBI!" she shouted at him. "We're going to arrest Security Chief Holcomb on suspicion of sabotage. Which way did he go?"

The guard, a young man in his twenties who was still waging a losing battle with acne, looked too terrified to speak. He pointed to the left. "Th-there," he squeaked.

Ayalla released him. "If you're lying, I'm going to come back here and shoot you."

"N-n-o, I'm t-t-telling the t-t-truth."

"Good. Then you'll live at least until tomorrow. I want you to stay here. You don't move unless I tell you to. Now give me that radio you're wearing."

He complied, fumbling the unit off his belt. He was desperately trying to untangle the earpiece wire from his epaulet when Ayalla grabbed the radio, yanked the cord out of its jack. "I don't need that part. Now stay!"

They began to run in the direction he'd indicated, knowing that they were many minutes behind Holcomb and no doubt he knew every closet and stairwell and passageway in the place.

"It's gonna be damn hard to find him in here," said Malcolm.

"I know. But at least we can alert the control room technicians that there might be a problem. Then we'll lock the place down, call for backup, and smoke him and his goons out of wherever they're hiding."

Ayalla had to stop as Malcolm grabbed her arm. "They don't have to hide."

"You mean they already drove out of here?"

"No. Remember what Benjamin said—there are passageways under the ground between here and the mission. What if they go out that way? While everyone's watching the roads over this way, they can walk a mile or so and come up there. If they have a car stashed, they're outta here."

"Maybe so, but first the control room. I want these people to start shutting down the reactor until we figure out what's going on."

»—«

Of all the sights poor Archibald might have expected to see in his underground prison—rats being the worst of his many fears—the list would not have included a Catholic clergyman.

Yet there he was like some sort of delusion born out of a drug-induced religious fervor. No doubt, thought Archibald, he'd lost his mind. The pressure on his fragile psyche was more than it could tolerate.

Then hope sparked within him. What if this was a miracle? Perhaps God was going to save him, and all that he'd done for the sake of the Society had been justified. He reached out his hands in supplication. "Father," he murmured. "Please help me."

"Of course, my son. I'll help you," said Richard La Cloche. "...help you to see God." From behind his back he swung the heavy-duty flashlight favored by security guards and police for its heft and durability. The long arc of the swing gave the weapon immense momentum, and it caved in the side of Archibald's skull before he could even comprehend what was happening. The whiplash of the blow fractured two vertebrae in his neck. Before his brain could fully register the intense agony of the blow, the neural pathways from his body's pain receptors had already shut down operations. He dropped to the dirt floor in a heap, like a marionette whose strings have been severed.

La Cloche stepped over him and rapped sharply and rhythmically on the door with the butt of the flashlight. After a delay, the locking wheel began to turn. The security guard was almost as surprised as Sims had been to see a man in priest garb, but La Cloche didn't give him time to ponder over it. "Where's Holcomb? Why was Sims out there in the crawl space?" he snapped.

"He's on his way down, I think. There's some sort of problem. He told me to put Sims in there to keep him quiet."

"What kind of problem?"

"FBI. They're here in the plant," snarled Zemecka.

La Cloche rode out the momentary surge of fear. They were quicker than he'd anticipated. No matter. Everything was in place.

The guard, who was staring through the door at the limp form of the plant manager was about to say something. La Cloche stepped close, facing him. "Permanent solutions are always better than temporary ones." The man never saw the flash of steel in La Cloche's hand and looked almost surprised at the prison-style shiv in his chest. With a practiced upward stroke, followed by a twist to the right, La Cloche sliced through the man's heart. Quick, easy, tidy. Very little blood, with lots of internal damage. He was still thankful for the skills he'd acquired in prison. God had been wise to send him there. He thrust the guard's body through the door and into the crawl space, dumping him on top of Sims. He considered saying the last rites over them, but since he hadn't the proper equipment—the oil, his stole—they would have to meet their Maker unshriven.

His keen ears caught the unmistakable whine of gears and cables as the elevator descended to the lower level. La Cloche pulled the door almost to the jamb, leaving an inch from which he could survey the hallway. He tensed until he recognized Holcomb's ungainly form trotting down the hall. The security chief was breathing hard, and sweat stains darkened most of his uniform shirt. He looked wildly around for the guard he'd left there and almost screamed when the hatch swung open and La Cloche stepped out.

"Oh, it's you," he said, gasping for air. "Where's Leonard?"

"I sent him on an errand."

"I hope he didn't go back up to the control-room level."

"Why?"

"Didn't he tell you? There's a couple of FBI agents up there, and they *know*—the sons of bitches know. They asked about my brother—and about *you!* Jesus. 'Cept they said your real name wasn't Bell—it was La Close or something like that. Come on, we've gotta get out of here."

His face frozen in disbelief, La Cloche stared at Holcomb. "What did you say?"

"That we gotta get out of here."

"No!" He trapped the man's biceps in his left hand with tremendous grip. "Before that. They said my name wasn't Bell?"

Holcomb looked into the Preacher's eyes, and fear boiled in his guts. "I don't know. Maybe I didn't understand them. I thought they said, um—"

"Said what!" La Cloche shouted.

"That your real name was something that sounded French-like, you know La Cloak, or La Close—I don't *know* French," he whined as the fingers on his arm tightened like talons.

La Cloche's entire body vibrated with anger. They'd done what they were not supposed to do. Somehow, after all these years, they'd discovered his true identity. But how? His fury was almost uncontrollable. He yearned to lash out at them, all of them. He forced his voice into as calm a tone as possible.

"How quickly will they be able to get down here?"

"I locked off the elevator. They can't call it. And they'd need a security passkey card to use the stairwells."

"I imagine they're smart enough to find one. And what about our little packages. Are they all in place as I instructed?"

"Yes, sir. Yes, they are. Holcomb reached into his pants pocket and withdrew a small gray plastic box. As soon as you flip those two switches, they're armed. Then all you have to do is press the white button." Holcomb shuddered. "But you won't have to, right? I mean, it's just a bluff, right? We get the money and then take off."

"I never bluff." He plucked the device out of Holcomb's fingers and tucked it into the pocket of his black suit coat. Then once more the vicious blade slid down out of his sleeve and came to rest in his palm. "And I'd never sell my soul for money."

Within seconds Holcomb had met the same fate as his employee. The look on his face was so startled as to be ludicrous, but La Cloche wasn't laughing. He had to act, and he had to act now. His timetable was considerably altered, but he felt alive, energized. His anger had already subsided beneath the excitement. So they knew who he was. It didn't matter. Killing had never seemed so easy, and certainly raining down destruction on the world had never seem so appealing.

He pushed Holcomb's body through the hatch, picked up the metal pry bar that the guard had used to jam the door, and stepped into the crawl space. Closing the hatch behind him, he spun the inside wheel and thrust the bar into it at a forty-five-degree angle. A more experienced person, a sailor perhaps, would have told him that the strategy was not foolproof unless he positioned the bar parallel to the ground so that it couldn't be shifted by rocking the wheel back and forth from the other side. But La Cloche was in a hurry and, he believed, a state of righteous and divine grace. What could possibly hurt him now?

»——«

Malcolm cussed a blue streak at the stubborn head technician who had steadfastly refused to begin a controlled shutdown of the reactor. He insisted that only Mr. Sims could order such a drastic action. Then he started quoting statistics about how many homes, businesses, and public services relied on San Peligro for power.

"You have an emergency plan, don't you?" Ayalla interjected. "Don't other suppliers fill the gap in the power grid if you have to shut down."

"Theoretically," the technician replied. "But I haven't been informed of any real emergency."

"We just told you, you pompous moron. This plant is a target. Your security chief has been working with convicted felons to cause some kind of destruction here. Less than fifteen minutes ago he ran from us and is hiding somewhere in the plant. By any chance do you find that alarming?"

The technician's face suffused with color. "There are regulations about shutdowns. I can't start a process like that without express authorization. Certainly not on the word of one cop and one FBI agent. The whole idea is absurd. You act like it's a matter of hitting an 'off' button. I'm telling you, there's a lot more to the process than that."

Ayalla had just opened her mouth to speak when a deep guttural rumble rolled beneath their feet. A few seconds later, the shock wave of the explosion smacked into the floor, lifting it slightly. The walls cracked. Acoustic tiles showered down on them. Everyone in the room was thrown to the floor.

"What the hell was…" The rest of Malcolm's question was drowned in the splitting shriek of the plant-wide alarm. An automated voice hissed through the static of damaged speakers on the walls: *"Warning. A fault has been detected in the primary coolant system. Commence immediate emergency shutdown. Warning. A fault has been detected in the primary coolant system. Commence immediate emergency shutdown. Warning…"*

Malcolm felt like throwing a chair at the speakers. Instead, he helped the chief technician to his feet. "Okay, *now* do you suppose we have an emergency?"

The man's mouth gaped open as he looked at the damage to the control room. "I don't understand. There's nothing in this system that could cause an explosion like this."

"Move!" shouted Ayalla. "Do it now!"

He scrambled past overturned chairs and tables to the central panel from which they monitored the status of the coolant system. Malcolm and Ayalla were right behind him.

"Are you shutting it off?" shouted Malcolm over the noise of the alarm.

"First, I have to make the sure the secondary coolant system is on-line. Without that, it doesn't matter whether I lower the control rods or not. They'd still keep heating up."

He flipped a row of switches and watched as the panel showed green lights for the backup coolant system. The valves were open, and cold seawater was flowing into the pipes and tanks. Only then did he open the cover protecting a button that would drop the rods completely into the coolant tank and shut down the nuclear reaction. He pressed it and watched the analog display as it mimicked what was happening beneath them. Slowly, all of the rods descended. The other technicians, though clearly frightened, were hurrying to their duty stations.

"Reaction is slowing," shouted one.

"Coolant temperature within nominal levels," reported another.

"Will somebody shut off that damn alarm!" said the chief technician. "I can't hear myself think."

In a few seconds, the horns and the automated warning message fell silent.

Malcolm looked at the chief technician, who was leaning on the panel, staring at the gauges, his face covered with sweat and dirt. "So, we're okay now? The reactor's safe?"

"As long as we can keep the control rods cooled off," he answered. "Thank God for the complete backup system." Malcolm turned to Ayalla, who was staring right through him as if she were completely focused on something invisible. "What?" he asked her. "What is it?"

She ignored him and tugged at the technician's arm to get him to turn around and face her. "What happens if the backup coolant system fails?"

He swallowed hard. "Um, that can't happen."

"What if it *does*?"

"Then, well, there's no way to control a nuclear reaction without coolant. If we can't pump water into the reactor and into the holding tanks for the spent rods, then..." He clearly didn't want to finish the sentence

"Then what?"

"A meltdown."

"Like Three Mile Island?" asked Malcolm incredulously. "Like Chernobyl?"

"Look," said the technician. "We've got fail-safes. That's why the backup system was installed. It's completely separate. The malfunction can't spread to the other system."

Ayalla gritted her teeth. "You aren't quite getting this, are you? This was not a mechanical failure; this was not a system malfunction. This was a deliberate act of terrorism. What we heard was no doubt an explosive device set off near the critical parts of the coolant system. Which means," she said slowly and deliberately, "that if someone can destroy one safety feature, they can destroy all of them."

"But why would anyone do—"

"I don't know why people do *most* things," she snapped. "But I suggest you start implementing whatever contingency plans you have, and alert the NRC. We'll take care of the local response." She walked toward the corridor to try and get better reception on her cell phone.

The technician watched her walk away, then he looked at Malcolm before dropping his eyes. "I'm sorry. I acted like an ass. I didn't know."

"Doesn't really matter, does it? Looks like even if you'd done what we asked, we'd still have the same problem. Look, how do we get down to the subbasement or whatever it's called?"

"I don't know if the elevator's still intact, but there's a stairwell. Thing is, the doors are all locked at each level. You need a key card to get through them."

"You have one?"

"It only works for doors between the control room and the staff exit. Access is sort of on a specific-need basis."

"How about the guards?"

"Their keys should work anywhere."

"Thanks."

Malcolm trotted out into the hall and past Ayalla, signaling her that he'd be right back. He found the young guard sitting on the floor where they'd left him. He looked terrified, but to his credit, he hadn't run off. Malcolm imagined a lot of people had fled the building when they heard the explosion. When you came right down to it, people knew just enough about radiation to be scared as hell of it. He certainly was.

"Hey," said Malcolm.

The guard stood up and was able to keep his feet, but only just. "Sir."

"I need your key card so we can get downstairs."

"You need me to show the way, sir?"

He looked so young and vulnerable Malcolm took pity on him. The kid reminded him of the raw recruits standing in line at roll call, trying not to look terrified that they were about to face the real world.

"No, the doors are marked. What I need you to do is go out front and direct traffic. The FBI will be rolling in along with a police SWAT team, so you need to tell them where to go. You can do that, right?"

The guard looked almost giddy with relief that he'd be allowed to get out of the building. "Yes, sir. I can do that."

"Good, and on your way out, would you check on Mr. Holcomb's secretary? She fainted earlier. Make sure she's conscious and out of the building. Tell everyone you see to evacuate."

"Sir?"

"Is it a meltdown? Is there going to be like a mushroom cloud?"

Malcolm quelled his impatience. "We're not sitting on an atomic bomb, kid. That's a whole different thing. But there is danger from leaking radiation, so get all nonessential personnel as far away as possible. Now go!"

The guard jumped like a startled rabbit and scurried down the corridor, his baton slapping against his leg, his key chain rattling.

"Amateurs," muttered Malcolm. Then he shook his head. For professionals, he and Ayalla hadn't accomplished much either. A bomb had gone off. Holcomb was missing. There was no sign of the plant manager, and everything was one big freakin' mess. He slipped the key card into his coat pocket, squared his shoulders, and headed back to get Ayalla. Next stop: See what was going on downstairs. God, he hated tunnels.

Chapter Twenty-Six

I have lived long enough, having seen one thing, that love hath an end;
Goddess and maiden and queen, be near me now and befriend.
—Algernon Charles Swinburne, *Hymn to Proserpine*

"What is that? An earthquake?" asked Laura as they stopped in their search for the tunnel entrance Father Rosario had marked on his map.

Connor, who'd been poking in some bushes, said, "I don't know. I hope that's all it is."

Laura snorted softly. "Hard to believe we'd actually be hoping for an earthquake."

"Better than Ricky Bell on a rampage."

"But what if it is? What if he's already started?"

"Then we'd better find that damn tunnel. If he's responsible for the rumble, then he's probably somewhere between here and the plant."

Laura's cell phone bleeped. She glanced at the display and punched the TALK key. "Ayalla, what's happening over there?"

Connor abandoned one clump of bushes and moved to the next, her ears tuned like radar to pick up some hint from Laura's side of the conversation. Part of her wanted to grab the phone and hear, but she restrained herself.

After less than a minute, Laura clicked off the call. "Bad news," she got right to the point. "Ayalla says there's been an explosion underneath the plant. The primary coolant system for the reactor isn't working. They've brought the backup on-line and are taking the reactor itself off-line. She and Malcolm haven't been able to confirm what caused the explosion. They're heading down to the lowest level right now. She's called her field office, and she called Benjamin. He's handling all the necessary notifications right now. He and the archbishop are already here. They're in Benjamin's car in the parking lot, and they'll be headed this way in a few minutes."

"Malcolm's staying in the plant?" asked Connor.

Laura took a deep breath. "I know. I'm worried about him, too. But he's doing whatever he has to do. He's not going to run away if there's anything he can do to keep this from getting worse than it already is. Besides, if they can find the plant entrance to the underground passage, then we could get this creep sandwiched between us."

"Unless we don't find our end of the tunnel, or there actually is more than one, which the map seems to indicate."

"There are times, darling, when pessimism is not the best way to go."

"I'm a natural pessimist," said Connor.

"I know, and I love you anyway. Now keep looking. I have a feeling we're right on top of it, so to speak."

No more than five minutes later, as if to confirm Laura's occasional clairvoyance, Connor didn't so much as find the tunnel entrance as fall over it—and then into it. An old round wooden cover, like those found over wells, had rotted away for years and could not bear Connor's weight. The edge of it disintegrated when she stepped on it, and her leg went all the way through.

"Damn!" she cried out. "What the hell!"

Laura dashed through the clump of bushes to find her lover with one leg trapped, flailing at the branches of the shrubs so she could sit upright.

"Wow, you found it," said Laura, trying not to seem amused.

"Yes, the hard way, I might add. How about a hand?"

Laura grabbed Connor's arms and helped her sit up, then squatted beside her to look at the door. "It's been here a long time, but the wood's finally rotted. The way it's buried just below ground level, we might never have seen it. Good work."

"Thank you, I'm glad I could oblige. I'll take good luck over incredible skill any day. Now do you suppose we could extract the rest of me? It makes me nervous having my foot underground where I can't see it."

"What? Why?"

"Who knows what's down there?"

"You think some creature is going to eat your foot?" Laura couldn't suppress a giggle.

"Oh, yeah. Laugh. You wouldn't think it was so funny if it were your foot dangling into a covered hole. There could be rats, or mice, or... chipmunks."

Laura let loose with a full-bellied laugh. "Oh, right. I'd forgotten those carnivorous giant chipmunks they have in California. We talking Theodore, Simon, or Alvin?"

Connor looked as if she wanted to stay annoyed, but Laura's laughter was infectious. She fell back on the grass with her own case of the giggles. "All right," she finally said, wiping her eyes. "You're right. I'm totally insane. I have no idea why we're even laughing. Considering what's going on over there," she pointed in the direction of the generating station, "shouldn't we be completely serious?"

"There's never a better time for gallows humor," replied Laura. "We're scared. We don't know what's going to happen. I'd rather chuckle than have a panic attack. Besides, think of all those endorphins we're releasing. We'll need them later, believe me."

"Point taken. And now could you get me out of here?"

Laura quickly helped Connor pull her leg free of the jagged wood and they knelt beside the hatch to see how they could open it. "How about something to use as a lever?" Laura suggested after several unsuccessful attempts to pull the hatch up by the single rusty iron ring set in its center.

"Would brute force be welcome?" Benjamin's voice was right behind them.

Connor turned around. "Any force is fine, but I still think Laura's right—we need to get some leverage. Where's the archbishop?"

"I asked him to stay in the car and do what he does best—pray."

"We need all the prayers we can get," nodded Laura. "Any more word from Ayalla or Malcolm?"

"No, and I don't expect any. Once they're down on the lower levels of the facility, I doubt they'd be able to use a cell phone."

"So we still don't know what happened over there," said Connor, looking toward the squat white domes in the distance.

"No, but let's keep following our hunches. I'm willing to bet that some sort of explosive was set off." He examined the wooden cover. "This hasn't been opened in decades, maybe a century or more. La Cloche can't be using this as an escape route."

"We figured the same thing," said Connor, "but at least it gives us a way in."

"True. But we need to find the other entrance as well."

Laura unfolded the map and traced the lines Father Rosario had made. "If this line ends here," she said, frowning at the faded markings, "then the main passage from the station splits into a Y just on the other side of the church. And the other branch should be in the botanical garden, or very near it."

"I think you're right," Benjamin nodded. "So let's work this door off and then find something lighter to cover it with."

As Laura went off in search of that "something lighter," he and Connor grabbed hold of the metal ring and heaved, once, then again. It began to move. On the third try, it broke loose from the soil and they almost fell over backward. They rolled it a few feet away and let it drop. "Not bad for an old man," said Benjamin, brushing the dirt and rust off his hands.

Not for the first time Connor felt a pang of sadness when she looked at her father. To her, he'd never been old. And even though his once-black hair was more gray than dark, he was still strong, fit, and vital. Already in his sixties, he could easily pass for someone ten or fifteen years younger. Still, someday he would be gone, and Connor couldn't quite bear to think of her life without him in it, somewhere nearby when she needed him.

She must have stared too long, for he waved his hand in front of her face. "Odd time for woolgathering, hon. What's wrong?"

"Nothing, just trying to figure out why we're here."

He smiled. "Are we talking 'why we're here' on this planet, or 'why we're here this minute'?"

"Maybe a little of both. Sorry. I'm being weird."

"You may be a lot of things, daughter of mine, but weird isn't one of them. Now what's keeping Laura?"

"Scavenging," came her voice from beyond a stand of trees. She emerged carrying a few smallish scraps of dirt-encrusted plywood and part of a fence rail. "There's a shed over there with some odds and ends in it. Will these do?"

"Admirably," said Benjamin. "We'll use the rail across the middle and lean the plywood on it. That should block out most of the sunlight. I don't want La Cloche homing in on it if we cut him off from the other end."

"Do you think we have time to be doing this?" asked Connor.

"Yes. You see, Ayalla told me that there has only been one explosion. And the plant is still fairly intact. The backup coolant system is on-line and functioning properly. So that tells me that we're waiting for the other shoe to drop. I doubt La Cloche is finished with what he's doing in there. But still, you're right, we need to keep moving."

Within a few minutes, they had camouflaged the tunnel entrance and began making their way toward the other side of the church. It was several hundred yards away, and they walked quickly and silently, each one scanning the area for signs of anyone else.

"Strange there aren't any tourists," Laura said quietly. "The other day when we were here there were at least half a dozen people."

"I suggested to the park ranger that he close the gate."

"Odd that he would agree," said Connor. "Ayalla and Malcolm said he wasn't the cooperative type."

"I had to get his boss's boss on the phone, and after that he was extremely cooperative."

"Why not just the man's immediate boss?" asked Laura.

"Because he didn't owe me a favor."

"Seems reasonable."

They walked quickly through the cloister and down the arcade, along which were the murals. Connor and Laura both averted their eyes as they drew abreast of the last mural, but Benjamin paused, turned, and walked backward for a moment. "Hmm. It's just as you described. The goddess figure, the people around her, the scepter."

The two women, a few paces ahead, stopped in their tracks. "You see it?" asked Connor in disbelief.

"Sure. Seems clear enough, a little primitive maybe."

They both turned and looked. Indeed, it was the disappearing image, the one they'd seen and then *not* seen. Were there time, they both would have stayed and kept it in sight just to figure out how it disappeared.

"At least now I'm fairly sure we're not crazy," whispered Laura as they reached the gate into the garden.

"Or else my Dad is as susceptible as we are."

"Okay," he said, consulting the map again. "Certainly it's at this end of the garden. This place has a lot of plantings, but its pretty orderly. Let's fan out a few feet apart and sweep a line from here to there. Then we'll pivot and come back at an angle to the first line."

Given Benjamin's strategic approach and the scrape marks in the dirt that were a dead giveaway if you were looking for them, they found the entrance within minutes. A false trellis concealed a door set partly in the ground at an angle—like the entrance to a root cellar under a house.

"Now what?" asked Connor.

"We go looking," replied Benjamin. He unslung the small pack over his shoulder and distributed flashlights fitted with adjustable filters to regulate the amount of light emitted from them. "We'll use one at a time. Keep it pointed at the ground and be very quiet. Sound could carry easily." He handed Laura a shoulder holster with the Glock 9-mm she used when she was on the job. She quickly shed her jacket, fitted the holster, and slipped the jacket back on. Benjamin tucked a similar weapon into his waistband. "I have one for you," he said to his daughter, "but I wasn't sure you'd really want one."

"I don't, but I'm not going to be a liability. At least I'm accurate with one of those, but I still hate them."

He reached into the pack and extracted an older Colt .32 semiautomatic. She checked the clip, the chamber, and the safety, then shoved it in the pocket of her coat.

"I'm ready," she said.

"Then let's go," replied Benjamin as he swung open the left half of the door and Connor opened the right half. In the strong sunlight they could make out steps leading downward.

"You know," said Laura. "If this is just the entrance to the monk's old basement, we're screwed."

"Truly screwed," added Connor, and followed her father and Laura into the dank passage.

»——«

"It's jammed from the other side," Malcolm grunted, heaving at the wheel in the center of the metal door. "I can feel it clanking against something."

"There's blood on the doorsill and on the floor next to it," said Ayalla peering at the substance on the tip of her finger. With no other option, she wiped it on the sleeve of her blazer. "Someone's been through here very recently."

Malcolm continued to rock the wheel back and forth, clockwise, then counterclockwise, again and again.

"What good is that going to do?" she asked.

"Maybe none. But you said Benjamin's coming from the other end of the tunnel. I imagine he expects us to be coming from this end. I don't like letting my friends down. And if there's a snowball's chance in hell this will work, I'll keep doing it." He twisted the wheel again. "Besides, I don't know that we have much else to do."

"We can head back upstairs and rendezvous with my guys."

"And do what?"

She sighed. "Nothing really."

"All right. Then grab this wheel and pull hard in your direction. Alternate with me."

They slammed it back and forth with only an inch of movement either way. They kept at it, even though Ayalla thought it a supreme waste of time. "Malcolm, don't you think we ought to—"

Her suggestion was interrupted by the sound of something sliding against the door, metal on metal. Malcolm yelled. "It's working. Keep pulling down on your side. Up, down, up, down." More metallic scrapes, then a bang against the lower part of the door and the wheel spun in Malcolm's enormous hands. "Yes! Yes! Yes!" He started to fling the door open, then waited to give Ayalla time to draw her weapon.

"I'll go high, you go low," he suggested.

"Would you rather go high with a weapon?"

"Yes, but it's a little late to run to the gun store."

She leaned down and slid her pants leg up to reveal an ankle holster. "It's petite but effective," she told him. "Eight in the magazine, one in the chamber."

"I love a woman who's prepared," he said, clicking the safety off. The small automatic looked like a toy gun in his huge hand.

Ayalla caught his longing glance at her 9-mm Glock. "Gun envy?"

"Yep."

"Ready?"

"Yep"

"Go!"

He opened the door and let Ayalla, in a low crouch, start through, leading with her gun. He was right behind and above her. Ayalla went over the threshold and knelt to the left of the door, sweeping the area from left to right. Malcolm did the same on his side, from right to left. There was no movement within sight. Then they saw the bodies. Near the door were two men in guard uniforms. Malcolm rolled over the top one.

"Holcomb," he said. "Don't know the other guy."

Ayalla bent over the man clad in a white shirt and dark tie and tilted his plastic security badge toward the light. "This is our missing plant manager, Archibald Sims. I'm afraid Mr. La Cloche was not the sort to share the glory or the ransom—or whatever he's after."

"I'd feel a lot better if we knew the answer to that," said Malcolm. "Since we don't, where do we go from here? We could check up and down this crawl space and see if we can find any more charges he could detonate."

"We'll leave that to the bomb sniffers," said Ayalla. "Maybe we can stop this bastard before he sets anything else off."

"What's he waiting for, I wonder."

"Either his timing is critical, or he wants to get farther away."

"He hasn't been gone more than a few minutes," said Malcolm, running his hands over Archibald's chest and throat. "This guy is still plenty warm."

"So there's a chance we have him between us and the others?"

"If they found the other end. And if La Cloche is taking it slow for some reason." He plucked the flashlights off the guards' utility belts and handed one to Ayalla. They started walking.

Malcolm spoke softly. "I keep thinking that there must be something significant about this day, or about the time. Something. If he's into all this Biblical prophecy stuff, he's probably decided on some dramatic gesture, but what?"

"I wish I knew. Then we'd also know how much time we have."

"I guess we'll have to assume, nowhere near enough for comfort." He picked up the pace, and Ayalla effortlessly lengthened her strides to match his. He rather liked that. That might bear thinking about in the near future—if there were a future, near or otherwise.

»——«

They'd reached the place where the Y branches split from the main passage, and Connor swiveled the filter on her flashlight to the almost-dark position. Pausing to listen, they heard not a whisper of sound in any direction. "So he could be hiding in the other branch of the Y even if he doesn't know about the other door," whispered Laura, her back against the rough rock and dirt.

"Here's where my secret weapon comes in handy," replied Benjamin softly. He eased the backpack off his shoulder and deftly slipped open the noiseless nylon zipper. He extracted a black rectangular box, and flipped its thin plastic cover back over on its hinge until the cover lay flat against the back. It resembled a handheld computer, but was larger than a standard PDA. Pressing one switch on the side, then a button just below the four-inch by four-inch screen, he waited for the unit to boot up.

Laura and Connor stood close on either side of him. "Is that what I think it is?" asked Laura.

"If you think it's the latest model of the XR-17-D scanner now being tested by the Navy Seals, then you'd be right."

"Scanner?" asked Connor.

"It detects movement and body heat and maps terrain directly ahead of you," said Laura. She peeked at the screen. "Does it show anything?"

Benjamin adjusted the contract and brightness on the view screen. "Nothing yet, but it's forming a three-dimensional image of the passage." They watched as the computer's scanners sent out pulses of ultrasonic sound and light beams invisible to the human eye. With each response the software interpreted the data and added to the schematic it was building. In less than a minute they had an electronic view at least fifty feet beyond them. They could, theoretically, walk in complete darkness, but Benjamin pointed out that the unit was experimental and might have little accuracy in detecting small but nonetheless dangerous obstacles on the ground in front of them. "We'd better use just a little light," he suggested. "If the scanner picks up anything, hide the flashlight."

Benjamin directed the scanner down the other "Y" branch. Readings did not indicate the presence of anything that gave off body heat. "This way then," he said, pointing in the direction that led to the nuclear generation station. "We'll take it slow." The unit was equipped to give an audible signal upon detecting heat or movement, so Benjamin put the earpiece in his ear, then plugged the cord into the side of the scanner.

"Be sure to keep the light away from your body," he reminded his daughter. "It makes a target." Staying a foot or two ahead of the others, with the scanner held before him, Benjamin started down the twisting passageway. Laura moved close to his left side. With both hands occupied, Benjamin would have no way to reach his weapon. Connor, guessing the reason for Laura's closing up ranks, did the same thing on his right.

He noted their proximity with a slight smile. "You two worried about me?"

"Of course not," said Laura softly. "I want to make sure nothing happens to that borrowed equipment. Must have cost the Navy a mint."

Connor squeezed his arm gently, and they moved slowly forward.

»—«

Richard La Cloche was no longer as sure of his invincibility as he had been a half hour earlier. According to his newly adjusted timetable (given the interference of the FBI bitch and her stupid cop friend), he should have already reached the passageway exit at the mission end. But in his haste to put distance between himself and the soon-to-be-destroyed power plant, he'd been careless. Having made the trip several times, he was thoroughly familiar with the occasional low-hanging tree root, or mound of dirt and rock, but he hadn't paid enough attention this time. It was almost as if he were outside his body. Some part of him had barked at him to slow down, shine the light farther ahead. Yet another voice, both familiar and unfamiliar, had goaded him to move faster.

Thus he'd come around a bend and slammed his forehead into a thick, gnarled tree root that looped down from the ceiling of the passageway. The impact had not only knocked him down but stunned him as well. At least that was the only way he could account for the missing time. He checked the diver's watch on his left wrist and the glowing numbers, though blurred, still indicated he'd been in the tunnel for more than forty-five minutes. Even with the door behind him barred, and the way ahead a secret known only to him and one dead priest, La Cloche felt tremors of fear in his belly that his grand scheme might unravel at the last minute.

He wasn't yet ready to detonate the second set of charges—the first two of that set would effectively destroy the only other coolant system on which the generating plant relied; the next three, ones he'd placed himself without Holcomb's knowledge, were directly beneath the containment structure floor. The C-4 explosive that had taken him fourteen months to obtain was carefully shaped so that its main force would tear the floor out completely and allow the entire reactor to plummet through. After that, the ensuing heat of the meltdown would send the core farther and farther into the ground until it generated a seismic event that would aggravate the Cueva Antigua fault directly beneath. Once that happened, he believed the destruction would continue unabated. The fault would become so unstable it would cause a veritable chain reaction along nearby faults.

Although he'd often toyed with the concept of martyrdom, he wasn't quite ready to experience it. He had to be almost within reach of the exit because another charge, a quarter mile into the tunnel from the plant would bring down the entire passageway. They'd never know how anyone escaped.

He'd laid the wiring for the detonator along the floor next to the left-hand wall. That had taken him three days, but it had been worth the effort. A detonation by radio signal such as the one Holcomb had prepared, wasn't feasible through this much rock and dirt. He'd opted for electricity. The twelve-volt battery waiting for him near the end of the tunnel would work fine. Hook up the wires, press the plunger, and run like hell. He could watch the fireworks from the mission.

La Cloche stood up and grabbed the wall for support before exploring the egg-sized lump on his forehead. His hands came away sticky with blood, and he felt the same warm wetness on his cheeks and eyelids from the profusely bleeding head wound. He'd have to find a place to clean himself up before he left the mission. He focused on the flashlight lying on the floor. Its beam was weakly yellow. "Damn it!" he said, trying not to jar his head. He'd dropped the light and it had been on all this time.

He picked it up, fighting a wave of nausea as he bent over. Then, with a deep sigh, he started walking again, this time with utmost care.

»—«

"Still nothing," said Malcolm in a low voice. He'd taken the point as they moved along the passage. "If La Cloche is in here, he's being damn quiet or he's way ahead of us."

"Then let's hope your friends are doing their job at the other end," replied Ayalla.

"They've never let anyone down yet," he said sharply.

"I wasn't dissing them, Captain. I only meant I hoped they found the other end of this damn tunnel."

"Sorry."

They walked another 100 feet before she said, "No, I'm sorry. I got off on the wrong foot with all of you. But I've been an outsider a lot in my life, and you guys are tight. I wasn't sure I even belonged on the investigation."

"You're the Feeb, remember. You belong on any investigation you want." He couldn't see her smile, but he hoped it was there. "And just 'cause the ladies and Benjamin and I are close doesn't mean it's a private club."

"Thanks."

"You're welcome."

They continued in silence, every sense alert to sound or movement ahead of them. By unspoken agreement, they began to move faster, even though their steps, particularly the ones made by Malcolm's sizable cop shoes, were becoming more audible. But somehow they shared a sense of urgency. At the next bend, they slowed down. Ayalla stumbled over a piece of uneven ground, and it was that moment of inattention that was both Malcolm's salvation and Ayalla's undoing. Malcolm had turned back toward her so that his torso was parallel with the wall. A split second earlier and he'd have taken a bullet squarely in the chest. It zipped past him and hit the FBI agent instead, flinging her back against the wall on the other side. Her flashlight crashed against a rock and went out. She slid down the wall, too stunned by the force of the bullet to stay upright. Malcolm hit the floor and scuttled backwards crabwise. "Ayalla!" he whispered. "Ayalla! Are you hit? Answer me!"

"Yes, for God's sake, I'm hit. But shut up!"

He felt for her and encountered a shoe, then a leg. Malcolm scooted up beside her. "How bad?" he asked.

"Hurts like fucking hell!" she hissed. "Can you spot him?"

"No. And I didn't even hear the shot."

"Son of a bitch is using a noise suppressor. Goddamn, I hate getting shot."

Malcolm stared into the thick darkness, as if by sheer willpower he could see whether the shooter was still waiting for them to move. Then they both heard it—footsteps receding toward the exit on the mission grounds.

"Looks like he doesn't want to wait around," said Malcolm.

"That could be bad for us if he's ready to blow up some more stuff."

"Can you move?"

"Not fast enough."

"What do you mean?"

"I'm losing blood." She pressed her hand to her upper chest just below her left collarbone. "I need to stay put. You can't carry me down the damn tunnel and have even a chance to catch this guy. So I stay here. You can send the cavalry later, or maybe my guys will find the hatch we came through and follow our trail."

"No."

"Yes. Don't argue. Give me your jacket. I'm cold."

Malcolm decided to risk a light. He examined Ayalla's wound, then helped her sit up so he could check her back. "Looks like a through and through, but you need a doctor."

"What I need is to not see this investigation totally FUBAR'd," she groaned. "So move your ass and find the bastard. Then you can save him for me. He's my fucking collar."

Malcolm wrapped his suit jacket around her. He had nothing with which to make a bandage. "Shit," he kept saying. "Shit, shit, shit!"

"Could you cuss a little more creatively?" she said through gritted teeth. "I hate boring obscene repartee."

"Sorry."

"Go! And here. You can have the big gun." She fumbled for the Glock and handed it to him. "I know you wanted the big one."

He pressed the backup pistol into her hand. "I'll be back as quick as I can," he said. "Stay put."

"Like I'm going for a jog," she muttered.

He retrieved her flashlight. Fortunately, it wasn't broken after all. When it glanced against a rock, the slide switch had gotten pushed into the off position. He put the light in her hand. "You can signal with this if you hear your guys coming from back there."

"And hope they don't shoot me. Would you please get going, you idiot!"

Malcolm hated leaving her, but she was right. And now that they knew La Cloche was armed and not in the least reluctant to shoot, he was worried about his friends. He believed they'd be coming from the other end, and La Cloche could easily kill all of them. He turned on his light, threw all caution to the wind, and ran.

»——«

La Cloche was stunned when he saw the light coming up behind him. He'd had to stop and rest again. His head was throbbing, and it seemed he'd stumbled over every rock he'd encountered. He was sitting perfectly still with his light off when he saw the brief flash. It wasn't possible that anyone had gotten through the door. Was there another access hatch? He was quite sure Holcomb, Sims, and the other guard were dead.

He drew the .45 from the shoulder holster that fitted so nicely under his custom-tailored black suit jacket. From his pocket he removed the silencer. Carefully he threaded it onto the barrel, then rested his arm on a rock. A few seconds later he saw the light again and fired. The light went out. He heard something else fall. Good, he'd hit him. La Cloche waited, straining to detect movement. He heard a rustling, a faint whisper. Was there more than one of them down there? He should wait. No, he should go. Panic set in. He had to get to the end, had to get to the battery and finish the plan. If he waited here…what if there were a dozen of them? He couldn't hold them off with one ten-shot magazine. He crawled around the next bend, got to his feet, and ran.

»——«

According to the Navy's newest tech toy, they'd covered only two-tenths of a mile, not nearly enough, yet they could only proceed so fast with only a dimmed light and a computer screen to guide them. Benjamin insisted they not get careless. "We may have a slight advantage in that he's not expecting us, but he has a very large advantage because he probably knows this tunnel. There may even be alcoves or side tunnels along the way where he can hide."

They continued at a stately pace, and Connor could hardly contain her own impatience. The darkness and silence were oppressive. She wasn't the least bit fond of enclosed spaces and had to fight to control her breathing and her heartbeat. But no way in hell would she have let her father and Laura come down here without her. If only they could move faster.

She wasn't paying close attention and butted into her father, who'd stopped abruptly. He held up his hand, signaling them to be quiet. They both edged close enough to see the screen. An amber light flashed at the top of the screen. Underneath, the words "Motion detected—120 yards."

Benjamin dropped to a squat and the two women did likewise. They continued to watch the screen as he pressed other buttons to extend the sensor-created schematic and display more of the tunnel ahead. But it only indicated a clear picture of the next forty yards. Then a sharp bend to the right. They couldn't see beyond it, nor was the unit yet receiving any data to indicate the body heat of a person. But the motion sensors continued to record the approach of *something*. Then that something paused.

"Back up," whispered Benjamin. "About twenty feet behind us, the tunnel's wider."

They took turns. Connor first, the Laura, and finally Benjamin. Just as he reached the cover of a waist-high outcropping of rock, the dangling shoulder strap of the device snagged on a jagged stone and he dropped it. The earpiece cord was yanked from the socket, and immediately the high-pitched beeping of its warning system filled the tunnel. Benjamin dived on top of it and stabbed at the power switch.

"Jesus H. Christ," he muttered after the echo died away. Laura and Connor were beside him.

"You okay, Dad?"

"Just stupid is all." He fumbled with the unit and replaced the earpiece. Let's hope this damn thing still works." It hummed to life, having been designed to take more of a beating than a three-foot drop and a 175-pound man landing on it. As he feared, there was no longer any motion detected ahead of them.

»——«

La Cloche had just reached the narrow alcove where the battery was hidden when the squealing noise erupted in the tunnel. He dropped to the ground, trying to ignore the pain coursing through his head. Then the noise stopped. He lay there, breathing hard. What *was* it? His mind refused at first to accept the premise that his escape had been cut off, that God had deserted him. Yet certainly that had been a mechanical, man-made noise and he could draw no other conclusion. They'd found him. Tears formed and coursed down his cheeks. He wanted to scream; he wanted to tear at the minions of evil with his bare hands. So much time, so much planning, so much fervent prayer on his knees before the altars of every church he'd passed along the way. Why?

Ever so slowly and carefully he pulled himself along the rocks and dirt into his little alcove. It was only slightly wider at the entrance than his shoulders, but instantly widened to more than three feet. This was where he'd chosen to conceal the twelve-volt battery and the electric switch that would detonate the C-4 charges and destroy the plant, the tunnel, and much more.

Without stopping to weigh the consequences, he began wiring the leads of the switch to the battery. Once he'd connected the bare wires of the cables running through the tunnel and back to the plant, all it would take was a quick twist and a downward thrust. He supposed he might make it out in the confusion. After all, he was a priest, come to give aid to the injured. And he was injured himself, surely an object of concern and pity. He reached for the bare wires.

»——«

Ayalla tried to not to expand her lungs too much. It hurt like hell to suck in air at all, but breathing wasn't optional. She tried to keep her mind off the immediate future, which didn't look all that bright. She ran through a few scenarios, most of which didn't prominently feature her survival. But at least she would die in the line of duty. Funny, though, that didn't sound quite as pleasingly dramatic or deeply soul-satisfying as she'd always thought. She supposed that imminent death, as opposed to hypothetical death, tended to clear up one's illusions rather quickly.

Trying to keep her mind off the pain in her upper chest, she began to play the flashlight along the walls of the tunnel, along the ceiling, then the floor. A spot of color caught her eye. She swung the flashlight back. In the dirt and behind a couple of smallish rocks, she could make out a patch of bright blue. Stifling a groan, she pulled herself closer and moved one of the rocks. Wiring. It was mostly black, which is why she hadn't seen it before, but here, for about ten inches, the insulating cover had been stripped away and blue and yellow-wrapped wires were visible within. Blue and yellow. She took a deep breath. Was it possible La Cloche had hooked up some kind of communication lines along the tunnel? But why? He could contact Holcomb anytime. No, communication wasn't the reason. Eavesdropping? Again, Holcomb would fill him in on whatever was happening at the plant. Besides, he probably had a full set of plans, just like the ones he'd sent with one of his terrorist threats. *Plans...blueprints...explosions....* She started to nod off again, then her eyes snapped open. How was La Cloche going to set off the other charges, if indeed there were others? She stared at the wires. *Oh, God.*

Utterly ignoring the next wave of pain that ripped through her as she jostled her fractured collarbone and started a fresh wave of bleeding from the open wound, she struggled to reach the pocket of her slacks. *Please let it be there. Please let it be there.* On her key ring was a miniature Swiss Army knife, more for the occasional hangnail or letter opening than anything serious. Her fingers closed on the key ring. *Yes!* She pulled it out with her right hand and brought her right hand over to her left to pry open the small blade. She tried not to think of how numb the fingers of her left hand were. She could barely feel the knife. *How ironic if I cut myself...like I'm not bleeding enough.* She finally had it open and inched closer to the wiring. She tried to saw at it. Hardly a dent. She'd have to pick it apart first and then cut each lead wire. She tried to breathe again. *Hard. It's so hard. Keep at it. First, the blue one.*

»——«

"Still not moving," murmured Benjamin. "No, wait—yes, he is moving. I don't know what he's thinking, but he's headed right for us. Stay down."

He rested the unit on the rock and drew his gun. Laura already had hers in one hand, her flashlight in the other. Connor, slightly behind and to the right of her father, was similarly prepared, though without anywhere near the confidence of the other two.

"When I say 'now,' turn on the lights and be ready to fire. If he's holding anything that even looks like a detonator, shoot to kill. Don't waste any time."

»——«

The once and future Father Lemarteau was almost finished when he heard heavy footsteps pounding toward him. He quickly extinguished the spare flashlight he'd stored in the alcove and only allowed himself to breathe when the steps went right past his hiding place.

»——«

Malcolm, winded and almost ready to drop from his exertion, couldn't believe he hadn't yet caught up with La Cloche. Good God, the man moved fast. And Malcolm's pace had been slowing despite his best efforts. But where the hell was La Cloche? His flashlight picked out a bend in the tunnel ahead. Maybe he'd at least get to the end and see some daylight.

»——«

Ayalla could barely see. The flashlight battery was almost out, but she didn't stop. She'd finally cut through the blue wire, and now the yellow one was about to come apart. With a last tug, she felt it separate. Her flashlight died, and along with it her hopes to live a long and healthy life.

»——«

Malcolm slowed for the bend and forgot to keep the light pointing straight down. It flared out in front of him. He figured the precautions were pointless by now. Better to see than get brained by a rock. No doubt La Cloche was long gone. And Malcolm had accomplished nothing except to leave Ayalla behind with who knew how serious an injury. It made him furious. He trotted around the corner.

»——«

The last thing the three of them expected was to be blinded by a flashlight. Benjamin's immediate reflex would have been to fire at the source of the light. Had he done so, Laura would have followed suit. But someone shouted, "No! Wait!"

Benjamin shone his toward the figure at the bend in the tunnel.

"Dear God in heaven," he shouted. "Malcolm!"

"Benjamin, is that you?"

»——«

La Cloche heard them. Benjamin…the man from Washington and his daughter and her lover. And the cop. *How appropriate they should all die together.* He closed his eyes, turned the plunger, and pushed down. Silence reigned supreme. It was perhaps the greatest anticlimax of his life.

»——«

Malcolm rushed toward his friends. "Did he get past you?"

"La Cloche?"

"Yeah."

"No, unless he got away before we even got here."

Connor couldn't quite focus on him. She still held the gun in her hand, the gun she might used to shoot her best friend. "It was you," she said. "It was you."

"Well, yeah," replied Malcolm.

"We could have killed you."

"I wouldn't have liked that."

"You idiot," she shouted. "You goddamn idiot. Running toward us like that."

"Hey," he said, grabbing her into a hug. "I'm sorry."

"You know what," she said. "I hate guns. I really, really hate guns."

"Benjamin interrupted. "Did you *just* come down that tunnel, I mean just this minute?"

Malcolm looked at him strangely. "Yes. I slowed down a little, but I never stopped."

"Shit!" yelled Benjamin. "Everyone get down."

"What is it?" Connor started to ask, but in the dim light she saw movement about twenty feet behind Malcolm. The gleam of metal aimed at her friend's back, a brief glimpse of a white face streaked with black. Connor raised her pistol, took one step to the side, and fired. An inhuman scream rent the air around them.

Malcolm looked back at the man lying on the ground, looked at Connor, then at the pistol. He raised one eyebrow.

"Okay," she said. "I hate most guns, but not *this* gun."

Chapter Twenty-Seven

Why this is hell, nor am I out of it:
Thinkst thou that I who saw the face of God,
And tasted the eternal joys of heaven,
Am not tormented with ten thousand hells
In being deprived of everlasting bliss!
—Christopher Marlowe, spoken by Mephistopheles in *Faustus*

Richard La Cloche wasn't dead, either by divine plan or because Connor's shot in the semidarkness went slightly awry. She'd actually only hit his gun hand, but the bones in his wrist were snapped in two, and he continued to weep as they led him out of the tunnel and into the botanical garden. Perhaps his mind had shattered along with his wrist, but he had nothing to say to them. His eyes were vacant, as if the animating spirit that gives all humans life had suddenly departed.

"I've got to notify the FBI team about Ayalla," said Malcolm. "I don't know if she'll make it."

"I'll start calling. You get in my car and drive to the plant. You might do better in person. Turn La Cloche over to the park ranger.

Give him a chance to do some law enforcement for a change."

Malcolm dragged the man along with him, heedless of his whimpers.

Connor, noting Malcolm's haste to rescue Ayalla, wondered if there were more to his concern than one colleague for another.

"So," she said to her father, "now what?"

He took the map from his shirt pocket and went to sit on a bench. "I think there's one more thing we need to do, and that's finish whatever Father Rosario started."

"You think the artifact is here?" asked Laura.

"I'm almost sure of it. I realized as I was driving here and talking to the archbishop that Enrique's Morse code shorthand was pretty odd. That's why I didn't quite understand all of it. But Johnston said something about the light shining on those domes at the generating station, and you know how we sometimes make those weird associations for no apparent reason?" They nodded. "I assumed that all of his Morse code stood for *English words*. But look here."

L...A...L...U...M...I...È...R...E

"*La lumière de sacré mère,*" exclaimed Connor. "He was talking about the plant, the big shrub in the middle of the garden. He's hidden the artifact somewhere around it."

They rushed to the center of the garden, to the dark, shimmering leafy shrub.

"But where?" said Connor. He wouldn't bury it anywhere a gardener might dig it up." They circled the perimeter.

"I don't know," said Laura. "I have a feeling he also wouldn't disturb this beautiful planting." She walked slowly around it again, then once more. "Here," she said finally. "A few of the branches are bent back. I wonder..." She stepped close and pulled the branches apart, then turned sideways and slipped through.

"Where'd you go?" Connor demanded as she came around. "Laura?"

"Hang on. I think I've got something. There's a flat stone here, funny but it looks just like something I've seen somewhere." They heard scrabbling noises. "Oh...wow! I think this is it."

Benjamin's cell phone rang. "What?" he barked, intent on Laura's discovery. Then Connor saw a scowl settle over his face. "All right. You hang on to La Cloche, and be careful. We'll figure out what happened to the ranger."

"What's wrong?" asked Connor.

"When Malcolm got back to the parking lot, he found the ranger out cold in his guard shack and no sign of the archbishop. The ranger's sidearm is gone."

"But I don't get it. If La Cloche had someone out here waiting for him, where is he?"

"I don't know," Benjamin shook his head.

At that moment, Laura worked her way back out of the center of the enormous plant. In her hands lay an ancient, battered wooden casket bound up with rotting leather cords. "I guess this is what everyone's tried so hard to find."

They stared at it. How could anything so small and nondescript have caused the death of so many?

"Shall we open it?" ventured Connor. "Or wait?"

"I don't think I can wait," said Laura.

From behind them, they heard a shout. "Put it down!"

The three of them whirled around to face the voice. It was Archbishop Johnston, and he gripped a heavy revolver with both hands. The gun was pointed right at them.

"I said, put it down! You can't have it!"

"Archbishop Johnston, what are you doing?" said Benjamin.

"I'm doing my duty. You can't have it. No one can have it. It's a lie. It's always been a lie. Don't you see? I can finally rest knowing it's been destroyed." He gestured toward Laura. "Put it on the ground and go away. I'll kill all of you if I have to."

She complied, but she didn't back away as he stepped closer. She stared at him and refused to move.

"Laura, do it. Back up!" hissed Connor.

"It isn't him," said Laura softly.

"What are you talking about?"

"It isn't the archbishop. It's the man, the demon, from my dreams."

"'Demon!' How dare you speak the word! I'm a man of God. All those years, decades, centuries, of waiting, waiting to be freed from my sins."

"You dreamed him?"

"Whoever he is, he's controlling Johnston. Look at his eyes. I couldn't forget them if I tried."

"Whoever he is, he's got a gun. Back up!"

"We can't let him have it. He's going to destroy something precious. I don't know what it is, but we can't."

"So what do you suggest we do?" asked Benjamin. All of their guns were tucked away again in Benjamin's backpack.

Laura started to speak, slowly, but precisely. "Mother God, deliver us from this evil. Deliver us from fear. We call on the Great Spirit. We call on the Divine Mother of all life. And She is with us."

"No!" the archbishop screamed. "No!"

"Yes," came a new voice and all eyes turned to its source. "She is quite right in calling on the love of the Mother." The figure of an ancient priest in a dusty cassock coalesced between the archbishop and the three who stood beside the great healing plant.

"You?" said Connor. "Father Angelico."

"That has been one of my names," he replied. "And I have been seeking that which you have found."

"Not again, Gandolfo, not this time," screamed the archbishop, who swung the barrel of the gun toward the old priest. "You tricked me once; you cheated me with death."

"No, Bellini, I did nothing to you. All I did was preserve a little piece of the truth that you wanted to obliterate from this existence."

"You're still trying to perpetuate the lie of the damnable whore!"

"Still doing what I am sworn to do," he said gently. "And I cannot let you harm these people."

"You can't save them," he screamed. Connor, Laura, and Benjamin steeled themselves as the archbishop aimed at them and the man's trembling finger squeezed the trigger. On each of their lips was a silent prayer, *Let the bullet be for me.*

But there was no bullet. Time froze, all movement stopped, there was no sound of any living thing. Through this void, the old mystic moved swiftly, his cassock soundlessly brushing the ground. He gently plucked the gun from the archbishop's hands and placed his palm upon the old man's brow. "Go now, Bellini, trouble not this soul again. Your time has passed and all your hatred is forgiven. The Mother waits to take you home."

He waited until he saw the vaguely defined shadow lift away from the archbishop, watched it float upward, watched it into the waiting arms of the angels of death. Then he led the man to a bench and made him sit before returning to the other three. The priest laid the gun on the ground and picked up the old casket.

The flow of time resumed. For the others, the entire scene before them had changed as if the blink of an eye. Connor stared at the archbishop, who was no longer armed. Benjamin was the first to see the gun on the ground at his feet. He picked it up and looked curiously at the old priest. "Who are you, really?" he asked.

"It would take more years than you have left in this lifetime—and there are a great many—for me to explain it to your satisfaction," said the old man with a smile. "But rest assured that, like the three of you, I'm on the side of the angels."

"I've heard that before," said Laura.

"Your journeys in the Dreamtime are legend," he said, his eyes twinkling.

"I suppose you're taking that," said Connor, pointing at the casket.

"Yes, I'm afraid it isn't time yet. Your world isn't quite ready for the most profound change it's ever known."

"Will you at least tell us what's inside?" she asked.

He nodded. "You love a mystery, don't you?" he said. "Then, very well. Within this casket are some notes that I left a long time ago, long before you were born, as well as some much earlier writings that were passed down to me. And also in it is a large chunk of amber."

"Amber?" Laura frowned. "Amber doesn't sound all that important."

"Except that locked within this particular piece are three chambers containing locks of hair and bits of skin from three individuals."

"Whose?" said Connor, almost afraid to hear the answer.

"The Apostle called Mary Magdalene, the one called Jesus, and the daughter they loved."

"But…" said Connor.

"How…" said Laura

"Surely you don't mean…" was as far as Benjamin got.

"You see. The world isn't ready to know that the message of the Great Teacher was not conveyed in its entirety, or in complete truth. Someday perhaps, when the descendant is found."

"The line continued, didn't it?" whispered Connor.

"Yes, indeed. I'd almost hope that perhaps one of you…But sadly, no. And somewhere, someday another great teacher will arise, this time in the form and body of a woman, and finally the separation will be dissolved, the great duality will diminish into oneness. The wheel of fortune and misfortune will cease to turn, and all will be reunited. This I promise."

"In our lifetime?" asked Laura.

"Time is relative," said the old priest, "especially to me. I must leave now. May the Mother-Father God be with you, and all the angels lift you up."

The light around the elderly priest brightened for an instant, and then his form simply dissolved.

»——«

Ayalla was unconscious when her fellow agents reached her in the tunnel. They puzzled over the Swiss Army knife clutched in her hand and when it was finally determined that her actions had prevented an unspeakable disaster, she received an extended recuperative leave as well as a promotion. She was happy about the latter, but not the former. The extra time off, however, did give her the chance to get to know a certain D.C. cop a little better. After two weeks she still wasn't sure she even *liked* him, but she was at least open to persuasion.

»——«

The long and violent career of Richard Renard La Cloche came to an end only three days after the terrorist attack on San Peligro Nuclear Generating Station. La Cloche, who remained in an almost catatonic state of shock over the outcome of his plans, had refused to utter a single word since his arrest. He sat completely motionless on the metal bunk in a tiny cell in the solitary confinement wing of the Orange County Men's Prison. La Cloche ignored the prison physician who came to change the bandage on his forehead and examine the cast on his broken wrist. He didn't touch the food trays that were slid through the slot in his door.

The prisoner also made no phone calls. Thus, authorities were surprised when an attorney appeared, demanding to see his client. After a quick consultation with the local FBI field office, the man's credentials were checked once more. They appeared in order. Unfortunately, La Cloche refused to leave his cell. He ignored the guard's explanation. To avoid later claims that they had violated La Cloche's constitutional rights by denying him counsel, the jail supervisor decided to stretch the rules and let the attorney conduct the meeting in La Cloche's cell. He was given an hour alone with La Cloche.

Ricky didn't look up when the guard admitted the dapper stranger to his cell. He continued to stare at the cinder-block wall, just as he had for almost seventy-two hours. The attorney sat down next to the prisoner and put his arm around him. At the central command post, the guard flicked his eyes toward the monitors displaying grainy images from video cameras throughout the facility. La Cloche's cell was covered. His particular unit was designed for suicide watch as well as solitary confinement. The guard saw the attorney sit and begin talking, his arm still over La Cloche's shoulders. "Trying to be his buddy," the guard snorted, doubting the lawyer would get any farther with his questions than the two dozen or so cops and agents who'd been through in three days.

In the cell, La Cloche began to stir, but the movement wasn't enough to draw the guard's attention. Ricky was hearing but not quite understanding the sibilant whispers of the man beside him.

"You shouldn't have meddled in what you don't understand. You put all of us at risk. You jeopardized decades of painstaking work. You've blasphemed against God. You're a fraud, La Cloche, nothing but a fraud. You deserve the worst penalty we could mete out, yet there isn't enough time for that. All of this must end right now."

Ricky's eyes closed for a moment. His heart thudded hard behind his rib cage. He was afraid, for he knew without doubt this man was here to punish him, just the way Ricky had punished so many others. He tried to work his lips and tongue, but it was almost as if in only a few days he'd forgotten how.

The stranger released Ricky's biceps for an instant, then squeezed it, as if reassuring him. The poor quality images on the video monitors outside could not convey the spasm of shock that passed over Ricky's face when he felt not one, but two sharp jabs in his arm.

"The first one will make it impossible for you to move, you will not even be able to blink. The second one is slower, but far deadlier." He stood up with his back to the video camera. "You will not have to wait long for death to claim you." He shook his head. "It's a far-too-merciful end." He loosened his tie slightly and worked his fingers between his shirt collar and neck until he pulled out a glittering gold crucifix. Ricky's eyes locked on to it. He yearned to reach out and touch the holy object. Yet already he couldn't feel his body. The stranger's smile was cruel and cold. "Perhaps it will be enough that you know your soul is damned for all eternity. You see, I could give you absolution. But I won't. Goodbye, Mr. La Cloche." He tucked the crucifix away and picked up his attaché case from the bunk. He placed a hand on Ricky's shoulder. The guard saw the motion and realized the attorney was probably ready to leave.

"That didn't last long," he muttered before heaving himself out of his chair to go an unlock the cell. The attorney was waiting for him, facing the doorway. The guard glanced over the man's shoulder at La Cloche, who looked much as he'd looked for three days.

"I didn't think he'd talk," said the guard.

"I did what I could," the visitor shrugged. "I'll try again tomorrow."

Two hours later, the prisoner died in his cell. The coroner found evidence of poison. The attorney, of course, was never found, though in all honesty no one tried very hard to find him. They confirmed that all of his identification was bogus in every respect, and then they dropped the investigation. He had saved the government the expense of a long trial and a great deal of embarrassment over the lack of security at San Peligro.

The phony lawyer resumed his normal duties as an aide attached to the Italian embassy in Washington, D.C.

Epilogue

L'amor che muove il sole e l'altre stele.
(The love that moves the sun and the other stars.)
Dante Alighieri, *Divine Comedy, Paradiso,* xviii

Malcolm, with Benjamin's help, compiled a list of Malleus Society members, a list that was eventually leaked to the press. On that list prominently figured the name of the congressman who had ruined Ayalla's father, the name Malcolm had seen when they were reading the files at the FBI field office. Ayalla enjoyed the news coverage of that revelation rather more than stories about her own heroics.

Benjamin, Connor, and Laura had reached a tacit agreement not to reveal what had happened during those last few minutes in the botanical garden of the old mission. The archbishop thankfully had no memory of his actions; fortunately, neither did the park ranger Johnston had hit over the head while he was "not himself."

The day before Connor and Laura left California for their home in Santa Fe and some dearly needed peace and quiet, they visited once more the church where Enrique Rosario had died. St. Mary of the Groves was still closed, but Archbishop Johnston had promised that it would be reconsecrated and another priest would take Enrique's place.

They entered by a side door and stood quietly in front of the old-fashioned altar in the side chapel devoted to the Lady. Like any old Catholic church building, it smelt of incense and musty age. They knelt for a moment on the ancient cushions at the altar rail and pondered the kindly face of the Mother.

"I got those pictures back from the photo shop," said Laura, patting the pocket of her jacket.

"What pictures?"

"From the mission. Of the mural...the thirteenth image, the one that disappeared on us."

"Did it come out?"

"Not exactly." Laura slipped the envelope of prints out of her pocket and pulled back the flap. "There are several perfect photos of the mission, and then there's this." She handed Connor a print. Instead of the colorful mural they'd both seen, the entire background was a light gray and cloudy. In the center was just the shadow of an image—a woman's face? "What do you think it is?"

Connor sighed. "I'm afraid to say. If I tell you what I *think* it looks like, well, next thing you know we'll be seeing the face of Jesus in a tapioca pudding cup."

"Oh, please," laughed Laura. "We may we a little weird, sweetheart, but we have at least one foot in the reality camp."

"Then I'd say this is the outline of her face, the woman from the mural. And that's all I'll say for now."

"Fair enough."

"Now I've got a question for *you*. Who do you think that old priest guy really was?" asked Connor.

Lauren pondered that for almost half a minute. "I think he was an angel I've met somewhere before."

"Next time you go, wherever that is, take me along."

"It's a deal."

They left the church hand in hand. And if anyone on the sidewalks disapproved, neither of them noticed.

Acknowledgments

Once again, I owe an immense debt of gratitude to my loyal in-house proofreaders (and kindly but honest critics), Sandra Satterwhite, Debra Elston, and Katherine Missell. Each of these women is a treasure in her own right. My life is immeasurably enriched by my knowing them.

To Dr. Marj Britt, my minister and friend, heartfelt thanks for teaching me so much in such a short time. How else could I have understood nonduality? You see, I *was* listening.

Angela Brown, my editor, spent many hours polishing the final manuscript. Her meticulous work and dedication to the craft of writing have been invaluable to me.

I must also acknowledge a wonderful community of people who have supported me emotionally and spiritually with love, nurturing, kindness, and prayer. To my entire Unity of Tustin family (especially Alys "Mom" Sullivan)—you lift up my heart and soul.